INITIATION OF FLAME

The heat built sharply in the chamber, then exploded into a twisting green torrent of fire. It swirled around me faster and faster, sucking the very air out of my lungs. My robe burst into flames in a heartbeat, then my vision dimmed and the world went black.

BOOKS BY MICHAEL A. STACKPOLE

*published by Bantam Books

THE DARK GLORY WAR

A Prelude to the DragonCrown War Cycle

Michael A. Stackpole

BANTAM BOOKS
New York   Toronto   London   Sydney   Auckland

THE DARK GLORY WAR: A PRELUDE TO THE DRAGONCROWN WAR CYCLE

A Bantam Spectra Book / March 2000

ISBN 0-553-57807-3

Published simultaneously in the United States and Canada

PRINTED IN THE UNITED STATES OF AMERICA

OPM   10 9 8 7 6 5

To the Memory of Gladys McIntyre
The only thing bigger than her imagination
was her heart.

ACKNOWLEDGMENTS

The author would like to thank the following people for their contributions to this work:

Tom Dupree, Anne Lesley Groell, and **Ricia Mainhardt** for providing me the opportunity to write this epic.

Dennis L. McKiernan and **Jennifer Roberson** for insights into the proposal, the series, and the thinking behind it all.

Liz Danforth, who willingly lets me share with her pieces of the tale as it goes together, and puts up with my muttering, musing, mumbling, and maniacal cackling when pretty much anyone else would be calling a psych ward to have me incarcerated.

CHAPTER 1

The day they gave me my mask was the first day I felt truly alive.

Though I received my mask over two decades ago, I remember the events surrounding it clearly. The tinge of winter had not quite left the air that year, so even as we were coming to Mid-Summer's Eve the days were cooler than normal. Many people were happy with the weather, since the previous year had been a scorcher, and some went so far as to suggest that the mild weather might have betokened the death of Chytrine, the scourge of the Northlands. I didn't care about the weather or the tyrant of Aurolan because this was my eighteenth summer, which made it special and me anxious.

The mask I got was not, of course, the first mask I had ever worn, nor would it be the last. It was a simple moonmask, as white as the orb for which it was named. If the gods smiled and I proved worthy, as the moon again became full I would be awarded my first life mask, and this moonmask would be a memento of my transition from childhood frivolity to adult responsibility.

It had been my intention, that morning, to wake early and dress myself, as befit my new station in life. I wanted to be able to greet my father as an adult in all but the mask he would bring. Unfortunately I awoke much too early, spent time in my bed wondering if I should get up or go to sleep again, then fell asleep and remained so rather solidly until, dimly, I heard my father's heavy tread on the stairs. Before I could rub sleep-sand from my eyes, the door opened and he entered my room.

My memory of his coming to me that mid-summer morning, bearing the mask, still endures and is one of my most favorite of him. All over Oriosa other children in their eighteenth summer were also receiving their masks. For many of them the presentation would be a family affair, but among the Hawkinses, fathers presented masks to sons, mothers to daughters, making it a more intimate and solemn occasion. I welcomed this moment of serenity before what I guessed would be a month of controlled insanity.

My father stood there, at the foot of my bed, looking down at me. His life mask, which he seldom wore in our house, had a fearsome visage. White temeryx feathers, with their shifting rainbow highlights, splayed out and back at the mask's temples. The cut of the mask's lower edge had been sharpened into a hawk's beak over his nose. This had been done both as a play on our name and the fact that Lord Norrington and his father before him had often used my father to hunt enemies the way another might loose a hawk on a varmint. Orphan notches had been cut by each eye and the brown leather had two green ribbons stitched into the portion covering his forehead. Those marked awards for bravery, one from Lord Norrington and the other from the hand of the Oriosan queen.

A hank of blond and silver hair hung down over the mask's forehead and bisected the ribbons. My father refused to wear a cowl, though entitled to do so, preferring to let others see his full head of hair. Through the mask's narrowed eyeslits I could see his brown eyes, perhaps the hint of a tear glistening in an orphan notch. He never cried from pain, my father, physical pain, anyway. But other hurts, or life's joys, could tickle a tear from his eyes.

Though he did not stand as tall as I, he was still a big man and broader through the chest and shoulders than I was. Growing up, he'd seemed bigger, and yet even as I grew into my adult size, I always thought of him as bigger than me. Though he was entering the twilight of his life, my father still possessed the strength of his youth and served as Lord Norrington's Peaceward in Valsina.

He raised his hands slowly, bearing between them the simple strip of white leather I would wear for the next month. "Arise, Tarrant Hawkins. At an end are the carefree days of your youth. Upon this mask, and many like it, will be written the story of your life as a man."

I threw back my blanket, and with only the crackle of the straw mattress and the groan of old floorboards to break the silence, I stood before my father. I plucked a piece of straw from the sleeve of my nightshirt, then ran fingers back through my black hair and snagged another piece. They fell to the floor as my hands returned to my sides.

I'd waited for this day forever, it seemed. The full moon closest to mid-summer marked the day we'd get our moonmasks. Everyone my age knew the full moon would fall exactly on mid-summer, which meant we would be blessed and special. Great things would be expected from us, and I hoped I would prove worthy of such an auspicious omen. Ever since I'd learned that the full moon would fall on mid-summer in my year, I had worked to prepare for this day and the rest of my life beyond it.

The problem was, however, that preparing for the unknown was not a simple task. I knew, in general, what would happen during my Moon Month. While I'd been barred from the festivities surrounding similar awards to my brothers and sisters, the results of their Moon Months were not hard to see. Noni, my eldest sister, had emerged betrothed from her month, while my older brothers had won positions in the Frontier Lancers and the Oriosan Scouts respectively. It seemed to me to be pretty clear that during their month they had been the subjects of negotiations or recruitment that set them on a path for the rest of their lives.

Reaching up, my father pressed the leather mask against my face, then raised my left hand to hold it in place. I turned in compliance with his pressure on my shoulder and felt him tighten the mask in place. A bit of my hair caught in the knot and pulled, but I knew that had not been an accident. *The hair and the mask are equally now part of me. I am the mask and it is me.*

"Turn around, boy. Let me look at you."

I turned back to face him and saw a proud smile broaden the lower half of his face. "You already wear the mask well, Tarrant."

"Thank you, Father."

He waved me back toward my bed. "Sit for a moment, I've got something to tell you." He lowered his voice and glanced back at the door, then crouched at my knees. "You're my last child to get a mask, but none have been so ready for it. In your training you've worked hard. You still make mistakes, you've still things to learn, but you don't quit, and your loyalty to friends, especially the Norringtons, well, that fires my heart, it does.

"Now your mother, she is fair to bursting with pride in you, but she's also fit to weep at losing you. You'll be remembering that, Tarrant, and you'll put up with her fussing about. When you're finally a man, she'll learn to retreat a bit—and likely you'll have an appreciation of her that you've not had before. For now, though, know your growing up is as difficult on her as it will be on you."

I nodded solemnly and felt the mask's tails gently slapping my neck. "I'd not do anything to hurt her *or* you."

"I know, you're a good lad." He patted my knee with a calloused hand. Liverspots and scars were woven together in his flesh. "You're also going to have to remember that you wear the mask everywhere, at all times, save here in your home, with your family. Yes, I know there are those who think shedding the mask amid friends is acceptable, but we're an old family. We've taken the mask since the days when one had to, and we're not surrendering a tradition for which our ancestors shed blood. Promise me, boy, that you'll always wear your mask."

I laid my hand on top of his. "You have my promise."

"Good." He glanced down at the floor for a moment, then nodded. "Your brothers, they're good men, but not quite as bright as you. When I gave them their masks, I gave them some advice about what will be going on in the next month. For you I've not got anything to say that you don't already know. For some people the Moon Month is a chance to start over. For others it's a chance to start. For you, though, it is a chance to continue learning and growing into the man you want to be."

He straightened, then looked down at me. "You know, Tarrant, I've no favorites among my children. I love you all, but I will say this: if I were out in the forests and lost, with frostclaws coursing me, there's one of you I know would find me and help me. That's you, lad. The others would try, don't get me wrong, but you'd manage it. By luck or pluck, you'd do it. For that reason among many I am very proud of you."

The pride welling up in my chest robbed me of words. I smiled at my father and he nodded in return.

"Come on, lad, I'll be introducing you to your family now." He opened the door to my room, then ushered me onto the walkway that provided access to the house's upper rooms. My mother and my two brothers had gathered in the entryway, at the base of the stairs—just this side of the entryway's mask-curtain—but I did nothing more than glance at them. In keeping with custom, they did not even acknowledge my existence.

I preceded my father down the stairs, then let him pass me. He cleared his throat and my unmasked kin smiled at him. "This being the fifteenth day of the month of Gold, I would like to present to you a new Hawkins. He is Tarrant."

I bowed my head to them. "I am pleased to make your acquaintance."

My oldest brother, Doke, wearing a semiserious expression on his face, offered me his hand. "Captain Doke Hawkins of the Frontier Lancers, at your service."

"And I am Sallitt Hawkins, Lieutenant in the Oriosan Scouts." Sallitt swept a hank of red hair out of his eyes and shook my hand. "Tarrant, you say? I once knew a Tarrant Hawkins. Bit of a bother."

My mother hissed at him. "Hush now, Sal. Pleased to be meeting you, Tarrant."

"The pleasure is all mine." I took my mother's heart hand in mine and kissed it gently.

She turned away quickly so I couldn't see her face. Dawn light pouring in through the front windows caught the long veins of grey running through her brown hair. I'd noticed them before and had even kidded her about them. But now, seeing them through the slits in a moonmask, I felt the first cold jolt of mortality. My mother and father had been part of my life forever—or, rather, until this day I had been part of their lives. Now I had my own life to live, one that would take me away from them. I was a seed fallen away from the tree, to sprout and thrive on my own, or to fail to do so on the same terms.

As if my mother could read my thoughts and wanted to counter them, she pointed to the rough-hewn table over by the kitchen hearth. "We would welcome you into our home, Tarrant. Please, join us."

I crossed the open room and sat at the guest end of the table. Placed there was a loaf of bread, a green apple, a tiny bowl of salt, a small wheel of cheese, and a pitcher of ale. Cups and plates had been set at four more places, but no food had been laid out at them. I sat, then the others, each watching me with a mixture of amusement and pride shining in their eyes.

First I took up the apple and carved a small wedge from it. It being a little early in the season for apples, the fruit tasted quite tart, but it had been the first solid food I had eaten after birth, so here I consumed it first after my rebirth. I chewed and swallowed, then quartered the remaining apple and passed it out among my kin.

Likewise I took the first piece of bread and cheese, then divided the remainder. I also poured the ale into each cup and added a dash of salt to each. I raised the cup of ale and offered the traditional moonmask toast. "To the nest become a stronghold, and the blood ties that bind this family together."

We all drank and solemnly set our cups down. The crackling of the kitchen fire filled the silence for a second, then my brothers chuckled and Doke reached for the ale pitcher. "Are you prepared for your Moon Month, little brother? Fretting the adventures you'll have?"

"Fretting? No." I smiled and could feel the flesh of my cheeks press against the mask. "What do I have to be afraid of?"

My brothers laughed again, and even my father joined in. My mother gave him a stern glance and laid a hand on his arm, then nodded toward my brothers. My father's laughter tumbled into a rumble, then died in a cough. He advanced his cup toward Sallitt.

"You'll be wanting to tease Tarrant, but you're old enough to know better, the both of you. You could have him thinking all manner of horrible things." My father drew back the full cup and sipped the foam off the top. "I think you'll recall he was quite respectful of you two during your Moon Months."

I remembered my father having pulled me aside during Doke's Moon Month. I was just a boy, a good ten years younger than Doke, and my father told me I was not to pester him about anything. "He's your brother, and that's just it. You'll be leaving him alone and not be asking about this and that. Understand?"

I said I did even though I didn't, but I also kept to myself all the questions I wanted to ask. Thinking back on it there at the table, I remember one of Doke's eyes having been blacked—badly enough that the bruise reddened his eyeball and extended well beyond the protection of the mask. And I remembered Sallitt, two years later, limping for the latter half of his Moon Month, which made him rather sour since he couldn't dance worth a lick at the various parties.

Recalling their injuries did make me wonder what I'd be facing. While I did know what the end result of my brother's Moon Months were, I really didn't know what they'd gone through during them. I mean stories of the parties and feasts were common knowledge. While, as a kid, I could not attend, everyone my age had seen the preparations for various events. Still and all, I didn't recall seeing much of either of my brothers during that month of their lives.

All stories that I knew concerning what one did during a Moon Month came from kin of merchants and tradesfolk. I'd heard of one girl who'd been shut away in a cottage spinning wool into yarn, or a baker's-boy who had been tasked with making as much bread as he could in a day. Those sorts of monumental tasks were really the stuff of fey stories, though, so I didn't set much store by them. The not knowing, however . . . that did start to get my stomach gnawing on itself.

Doke looked over at me and smiled at the trace of concern his question had sparked. He settled a big hand around the back of my neck and shook me playfully. "Don't you worry, Tarrant. Nothing that will happen to you hasn't happened to many before. They survived, as will you."

"Just survive? I would like more than that."

"So would many others, Tarrant." My father gave me a big smile. "But, survival comes first. Remember that and you'll be starting ahead of your fellows. Be yourself, and they'll never have a chance to catch up."

CHAPTER 2

Valsina, like any other Oriosan city or town, hosted a moon-mask gala on Mid-Summer's Eve. The city-sponsored gala was not the only one held that night. Various guilds or religious sects held their own, but the city affair was by invitation only and involved the children from the finest families, a few of the brightest guild offerings, and a dozen or so people chosen by lot. Back then I didn't see that these "lucky ones" were really allowed to attend as curiosities. It was expected that the one night they spent in our company would likely be the highest they would rise in their lifetimes. In my excitement I missed the cruelty entirely.

I spent the day as most others my age did, moving through a prescribed series of activities meant to reflect the new me. I began with a hot bath and good scrubbing, using a special cake of soap that had enough lye and grit in it to grind down the hoof of a horse. It left me red all over and tingling. My brothers helped me get over that feeling by dousing me with frigid water to rinse off.

I washed my hair, too, and my mother trimmed it up some. I didn't go as far as some folks did, shaving their heads completely, but my mother allowed as how that was right since I'd been born with a full head of hair anyway. There were folks, generally out in the hinterlands, who actually bashed a tooth out of their moonmasked children, since few folks are born with teeth, but in the city we didn't go that far. The rebirth was symbolic, after all, and we were coming into adult life as adults, not newborn babes.

I got dressed in a new set of clothes, from tunic and trousers to stockings, boots, and belt. The tunic was green, of the same shade as those worn by Lord Norrington's retainers, and the trousers brown, though not as dark as the boots or belt. I wasn't allowed to wear so much as a knife. Tradition had it that a moonmasker shouldn't be saddled with the weapons of war, preserving innocence and all. I suspect there's a more practical reason, though, since not a few moonmaskers get puffed up by their status and are giddy enough to do stupid things like challenge others to duels.

From home, with my mask in place, I made my way to the Godfield area of town. Valsina itself started in a small valley at the convergence of two rivers, and spread out over the years to cover the surrounding hills. Beyond it to the south and west are the Bokagul Mountains—home to one group of urZrethi, though I'd never seen any of them when I was in the mountains. From there the rivers flowed north and east across the plains. At Valsina the Sut and Car Rivers become the Carst River, which twists on into Muroso on its way to the Crescent Sea to the northwest.

The city itself is over five hundred years old. The original walls form a triangle in the middle of the city. Things spread out from there, with the architecture becoming less massive, less martial, and varying from elegant, like the Norrington Manor on South Hill, to more rundown and dismal along the river. Godfield lies just north of the Old Fort and is lined with temples and shrines. Despite being one of the older sections of town, the buildings are newer and quite impressive, but that's because most of them have tumbled down or gone up in flames at one point or another, allowing their congregations to start over and thus outshine the competition.

The Temple to Kedyn, the warrior god, had been built broad and strong. The grey and white stones used to build it were both crudely quarried and dragged from the fields wherever they lay. In some cases they were even hauled a long distance from the site of some memorable battles. The stones were then fitted together, with edges smoothed and outlines softened, leaving their natural shape mostly intact, but uniting them with the other stones to form a cohesive whole. Doke had once suggested to me that the builders intended the structure to suggest that different people, united in a cause, would be stronger than any individual alone, and that seemed to make sense.

Of course, anyone growing up in Oriosa and destined to take the mask read a lot of symbolism into almost anything. We tended to look for added meaning in things, trying to find intent when nothing more serious than an accident had happened. I'd heard my father often say that men of other nations hated that trait in us, and suggested we looked too hard for meanings. But he also said the ones who complained the loudest were those who didn't want their hidden plans discovered.

I mounted the steps to the temple and bowed my head as I entered. Heavy pillars supported a tall ceiling and each ended in a cap shaped like the blade of a broad-ax. Stairs in the corners led up to a broad balcony, known as the priest's-walk, which provided access to upper chambers. The priests maintained their personal quarters up there, as well as offices and storage space for seasonal decorations.

The dome over the far end of the temple had been shaped to resemble the underside of a shield. A statue of Kedyn lurked beneath it. All massive and terrible, the statue's base rested in a depression that had been sunk below street level and had steps leading down to it. Sand covered the stone disk that formed the base, and in it were scores of glowing coals sending thick ribbons of musky incense drifting up over Kedyn's form. Scars crisscrossed his body where the cloak of dragon flesh did not cover it, and the helmet crested with dragon's claws hid his face in deep shadows. Kedyn wore no mask here in Oriosa, but his body bore the signs with which we would have decorated a mask. He was matched to us and us to him.

Murals depicting well-known battles or the exploits of famous heroes decorated the interior walls. Scattered throughout the main floor were statues of heroes and, in a few places, stone slabs marking the graves of Oriosan heroes from Valsina and the surrounding county who were deemed great and brave enough to be buried in the temple itself. No Hawkins had yet earned that honor, but my father said it was because we had the misfortune of surviving the sort of heroic acts that usually killed others and earned them a place in the temple.

My mother, in raising us all, encouraged us to continue in that tradition.

Off to the right was a small shrine to Gesric, the godling of retribution, and one of Kedyn's children. Back and to the left was another smaller shrine to the crone Fesyin, Gesric's half-sister. She'd been born of a union between Kedyn and the female aspect of death. She governed pain, and many were the ill and maimed who made offerings to her to relieve their suffering. Her shrine stunk of *metholanth* incense, which did not mix well with the muskier stuff offered to Kedyn.

I crossed to where one of the acolytes sold little charcoal biscuits shaped like a shield and thimblefuls of the incense powder favored by Kedyn. I offered him a fresh-minted Moon coin—a gold coin that I was honor bound to offer only once to any purveyor of goods in the city. The acolyte refused payment and gave me the charcoal and incense with a quick blessing. It was understood that in the future I would compensate, by action or through money, the kindness of everyone who refused to take my Moon coin—and by the next full moon it would be accepted as payment without a second thought by any merchant I offered it to.

I took the charcoal shield down the steps to the base and held the shield in the flame of an igniter. I waited until the edge had caught, then blew on it gently. Sparks jumped from the slowly expanding crescent until the coal burned bright red. I placed it down in the sand, elevating the unburned edge ever so slightly, then knelt and bowed my head.

It is said that the first prayer offered to a god by one of the moonmasked is the prayer most likely to be granted. Most folks say this with the assumption that the gods, who remain largely unseen and unheard from, favor the innocence with which such prayers are offered. Others, who have known some of the more self-confident of the moonmasked, assume the gods perversely grant that first prayer since most people discover it is not truly what they wanted or needed. And still others assume that the gods, like most moonmasked, are just silly and enjoy granting prayers that the faithful have no way of handling.

I had given long and considerable thought to the prayer I would offer. The warrior god was the god to which the Hawkins men paid their respects, and he had done well by us. The prayer I offered then would be the same as a prayer I might offer in the field, but here it was meant to cover my entire life instead of provide support in an immediate situation. I had my choice of the prayers for any of the six Martial Virtues, and sorting through them had not been a simple task.

No one prayed for Patience, though my father said that particular invocation was useful in the field when more waiting was being done than fighting. Many folks prayed for Mien—that collection of physical attributes such as strength, speed, and endurance that were crucial in combat. Courage and Spirit were also popular, as was Battlesight, or the ability to see and plan clearly for the campaigns to come. Each of them had their attraction for me, but I rejected them in the end. Physically I was well suited to being a warrior. I understood war and how it was waged, and realized that if I lived I'd learn more all the time. Courage and Spirit were things I thought I possessed, but at eighteen summers of age, there was no way to know for certain. Still, the arrogance of youth allowed me to imagine myself as not lacking in those areas.

What I asked for was Control. As I faced life and war, I wanted no illusions, no fog of war to confuse me, no momentary madness to leave me wondering where I was, why I was there, and what I should be doing. I wanted the clarity of mind that eludes many and without which all the other gifts would be useless. I knew that if my prayer were granted, I would find no escape from the madness that was war, that I would have to live with memories both exquisite and horrible, but better to live with them than not to live at all.

Over the years I have been given to wonder if my choice was based in innocence, arrogance, or some sort of delicious insanity that compelled me to want to know just how completely mad I should be.

I curled my left hand into a fist and clutched it to my breastbone, as if I were holding a shield covering my chest. My right hand poured the thimble of incense on the charcoal, then I extended my right arm down and away from my body, as if I were pointing a drawn sword at the ground. The incense began to smolder, pulsing a guttering ribbon of white smoke into the air.

"Most divine Kedyn, hear my prayer." I kept my voice low, so as not to disturb the warriors to either side of me. "You are the wellspring from which all heroism flows. Your mind possesses the razored edge that parts fiction from fact, rumor from truth, fears from reality. I beseech you to hone my mind that I may see clearly, think clearly, and know in my heart and head what I must do, when I must do it, and how it will be best done. With your aid I will never shrink from battle, shirk my duty, or abandon those who most depend upon me. This I pledge on my honor, now and for all time."

I glanced up at the statue. Smoke gathered around it like a thunderhead and I waited for a quick lightning strike. I got none, and realized I would have no sign of my prayer being heard or granted. Then I smiled as I wondered if that realization itself confirmed that Kedyn had granted me Control. *Or it could just be self-deception, which would be evidence of the opposite?*

Rising from my place, I ascended the steps again and presented myself to the acolyte. He took out a small carved stamp, inked it, and pressed it to my moonmask, below my right eye. It left there the tridentine sigil that marked my affiliation with Kedyn. I bowed to him, then wandered out of the temple.

As I emerged from the temple, two moonmasked youths sitting at the base of the temple steps rose and started up toward me. Both wore clothes with a similar color scheme to mine, but their garments had been fashioned of silk that flashed in the sunlight. Each wore a big grin and had temple marks on their moonmasks.

I recognized them instantly, but had to play through the

charade of our being moonmasked. "Good day, my men. Who under the moon are you?"

"I am Rounce Playfair." Rounce stood almost as tall as me, wasn't nearly as big as I am, but almost made up in quickness what he lacked in strength. His brown hair had been trimmed short, in a style I knew his father favored, but his brown eyes sparked with enough mischief that I knew he'd not taken his shearing badly. His moonmask bore the mark of Kedyn, which surprised me, since I thought he'd have tended more toward Erlinsax, the goddess of wisdom, or Graegen, the male aspect of justice.

"And I," offered the shorter, blond man, "am Bosleigh Norrington." Leigh's blue eyes sparkled as he sketched a quick but ornate bow. He surrendered nearly a hand-width of height to me and nearly twenty pounds. His moonmask likewise had been marked in the warrior temple, but there never was a choice for Leigh. Despite being somewhat small and not all that fast, he was Lord Norrington's son, and that meant a warrior was all he could ever hope to be. Luckily for Leigh, it was all he had ever *wanted* to be. Though no one thought he'd be the warrior his father was, most figured he'd manage to uphold the Norrington honor nonetheless.

"Pleased to meet both of you. I am Tarrant Hawkins." I drew myself up to my full height, then frowned slightly. "Why the warrior mark, Rounce? I didn't think you were inclined toward a warrior's life."

Rounce shrugged. "The warrior virtues help those dealing with conflict, Tarrant. Business is conflict, hence my choice. Besides, Leigh pointed out that the trident has three tines, so the three of us should stick together. We'll be stronger that way."

"True enough." I nodded toward Leigh. "So wither are you bound, my lord?"

Leigh struck a noble pose, though his being a step below me and that much shorter made it seem a bit ridiculous. "There is a tailor who is completing my costume for this evening. I'll give him moongold for it—my family pays him enough each year he can well afford to let this one suit of clothes go by without payment. Then back to the manor for something to eat before the gala. You'll come with, of course. Rounce is coming, and some of the others. Do say you'll come. I won't take no for an answer."

I sighed. "I will try, Leigh, but no promises. My sister Noni and her children are coming, and my mother hopes Annas will be there, too."

"Well, far be it from me to spoil a Hawkins gathering." Leigh's eyes brightened. "You should bring them all, even Noni's brood. Your father is my father's Peaceward; you'll all be welcome. You simply must come, all of you."

"I will try, Leigh."

Rounce leaned a forearm on Leigh's shoulder. "That's what he always says when he knows he won't join us."

I grinned. "My father, he is stuck in his ways. It's the way of his generation, not Lord Norrington's or ours. . . . The only way he'll go to Norrington Manor is if he is on official duty or if Lord Norrington asks him to be there. It would practically take an armed escort to get him to bring the family."

"Well, then, Tarrant, when we have taken our father's places, the rules will be changed, won't they? Open doors and all that, I think. I won't have it any other way." Leigh slipped his shoulder from beneath Rounce's forearm, then laughed as Rounce stumbled. "Come on, Rounce, we have things to do. We shall see you tonight, then, Tarrant, yes?"

I helped steady Rounce. "I will plead the case to my father, Leigh, but make no promises. If I do not see you there, I will find you at the gala."

"Good, then." Leigh threw me a sloppy salute. "Tonight our lives truly begin, and the world will never be the same."

CHAPTER 3

ruth be told, I would have welcomed some sameness to the world, if only because of the tear in my mother's eye as she smoothed the breast of my doublet that evening. I knew then that my growing up hurt her in ways I could not imagine and, worse, could do nothing to counter. I'd tried to head things off by talking to my father about Leigh's invitation, but he was unswayed—as I'd expected. Instead I remained with my family, catching my mother getting misty-eyed despite the joyful fellowship of a family come together once again.

Valsina's gala was held at Senate Palace. The large and rather ornately decorated building had steps that led up into a rotunda. Portraits and statues of leaders decorated it, but the most striking feature was the gallery of masks that matched those of the Senators serving in Upper and Lower Assemblies. The sixteen members of the Upper Assembly were nobles elected by the Lower Assembly, which was made up of trades-folk and nobles from cadet branches of the houses. Each had to be able to trace his family back to the time of the Great Revolt, and while many folks in Oriosa could do that, only those who had amassed a certain amount of material wealth ever reached the Senate floor.

On this night the Upper Assembly's small gallery, which sat above and behind the entryway to the Lower Assembly floor, had been staffed with musicians who played a host of songs which had been sanctified by their antiquity. To enter the gala, I passed through a long corridor that led beneath the orchestra and brought me out at the head of some long steps going down to the rectangular assembly floor. A wide-railed walkway ringed the room to provide space for spectators wanting to study the Assemblies in action but, unlike tonight, chairs were not usually provided.

I paused at the head of the stairs as a masked chamberlain in red pounded his staff against the floor twice, then announced me. "I present Master Tarrant Hawkins." Mild applause, mostly from the spectators, followed the announcement, then I descended the steps.

The room spread out wide on either side of me. A massive castle of ascending high benches split the far wall as the stairs did at this side. The hardwood platforms rose one above the other, front to back, and normally housed the Assembly's Speaker and his various deputies, but this night were festooned with flowers. A big, round silver mirror, reminiscent of the moon, hung from the Speaker's seat and provided us with a view that gathered us all together and shrank us down to nothing. Tables laden with food and drink surrounded the Speaker's platform as if breastworks to hold us at bay.

I quickly spotted Rounce and joined him at a table where a servant pressed a goblet of wine into my hands. The vintage was a red that was both dry and hearty, though it had a touch of sweetness and the faint flavor of berries. It was a wine that had aged, which surprised me, since the moonmasked often got brand-new wines that had yet to mature.

I smiled at Rounce. "Good wine."

"I know, I picked it out." He bowed his head to me as applause descended from above in the wake of another entrant being announced. "The Speaker asked my father to supply the wine for this evening, and he intended to use the first pressing from last year, but I prevailed upon him to go deeper in the cellar. He almost balked, but I reminded him that what moongold buys now, real gold will buy later, and having us remember the wine as good instead of symbolic would be best."

"Good thinking." I sipped more wine and raised my goblet in a salute to him. "Though thoughts like that are what made me wonder about your tridentine mark."

He gave me a quick smirk. "Armies need quartermasters, don't they?"

"My father never reported having good wine in the field."

"Then I'll have to change that." He held his goblet in both hands and looked down into it. "I thought about Graegen, as you suggested, or even Turic . . ."

"Turic? You'd pledge yourself to Death?"

"The female aspect is more concerned with change than death, but you can't say that death has not changed my fortunes. Here I started life as the first son of a merchant who had a noble for a cousin, then an illness takes that branch of the family and suddenly we're elevated. I'm not really different than I was before, but . . ."

I nodded. I had seen Rounce in Valsina before his family's elevation when I accompanied my mother on her trips to market. Playfair & Sons Traders were known as honest merchants, but Rounce and I were just kids who eyed each other suspiciously. When his father became a noble, the family firm became Playfair & Sons Trading Company, and Rounce was expected to move into new social circles. He ended up in the same student battalion as Leigh and I. Being bigger than most others since we'd gotten our growth early, we were thrown together in many exercises, thereby becoming friends.

"As my father says, Rounce, 'It's not the man in the prettiest uniform before the battle that's remembered, but the man who's still standing after it.' You're one of those who will still be standing."

"Only if you're holding me up." Rounce slapped me on the arm. "By the way, be prepared. You were missed at dinner and Leigh might be in a bit of a mood."

"And this would be unusual because . . . ?"

Rounce laughed, then pointed up at the top of the stairs. "You'll see. Here's our little Leigh now."

The echoes of the staff reverberated through the hall. It

took the third staff-strike to kill the murmuring voices, and the fourth buried them in silence. The chamberlain waited a heartbeat or two to guarantee no ghost of conversation lingered, then made his announcement. "I present Lord Bosleigh Norrington."

Leigh, at the top of the stairs, bowed handsomely as hearty applause washed over him. The night's dress code had required us to wear something other than our moonmasks that was white—which Rounce and I accomplished with our shirts. Leigh had gone a considerable step further, decked out in a full jacket made of white satin, with lace at the throat and cuffs. His pants likewise were white satin and ran down to his knees, where they met white stockings. His shoes, which were low cut, had been cobbled together from white leather and had big silver buckles.

He descended the stairs at a leisurely pace, smiling and waving at those below, bowing his head at the spectators above. Leigh was in his element, with all eyes on him. It had been that way since his birth, to hear my father tell it, since he was Lord Norrington's firstborn and a son. The boy had grown into a man used to such attention, who was, in many ways, uncomfortable when he didn't get it.

Rounce and I looked at each other and laughed as Leigh reached the floor. He continued to make his way toward us, pausing to bow to the girls who giggled at him. His progress through the crowd took long enough for me to nearly finish my wine. Rounce had started on another full goblet by the time Leigh arrived.

Leigh bumped against me, then looked up and smiled. "Oh, Tarrant, there you are—I'd expected you to be off eating something. And you, Rounce."

I grinned. "Make it sound as if you weren't looking for us."

"Well, I was, of course, my dear friends, but I can't let *them* know that." His eyes rolled up to sweep the spectators' gallery. "It would not do to let them think I am so fragile that I cannot exist without my friends."

Rounce rolled his eyes. "Keep talking like that and you won't have any friends."

"Don't be offended. You know I jest."

"Just a little too often, Leigh." I stepped out of the way to provide Leigh access to the wine table. "Your pleasure, my lord?"

Leigh sniffed and moved past me. "Well, arriving is such dry work . . ."

I glanced past him at the spectators' gallery and did feel a little uneasiness coil in my stomach. All the spectators wore fine clothes, but they were cut from cloth dyed bright red. Their masks covered their faces in full and were without decoration, completely obscuring their identities. While some individuals, like the Assembly Speaker, were corpulent or remarkable enough to be recognizable, most of the observers sank into a red sea of anonymity. They were there not to be seen, but to watch us and decide our fate. What they saw at any point might determine which regiment would offer me a chance to join it, or what merchant house might vie for my services. Leigh's concern over the spectators mocked their import, since his life was already decided. It dawned on me immediately that I had no such assurances, so I finished my wine and began looking for a woman to guide to the dance floor and show I could be well mannered.

Leigh managed, in that moment, to provide me an opportunity to show off my more martial side. He'd been making his way down the table, bending to sniff the various vintages. Rounce stood with him and Leigh would announce a district and year for each wine offered, with Rounce confirming each judgment. This continued until Leigh bumped into someone on his right and, without even looking at the person, snapped at him in a rather imperious tone.

"Give way, sir, for my mission is most urgent."

"While most take their wine through the mouth, looks as if you sniff it up, ay?"

Leigh's head turned slightly in the speaker's direction, and I knew he caught a glimpse of the man's black homespun trousers and polished but well-worn boots. Unfortunately, bent over as he was, Leigh wasn't in a good position to judge just how big this man was. "I said, give way, good fellow."

"Not 'sir' no more?"

Leigh turned and straightened up, then was forced to crane his neck back to look up past the man's heavily muscled chest and shoulders to his face. A thick shock of red hair capped the man's head, and freckles could be seen spreading over his cheeks below the moonmask. Green eyes glittered emeraldlike in the mask, and I spotted a trident below the right eye. The man wore a black linen tunic, with a band of white cloth tied around his left biceps. An evil grin split his face.

"Perhaps, *good fellow*," Leigh persisted, "I should acquaint you with the manners prized in society."

The man raised his right hand and curled it into a fist that would have filled a fair-sized mixing bowl. "Perhaps I should acquaint you with my fist."

"Easy, friend, easy." I stepped forward and wedged myself between him and Leigh. "You've been lucky enough to be chosen to be here tonight. Stretch that luck and avoid a fight."

"I ain't your friend."

"No, but we *all* are marked by Kedyn. That must count for something." I grinned up at him and offered him my right hand. "I am Tarrant Hawkins."

The larger man nodded his head slowly, then opened his right hand and engulfed mine in his grip. "Naysmith Carver, armorer's apprentice. Have a mind to be using what I made, not be making more." A smile slowly followed his words and I shook his hand heartily.

Freeing my hand from his, I turned, forcing Leigh and Rounce back a bit. "Bosleigh Norrington you have met. This is Rounce Playfair."

"Pleased," Rounce offered.

"As well." Naysmith glanced down at Leigh. "The wine to the end is the best, if you be continuing down that way."

Leigh blinked, then nodded. A smile grew on his face as he slipped round me and past Naysmith. "Say, Nay—oh, my, that rhymes—say, Nay, how went your day?" He laughed to himself. "So lyrical, that."

Naysmith's eyes narrowed.

I held a hand up. "Forgive him, please, Naysmith. He's just excited and gets like that. Mid-Summer's Eve and all."

"A good slap will fix that, ay?"

Leigh plucked a goblet of wine from the table and turned back toward us. "But only the finest slap for me."

Naysmith's right hand flexed, and I had no doubt his best shot would spin Leigh's head around like a weathercock in a gale.

I sought to distract the big man. "What company were you hoping to join, Naysmith?"

"I answer to Nay—too many Smiths about." Nay shrugged. "Home Guards, if I must. The Norrington Foot Guards is best. See more than Valsina."

"Not the Frontier Lancers, or the Oriosan Scouts?" Leigh regarded us with a broad smile on his face. "The Heavy Dragoons could use someone like you, though I doubt there's a horse that would carry you."

"Some do, some don't." Nay tossed off the rest of his wine and started to wipe his mouth on his sleeve, but thought better of it. "Riders worry about sticking and stabbing. Been laboring for years with a hammer. Bashing and laying about with a maul is for me."

"Your strength will serve you well in war." Leigh finished his wine and returned the goblet to the table. "How will you fare at a ball, though? The watchers have seen we can drink, so shall we thrill some of these ladies with a turn about the floor?"

Knowing Leigh the way I did, the hint of cruelty in his question wasn't lost on me. While there wasn't a girl present who wouldn't be overjoyed to be seen on Leigh's arm—or Rounce's, for that matter—most of the girls were from a class that would scarcely spare Nay a look. Even those girls who had learned the skills necessary for a trade would be interested in marrying, and none of them at this age had anything but dreams of bettering herself through matrimony. While all would have said they would marry for love, a title or money or lands makes a suitor very lovable indeed.

Nay looked over at the blizzard of dancers swirling in time to the music. "Don't know this step."

His voice carried no surrender with it, and Leigh picked up on that immediately. "Name a step, then, and I'll call the tune."

"Don't know as how it has a name." Nay folded heavily muscled arms over his chest. "We dance it to the song 'Firetoes.'"

Rounce hummed a moment or two, then nodded. "Firelight Dash is the step, Leigh."

"Firelight Dash it shall be, then. Gentlemen . . ." Leigh waved us in his wake. I let Nay slip in after Rounce and before me, which earned me a frown from Leigh. "I meant you to come as well, Hawkins."

"I gathered, my lord."

Nay glanced back over his shoulder at me. "Which is it you're called?"

"Tarrant when he's being nice, Hawkins all other times."

"Must hear Hawkins a lot, then."

"Easier to rhyme than Tarrant."

"I heard that." Leigh turned quickly and stuck his tongue out at me. "Along came Nay and Tarrant, the fearful giant and the ant . . ." Spinning around again he darted up the stairs and spoke to the chamberlain, who then spoke to the lead musician. Leigh all but skipped back down the steps.

"It is set." He smiled and waved a hand at a line of young women. "Gentlemen, choose your weapons."

Leigh and Rounce immediately plunged into a cloud of giggling girls. Nay looked back to our left, toward a small knot of girls who were dressed as he was, but I caught his arm. He looked down with his face twisted in puzzlement, but I gave him a reassuring smile. "I have an idea, if you're game."

Nay grunted and nodded.

I led him over to a pair of twins, May and Maud Lamburn. The flaxen-haired beauties had bright blue eyes peeking out from beneath their moon masks. Though small enough that I dwarfed them, and close as twins always are, they were also known for a keen sense of competition. If I asked one to dance, the other couldn't stand to be left alone, so she would accept the next invitation offered.

And, on top of that, both of them danced very well.

"May, I would request the pleasure of this dance."

May took my hand with a smile and a nod. "I am honored."

I smiled at her sister. "Maud, this is my friend, Naysmith Carver."

"If your ladyship would permit . . ." Nay offered her his hand and she took it.

We escorted our partners onto the floor and took up positions behind Rounce and Leigh. Rounce had asked Lindsey Cotter to dance with him, but that was no surprise. He'd been sweet on her for the better part of a year. Leigh, on the other hand, had asked Nolda Disper to join him, though for size she would have been a better match with Nay. Still, with her long hair so blonde it was almost white, and her skin a gentle damask, she and Leigh seemed of a type. Her pale blue eyes proved a few shades lighter than his, and the hard nature of her stare would have chilled me to the bone.

Our partners knew the moment the first violinist put bow to string that the four couples were in a competition. The Firelight Dash is one of those festive, long-stride galloping type dances, with quick turns and laughter and gay abandon. The full-skirted gowns the girls wore that night were not well suited to it, but there Nay and I had an advantage. As we spun across the floor, whisking our partners around this way and that, we could lift the Lamburn sisters clear of the floor, freeing their trapped feet—and keeping them out from under my feet, as well.

Leigh, to his credit, realized he'd been overmatched from the start, so kept to the center of the floor and let the rest of us circle him and Nolda. He led her through a version of the dance that was more stately than frenetic. His turns let her long hair sweep out in a wondrous display, and his frequent bows in her direction made her the center of attention. He showed her off to her benefit before all, while the rest of us became fast-moving fish in an ocean of white.

I admired him for thinking that quickly. I also pitied him because Nay, Rounce, and I were having great fun in the dance. Somewhere in it, as the music took hold, all the anxiety I had been feeling about the night and its import drained away. I let my laughter mingle with everyone else's, then drew it all back in and let it live in my heart.

The song ended all too fast as far as I was concerned. May

had weathered well my clumsy leading through the dance, and even gave me a smile when I bowed to her. Nay and I both nodded to the twins as they curtsied to us, then we let the Lamburn sisters return to the coterie from which we had drawn them. Other girls surrounded them, insulating them from music with a cacophony of giggles which, for some reason, started a bit of a blush creeping up my cheeks.

Nay slapped me on the back. "Not a bad stepper, that Maud."

"Thanks for helping me keep the peace there."

"That was it then, not dancing?" Nay grinned ever so slightly, then rubbed a hand across his chin. "If you like, there are two other girls, my master's daughter and friend, we could give a whirl."

"A fair trade, I think."

We turned and started toward the group of girls Nay had looked at before, but Rounce caught up with us and Leigh cut us off. "Where are you going?"

I fixed Leigh with a gimlet eye. "This *is* a gala, so we're off to enjoy ourselves."

"Ah, Tarrant, I had such high hopes for you." Leigh shook his head mournfully. "This is not a gala, this is a livestock auction. They watch, they choose."

I wrinkled my nose. "I'm not sure I like the sound of 'livestock auction.'"

"Neither do I, dear boy, but at least we have a bid." Leigh held up a folded slip of paper. "I was given this just now."

I took it from him and unfolded it. Rather than chance Nay's not being able to read, I read it aloud in a hoarse whisper. "Your demeanor and spirit impress us. Midnight, in the west garden, by the north gate."

Nay ran a hand through his red hair. "Invite to an alley bashing, sounds like."

"Hardly, my big friend." Leigh took the note back from me. "We're being invited to glimpse the future. And I think, for us, it will be a most pleasant one indeed."

CHAPTER 4

The full moon stared down dispassionately at the four of us as we waited at the garden's north gate. Moonlight glowed off Leigh's outfit, making him look like an overdressed ghost. Rounce kept glancing back at the dark edifice of the Senate Palace, silently lamenting that the plans he'd had for ending the evening with Lindsey Cotter would not come to fruition. I sat myself down on one of the carved granite benches and sniffed night-blooming *yismyn* flowers.

Nay shuffled his feet and paced nervously along the gentle curve of the crushed marble walkway near the gate. He'd get as far as Leigh, then turn on his heel and march back toward the gate. Leigh, Rounce, and I had assured him that he was included in the message Leigh had received.

Nay had countered, "A trident only has three tines."

"But it also has a haft, which is bigger than any of the tines, and that describes you, Nay." I patted him on the arm and was a bit amazed at just how hard his muscles were. "You really are meant to be with us."

Leigh had agreed. "Come now, dear fellow, do you think I would be wrong about such things? The invitation was for my companions, and you are one of them. You've danced with one of the dreaded Lamburn sisters, so you are clearly valiant."

Nay scowled. "Don't like an invite what doesn't say who sent it."

Laughter rolled melodically from Leigh's throat. "Oh, but that's the joy of the day, Nay. It's the mystery of it all. Look at the watchers, secure in their anonymity, all wrapped up in red secrets. You know why they wear red, don't you? It's the color of blood and the color of life. It's to stress their import and to show how they have the power to make our lives or destroy them."

He lowered his voice and all of us had to lean down to his level to hear him continue. "The man who gave this note to the chamberlain had a military bearing. Even the script is the type they teach officers so orders will be clear. We've clearly understood their order. We didn't drink too much, just danced, showed we are not out of control. We'll be the winners here, all four of us, tines and haft together."

In the garden Leigh had stationed himself on the walkway to prevent Nay from bolting. I think Nay fascinated Leigh because the man clearly was not frightened by him, nor did he particularly care if he offended the son of the city's highest noble. Instead Nay seemed more frightened of doing something that would prevent him from reaching his dream. Being with us when he shouldn't be could certainly do that, but running away when he should be with us would also doom him. He bounced back and forth between those two alternatives, and only Leigh's having positioned himself to cut off any retreat forced Nay to remain with us.

Which, from the occasional smile that graced his moonlit face, I judged to be what he wanted to do anyway.

The north gate itself was not one of the garden's best known features. A small, iron-bound oak door had been set in an arched doorway. Ivy covered the wall around it, and curled tendrils reached for the door itself. I'd not seen it before from this side, and I couldn't recall having seen it on the handful of times I'd been walking along High Street.

Crickets competed with crunch of stone beneath Nay's feet until Leigh hissed: "Quiet; listen."

I heard nothing at first, then, from the other side of the wall I caught the muffled thump of horses' hooves on cobblestone and the occasional squeak of wagon wheel on axle. The hoofbeats should have been sharp and clear, so I assumed rags had been tied over the hooves to kill the sound. That realization puckered my flesh.

Nay stared hard at the door and whatever lay beyond it. "Not liking this at all."

"All part of the game, old shoe." Leigh tried to keep his voice light, but he still ended up wiping his palms on his jacket.

I stood as a key rasped in the lock. Ivy leaves bounced and shimmered in the moonlight as the door opened outward, pulling free of clinging vines. From my angle I could see nothing through the doorway, but Nay bobbed his head, then nodded. He flashed me two fingers.

I smiled. *Smart man. He can see two people, but doesn't think they need to know they've been seen.*

A voice disguised in a hoarse whisper snapped an order at us. "Come on now, the four of you. No time to waste."

Leigh flashed a quick knowing smile at Nay, then strolled through the doorway as if he had not a care in the world. Rounce followed him, bowing his head to get through. Nay had to stoop and shift his shoulders at an angle, and I let him precede me so he'd not have any excuse to run off. I came last and heard the door squeak shut behind me.

The wagon I'd heard roll up had been a big, boxy affair, the kind that serves as both shop and home for tinkers and traders who make a circuit through the hinterlands. I saw that rags *had* been tied around the hooves of the team drawing it and likewise had been wrapped around the wheels' iron rims. The wagon had no windows that I could see, and I only saw the door as I came around the back of it. The door itself had been hinged at the bottom and served as a ramp for walking up into the interior. Two men, hooded and cloaked and masked in shadow, guided us up the ramp. Not unexpectedly, the ramp rose behind me, cutting off the light from the street before I'd gotten much of a look at the wagon's interior.

What little I did see didn't tell me much. Two padded

benches lined each side, but the box remained otherwise un-
decorated. There did appear to be a small window at the top
of the forward wall that would let someone communicate with
the driver, but the panel covering it was closed. When the
ramp closed, I heard a bar being dropped behind it to keep it
shut. Someone slapped a hand against the back of the wagon,
then we started off with a lurch that spilled me to the floor at
my companions' feet.

"Really, Hawkins, time enough to thank me for including
you on this adventure later. No need to prostrate yourself
now . . ."

I made sure to press down heavily on Leigh's thigh as I
climbed to my feet. "I have no intention of letting you believe
I'm ungrateful, Leigh."

"I see that." He hissed with pain and gently shoved me
back. I stumbled into Rounce's lap, then slid off to my left and
onto the empty half of a bench across from Nay. "Well, quite
the interesting little start to our adventure, is it not, gentlemen?"

I twisted around and settled my back against the rear of
the wagon. "I'm fairly certain Rounce would prefer Lindsey's
warm kisses to this cold box."

"I'll just carry on bravely, Tarrant, and she'll reward me for
it."

"Quite so; that's the spirit." Leigh's voice shifted in tone to
something a little less warm. "What think you, Nay?"

"Don't know as what I'm supposed to think." Nay sniffed
twice. "Racing along like this, we'll be out of the city soon."

I nodded. The wagon had kept on rather straight, only
making the few jogs that High Street did as it headed to the
West Gate. This time of night it would run into little if any
traffic on the way, and if we were meant to travel out of the
city, I had little doubt those taking us would have the authority to speed on through the gate. "If we head west, we'll be
into the forests before much time. Anyone have an idea what
they'll do with us?"

"Dear boy, for us to have any idea of what they will do
with us would be for us to be privy to information we're not

supposed to have." Leigh laughed carelessly. "I could *speculate* about what they might do with us, if you wish."

I was determined not to give him the satisfaction, but a wheel hit a pothole, jouncing me up and landing me on my backside hard enough to force a quick yip from me.

"Oh, prize to the wolf-yipper. That's it exactly."

"Leigh, explain it, if you please, for those of us who aren't as fluent in wolf as Tarrant is."

"It is simple, dear Rounce. They will be taking us deep into the wood and will drop us off in some spot from which we will be forced to make our way home. The journey will call upon us to work together to survive, and will demand from us all our survival skills. We'll have to find food and water, all those things. It will be a fun outing."

My eyes narrowed. "You knew this very much in advance, didn't you?"

"Know? No."

I leaned forward. "If not, why did you choose to wear a coat this evening, one thick enough to keep you warm if we're a couple of nights out in the woods?"

"Well, I might have guessed a coat would be useful, but not as useful as you think." Leigh's hand slapped against the wagon's wall. "This coach will travel twice as fast as a man can walk in an hour, or perhaps three times. I have no innate sense of time . . ."

"That's right," Rounce growled, "which is why you always manage to be late."

"That notwithstanding, Rounce, the simple fact is that you or Hawkins or even our new friend will likely be able to look at the moon when we are released and can guess how long we have been traveling. At best, I would imagine, we will have eight hours of walking back."

"Puzzle that out yourself?"

"Indeed I did, Nay." Leigh snickered in his corner. "And it helped that my father is holding a dinner tomorrow in my favor—*our* favor—and he would not have scheduled it when he did if he expected me to be late. Or later than usual."

"Don't like the sound of this at all." A thundercrack reverberated through the box: Nay's fist pounding the side. "Should have warned us."

"Dear friends, did I not suggest you avoid too much wine so as to be clear-headed for this adventure? I did, didn't I? If I'd not warned you, you'd all be besotted right now."

"I must have been besotted to be here." I let a low growl rumble from my throat. "If you'd hinted, Leigh, we could have eaten more. We could have slipped some cheese into our pockets . . ."

"Stuffed bread up your . . . shirttails."

"My, my, rather testy. Be careful, my friends, or I might not lead you back to Valsina."

"Be going my own way. Don't need you, Leigh."

"Will it be the Nay way for you two, as well?"

"I think we should all calm down a bit here. Let's remember that tines and haft thing, shall we?" Rounce's words came firm and cut through the growing tension. "If they wanted four of us, presumably there are some challenges out there that require four of us to handle. I know Hawkins, Leigh, and I have spent time in the countryside, out hunting, living off the land. What's your experience, Nay?"

"Done my time woodcutting." He fell silent for a moment, then plunged on. "My mother, she makes cures, so I know to harvest some plants and roots and berries."

"Good, that's a skill we don't possess." Rounce yawned. "I don't know about the rest of you, but I've had a long day. Getting to sleep in this wagon may not be easy, but I'll suggest it. If Leigh's right, and chances are he is, we've a longer day before us tomorrow."

"Well, I'm all for sleep, gentlemen. Perhaps I'll dream up a way we can return in style. Wouldn't that be something?"

I shook my head. "It would, Leigh, but I'll leave the dreaming to you. I have a feeling this exercise will be rooted more in reality than anything else."

Though I tried to remain awake during the journey, the day did catch up with me and I drifted off. Just prior to that we had taken a turn that should have put us on a southwesterly jog, and we'd begun to climb into the foothills of Bokagul, but that's the last thing I remember before the wagon stopped and cool air flooded in through the open doorway.

I rolled off the bench and started down the ramp. Yawning, I nodded at the two men standing in the moonwashed forest road. Given the moon's position I figured we'd been on the road for the better part of three hours, which put dawn another three hours off.

I flung my arms wide to stretch. One of the cloaked figures drifted forward and gave me a hearty shove in the flank. I stumbled toward the side of the road, intent on remaining on my feet, but I ran out of ground.

I tumbled into a ravine, passing first through a screen of thorny blackberry bushes. I hit on my knees beyond that, snapping some deadfall branches, then began a somersault that bounced and tossed me down the steep hill. Somewhere in all that I clipped a sapling with my right thigh. This started me spinning wildly, caroming me off this tree and that and finally dumping me in the grasp of a lone pine's gnarled and exposed roots.

I heard more crashing around me and at least one splash. I tried to stand, but my right leg apparently decided it was done for the night, so it collapsed. I slid facefirst down to the stream running through the ravine's heart. My fingers sank into cold mud, but didn't sink so far that I got a dunking.

I heard more splashing, and then a laugh. "Just as well you didn't stuff bread in my coat, as it would be soggy mush right now."

"A match for your brains, then."

"Well done, Nay . . . with your wit, me you may yet slay. Triple rhyme!"

"Rounce, you with us?" I looked around and could see Leigh sitting in a pool and Nay crouched on a rock at the stream's edge. "Rounce?"

"Here." From further upslope he made his way down to us. He leaned on trees as he came and held his left arm across his chest. "Anyone else hurt?"

"Just my pride."

"Likely a mortal wound on you, then." Nay pitched a small pebble toward Leigh. "Not hurt either."

I pushed back from the stream and tried to gather my legs beneath me. I was finally able to stand, but the lower part of my right leg still felt a little numb. "I'll be fine pretty soon. What's wrong, Rounce?"

"Hit a tree on the way down. I think I broke a rib."

Nay stood. "Coughing blood?"

"Not so far."

"Good thing." Nay walked down toward Rounce, then veered off and snapped a sprig off a low bush. He stripped off all but the newest of the fat, round leaves at the tip, then folded the twig in half until it cracked. He plucked the leaf off and extended both the twig and leaf to Rounce.

"What is it?"

"Fesyin Bane. Broke the twig like the rib. Press them together to draw off the pain. Pulp the leaf and tuck it in your cheek."

I sniffed. "Smells like *metholanth*."

Rounce accepted the leaf and chewed it, but waved away the broken twig. "The leaf will do."

Nay lifted his chin. "The twig draws pain."

Leigh splashed his way over. "I see our big friend is superstitious. Perhaps, Nay, you think I should thank the spirit of this stream for stopping me without injury."

"Spirits ain't godlings." Nay pressed the twig into Rounce's left hand, then laid it against his ribs. "Broke twig draws pain."

Rounce looked at me, but I just shrugged. "Can't hurt."

Rounce nodded. "It is feeling a bit better."

Leigh flicked wet hair off his forehead. "Take you into the wildness and you become savages, all of you. Fear not, this way to civilization."

Rounce fell into step behind him. "Think he knows where he's going?"

"I don't know." I limped into line after him. "He was smart enough to figure out what would happen to us."

Nay, behind me, tapped me on the shoulder. "Not that smart."

"Say what?" Leigh glanced back at us. "What makes you think I'm not that smart?"

"Your shoes."

I laughed and Rounce joined me for a moment before he hissed and grabbed his ribs. "Nay's right, Leigh. Those shoes aren't suited to hiking back to Valsina."

"Perhaps he knows a cure for blistered feet."

"Suffering." Nay's hearty chuckle warmed my heart. "Builds calluses and character."

"Character? Piffle! I have enough character for—"

An unearthly shriek split the night. The four of us yelped in response, then took off running toward it. Nay and I quickly passed Rounce, but Leigh and Nay drew ahead of me with ease. I kept after them and watched them scramble up a small hill. They silhouetted themselves against the moon, then Nay's big form reeled to the right and dropped to its knees. I watched his body twitch and his head dip, and I knew he was vomiting.

I reached the crest of the hill and stood beside an unmoving Leigh. Before us, in a small depression in the top of the hill, lay the body of a man. A shredded cloak lay a short way away from him and his bare face stared up at the sky. Without a mask on, there was no way Leigh or I could recognize him. Blood soaked his clothes and the ground, but in the moonlight both it and his clothing took on the same dark burgundy hue.

A sword lay on the ground with its hilt near his right thigh. He could have reached down for it, were he still alive—and if he still had his right arm. He wasn't and didn't.

Rounce came up on my right. "Oh, by the gods. He's dead, isn't he?"

"Very dead, but the thing that killed him isn't." I looked around at my companions. "I think this test of our survival skills just got a lot harder. Chances are real good that tomorrow we'll be very late for dinner."

CHAPTER 5

"Being *late* for dinner is not my concern. *Being* dinner is." Leigh stooped and picked up the sword. "Hawkins, get the dagger on his belt. There's another in his boot for you, Rounce."

"In a minute, Leigh." I walked over to Nay and dropped to one knee beside him. He remained down on all fours and twitched when I settled my left hand in the middle of his broad back. "How are you doing?"

He turned his head to look at me and the moon leeched all the warm color from his face. "Hain't seen someone done like that."

"Neither have the rest of us."

He half-laughed and spit. Little ropy lines of mucus dripped slowly down from his mouth to the pine needles covering the ground. "So much for my prayer for courage being granted."

"I'd not judge Kedyn that harshly. After all, you only took a step or two away and puked. If you didn't have courage, you might have run screaming." I got my hand under his right arm. "Ready to get up? Wipe your mouth."

Nay swiped his sleeve across his mouth, spit twice more,

then staggered to his feet. He turned and looked at the corpse and almost heaved again, but managed to keep his gorge down. "Thanks, Hawkins. Be fine now."

Rounce tossed me the dead man's belt, complete with an empty scabbard and the sheathed knife. I looped it over my right shoulder. "Are we going to bury him?"

" 'Spose we ought to." Rounce nodded as he slipped the boot dagger into his own boot top. "Leigh?"

Leigh, who had been crouched examining a patch of earth, grabbed the sword's quillons and levered himself upright. "I don't think it will matter much since there aren't that many stones around here. The thing that killed him won't have trouble digging him back up no matter what we do."

"You find a track?" I skirted the body and came over to look at the place where the leaves and needles had been scratched back to the bare earth. I squatted and let my fingers trail over the trio of parallel tracks, but I'd never seen anything like them before. "What is it?"

Leigh's silhouette shifted its shoulder uneasily. "I don't know for certain, but my father once described something like this."

"What do you think it is?"

"A temeryx."

I shot to my feet as a chill rolled down my spine. "A frostclaw this far south? And in summer?"

"I no more like the idea than you, dear Hawkins, but it *has* been a chilly summer." Leigh pointed the sword back toward the body. "Check his back. You'll find claw marks there, too."

"But there aren't any feathers. It can't be a temeryx."

Leigh shook his head. "Fine, have it your way. It was a rogue bear, one with only three toes on each paw, which snuck up on a man, killed him, bit off an arm, and then ran off before we got here."

My mind refused to believe a frostclaw could be all the way down in Oriosa—less because it wasn't possible than because if it were true, the chances of our making it home were growing smaller. Of course, I'd never actually seen one of the beasts, and I was certain the stories told of them made them out to be nastier than they possibly could be, but whatever had killed the man had certainly worked quickly and quietly, in keeping with the descriptions of temeryces.

Nay toed the dead man's booted foot. "What was he doing out here?"

"He's dressed in red, like the watchers from the gala." Rounce picked up the man's cloak and fastened it about his own neck. "Perhaps they sent him out here to watch us and report back."

"Makes sense to me." I shifted the belt around and fastened it about my waist. "If it returns for more of its kill, I think I want to be far away from here."

Rounce frowned. "We can't just leave his body for that thing to eat."

Nay snorted. "Not liking the idea of carrying a frostclaw's dinner with us. And that cloak has blood on it."

The cloak puddled around Rounce's feet. "Thanks for pointing that out."

"Well, gentlemen, our course is clear. We head east-north-east as quickly as we can." Leigh pointed the sword in the direction of Valsina. "We'll have to be alert and quick."

Nay folded his arms across his chest. "You having the sword . . . You must be the best swordsman among us, then?"

Rounce shook his head. "Hawkins is better, actually."

"Then why does Leigh have the sword?"

"I have the sword, dear Nay, because I am a Norrington." Leigh's surprised expression clearly suggested he had no idea why Nay would think anyone else would be entitled to carry it. "Perhaps you somehow think you should wield it?"

"No." Nay walked over to a fallen tree and snapped off a thick branch about a yard and a half long. "Do fine bashing with this. If Hawkins is better with the sword, though, it should be his."

I held my hands up. "Let Leigh keep it. I may be better, but he's not bad. Being his father's son, he's likely heard lots about frostclaw killing, so he can put it to better use."

Leigh spread his arms. "Anything else, or shall we go?"

"After you, my lord." I waved Leigh forward, then fell in

behind him. Rounce came after me and Nay brought up the rear.

Though it wasn't the sort of hot and humid summer night I was used to, it was not really cold. Even so, I felt chilled to the bone. My left hand rode on the hilt of the dagger, ready to draw it in an instant. My ears strained for any hint of sound that couldn't be put down to the tread of my companions or me. Though the moon provided light, it didn't provide enough, and walking down the north face of a hill plunged us into a moon shadow so deep I almost lost sight of Leigh's ghostly form ahead of me.

We didn't talk as we marched along. I told myself it was because I wanted to keep quiet so the frostclaw wouldn't track us. While I wanted that to be true, I knew it wasn't. I was afraid, deeply afraid, and I didn't want the others to know it. I didn't know if they were as fearful as I was, but I took their silence as a sign that they each knew how dangerous our situation was.

Try as I might, I couldn't hear or see or smell anything of a temeryx, but back then I was woefully unprepared to spot the beast. We were moving into the wind, so I had no chance of catching the dry, heavy scent of it. We were making enough noise to hide the approach of cavalry, much less a creature that is more quiet than falling snow. And, as for seeing it, the creature didn't want to be seen until it struck, so unless I could see through to the other side of the hills, I had no chance of spotting it.

We were strung out along a deer path running along the side of a hill when it struck from up-slope. Nay started to cry out, which brought me around to the right, looking back up the hill. I caught movement in the shadows, but it came so fast I couldn't focus on it. The temeryx leaped at Rounce, its clawed hind legs reaching for him. Before I could complete my turn, it had carried Rounce off the trail and was chasing his rolling form down the hill.

How to describe a temeryx? From tip of its toothy muzzle to tail, the feathered beast is ten feet long, standing six at the head. The rear legs are cocked back like those of a bird, and the forelimbs are these small, hook-clawed things that aren't strong, but useful for holding prey. The hind legs are thickly muscled and the interior toe on each has a big sickle-shaped claw that slices through flesh and muscle quicker than a sword. The narrow head has eyes set forward and a long muzzle with rows of sharp teeth.

The temeryx's black feathers half hid it, but Rounce's screams told us where it was. The beast leaned forward, ducking its head down to snap at and worry Rounce's left leg, then its head came up and the creature hissed open-mouthed at the sound of Nay and me running toward it. Its tongue writhed like a snake and the hiss made my flesh crawl, but I was moving too fast to stop.

Nay's club came up and through with a blow that snapped the frostclaw's jaw shut. His blow tumbled the creature off Rounce and sent it staggering a step or two down the hill. It waggled its head and clawed at it with its little forelimbs, then tried to turn toward me, but its stiff tail smacked against a tree, freezing it in position.

I dove at it, sailing above Rounce's thrashing body, and hit the frostclaw in the right flank with a diving tackle. I got my right arm around its neck and hooked my legs inside its thighs and down around its belly. The dagger in my left hand flashed down, stabbing a full handspan into the monster's chest.

The temeryx shrieked and twisted around to the right, trying to pitch me off. Its little claws caught my right sleeve and shredded fabric as the beast tried to pry my arm free. I tightened my grip, trying to crush its throat, but its thickly muscled neck defied me. The temeryx smashed itself into a tree, battering my right leg, but I hung on, stabbing and stabbing and stabbing until my left hand, slick with blood, lost its grip on the dagger. The weapon spun off into the darkness.

Though blood gushed from its side with every exertion, the beast still bucked and leaped and whirled beneath me. Jolts ran through it as its tail or flanks hit trees. The back arched as the frostclaw leaped, then landed stiff-legged to drive its spine up into my chest and groin. Each bone-jarring landing would pitch me up a bit, then the temeryx would spin, trying to flick me off. I hung on tight, though, thrusting the fingers of my left hand into the hole I'd opened between its ribs. The ribs crushed down and pinched my fingers, but I refused to let go because I knew the second I flew off, it would pounce on me and tear me to pieces.

The month of anticipation before mid-summer had seemed to take a year to pass for me, but it was a heartbeat compared to the time I spent on the frostclaw's back. My right leg came free for a moment, unbalancing me perilously to the left, but the temeryx caught its tail on another sapling before it could spin me off. Its foreclaws raked the flesh on my forearm, igniting fiery pain, but it couldn't pull my arm away. Finally the temeryx stumbled and crashed down on its right side, with both of our spines pointing downhill. We began to slide in that direction, so I heaved mightily and rolled the beast over the top of me so that when we hit a tree, as I knew we would, I'd not be between it and the wood.

I clung on through a final impact. The temeryx's limbs thrashed and its lungs worked hard to fill with air. I tightened my knees on its chest and after a couple of labored breaths, it stopped fighting. The fingers of my left hand felt a strong heartbeat become ragged, then flutter and die. But even with that assurance that the creature was dead, I waited for the final jerking of its body. Until Rounce's cries overrode the pounding of my own heart, I refused to believe the monster was truly dead.

Finally, I pulled my left hand from its side and my left leg from beneath it. I rolled onto my back and trembled and wanted to vomit. My jaw quivered and faint wisps of steam rose from my blood-slicked hand. I glanced at the dead monster, then shoved myself further from it, coming up on my hands and knees.

I started the crawl back up the hillside. Leigh and Nay crouched over Rounce, not sparing a glance in my direction. I'm certain they felt the creature had made off with me and that I'd never be seen again. As it was, covered in its blood and mine, I looked more dead than alive.

Halfway up the hill I managed to get to my feet again and lurch further upward. Leigh nearly jumped out of his skin as I touched his shoulder and left a bloody handprint on his jacket. "It's dead."

"So are you, by the look of it." He stood quickly and looked me over. "You killed it? All by yourself, you killed it?"

"I had help from Nay." I dropped to my knees and looked at Rounce. "Oh, by the gods. Rounce's not dead, is he?"

Nay, kneeling at Rounce's feet, shook his head. "Fainted from the pain."

I nodded. A couple of cuts on his right flank showed where the temeryx had hit him in the initial attack, but they looked as superficial as the cuts on my arm. What looked the worst was the mangled, bloody mess the thing had made of his left knee. The angle of his foot in relation to his hip told me bones had been broken, crushed in the temeryx's jaws. Blood oozed up through the wounds and soaked the fabric of his pants. Nay finished slicing open that leg of the trousers with Rounce's knife, then cut it away above the wound.

Leigh stared down at the ruined leg. "It's my fault."

I glanced up at him. "How so?"

"I was leading. I couldn't get back; he got taken. My fault." Leigh's eyes narrowed as he chewed on a thumbnail. "I have to fix it. I have to make it right."

"Want to make it right, Leigh?" Nay wiped the knife off on his own tunic. "Here's a start. That's Fesyin Bane over there. Hack off a branch."

Leigh complied with Nay's command. Nay took it and began to strip off leaves, stuffing them in his mouth. He tore away smaller branches and handed them to us. "Chew the leaves into pulp. Pack his wounds with them."

We quickly complied, and I noticed the edge on my pain dulling as I did so. I spit a mouthful of chewed leaves into Nay's hands. He smeared them over the wound and started us chewing more. After we'd produced enough for a poultice, Nay wrapped the leg in the torn trouser material and tied it up tight. He then cast about for two stout sticks and tore the sleeves off his own shirt. He used them to fasten the splints around Rounce's leg, above and below the knee, keeping it stiff.

I got more *metholanth* and chewed it up to salve the cuts on my forearm, and wrapped it with the tattered remains of my shirt's right sleeve. With that task done, I looked around for Leigh and found him trudging back up the hill from where the temeryx lay. He nodded to me and tossed the things he was carrying on the ground before us.

He'd chopped all four paws off the temeryx and had plucked a half-dozen teeth from its jaws. He'd also torn a fair-sized patch off its hide. He stabbed the sword into the middle of the pile, then knelt and began to unbutton his jacket.

"This is the plan, gentlemen." He peeled his jacket off and laid it over Rounce's chest. "The two of you will make a stretcher or sled to drag Rounce along."

Nay frowned. "And you'll be . . . ?"

Leigh heaved himself to his feet. "I'll be running to Valsina to get help." He held up a hand to forestall protest. "Ask Hawkins here who's got the most endurance and can run the longest among us. The sword stays with Hawkins, in case there's another of those things around. I'd take Hawkins' dagger with me, but it's gone."

I nodded. "Sorry. It does make sense to have you go ahead, though. No offense to your healing skills, Nay, but Rounce is in serious need of help."

"True enough. One thing wrong, though."

Leigh arched an eyebrow. "And that is?"

Nay reversed the boot dagger and offered the hilt to Leigh. "Club's good enough for me. Take it."

Leigh's hand closed about the hilt. "Thanks. I'll get help, I really will, and fast, too." He tossed us both a salute, then stooped and picked up one of the temeryx's hind claws. "They'll come even faster if they see this. Keep on east-north-east. I'll carve blazes and pile rocks at stream fords, so I can backtrack to you."

"Go, Leigh. May the gods speed you on the way." Standing, I drew the sword from the earth and slid it into the empty scabbard on my belt. "Beware the frostclaws."

"Ha," he laughed as he started off. "I'm a Norrington; it's me *they* should fear."

I watched him crashing off into the brush until darkness swallowed him and the sound of his passing faded. "Think we'll see him again?"

"If we don't, if there are more frostclaws about, chances are no one will ever see us again either." Nay shrugged. "No matter. Worrying about that won't get Rounce to town."

"Well said." I gave him a smile and we set about making ourselves a way to get Rounce home.

CHAPTER 6

We made a drag-sled out of two stout saplings that we hacked down with the sword. We ended up butchering the temeryx, pulling off the hide and cutting loose the long sinews that ran along the back of its legs and that helped stiffen the tail. We used the sinews to lash pine boughs on the sapling poles, then we laid the temeryx skin on it, feather side up. We put Rounce on it, using his belt to tie him in place, then made a harness out of our belts and the sword belt with which one of us could drag the sled.

Nay put himself in the traces first and I led the way, following Leigh's blazes. Leigh did pick out a fairly easy course, taking into account the fact that we'd be carrying or dragging Rounce behind us. The trail wound through the valleys between hills, giving us plenty of opportunity to see any temeryces that would be attacking—at least, after the sun came up. In other places, where trees were spaced enough to let us pass, the path took us through the sort of grove that would make twisting and turning tough for one of the stiff-tailed beasts.

I looked back at Nay. "I'll take over and drag him whenever you want."

"Good to go a bit more." He swiped a hand over his brow,

smearing dirt through the sweat. "Thought you were dead when you took the temeryx."

"So did I, but I didn't really have a choice, did I?"

"Always a choice. It had a meal. We could have moved on."

I spun on my heel. "That meal was Rounce and I wasn't going to leave him. And, despite what you suggest, you weren't going to leave him either. You hit it before I did."

"Funny what fear will make you do. Glad it was you there in line, not Leigh."

I started on walking again. "If Leigh had been there, he'd have gone after the temeryx. Leigh can be . . . annoying, but he doesn't lack for courage."

"Not what was suggested, Hawkins." He grunted as we began a bit of a climb. "He'd have used the sword against it. Not the right weapon. Gotta be close, like you, with a dagger, or away, with a lance."

"That's pretty insightful." In close the temeryx couldn't bring its formidable weaponry to bear. Skewered on a lance or spear, it would be too far from its killer to do any damage. At medium range, as Leigh would have been, the creature could have leaped at him, and even if he impaled it on his sword, the beast would have raked its claws through him. "Of course, I'd not have had it if you'd not addled it with that lick you laid on it."

"Did get a fair piece of it." Nay chuckled lightly. "Next time mayhap I'll have something stouter than a piece of dead-wood."

"You're looking forward to a next time?"

"Nope, but no reason to assume there won't be one."

I pondered that point in silence as we continued on. Nay never let me drag the sled, but I did take the back end of it to lift up as we forded streams. The water got no deeper than our knees, so keeping Rounce dry wasn't a problem. The water was cold, however, so we needed the exertions of the walk to keep us warm.

By dawn, with the sun flooding bloody light into the eastern sky, we'd made it about three miles toward Valsina. Rounce hadn't awakened and that concerned me, but Nay said

it was the Fesyin Bane poultices that were keeping him asleep.
Given how much pain he'd be in if he was awake, sleeping was
best, but the dawn revealed a greyish pallor to his flesh and he
was feverish. Nay soaked some moss in a stream, wrapped it in
a sleeve from Leigh's coat, then placed it on Rounce's forehead
to cool him off.

We got another couple of miles before the rescuers found
us. Some were on horseback, but most were on foot, and had
come west along the road the wagon had used to deliver us
into the forest. Leigh had tied his shirt around a tree at the
side of the logging road where his path cut across it, then had
continued cross-country to cut distance off his trek. The rescuers had brought several wagons with them, which waited on
the road, to carry the searchers out to us and, presumably, to
carry us back. They also had brought along a string of spare
horses.

One of Lord Norrington's huntsmen, dressed all in green
leathers, found us first. He blew a blast on the small brass
horn he wore on his right hip, then shucked off a pack and
drew out a silver flask. He offered it to me, and I sniffed it first
before I drank. I drank sparingly, but gladly let the brandy
burn its way to my belly.

I wiped my mouth on the back of my hand, then gave the
flask to Nay. "It's brandy."

Nay tipped the flask back and took a long pull on it, then
his eyes bugged out. Bringing his head forward he swallowed,
then coughed a couple of times and swiped at the tears
streaming from his eyes. He fixed me with a green glare and
whispered hoarsely, "You meant it was *real* brandy."

"I did."

He looked away from me and toward the east as hoofbeats
drummed loudly. A magnificent black stallion crested the hill,
spraying dirt and rusty pine needles about as he dug his
forehooves into the ground. The bridle and saddle were black
leather chased with silver, likewise the saddlebow-scabbard
and quiver at the horse's left shoulder.

Astride the horse's back sat a tall, lean man with a piercing
brown gaze. He wore a hood of green leather that matched the
verdant suede of his personal mask. Ribbons adorned the

mask and temeryx claws hooked down from above the eye-holes as if they were eyebrows. His mouth was set in a grim, thin-lipped line and he intently studied the two of us, tattered and tired and sweat-soaked.

I immediately dropped to a knee and bowed my head. I glanced at Nay, then flicked my left hand at him, directing him to follow my lead. Nay did, and keeping my head down, I waited for the man to address us.

The saddle leather creaked as the man dismounted. His horse snorted and shook his head, jingling the tack. Sticks cracked beneath the man's booted feet, then he stopped before me and I felt his gloved hands on my shoulders. "Rise, Tarrant Hawkins. Today there is no reason for you to be on bended knee before me."

"My Lord Norrington is too kind." I slowly rose, then stepped back and rested my left hand on Nay's shoulder. "This is Naysmith Carver."

"Rise, Naysmith Carver. You have both done great things here."

I shook my head. "No greater than what Leigh . . . Bosleigh did in summoning help. His run—"

Lord Norrington held a finger up to silence me. "I know very well what my son did, and of him I am very proud, but the two of you . . . My son tells me that you attacked a temeryx armed only with a stick and a dagger. And in the dark, no less."

Nay shifted his feet nervously. "Had it been light, my lord, it might have been different."

"I have found, Master Carver, there are few men who brave horrors at night who will then run from the same in daylight." He turned and gathered up his horse's reins. "You two will come with me. We have horses for you, or you can ride in the cart, as you will. We even have a large horse for you, Master Carver."

Nay frowned. "But Rounce . . ."

Norrington turned and smiled. "My people will take care of him. Sandes!"

The huntsman who found us looked up from where he knelt next to Rounce. "Yes, my lord?"

"Convey Master Playfair to the cart. Abandon the sled, but bring the pelt and the other bits they took from it. We'll need that."

"As you command, my lord."

Other huntsmen who had been summoned by the horn came running up to where we were. Nay shrugged himself out of the harness and came up on my left, placing me between himself and Leigh's father. I had known Lord Norrington since I was too young to clearly remember anything. I knew him as Leigh's father and my father's master, and my father was inclined toward strict formality where Lord Norrington was concerned. Lord Norrington was a bit more forgiving on that count. While his invitation to walk with him didn't surprise me, the fact that he did not mount up and treat us as the moonmasked youths we were did seem out of the ordinary. Even so, his voice came warm and familiar when he spoke to us, as if we were his friends rather than friends of his son.

"The pelt you have there, the feathers are sable. I've heard it said they can be that way, but n'er have I seen it." He stroked the point of his chin with his left hand. "Could be it's a fledgling, but the pelt is full-sized. Or, perhaps, they molt into a summer plumage, then again into their white for winter."

I nodded my head. "I suppose it could be, my lord."

Norrington threw his head back and laughed. "Very good, Hawkins, don't offer an opinion if you don't have one. Your father has taught you well. And you, Master Carver?"

"Better to be silent and thought a fool, than to speak and remove all doubt, my lord."

"Listen to me, boys . . ." Norrington paused and shook his head, then lowered his voice. "Here I call you boys when you are clearly men. Forgive me and hear me: what you have done here is rare, very rare. I know of perhaps a score of men who have been involved in a temeryx kill—your father among them, young Hawkins. I've killed a half-dozen myself, most with a bow. I got one with a lance from horseback—I wear its claws in this hunting mask. Another I took with a spear, on foot, but I will tell you now I only did it because my horse had broken its leg and I was reduced to walking against my will."

He watched us both carefully as the import of his words sank in. "There will be men who seek to devalue what you have done, to say you are mistaken, or that you have lied. 'Exaggerated,' they will call your exploit. These are petty men and ones to stay well away from. Others—true men like your father, like others in Valsina—they will know your hearts from this act. So, no matter what you hear, do not doubt yourselves. A day into your Moon Month you have displayed more about yourselves than others could in a century."

Nay cleared his throat with a low rumble. "Thank you much for your kindness, Lord Norrington, but making too much of this ain't right. We did what we had to. No thinking on it. No knowing how much it might pain us. Now, Leigh, he knew his task. He took it on himself to save us."

"Again, I know what my son did."

"How is Leigh?"

"You can see for yourselves." Norrington smiled. He pointed off across a small valley to the logging road and the trio of wagons that had been brought up. "He's in the first wagon. He insisted on bringing us back here. Go on, he'll be glad to see you."

Nay and I took off running, passing a pair of magickers heading off in the other direction toward Rounce. We scrambled up the hill, then along the road to the rear of the wagon. It had a boxy bed with wooden sides two feet high and a canvas covering over a wooden framework that rose six feet above the bed. Reaching the endboard, we pulled back the flaps and found Leigh.

He was seated on a half-dozen pillows that propped him up in a sitting position. He looked tired and had a red welt on his right cheek where it looked as if a thorny bush had raked his face. Similar welts crisscrossed his hands and his shins, which had long since been stripped of stockings. His feet had been swathed in white cloth, some of which had pink patches showing—mostly on the heel and along the sole.

He smiled at us. "When I heard the horn, one blast, I knew they'd found you. And this close to the road, I knew you had to be alive. Rounce?"

"Alive as well. Your father's people are bringing him in. Magickers were going to him as we came along."

"Good. I told them what you'd done with the *metholanth* and they said that was probably as good as you could have done, given the circumstances." Leigh shrugged. "They dabbed some tincture of it on my feet, too."

Nay smiled. "Told you them shoes weren't right."

"Oh, and the shoes quite agreed with you, Nay. They came apart a mile or so east of here." He barked a quick laugh. "I paid for them with moongold, so I suppose I cannot complain. Perhaps a temeryx will snap them up and choke on them."

I laughed aloud. "I don't think that's very likely, do you? They'll long since have decayed before another frostclaw is found in these parts."

Leigh shook his head. "My father didn't tell you?"

"Tell us what?" I looked at Nay and he stared blankly back at me. "What was he supposed to tell us?"

"My good fellows, you don't imagine my father brought all these huntsmen out just to find you, do you?" He waggled a finger at us. "No, no, no! It seems that frostclaws hunt in packs. Where you find one, you find at least three more. No, my friends, we're here with the huntsmen to find the other frostclaws and kill them. The fun we had last night, it was just the prelude, and we are in this little opera until the very last note is sung."

CHAPTER 7

The hunters returned to the wagons along with Rounce. One of the magickers got into the wagon where they placed Rounce, then it was turned and sent back to Valsina with four outriders. The rest of us piled into the other two wagons—with Nay and me riding with Leigh. We all set off along the road to the point where we'd been dropped off.

I got a little sleep during that run, then woke up when the wagons stopped at our drop-off point. Two other wagons and more riders had been sent ahead and were waiting for us. Nay and I left our wagon and accompanied the others to the site of the first kill. Of the watcher who had died on the hilltop we could find only his tattered cloak. The huntsmen located a couple of other bare patches of earth that yielded temeryx prints, including one with only two claws, indicating an animal that had been injured.

Sandes looked up from that particular track and nodded. "There certainly was more than one. The others tracked the first beast here to its kill and took the food away."

Lord Norrington stroked his chin. "Can you tell how many?"

"At least two is my guess, possibly twice that number."

I didn't like the sound of that, but said nothing since the hunters' muttered musings sounded dour and grim. Nay and I then led them to the site of the second attack and our kill. We found its body where we'd left it, though something had been worrying it. Sandes asked if Lord Norrington wanted him to further butcher the animal for food, but Leigh's father demurred.

"We've provisions enough, and I don't want too much confusion when we seek out the rest of the pack. Later we will have more and fresher meat."

We all hiked back to the wagons and discovered that some of the hunters had crossed the road to the side away from the ravine and, in a fairly level spot, had set up camp. They had three fires burning and had pitched several tents, including a fairly large one with a central pavilion and a couple of smaller tents coming off it like spokes from a hub. As we came into the clearing, Leigh emerged from the large tent, walking rather gingerly, but smiling nonetheless.

In our absence he had changed from the tattered clothes he'd worn previously to a set of green hunting leathers. The stark white of his moonmask contrasted sharply with the deep green of the leathers. He wore a sword and dagger on a belt around his waist, and his feet had been clad in soft leather boots that laced up the front and had a fringe around the top. A folded pair of gloves hung from his belt.

"Welcome back to our home away from home." He waved a hand at the large tent. "You've each been given one of the wings here—Hawkins to the right, Nay to the left. There is a change of clothes for each of you."

Nay covered a yawn with the back of his left hand. "Nightclothes would suit right now."

Lord Norrington came up from behind and clapped both of us on the shoulders. "Yes, please, get some more rest. Three hours until noon, then we will be hunting."

I had to pass through the main tent to reach my little tent, and I could not help but be impressed with what I saw. A series of carpets had been overlapped to form the floor. Many had intricate designs on them—the sort of thing that came from Naliserro or Savarre—and the rest were plain. All were well worn. A long dining table complete with twelve chairs had been set up, but I noticed that all of them could be taken apart and broken down for easy storage and transport. An easel dominated one corner, and on it had been placed a board to which had been tacked a map of the area, with small pins stuck into it at the sites of the kills.

The rather stark nature of the furnishings both did and did not surprise me. I knew, from having been at Norrington Manor, that Lord Norrington could afford the finest furnishings from anywhere in the world, so the simplicity and pure utility of these pieces suggested a tightfistedness on his part that I knew wasn't true. By the same token, in the field, these furnishings were exactly what he needed. While he was a man who could enjoy the finer things of life, he let various situations dictate what he demanded.

My little tent was very simply appointed, with a carpet rolled over the ground and three thick blankets folded on top of a small chest that I assumed held my new clothes. I pulled off my party costume and wrapped myself in one of the blankets. I used the other two to form a pillow, and despite it being mid-morning, I dropped immediately into a dreamless sleep.

The sun hung straight overhead by the time I emerged from the tent. My new hunting leathers fit me better than Nay's fit him. His were tight across the shoulders and through the arms, but he shrugged off the problem. We both grabbed a small loaf of bread, a hunk of cheese, and an apple from the provisions table in the clearing, then joined the rest of the hunters. We all seated ourselves in a semicircle facing Lord Norrington and a wizened, stoop-shouldered old man with long white hair and enough knotted mage-braid hanging from his mask to let us know he was a magicker of considerable power.

Lord Norrington waited until a few stragglers sat down, then addressed us. "We are here to hunt for frostclaws. We want to find them this afternoon, because while the sun is up we will have an advantage. In their native northern range, during the winter, there is very little sunlight available, so they have big eyes to gather in the light. Here and now the sunlight will be a bit more than they can bear, so we will be hunting for their lairs."

He reached down and lifted the skin from the temeryx we'd killed. "Frostclaws hunt in a pack, and packs are believed to be formed from a single clutch. All the frostclaws in a pack will be related to each other, and this will make finding them easier. Archmage Heslin will explain."

The old man shuffled forward and plucked a feather from the skin. "Blood knows blood. If you can see in the aetherrealm, you can see the way the lines are mixed." He squinted at us, enlarging one brown eye as he closed the other. "You and you, you're cousins, and you and you are brothers, eh?"

The huntsmen he pointed to with a crooked finger gasped in astonishment.

The old man cackled gleefully. "The temeryx feather here is linked to those of its bloodkin, and I will be fixing feathers to show you the way to go after them."

One huntsman raised his hand. "Will you be enchanting our weapons to kill them?"

"If such a spell existed, why would I need any of you here?" His riposte brought a ripple of laughter. Heslin waited for it to subside before he continued. "They won't be easy to kill, but not hard for you, either. Finding them will be difficult, but I'll see to that. Get yourselves fed and outfitted, then you'll have your feather and go."

Norrington held a hand up and circled it. "Break into your groups, get yourselves armed, and then we move out. You have a quarter hour."

Two lesser mages joined Heslin and started to pluck feathers from the edges of the skin we'd harvested. Sandes walked over to the trio of us and pointed toward the largest of the wagons on the road. "You three will be with my group. Let's get you armed."

The large wagon proved to be a wheeled armory with multiple racks of weapons and tack. Bearing in mind the conversation Nay and I had had concerning how to fight frostclaws, I asked for a long dagger, which I sheathed at the small of my back. On my right hip I put a quiver of thirty arrows, each one featuring a razor-edge broadhead, black shaft, and red feathers. To shoot the arrows I took a horsebow. The compact recurve weapon had a short but stiff draw that would put an arrow through a man armored in mail at a hundred yards or so.

Sandes looked at me curiously. "No sword?"

I shook my head. "If I have to run, I don't want it tripping me up. Besides, Nay pointed out that a sword against one of those things would be suicidal, so I'll do without."

Leigh laughed at my comments, but did shift his sword belt up so it looped over a shoulder and across his chest. He fixed the scabbard to it so the blade's hilt projected above his right shoulder. He drew the double-edged broadsword without trouble. To the sword he added a light crossbow that had a goat's-paw—a levering device that would let him cock it quickly. A quiver of bolts went on his right hip and a dagger was sheathed on his left.

Nay stayed away from bows and instead drew a boar spear from the stock of weapons. Eight feet long from butt to tip, the weapon featured a broad, dagger-bladed head and a wide crossguard that would prevent a creature from sliding down the spear to get at the man carrying it. The stout oak shaft promised the weapon wouldn't break beneath the weight of a charge. And the point on the butt-cap would let Nay plant the weapon in the ground as he crouched to take a charge, letting the earth accept the brunt of the force. He augmented the spear with a hatchet and a dagger.

Once armed, we moved to where Heslin and his associates worked. I wondered exactly what they were going to be able to do for us, since we all knew that human magickers rarely lived long enough to master spells that could directly affect living creatures. While stories of mages casting spells that exploded fireballs to kill various brigands or Aurolani creatures did abound, combat spells appeared to be an exception to this general rule. More complex and delicate magicks, such as those that could heal disease or cure a wound, required control that most humans never attained.

But, as we discovered, the spells that would help us did not so much affect the temeryces as much as were affected by them.

At the mage's direction, Nay presented his spear first. An apprentice used flax thread to dangle one of the temeryx feathers from the crossguard. Heslin then raised his left hand and circled his thumb and forefinger around the feather. He began mumbling under his breath and slowly swept his hand down over the feather.

A light golden glow seemed to spread from his palm and infuse the midnight feather with golden highlights. As his hand came past the end of the feather, the golden glow faded and the highlights sank into the feather as water sinks into sand. Then, all of a sudden, the feather twisted and bounced as if being buffeted by a light breeze, even though the air remained completely still.

Heslin nodded, then pointed in the direction the feather wanted to drift. "The frostclaws will be off that way. Follow the feather. As you get closer, it will get more active. When it palsy-twitches, set yourselves."

He enchanted feathers for the rest of us as well, repeating his instructions. He fastened mine to the upper end of my bow and Leigh's to the hilt of his sword. Sandes and two other of the half-dozen hunters accompanying us carried spears like Nay; the rest had bows like mine.

The whole company had broken down into three groups. Two of them—one led by Norrington, the other led by one of his deputies—mounted up on horses and headed out in both directions on the logging road. As per the plan, they would vector in on the temeryx lair, coming at it from two sides. The third group—nine of us on foot—was to head straight at it from the camp, ostensibly to catch any creatures that broke for freedom in our direction.

As he set off, I looked at Sandes. "You don't mind that you are nurse-maiding us and won't get a chance at a frostclaw kill?"

The round-faced man smiled. "Lord Norrington honors me by entrusting you to my care."

"That's not really an answer."

Leigh slapped Sandes on the right shoulder. "Leave him

be, Hawkins. The man has been my father's chief hunter for two years now, and he will marry a month from now, won't you, Sandes?"

"I will, my lord."

"So, being allowed to herd us youngsters and keep us out of trouble is practice for the coming years. Besides, if we see no frostclaws, I'm certain Sandes can find us something else to hunt. We'll bring back a buck or two for the victory celebration."

I frowned. "How will we know when the hunt is over?"

Leigh pointed at the feather on my bow. "When the temeryces are dead, the feathers will stop moving."

"Won't be soon enough." Nay pointed his spear along the feather-path. "Goodman Sandes, might be safer if we keep to the nursery groves. Cuts down their turning."

Sandes nodded in agreement, so we shifted our course to move from protective stands of trees to other positions that were defensible. This slowed our progress, but I didn't mind. I moved ahead with Sandes, watching as he picked out our course. He kept our exposure to attack minimal, and as a tactical exercise, I learned a lot from him.

It was an exercise that saved our lives.

For reasons we had no way to anticipate, the temeryces did not stay laired through the afternoon. We received the first inkling of this when our gently drifting feathers began to dance a bit more heartily. Sandes called an immediate halt, with him and me on the top of one hillock, the other five huntsmen in a grove on another, and Nay and Leigh caught fording a small stream that split one hillock from another.

Even though our forward progress had stopped, the feathers' jerking increased.

"They're coming at us!" Sandes waved to Leigh and Nay. "Move it, get up here."

I stepped up to the fallen log that lay across the northwestern edge of our hilltop. In the distance I caught little flashes of movement, and I knew it was more than the feather tugging at my bow. "I see something coming in. Fast." I fitted an arrow to my bow and drew it back.

The first temeryx came into view as it splashed across the

stream about twenty-five yards down from Nay. I let fly and missed its breast, but did stick it in the left thigh. The creature shrieked and slipped off a rock, to splash down in the water. It scrambled to its feet again, leaping up and away as Leigh's quarrel struck sparks from a rock in front of it.

Two more temeryces burst into the open as the first started charging up the streambed. The huntsmen on the other hill shot at them, with a trio of arrows catching one frostclaw in the right flank. It flopped down and thrashed, its feet clawing mud and stone from the bank. The third temeryx leaped over its dying companion and sped forward.

I drew another arrow back and tried to track the running frostclaws, but trees gave me only fleeting glimpses of them. I glanced back at the clearing where I'd gotten my first shot to see if there were more, but I saw no others. Another target *did* present itself, and I let fly with only a second's hesitation, even though I could not identify the creature at which I shot. I just figured that anything running *with* the frostclaws instead of *from* them had to be bad.

My arrow took the child-sized creature high in the chest, lancing down from right shoulder toward its left hip. The broadhead pierced its brown, downy pelt. The creature opened its mouth in a scream, spraying out blood where there should have been sound. It spun around, then crashed down between two rocks.

Shrieking furiously, the first frostclaw leaped at Nay. The scream was enough to curdle my blood, but Nay calmly dropped to one knee and set the butt of his spear in the streambed. He hauled back, directing the spear-point into the frostclaw's narrow belly. The beast slammed down on the crossguard and the butt slipped. Rear talons clawed forward, barely missing Nay's shoulders and head. Wrenching the spear hard to the left, Nay smashed the temeryx into large rocks at the stream's edge and ended up sprawled facedown in the stream for his effort.

The other frostclaw came on hard. One of the huntsmen put an arrow into its tail. Leigh hit it with a quarrel in the left shoulder, ruining that foreclaw and knocking the beast against the stream's far shore. Two more arrows whistled past it, but the creature's crouch kept it too low for the archers to hit. The frostclaw hissed horribly, opening its mouth to display its fearsome teeth.

Then it gathered itself and sprinted at Nay.

CHAPTER 8

Nay rolled onto his back, reaching for his hatchet, and yelped in horror at the monster streaking at him. I had no shot—neither did the archers on the other side—and Sandes, though sprinting down the hill toward the stream, would never get there in time to save him.

His sword flashing silver and gold in the dappled sunlight, Leigh leaped over Nay's form and splashed down in the stream between him and the temeryx. Leigh bellowed loudly at the frostclaw and waved his sword back and forth. Hunched forward, he darted at the beast, extending his sword forward, set to impale it.

The frostclaw drew up short, rearing back and thumping its tail into the ground. Leigh skidded to a halt in the streambed, dropping to his left knee and hand while still keeping his sword extended in his right. The temeryx dipped its head forward and snapped at the blade. Leigh slashed once quickly at it, but missed the throat as the creature pulled back. The temeryx snapped at him again. Leigh cracked it across the snout with flat of the blade, then stood and slowly started to retreat.

Blinking its large amber eyes, the temeryx watched him go.

Nostrils flared as it drank in his scent, and it took a tentative step in his direction, then another. Leigh quickened the pace of his retreat. The temeryx started to trot toward him.

Leigh caught his heel on a stone and toppled backward. He never lost his grip on the sword, but his attempt to regain his balance left him flailing his arms. He landed flat on his back, his arms and legs spread, his belly open and unprotected. The temeryx saw this, shrieked, and leaped for him.

The huntsmen on the far side of the creek crossed three arrows through the beast's chest, but its legs still arched toward Leigh. The big sickle-shaped claws on the interior toes remained cocked. As it descended, dying though it may have been, the temeryx reached a foot toward Leigh. When it touched him, it would rake through clothes and flesh and muscle, opening his viscera to the air.

But the temeryx never hit Leigh.

Sandes, sprinting full out, dove forward and drove his spear into the frostclaw's belly. With all of his weight behind the lunge, Sandes deflected the temeryx, boosting it a bit higher and then dropping it on the far bank of the stream. Sandes released the spear, letting the shaft whip water into a froth with the creature's death throes, and turned immediately to haul Leigh away and to safety.

I scanned the forest for more movement, but saw nothing. More importantly, the temeryx feather tied to my bow had stopped moving. Keeping an arrow nocked in the bow just in case, I retraced my footsteps to the streambed, half-sliding down the hill in my haste. Leigh pulled himself up onto a rock and let water drip off him, then shook his head and sprayed me and Nay with water from his hair.

I arched an eyebrow at him. "That was the most brave or most stupid thing I have ever seen."

"Really?" Leigh's chin came up. "All I know is that it took you all long enough to do your parts."

"What are you talking about?"

"Why, my dear Tarrant, I'm talking about shooting the thing." He pointed at the dead temeryx. "You didn't think I meant to try and kill the thing with my sword, did you? No, I only wanted to distract it from Nay long enough for you to shoot it."

I narrowed my eyes. "I see. But, if you had managed to kill it with your sword, you never would have told us it was unintentional, would you?"

A sly smile grew on Leigh's face, but he turned toward Nay instead of answering me. "You are unhurt?"

Nay nodded slowly. "Don't know how to thank you. That creature, never been so close to death."

Leigh dismissed Nay's concern with a casual wave of his hand. "Think nothing of it, Naysmith. As Hawkins will confirm, I often act the ass, though I seldom realize it and less seldom admit it, even to myself. Despite how we met, you have shown you are a good man. It is my obligation as a Norrington to protect good men like you." A smile grew on Leigh's face. "And it is my pleasure to protect the life of a man I consider a friend."

Nay's brow furrowed as he considered Leigh's words, then he nodded once, solidly. "A Norrington for a friend. More than anyone would expect from a Moon Month."

"Oh, and you'll have more. You'll be featured in a poem I'll compose, I think. You, too, Hawkins." Leigh pressed his hands together. "I will call it, 'How to Vex a Temeryx.' Good, no?"

"I can't wait." I shook my head and splashed my way over to Sandes. "I shot something else, further downstream. I don't know what it was, but I know it wasn't right."

"Let's go."

The two of us trudged down to where the creature bobbed in a shallow pool. The thing measured no more than four feet from crown to toes, but was more heavily muscled than a child of equivalent size. It had large eyes that were all black, a little bit of a muzzle with its nose a black triangle at the top, very much like a dog. Parts of its face, its palms, and feet were bare of fur, revealing flesh the color of a blood blister. It had sharp peg-teeth, with the lower canines being longer than the upper, and the hands were very human, though they lacked the littlest finger. The creature had big bat ears which folded back into the fur on the sides of its head.

It could easily have been described as a little boy in a baby bear costume, though it ran more to lean muscle than fat. What defied that description was the fact that it wore a beaded armband from which hung a half-dozen black temeryx feathers. Around its waist it also had a slender belt from which hung two pouches that contained herbs, rocks, and unidentifiable animal flesh in neat little packets.

Sandes dragged the thing to the shore, then squatted by its head. "I don't know as how I've ever seen one of these before, and certainly not with dark fur like this." He reached a hand down and parted the fur on its shoulder, then nodded. "White at the roots."

"Meaning?"

"Meaning the creature colored its fur to be able to move through the forests more easily." He wiped his hand off on the leg of his trousers. "I think you've shot yourself a vylaen."

A shiver shook me. "But they live in Aurolan, past the Black Marches and everything, way up north."

"So do frostclaws. They're both Chytrine's pets, damn her black soul." Sandes raised his huntsman's horn to his lips and blew three quick blasts on it. He waited a moment, then blew three more. After a moment or two, the pattern of three and three came back at him from two different places in the forest.

Sandes toed the vylaen's body. "Lord Norrington will know what to do."

Lord Norrington and his party came riding in from along the temeryx backtrail. A couple of the horses had cuts on them, and at least one man had his shoulder bandaged after having been hit by an arrow. Strapped across the backs of a couple of horses being led by their former riders was one temeryx and three other bodies which I did not get a good look at initially.

Lord Norrington rode over to where Sandes and I stood. He dismounted, passing his stallion's reins to Sandes, then he dropped to a knee beside the vylaen. Leigh's father made a tiny clicking sound with his mouth as he thought, then stood abruptly and looked at me. "That's your arrow, Hawkins?"

"Yes, my lord." I turned and pointed back up at the hillock. "I was up there when it came through. I had no shot at the temeryces and I guessed that any creature running with them instead of from them just wasn't right."

"Very nice shot, Hawkins. And you're correct about this vylaen being out of place and allied with the frostclaws. I'll want Heslin to check, but I think the armlet there with the feathers linked the vylaen to them. Vylaens also have a very high-pitched voice—dogs can hear them, and frostclaws I suspect—so it may have been giving them orders including plans for attack on your position here." He clapped me on the shoulders. "Shooting it probably saved you all."

"Speaking of saved," I said as I pointed upstream toward Leigh, "your son saved Nay from certain death."

Lord Norrington cocked his head to the right. "Did he? Well, that will make for a good story tonight, I think, and one that will likely grow as time goes on."

He turned to Sandes. "How many did you get?"

"Three temeryces, my lord. Archers took one clean, Master Carver took one on a spear, and your son held the third long enough for the archers to get arrows into it and me to stick it with a spear." Sandes nodded his head toward the riders who had followed Lord Norrington in. "I see you got one."

"We did, yes, Jempson, with a spear—from horseback. The others are three gibberkin." Lord Norrington read the blank look on my face. "They're akin to the vylaens, but bigger, more bestial, with mottled fur, bigger teeth and muzzles. Elves call them *ominirs*, but the man-name comes from their constant gibbering and howling. These ones, it appears, were altered enough that they could only manage a bass whisper. One of them got an arrow into Swinbrook, but he'll survive."

"Yes, my lord." Sandes patted the stallion's neck. "What do you want me to do with the vylaen and the frostclaws?"

"Have your men dress them all out, including the gibberkin. Save the teeth, hands, and feet—we'll need them. Burn the vylaen and gibberkin bodies. We'll roast the frostclaws."

I blinked. "We're really going to eat them?"

"Become a warrior like your father and you'll eat much worse in the field. Frostclaws actually taste fairly good, wouldn't you say, Sandes?"

"I fix it the same way I would a hen, my lord." Sandes pulled a coil of rope from the stallion's saddle and tossed it to me. "Truss up his feet and we'll drag him back to camp. Do a good job and I'll see to it that you get a slice of the frostclaw liver fried up with some of the wild onions here. It'll be a meal you won't forget."

Sandes was correct. The meal that night was one I'd never forget, but not just because of the liver and onions. While the food did taste good, the company made it better. We all regrouped at the campsite and everyone set about their various tasks, from fetching firewood to slaughtering the creatures and dressing various wounds on hunters and horses alike.

The third hunting group had brought in two more gibberkin and another temeryx, which accounted for six of the beasts. That matched the number of feathers on the vylaen's armband, so I took that as a hopeful sign that we'd gotten all of them. I would have been more pleased if a full half-dozen gibberers had been brought in as well, but we had no evidence to suggest how many of them had been in the group to begin with. Someone even suggested that the sixth gibberer might have been fed to the frostclaws at some point to keep the others in line.

Heslin did confirm lingering traces of magick on the armband and suggested a simple solution for why the temeryces were out in the afternoon. As the two mounted hunting parties closed on their lair, the armlet might have allowed the vylaen to detect the magic being used to locate the temeryces. Given the local terrain, the easiest direction for them to head out was toward us, and we were undetected at first because we'd not moved close enough to the vylaen.

"If he had worked other magick to order the frostclaws about, he might not have detected you at all until much too late." The mage pressed his lips together in a thin line. "This was not a casual hunting party. This was something more."

"More to be discussed later, I think, Heslin." Lord Norrington cut off that line of discussion rather quickly. "Perhaps back in Valsina you will be able to learn more about the vylaen's magick."

That the vylaen had left two temeryces and a handful of gibberkin to hold off the mounted hunters while escaping in our direction underscored the fact that no one had expected our little group to be in any danger that day. We'd been along on the hunt because, after all we'd been through, they couldn't very well not bring us. Because of that, what we accomplished earned the respect of the assembled men.

Leigh and I had been out on hunts before and had been grouped around a campfire with huntsmen just as we were that night. Because we had been children in their eyes, wearing courtesy masks marked with our families' crests, they had spun great tales for us. They told us of feather-trout, fish that lurk in trees and have to be shot with a bow and arrow, and stag-hares, which have a set of antlers and are so fierce they fight off wolves and bears. They would listen to our stories of shooting a deer or catching a fish as solemnly as if it were the first time they'd heard of such a thing, then dissolve into laughter.

After the temeryx hunt, we were no longer seen as children. We had been with them when they faced some of the nastiest creatures in the world—and creatures that hadn't been seen so far south in over a century. Sandes praised my prowess with a bow and other huntsmen said they'd never seen as much strength as Nay had shown in spearing his temeryx and dropping it to the side. What little chiding there was came good-naturedly, and was in line with the ribbing the other huntsmen, including Sandes, got for what they had done that day.

By far, though, Leigh earned the majority of the accolades handed out around the blazing bonfire that night. Every one of us who had been there shared our version of what he did. We had all been amazed as he put himself in the path of certain death. His bellowing back at the temeryx had heartened us all, and his pressing an attack surprised us, but also brought smiles to our faces. When he retreated, well, each of us knew we had to find a way to help him, to preserve the man who had displayed such faultless courage.

Leigh drank it all in and, just for a moment, appeared embarrassed by what was said. I think perhaps that, for the first time in his life, people were seeing him as Leigh, not Lord Norrington's son. That night, by what he had done, he had emerged ever so slightly from his father's shadow. I don't think he'd particularly chafed to be there before, but dwelling in a shadow can be rather chilly. Coming out into the light on his own had to feel good.

At the end of our storytelling, Leigh himself got up and regaled us with what he had been thinking during the attack. "Well, there I was, wasn't I? The damnable beast had just shrugged off the bolt I put into him and somehow overlooked that grievous wound from the arrow in his tail. He looked at Nay just lying there and must have thought he was seeing the biggest green trout ever to swim. Having had a long run, he was hungry and went for Nay, but I couldn't have that, could I?

"So, leap forward I did, waving my sword about, trying to tell it that Nay wasn't a trout at all, which I thought obvious because he had more arms and legs than a trout. Well, the beastie hissed at me, 'Yes he is!' I bellowed back, 'No he's not.' Oh, didn't know I spoke temeryx, did you? Well, it wasn't until I'd advanced to drive my point home and it hissed at me again that I realized I didn't speak temeryx either—or not his dialect anyway. So I backed up and quickly threw myself on my back in hopes of splashing up a trout the beastie could eat, and you fine fellows skewered him four ways to Mansday, didn't you?"

Leigh accompanied his recital by dancing backward and forward. A short stick with a burning ember glowing red served as his sword and wove the point through a hypnotic series of nonsense sigils. We all laughed at the right places, and he played to our amusement. He even got a laugh or two from his father. He bowed at the end, and consigned his wooden sword to the fire before returning to his father's side.

Lord Norrington stood and ruffled his son's blond hair. "Gentlemen, it was a good day had by all. Finding these creatures here is an ill omen, no doubt about it, but a worse one would have been our having missed them altogether. I don't know what the future will bring because of these discoveries, but today you were all heroic and your deeds will not be soon forgotten."

CHAPTER 9

During our return to Valsina I began to realize just how out of the ordinary what we had done really was. While with the hunting party we were all just part of a whole. The hunt had been our world and we'd all shared the same experience, so it didn't seem that special. Our return to town brought us back in contact with people who did not have our perspective on the event.

Rounce's return to the city had started the rumors of temeryces roaming the countryside, so farmers and herders seeing us pass came over to ask how the hunt had done. Lord Norrington remained stoic and polite, telling them he was well satisfied with how the situation had been handled. "Nothing at all to worry about now."

At Valsina's outskirts, people began to fill the edges of the streets to see us pass. There really was not that much to see, just a stately progression of huntsmen on horseback and several wagons. All of the skins and other relics had been packed away in one of the wagons, so no one got to ooh and ahh over grisly trophies. Even our injured men rode along without any visible bandages, so it appeared as if we'd gone out and dealt with our task with very little in the way of difficulty.

As we moved near Old Town, Lord Norrington sent Leigh, Nay, and me off to see our parents and let them know we had survived. The three of us had already agreed to go to Kedyn's temple to offer thanks for our success, but Lord Norrington said that could wait until later. From the temple we planned to visit Rounce, but Lord Norrington noted that waiting until the evening or even tomorrow to visit him would be better, since he had been gravely injured and likely would take a long while to recover.

I smiled and patted my horse on the neck. "I will go see my father, then, and return this horse to your manor before we go to the temple."

Lord Norrington shook his head. "The horse is yours, young Hawkins, and the tack as well. That goes for you, too, Master Carver. That first night your quick action saved Master Playfair, yourselves and, most dear to me, my son. This is the least I can do to show my gratitude to you."

Nay's jaw dropped open. "My lord is too kind."

Leigh scowled. "Ha! Saving me is only worth a horse and saddle?"

Norrington glanced at his son. "I said it was the *least* I could do, Bosleigh; I did not say it was all I would do—but else is a matter for another time. Farewell to you both. Until I have the pleasure again."

I nodded to him in a salute, then reined my horse around and rode toward my family's house. I stopped at the closest stable and arranged a month's stabling for the glint of moon-gold, then rushed off. A group of younger boys, one of whom had seen me earlier, crowded around the front door, but I shooed them off. They retreated reluctantly, with a larger one disdainfully dismissing the stories about my having killed a rabid drearbeast as obvious fantasy.

I knocked, then entered through the door and mask-curtain beyond. I caught my mother in a big hug as she came toward me from the kitchen. She clung to me fiercely, her silent sobs sending tremors through her body. I felt the dampness of her tears on my neck, so I kissed her ear and held her tightly. Eventually her grip on me slackened and she pulled back, brushing away tears with her thumbs, then wiping her hands on her apron.

"Are you hungry, Tarrant?" She turned from me and pointed toward the hearth. "I have beans bubbling and some bread baking. I didn't know when you would be back. Your brothers are on alert and your father is at the Lord Mayor's Hall planning what to do if the Northern Horde gets this far."

"I'm fine, Mother. Just a few bruises, a few scrapes."

She crossed to the black, cast-iron pot hanging in the hearth. She swung it out, lifted the lid with her apron guarding her hand, and stirred the fragrant brown thickness of beans. "I know that, Tarrant, but after what was said about your friend Rounce . . . Well, a mother worries."

She turned back toward me, pot lid like a shield in one hand, glistening wooden spoon a sword in the other. "I will always be your mother and I will always worry. Know that. Know it is because I love you."

I nodded. "I know." I drew up a chair back from the table and sat. "How is Rounce?"

"One of the Baker girls took some bread to the family and said that Rounce is going to live. He won't lose his leg because of some quick thinking out there."

"Nay worked up a poultice."

"Nay?"

"Naysmith Carver. I met him at the gala. He was an armorer's apprentice, but he wants to be a warrior. I suspect now he'll get his chance." I smiled as my mother set a steaming bowl of beans in front of me. "Thanks, but I can wait for my father."

"I don't know when he will be back, so eat now." A smile softened my mother's expression. "Your father told me, when we got word about what had happened, that he'd expect you to be able to handle yourself. He said you would be fine. I didn't doubt him, but . . ."

She hesitated, lost in remembrance of what she had feared, then she sniffed once, more angry than sad. "No matter, you'll eat now . . ."

"Well, I am hungry. Camp food is fine, but . . ."

"That's right, Tarrant Hawkins. All this warring and fighting and killing and the romance of it might fill your mind, but surviving means you need more, which includes substantial things in your life. Like beans in your belly."

"And a mother who cares enough to see to it I get them?"

"Very good, Tarrant, very good." She nodded carefully, then stirred the beans again. "Perhaps your father was not far wrong at all."

Leigh, Nay, and I all met at the temple at sundown. I had with me a covered crock of beans that my mother insisted I take to Rounce's family. One of Kedyn's acolytes guarded it for me as the three of us bought charcoal and incense—paying good coin for it this time—and descended to offer our thanks to Kedyn for our success.

I knelt there solemnly, my shield arm across my chest and my sword arm pointing toward the ground. I began a standard prayer of thanks, but an idle draft wafted smoke into my face and I breathed deeply of it. I remember coughing, but felt a distance between myself and my body. I found myself drifting back over the events of our adventure, reliving the pains and fears, the exertion and exhilaration of the hunt and the kill. I recalled everything with incredible detail, remembering things I didn't know I'd seen or heard. My fingers twitched as I felt the temeryx's heart stop beating, and then my mind snapped back into the present.

I glanced up and followed the incense ribbon from my charcoal shield as it rose and washed over Kedyn's face. The smoky trail twisted and writhed, seeming to carry to him all I had experienced. I didn't expect a sign that Kedyn noticed me or cared about me, and I got none. The gods seldom meddled in the affairs of men, preferring to leave that sort of activity to the godlings and *weirun*—spirits of place that inhabit the world. Even so, I took my recollections as a sign that my prayer for Control might well have been answered.

I stood, bowed, and made my way back up to the main temple level. There I found Nay and Leigh speaking with a cadaverously slender priest. Kedyn's priest wore a black robe of rough-spun wool; he had shaved his head, but wore a mustache and goatee as dark as his robe. He held my pot of beans under one arm and, with the other hand, beckoned me close.

He kept his voice low. "Forgive the intrusion, Master Hawkins, but I have been asked to conduct you from here. As I have explained to the others, your celebrity has preceded you. You were seen coming in here and, even now, an anxious crowd has gathered outside to question you about the events of the last two days. If you will follow me?"

The priest turned and Leigh immediately set off after him. Nay and I exchanged glances, shrugged, then joined the procession. The priest led us off through an arched doorway and down stairs that took us below street level. They ended in a corridor that stretched out to the right and left, though the priest cut back beside the stairs and under them to a hidden corridor. What I had assumed to be solid block steps were, in fact, stone slabs that had been cantilevered into the wall, providing the open space. I plunged into the darkness with the others.

A bit further down the corridor, which was only lit by the dim glow of fungi on the ceiling, I saw the priest's silhouette. He pointed further along. "There is a circular stairway that leads down and out. Keep your hands on the central axis as you descend."

Leigh led the way, with Nay next and me bringing up the rear. I was a couple steps into the dizzying descent when I realized the priest was not behind me and that he still had my mother's beans. I turned and started back up the steps. I saw the opening into the corridor I'd walked down closing and the bright green image of a bird with wings unfurled and upswept on the wall. In a heartbeat the image vanished and I realized that the whole stairwell cylinder had shifted ninety degrees as we were descending. Had I not turned around and seen what I did, I would not have noticed the shift.

From below I heard Leigh's voice. "Not quite what I expected as a way out."

"Nope."

I descended quickly and came out into a small room. Once I left the stairwell, the cylinder turned again, cutting us off. Opposite us appeared to be an image of the bird again, this time looking as if translucent green stone had been carved to fill holes cut into the wall. Its glow built to brightness, illuminating the trio of hooded robes hanging on the wall. The robes took on a greenish cast because of the light shining on them, but I suspected they were really as white as our moonmasks.

Nay turned to regard the both of us. "Any idea what is happening?"

I shook my head.

Leigh's eyes narrowed. "It's obvious, isn't it? We've attracted the attention of a Society."

"A Society?" Nay's shoulders slumped a bit. "They exist, sure, but no trade is marked by this symbol."

Leigh held up a hand and waggled a finger at Nay. "Those are the Lesser Societies, Nay, the public ones. Every trade has one and accepts only the best of the guild into them. They grew up after the Great Revolt, as a response to the Major Societies. Before the revolt took hold, long before it, secret societies brought together the leaders of the day, allowing them to talk and plot. Some say the societies even predate the Estine Empire. I don't know if that is true, but the empire's incompetent leadership certainly necessitated their spreading and flourishing."

"Everyone knows that, Leigh." Nay folded his arms across his chest. "That's where the wearing of masks originated, but after the revolt, they were done."

"Not exactly. Instead of vanishing, they spread, moving into nations that had never even been part of the Estine Empire. The societies are a means for people of differing nations to exchange ideas even though their nations might be hostile to each other. They serve as shadowy embassies that can circumvent official conflicts as needed."

I raised an eyebrow. "What do they want?"

Leigh smiled. "Us, apparently."

The bird image took on a golden hue. A disembodied voice echoed distantly as if speaking to us from the bottom of a well. "You stand on the threshold of your future. Strip away your old selves and don these robes to become the men you are meant to be."

Leigh leaned back against a wall and began to tug off his boots. He looked up when he'd gotten the first one off, then tossed it aside. "Well, take off your clothes and put on the robe."

"Are you sure we want to do this, Leigh?" I nervously fingered the lacings on my shirt. "We don't even know who they are."

"We don't, Hawkins, but we know some of the people they must be." He started on his other boot. "What have we done to attract this attention? We've been out on that hunt, killing temeryces—which is a wonderful word to rhyme, by the way—and vylaens and gibberkin. Everyone in Valsina probably has heard some variation of a rumor about what we've done, but these people wouldn't invite us here based on rumor. We're here because they know what we did."

I nodded and pulled the hem of my tunic from the top of my trousers. "Which means they spoke with someone who knew what we did, like your father or Heslin."

Nay smiled and sat down to kick his boots off. "And they took us from the temple. Only a few people knew we were going there and when."

"Exactly." Leigh slipped off his pants, tugged off his tunic and peeled stockings from his raw feet. Standing naked except for his mask, he reached for a robe. "Two nights ago they watched us, last night they evaluated us, and tonight they want us. We've come far in just three days of a Moon Month, my friends. Just imagine where we will end up in a lifetime."

CHAPTER 10

We stood before the glowing golden bird emblem, wearing only the robes we had been given and our moonmasks. I certainly had no idea what to do next, and the voice did not return to help us. I started to reach a hand toward the symbol, to see if I could feel heat from it, but Leigh moved quickly to preempt me. He touched the symbol, then withdrew his hand quickly, as if he'd stuck a finger on a needle.

The stone panel slid slowly upward, revealing a small chamber that would only accept one of us. Nay and I took a step backward, inclining our heads toward Leigh. He stood stock still for a moment, then looked at us, blinking away surprise. His blue eyes became crescents, then he nodded and stepped into the chamber.

The wall again descended.

I heard no scream, no sounds of his struggling to get out, which did hearten me. It made no sense, after all, for our hosts to go to the lengths they did just to kill us when a dagger in the dark or poison in wine would have been less troublesome. Despite that line of logic, I couldn't shake a flesh-puckering sense of foreboding.

Nay waved me forward, but I shook my head. "You go before me."

"Not sure if they want someone of my low birth."

"If they didn't want you, you'd not be here. The priest could have separated us easily enough, or they could have taken us at another time." I smiled easily at him. "Besides, Naysmith comes before Tarrant in the alphabet, as does Carver before Hawkins. If you precede me, we make it easy on whoever keeps their records."

Nay frowned. "By that reckoning, Leigh should have been last. Then again, he is a Norrington."

"Just assume his first name won it for him; it's easier that way." I nodded to him. "I'll see you on the other side."

Nay touched the emblem and the wall swallowed him.

I hesitated for a moment, taking one last look around the room, and at the piles of clothes that we had worn into the place. We had been directed to shed that which marked us as who we had been, so we could become the men we were meant to be. I knew the Moon Month was part of that process, but stepping through the wall became an active rather than passive move. It made things come faster than I expected, and while part of me was pleased to be moving forward quickly, another part of me hoped I wasn't running so fast I wouldn't be able to keep up with my legs.

I pressed my hand against the emblem and kept it there despite the tingling pains trickling into my fingers. It was a petty victory over Leigh, and one only made possible by seeing how he had reacted, but I was glad to have won it. Leigh had been a life-long companion and friend. His self-centered nature was something I had lived with forever, and I had learned to ignore the trivial and warn him away from the malignant manifestations of it, but there were times he could get under my flesh. I stored up little victories like this to salve my soul when he annoyed me.

I stepped into the chamber and the wall sank to the floor behind me. It closed me in a tight chamber that felt hot and the air heavy. I could breathe, but as I expanded my chest, both it and my back touched the front and rear walls respectively. I could move my arms only an inch or two and shift my feet about the same. As the air thickened, I felt as if I'd been buried alive, and part of me wanted to scream.

But I'd not heard Leigh scream, so I refused to surrender.

The voice returned. "You have been chosen to join an elite assembly of men and women, most of whom you do not know and never will know. They all labor in the same cause, pulling in the same direction, to stave off the collapse of civilization into murderous barbarism. The correctness of their mission is not in question, merely your willingness to join them. Are you willing?"

"I am."

"You, Tarrant Hawkins, will swear a solemn oath. If you betray us and reveal what you know of us, your right hand will wither, your right eye grow dark, your tongue will swell up to choke you, and your ears will bleed. Say it."

"I, Tarrant Hawkins, swear that if I betray the society and reveal what I know of it, my right hand will wither, my right eye grow dark, my tongue swell until it chokes me, and my ears bleed."

A golden glow began above my head, then descended over my body. It tickled as it moved down and in its wake left my limbs tingling as if they had been asleep. My legs could not support me and I went limp. Somehow the chamber adjusted for this and I quickly found myself seated on the floor, with my knees under my chin and my arms flopped around them.

I should note that writing the words you are reading could be taken as a violation of my oath. My right hand remains strong, my right eye bright, my tongue has not swollen, and my ears do not bleed. I can only conclude that either the society never had the power to enforce that oath—something I do not believe—or that whatever mystical agent governs the oath does not consider what I am writing to be a betrayal.

The heat built sharply in the chamber, then exploded into a twisting green torrent of fire. It swirled around me faster and faster, sucking the very air from my lungs. My robe burst into flames in a heartbeat, then my vision dimmed and the world went black.

I awoke covered in sweat and bathed in a translucent blue glow. I still sat with my knees clutched to my chest, now

utterly naked. I reached out with my right hand, moving only
a couple of inches, and touched the glowing blue wall that
defined the edges of my world. It felt firm and rasped slightly
against my fingertips, but I sensed a fragility there as well. I
pressed a finger against it, the flesh beneath my nail going
white for a moment, then the wall cracked. I applied more
fingers and pushed a bit harder, breaking away a small triangular piece.

Cool air flowed in through the hole, bringing a smile to my
face. I picked away at the hole, enlarging it carefully. When I'd
cut a bar across my oval prison's wall, I set my elbows against
it and pushed them outward. More of the shell cracked. I
smashed my head up and back, then cranked my arms around
as far as they would go. Another flip of my head cast the top of
the egg off and I stood.

To my left Nay smashed a fist up through the top of his
blue egg, then kicked his way free of the front of it. Beyond
him Leigh emerged through the top of his egg, much as I had,
then kicked his feet free and stomped the eggshell into dust.
Standing there, watching them emerge, I tried to brush off the
ash of my robe, but only smeared it along my sweaty flesh.

The three of us occupied the central of five positions at the
edge of a bowl-like depression. The bowl descended through
three stepped levels, with men and women wearing brilliant
red-, yellow-, and orange-hooded cloaks standing on all of
them. At the bowl's center rose a circular dais upon which
stood two men. They wore the same sort of robes their fellows
did, though one's cloak was edged in blue and the smaller
man's was edged in black. Beyond them, beneath the side of
the bowl facing us, an arched passageway led deeper into the
facility.

A hand emerged from beneath the smaller, stoop-shouldered man's cloak and pointed toward us. "Behold, my brethren, from the flames we have eggs, and from the eggs we have
new Minor Hatchlings. You should know them to be Bosleigh
Norrington, Naysmith Carver, and Tarrant Hawkins. Study
them, guide them, seek aid from them. Reveal to them no
secret before their time, report those acts which do them

praise or no credit and, in whichever way you are able, see to it that they have done no harm."

As one the people gathered in the room reached up with their right hands, touched their foreheads, then brought the hand down, palm open and up, to linger at waist height for a moment before returning beneath the cloak.

The little man resumed speaking. "There, you three have seen the first of our signs, the most important one. It conveys an understanding of what has been said, and a willingness to comply with the obligation therein. Were the descending hand closed into a fist, or the face turned away from the rising hand, a lack of compliance or a failure to understand would be indicated. Do you follow?"

I touched my right hand to my brow, then lowered it with a palm facing the center of the room, as did my two companions.

"Good, very good, all of you." The old man bowed his head respectfully in our direction. "We are the Ancient and Most Secret Society of the Knights of the Phoenix. In the time when the *weirun* fashioned themselves into the world and the gods had not risen from their dreams, many magickal beasts roamed the world. The dragons are still among us today, but other creatures have passed into legend. One of these, the phoenix, builds a nest, immolates itself, then is hatched anew from the ashes. So it is that we have gathered together, across the world, to guarantee the rebirth of that world when it is faced with crisis. We are guided by Erlinsax's wisdom to pursue Graegen's Justice, often employing the skills granted to us by Kedyn to accomplish our ends. Do you understand?"

Again we repeated the gesture we'd learned.

"Very good." The small man opened his arms. "Who among you has proposed we accept these Minor Hatchlings into our flock?"

The man standing behind him spoke, and I recognized Lord Norrington's voice instantly. "I did, Most Revered Flock Lord."

"And the reason you commended them to us?"

"Though yet tender in age and unseasoned in the way of war, these three slew temeryces and a vylaen. Their quick thinking and selflessness saved the lives of comrades and allowed authorities to be alerted to the danger lurking in Westwood. Because of their actions, this danger has been destroyed, and we are now aware of greater danger to the world."

The small man, who I came to suspect was Heslin, turned a full circle to study the other Knights gathered in the assembly hall. "Does anyone speak against them?"

Silence answered him.

"Does anyone speak for them?"

A Knight below us took a step forward. "I would ask leave to speak in their favor, Most Reverend Flock Lord."

"Granted, Greater White Phoenix."

"Brothers and sisters, we have all heard the tale of what these three did. It is within our power to acknowledge that the acts they have performed are beyond the expectations we demand of Hatchlings. I would suggest we accept them as Minor Fledglings, making it incumbent upon them to learn all knowledge they must possess for their new rank, and the rank they have passed by."

Heslin again looked around the room. "Does anyone speak against this elevation?"

Silence reigned. He nodded slowly, then looked up at us. "You have been granted a great honor here, one which you will come to appreciate more and more as you progress in your knowledge. As a Fledgling there are three things you must know immediately. The first is this."

Heslin threw back his hood. Underneath was a simple black mask the same size and design as our moonmasks. He closed his left eye and touched his left index finger to it. "If you see this done and then the person points at something, be it nothing more than spilled wine, or as serious as spilled blood, you will turn a blind eye to it and speak of it to no one save if commanded to do so by an assembly of Knights. You will endure whatever temporal punishments are meted out for your silence, knowing that you are furthering our cause."

He then touched his left index finger to the outside corner of his left eye and brought it back to touch his left earlobe. "If you see this done, know that the person doing it is one of us and wishes to speak in private with you. You will, at your earliest convenience, without raising alarm or attention to yourself, seek this person out and speak with him—always within the strictures of silence demanded of you."

The mage then reached out with his right index finger and drew a shape in the air. It burned with a golden light similar to the emblem on the wall. He started with a horizontal line, then added two shorter vertical lines that touched it a third of the way in from both ends. At the left end he drew a short vertical line that descended below the horizontal for as far as the other verticals rose above it.

"This symbol you will recognize as marking the Fledgling entrance to one of our meeting places. If you see it, know that your presence is demanded. Touch it and you will be taken to the place where you may best serve the society. Do you understand all these symbols?"

Raising my hand and lowering it I indicated my understanding. Nay and Leigh did likewise.

"Good. As Fledglings you will be tutored in our ways— here in our assembly hall, or in other assembly halls. Your duties are simple at this stage: obey your superiors, pursue all lawful duties, and provide succor to those who require it of you. The Most Ancient and Secret Society of the Knights of the Phoenix is proud to have you among us."

Heslin applauded us and the others joined in. We did nothing but smile as they clapped. It did not occur to me except when they were filing out, with their colorful cloaks melding into a riot of color, that I was stark naked. I looked down and took some minor comfort in the fact that, given the grey ash smeared over me, and the dim light this high in the bowl, much of my nakedness had been clothed in shadow.

Heslin, Lord Norrington, and a third man whom I quickly recognized as my father ascended the stairs toward us. My father wore a big smile, whereas the other two kept their expressions more under control. Each one of them carried a cloak that was mostly brown, quilted together out of feather-shaped strips of cloth. Only the lowest rank of feathers had been made of yellow.

Heslin held his cloak up to Nay. "These cloaks you will

wear here, marking you as Minor Fledglings. When the hides of the temeryces you slew are tanned, a mantle of temeryx feathers will be added to each."

My father gave me my cloak. "You don't know how proud you have made me, Tarrant."

I smiled at him. "And you don't know how happy I am to hear that. I promise I will continue to do so."

"As will you all, I have no doubt." Lord Norrington reached beneath his cloak and drew out three black temeryx feathers. "You are each entitled to affix one of these to your moonmask. It should put an end to the rumors of what you did or did not do out in Westwood."

"A feather won't still tongues that wag."

Lord Norrington nodded. "True enough, Nay, but they might slow them." He turned and waved the way back down the stairs. "You can clean the ash off and dress again in your clothes. I believe you were all off to see your friend, Master Playfair. He has been told you were delayed, and the pot of beans is already there."

"Thank you." I almost started to say that Rounce would be surprised to hear what had happened to us, but I realized I couldn't say anything about our initiation to him. Another thought followed on the heels of that one as quickly as a wolf taking a lamb. "Rounce will never become a Knight of the Phoenix, will he?"

My father stiffened, then shook his head. "The injury to his knee is not good, Tarrant. He won't lose the leg, but it will never work right. His father might send for an elf to magick it back together, but there is no telling if one will come or would be successful."

Lord Norrington rested a hand on my father's shoulder. "His injury would not bar him, but we tend to draw members from the military. Your friend, he's a good man, and will have a future. It will probably not be with us, but others of the Great Societies will see his worth."

Nay's head came up. "Other Great Societies?"

"There are others, all of whom agree with our ends, but differ as to the methods to reach them." Heslin pressed his hands together. "We are at war with none of them, though our differences do make cooperation difficult at times. It is nothing with which you should be concerned at the moment."

The mage lifted a hand. "There is one last thing to keep in mind: you know who we are, and other Knights may make themselves known to you. Inquire of no one if they are one of us. Be discreet in making your signs and pursuing your duties. While we have no true enemies, we are not always seen as friends. Yours is to wait and watch and learn; that is enough for now."

I touched my hand to my brow, then displayed my palm. Nay and Leigh had done so as well.

Heslin nodded. "It looks as if this clutch is quick and full of promise. This is good. Given what brought you to us, we have never needed such as you more than now."

CHAPTER 11

We went to see Rounce that night, and several times over the next couple of days. I can remember how his face would light up upon seeing us and he would thank us for having saved his life and his leg. I did not doubt, then or now, that he was sincere in his thanks, but I always caught a hint of bitterness beneath his words. The healers had bound his knee up tight in a canvas splint with oaken stays, keeping it straight and stiff. Even though Rounce could get up and put weight on it—a little anyway, though he mostly got about on crutches—we all knew he would never walk right again.

Rounce would never be a warrior, and even though he might not have been perfectly suited to that life, the fact that he had been denied it so quickly and definitively always left him wondering what might have been. In all the chronicles of the events that took place subsequent to his wounding, he was only mentioned as a victim—sometimes even misidentified as a shepherd or woodsman the three of us had rescued. That temeryx might not have killed Rounce, but it killed the person Rounce could have been, and the survivor left behind would forever muse about how things would have been different had he been in my place or Leigh's.

Within two days of our return to Valsina it was decided that someone had to bring news of what had happened to the Oriosan court. Normally that would have meant a sixty-league journey to the capital, Meredo. At an easy pace of five leagues a day, it would take us twelve days, or just over a week. Unfortunately for us, the queen would have already set out for the Alcidan capital of Yslin, to meet with the other rulers for the Harvest Festival—an international festival held every four years at a different site.

The news we had to convey—that an unusual group of Aurolani creatures had been found in Oriosa—was deemed momentous by the Lord Mayor and the other local nobles, so an embassy was to be dispatched to the queen, to inform her and her fellow royals about this threat. Lord Norrington was tasked with putting the group together and he selected Nay, Leigh, and me to be part of it.

While I was honored beyond words to be included, I didn't think it was right and was determined to refuse. I reasoned that I had no place going and speaking with royalty of any stripe. Moreover, my Moon Month had barely begun, and there was a harvest to be brought in, and I wasn't at all comfortable with leaving Valsina when more foul creatures might be lurking about.

My father listened to my protests silently, then shook his head. "You have no choice in this matter, Tarrant. Lord Kenwick Norrington is my liege lord. We are his to do with as he wishes. While I would be most pleased to accompany you all, I am Valsina's Peaceward. My place is here, preparing the city for the worst your discovery augers. Your place is with him, on the road, going to Yslin."

"But my Moon Month—"

"Ah, there we have the crux of it, yes?" My father chuckled. "All the galas, all of your being lionized for what you have done. The feasts you'll miss. The trysts. Hardly seems fair, does it?"

I glanced down at the floorboards. "Well, no."

"Life isn't about fair." My father's voice took on a stern edge. "What happened to Rounce isn't fair. Sure as there are ten days in a week, he'll live with the consequences of it, no reprieve because of a Moon Month. You'll be doing the same thing. Life's intruding on your fun. Were it up to me, I might wish it different, but it isn't and I don't.

"You have a duty, Tarrant, to Lord Norrington, the people of Valsina and of Oriosa. And a duty to yourself. If you were to stay here, you'd not have a chance to see how far you could go."

I frowned. "You're staying here."

"But I didn't always stay here. I'm on the backslope of the mountain of my life, you're just in the foothills. You've got to make the climb."

I accepted what he told me and realized that I was being selfish and a little scared. The Moon Month was supposed to be a transition period, and I was feeling a bit cheated out of not getting at least a month. But my father's comment about Rounce brought home just how petty that idea was.

Our expedition shaped up quickly. Lord Norrington picked Heslin and two of his apprentices to travel with us, in addition to four huntsmen and ten soldiers. We each brought with us three horses, basic necessities such as blankets, wet weather gear, armor and weapons, as well as food for all of us and grain for the horses. Rounce's father saw to the provisioning and even bartered some of his goods with an armorer so that Nay and I could get our basic needs met. He said he would accept no payment from us, but Nay and I both gave him our moongold, seeing as how it would do us no good on the road.

In terms of armor and weaponry, I ran toward things that would allow me to preserve my speed and maneuverability. I accepted a long mail surcoat and coif, with an open helm to go over my head, then gauntlets, bracers, and greaves. I chose a padded leather gambeson and trousers to wear beneath, and for everyday protection. I included a horsebow and three sheaves of thirty arrows each, a sword, a small ax, and two daggers as my personal armament. The sword was a yard and some long, with thirty inches of double-edged steel for a blade. A simple crosshilt protected my hands and the hilt was long enough for me to use two hands on it if needed.

Leigh and Nay equipped themselves the same as I did,

though Nay opted away from a sword. Instead he chose a hideous-looking maul a good four feet long, with half a foot of triangular steel spike on top of that. The maul's top eight inches had been wrapped with steel, about doubling the stout oaken haft's diameter, and four narrow strips of steel ran the haft's length to turn swords and axes looking to chop into it. The maul weighed at least twice what my sword did, though Nay twirled it around as if it were a willow wand.

Taking leave of my parents was not easy, and I was pleased I did so at home and not in front of my traveling companions. My father, mother, and I ate breakfast barefaced that morning. My mother made certain I had plenty to eat and constantly reminded me about what to do if I found myself chafed, sunburned, with a variety of rashes, bumps, bruises, or even the occasional cut. She also extracted from me promises to mend my clothes quickly, so I'd be seen as more than a beggar, and to send word back to her as I could about how I was faring.

My father filled me in on things he knew about various members of the expedition and told me to learn as much as I could from Lord Norrington. He also demanded that I take care of my horses before I cared for myself and to be diligent in my duties around the camp. He told me that no one ever complained if water buckets were filled fast, or if more firewood was gathered than ever would be used. He also warned against complaining about the food, no matter how vile, and suggested a dozen different ways to stay awake when on a watch in the deepest night.

And he admonished me against cruel gossip and told me to watch over Leigh as if he were my brother. I knew the two things were linked, since unkind folks had whispered that Leigh was small and given to frippery because his parents were first cousins. Such things being said had always angered my father and I knew they stung Leigh, so I'd always refrained from any mention of that and had truly treated him like a brother.

Now that I was going away from home, I felt as if this last bit of advice was my father passing on to me part of the duty he felt to the Norrington household. With a solemn nod I let him know I'd shoulder that burden gladly. He smiled and nothing more was said.

I kissed both of them good-bye and brushed my mother's tears away before donning my moonmask. My last vision of them, before the mask-curtain slid down to hide them, was of them holding each other, wearing brave smiles, waving at me. I gave them a salute, then opened the door and let the sound of the latch opening and closing behind me hide my mother's gentle sobbing.

We met at Valsina's South Gate and immediately set off. We would skirt the Bokagul, less out of any fear of dealing with the urZrethi than just wanting to avoid the trouble of riding through the mountains. Men and urZrethi had fought a terrible war centuries past, and although a peace did exist between us, both sides largely kept to themselves. Despite living in the shadow of the Bokagul Mountains my whole life, I'd never seen an urZrethi, and only heard my father speak of meeting them a couple of times.

We'd head west once we'd passed the mountains, passing north of the ruined city of Atval, then go along the border road to Yslin. The entire ninety-eight-league trek would take us eighteen days. We would arrive in Yslin in the middle of the Harvest Festival.

The early part of the journey proved uneventful. We camped out some nights and took over the inns in a few small villages on others. Since our road provisions consisted of dried beef, cobbles—little, round biscuits baked hard enough to serve as paving stones—flour, rice, and millet, taking meals in the taverns offered us variety we all welcomed. Being able to stable the horses and get them more grain instead of just field forage was also a welcome change.

When asked why we were traveling south, Lord Norrington told innkeepers that he was taking the three of us moonmaskers to the Harvest Festival in Yslin to broaden our view of the world. This explanation proved immensely entertaining for tavern denizens, who all took it upon themselves to discuss every Harvest Festival story they'd ever heard. Some of them were good, but quite a few dulled after the first telling, and we heard them night after night.

We also learned a lot about local happenings. So far the news from Valsina had not made it south, so no one knew what we'd done. The black temeryx feathers on our moon-masks were taken to be from overly large ravens, and a few folks poked fun at us for that. Leigh bristled at such things, but his father kept him in line. Nay and I just fell into a pattern of spinning out a tale of our war with the ravens. It grew with each telling and, truth be told, was more entertaining than most festival stories.

Back on the road, as the three of us were riding with Leigh's father, I asked Lord Norrington when the last time was that temeryces and vylaens and gibberkin had been found in Oriosa.

He pursed his lips for a moment, then looked at me. "In truth, I do not know. You've heard the stories of local news, how some shepherds have found sheep dead or how farmers have lost calves. Could be that's the work of wolves, or it could be temeryces. They could have been here for years and we've not known it. I doubt it, though, since they seem quite bold.

"As for confirmed sightings, you would have to go back a century or so, at the time of the last Aurolani invasion. Among the Aurolani a leader rose up, a vylaen-urZrethi mongrel, if the stories are true, named Kree'chuc. He gathered a vast army and descended through a pass in the Boreal Mountains. They swept over Noriva—what we call the Ghost Marches now—and conquered Vorquellyn. No one thought they could do that, no one thought the Aurolani could master ship building or sailing, but they had.

"They sailed on south, bypassing Fortress Draconis, to attack Sebcia and Muroso."

Leigh frowned. "I thought Fortress Draconis was meant to protect the Southlands from invasion. It failed."

His father shook his head. "Fortress Draconis is perfectly positioned to cut off supplies flowing south, which it effectively did. After the elves smashed most of his fleet, Kree'chuc's army had to live off the land. His forward troops moved into Oriosa, but urZrethi from Bokagul and Sarengul halted their advance. Human forces then pushed in through Saporcia and drove the army back through the Black Marches.

Troops from Fortress Draconis harried them all the way to the pass, then a strong Aurolani force held them back."

"Kree'chuc was killed at Yvatsen Bend." Nay smiled. "He thought he held the only ford for many leagues. Thought he was safe with the river bend between us and his army."

Lord Norrington nodded. "You know the history of the Twilight Campaign?"

"My mother's father knew the tales. Had them from his father. Wanting to be a warrior comes from that."

"If your great-grandfather was part of the Twilight Campaign, you are heir to a noble tradition." Lord Norrington gave Nay a broad smile. "And you are correct. An urZrethi host shifted tons of stones to make another ford, then the army crossed to Kree'chuc's rear. They drove his forces back against the river, shattering them and killing him. Our army then headed north, joined with the troops from Fortress Draconis, and pushed on, bent on slaying his foul mistress. Chytrine raised an army and blocked the pass."

Leigh frowned. "If we broke the Aurolani army, why didn't we free the Ghost Marches and Vorquellyn?"

Lord Norrington shrugged his shoulders rather stiffly. "It happened long before my time, so I don't know for certain. The immediate reason for the lack of a fight was an early winter. The army headed home. The Twilight Campaign cost a lot of lives and created a lot of misery, so few were the rulers willing to repeat that sort of hardship for their people.

"Other problems took over later. Okrannel felt secure behind its mountain border with the Ghost Marches and didn't want to invite an army in. Given how armies tend to feed off the locals, that's not hard to understand. Also Noriva and Okrannel used to fight a lot over the bay between them, so not having the lords of Noriva returned to their lands meant one less problem for Okrannel's leaders."

Leigh's eyes got a distant look. "Wouldn't a seaborne invasion have worked?"

"It might have, but that sort of thing is very difficult. The logistics . . ."

I narrowed my eyes. "Is this something that is being considered?"

"Considering it is an exercise that has kept many warriors from boredom while garrisoning some far-flung fortress." Lord Norrington laughed lightly. "Perhaps we can work out details on our journey."

"That was the reason Vorquellyn was never freed?" Nay's eyes hardened. "It is an island."

"It *is* an island, but that is not the only reason for its remaining under the Aurolani banner." Lord Norrington unstoppered his canteen and drank, then wiped his mouth off with his right hand. "The elves live in their homelands, of which Vorquellyn is one. Their holdings used to be much larger, but they retreated to the present enclaves as humans spread further. When they reach the right age, roughly akin to your reaching your Moon Month, they undergo a ritual that ties them to the homeland of their birth. It is a magickal bond. If their homeland suffers, so do they, so they steward the land far more diligently than any other species.

"When the Aurolani forces overran the island, those Vorquellyn elves who had been bound to the land and survived the attack were in much pain. Some died of being heartsick. Others just headed west. What they did when they reached the ocean, no one knows; they just vanished. The others, the youngers, though, they could not be bound to any other homeland, though other elves offered them sanctuary. The Vorquellyn elves, they're very different."

He sat back in his saddle. "You three have never seen elves, have you, or urZrethi or any of the other species."

I smiled. "You mean, besides gibberkin and vylaens?"

"Point taken."

"Not me."

Nay shook his head, as did Leigh.

"Perhaps in Yslin we will see some. Envoys attend the festival from time to time." Lord Norrington stroked his chin. "By the end of your Moon Month you will see more of the world than most people do in a lifetime. Perhaps—"

Whatever he was going to say was cut off by one of the outriders from our northern flank reining up before us. "My lord, we've cut across signs of travelers in the woods."

"Human?"

"Gibberkin, I think. Day-old sign." The man shook his head. "At least a dozen, running parallel to us."

Lord Norrington's eyes tightened. "The road is fairly open, so it would have to be a night attack, and they wouldn't have delayed that sort of thing if they were just raiding."

Heslin came riding up. "Trouble?"

"The outriders have come across gibberkin sign. They've been tracking us."

The mage nodded. "That assumes they know who we are and have watched us from Valsina. Do you think one of the gibberkin escaped us in Westwood?"

"It works as an explanation. The sign also suggests there were more parties working in Oriosa, and they may have been tracking us until they found the strength or place to ambush us." Leigh's father stood in his stirrups and looked around the broad valley through which we rode. "No cover, no real defensible position. The forests could be full of Aurolani creatures."

Heslin pointed south across the low hills bordering the valley. "The ruins of Atval are perhaps a dozen miles ahead."

"Atval?" Lord Norrington shook his head. "We would have to be insane to chance it."

"Or desperate." The old mage smiled. "If they know of Atval, they won't have cut the path off to it, since they won't expect us to go for it. If we do, we might be able to fight them off. And even if the doom that came to Atval visits it again, chances are the Aurolani force will be destroyed, too."

"It's better than dying in a meadow." Lord Norrington looked at the outrider. "Cooper, bring everyone in. We're riding for Atval. Spread the word, armor up, change to fresh horses. We'll be riding hard to make it by nightfall."

"As you wish, my lord."

Norrington looked at Heslin again. "Are you certain about this?"

"If one has to die, why not go out in a blaze of glory, eh?" The mage cackled dryly, then reined his horse around and rode back toward his apprentices.

I felt my mouth grow dry. "What did he mean?"

"Blaze of glory? It's a joke, and a bad one."

"No, what did he mean when he mentioned 'the doom

that came to Atval'? He said it would get us, too. That's not possible, is it?"

"Oh, it is, Hawkins, very possible." Lord Norrington sighed heavily. "After all, the doom that came to Atval was dragons. They laid waste to the city and declared that no man shall ever live there again. If we take shelter there, we might survive the gibberkin, but if the dragons come enforce their decree . . ."

I nodded. "Our Moon Month will be eclipsed."

"Totally and completely, Tarrant."

CHAPTER 12

The Black City of Atval hung like a cloud on the horizon. Because it was built on a rise in the landscape, we were able to see it once we crested the hills. As we rode toward it, I waited for details to sharpen, but they never did. The whole city seemed liquid shadow, though the sun's death did splash bloody red highlights over the western surfaces.

Established well before the Great Revolt, Atval had been a simple settlement in the middle of plains that had served dragons for years as prime hunting grounds, but the leaders of the city struck a bargain with the dragons. They managed the bison herds, providing the dragons with thousands of the beasts each year without fail. The city prospered and walls that had once been wooden became made of stone. Massive battlements were raised and men decided their city had become formidable enough that they no longer need fear dragons.

A leader rose among them and led the people in a revolt against the dragons. They withheld their tribute and attacked the dragons sent to collect it. Legend says at least one dragon died—and stories hint at something that was more murder than a killing. For a short time, the people celebrated their grand victory and the leader who had won it for them.

As we drew close, the folly of their decision could not have been made more clear. The city itself remained recognizable in general shape, with huge walls and open gates, wide streets, monuments raised in central squares, buildings high and low spread out in an orderly fashion. What remained terrifyingly remarkable about it all was that the city might well have been fashioned of black wax, then placed too close to a fire. All hard edges had been softened, the crenelations on the walls melted down so the trails of molten stone could be seen. Roof tiles had run like water and frozen into stone daggers hanging like icicles from eaves. Square windows had been reduced to sloppy, sag-sided boxes, and proud archways had been softened into defeated holes.

As we rode into the city, Leigh pointed at what appeared to be rafters that somehow had survived the dragons' assault. "How is it possible the wood survived?"

"How is it possible any of this survived?" Heslin reined up short. "Dragonfire is tinged with magic. It can destroy, as it has done, or can be used to reshape stone—as they do when they form their halls in the mountains. Here they drove the people out, then reshaped the city as a warning. No man, no creature that walks on two legs, will ever be permitted to take up residence here ever again. Dragons, who trust occasionally, never forgive betrayal."

Leigh sighed. "But we didn't do anything to any dragons."

Heslin laughed. "And you would distinguish among dragons and their clans when you hear stories of raids?"

"Ah, no."

"Neither do they, at least, not when it comes to Atval. A dragon was murdered here. Those who did it thought the dragon's death would discourage other dragons." The old mage waved a hand toward the city. "They were wrong. The place reeks of dragon magic. They will know we are here, but how swiftly they will respond, I do not know."

Cooper, the outrider who had located the gibberkin sign, pointed along our backtrail. "They're coming in. Looks like multiple groups coming together. Gibberkin and temeryces, probably vylaens, too."

Leigh's father rode back to the gate and peered out. "No drearbeasts or hoargouns, but there must be a hundred of them at least. We need to find a building we can defend."

"Temple to Kedyn?" Nay pointed toward the center of the city. "If fighting there does get us help, the gods might at least be amused."

"As good a choice as any. Cooper, keep Alder and Darby here with you. Sign is moon, countersign is sun. Get us a count on them and then join us at the temple—and don't wait to come until they're right on your heels. I'd rather error in your count than not getting it at all."

We took the outriders' spare horses and rode with them into the city and up the broad steps of Kedyn's temple. Riding into the building, which was not quite as large as the temple in Valsina, we got our first indication of how complete the dragons' destruction of the city had been. The building itself showed the ravages of their fire, but inside the furnishings had also been affected. Tables and chairs were half-melted, but now made of stone. The statues of Kedyn, Fesyin, and Gesric had flowed down over their pedestals as if they were sandcastles overwashed by waves on a lakeshore. That the destruction had been so precise, leaving the structure sound while obliterating those things that defined its purpose, spoke very loudly to the dragons' contempt for all things human.

Once inside we gathered the horses down in the worship bowl and set about erecting barricades at the doors. Lord Norrington dispatched scouts, including Leigh, to seek out all entrances to the building. While the stone furnishings were heavy and hard to move, once we got them into position, we knew the Aurolani forces would have a hard time getting past them. I was sent up a stairway with four other archers to the second-story priest's-walk. There, I would be able to shoot out through the windows or down into the nave if the Aurolani broke in through the front.

Down below, Heslin and his apprentices managed to magickally rekindle some of the votive fires that once would have brightened the whole of the temple. Half-melted and misshapen as the sconces were, the ones that did work guttered with low flame and twisted shadows slithered throughout the temple. While they did dispel the gloom, they really gave us little more light than I would have expected of the sun a half-hour before it rose.

While Lord Norrington had been in charge of the hunt for the temeryces in Westwood, this was the first I saw him in a purely military situation. He made decisions quickly and definitively, though he sought advice from others and modified plans based on what they told him. The choices he made seemed most sensible to me, and the fact that he'd arranged for signs and countersigns and fallback positions made me feel as if the whole situation were under control. I knew we would be in a desperate fight, but I never had the feeling we were staging a defense in which we would all die.

That opinion underwent some revision when the gibberkin arrived—Cooper and the others reported having seen at least two hundred. I'd seen gibberers before, in Westwood, but they'd been dead. Their bulk had been easy to dismiss as fat, but the gibberkin stalking down the streets had muscles rippling beneath their mottled and matted fur. Their tall, black-tufted ears flicked this way and that, and they raised their broad muzzles to sniff the air. The gibberkin growled and snapped at each other, one or another giving voice to a blood-curdling noise that married a wolf's-howl with lunatic laughter. Most went unarmored, but all carried short spears and murderously long knives. A few had bows, and my companions and I silently agreed they would die first.

I nocked an arrow and drew it back to my chin. The bowstring pressed against my lower lip. I sighted in on a stout gibberkin who pumped his bow in the air and gave voice to one of the hideous screams. I loosed my arrow and cut the scream off. The arrow ripped into and out of his neck, spraying black blood over his compatriots and sticking another gibberer in the thigh.

Other arrows struck down gibberers, then the horde surged forward and up the steps in a seething mass. I shot arrow after arrow into it, never really having time to pick a target, but knowing I could not miss. The mob stopped for a moment and, from the shouts from below, I assumed the front line had hit our barricade. Shouts turned to screams and bestial yelps. Husky laughter from below and the dragging of thrashing gibberkin to the rear ranks of their formation told me we'd held and my friends were inflicting serious wounds below.

Again and again the gibberkin horde flowed up the stairs. Shrieking and yowling as if the sound alone would kill us, they rushed the barricade. They hurled rocks and arrows, axes and spears to drive our men back. The archers and I continued to feather them, doing our best to pick off vylaens or the few temeryces we saw.

Shouts from down below brought me around. From off on the left I saw a bright flash, then a burning temeryx sprinted into the nave. Its claws scrabbled against the stone floor, and as the fire consumed it, the creature slipped and fell. Acrid black smoke rose from it, then two more temeryces appeared and ran at our barricade from behind. In their wake I saw one of Heslin's apprentices face down in a growing pool of blood. The other supported the old man with one arm, touching a simple staff to another temeryx and causing it to burst into flame.

I loosed an arrow at one of the temeryces and split its breastbone. It flopped to the ground, spending its momentum by sliding into and undercutting one of the outriders. Another man whirled and beheaded the dying beast with a single sword stroke. He died moments later as the other temeryx leaped and slashed his chest and belly open.

Soldiers turned from the barricade to deal with the attack from our rear. Vylaens outside shouted new orders in a foul, harsh tongue. The gibberkin snarled savagely and assaulted our line one more time. They slowed for a moment, letting me pin one's breastbone to its spine with an arrow, then the gibberkin surged forward again. They didn't stop and I knew our barricade had been breached.

I turned and directed my shots into the temple's nave. My first shot split the spine of one gibberer, dropping him at Lord Norrington's feet. Leigh's father ducked the mighty crosscut aimed at his head by one, then slashed his sword through its legs. The blade then came up in an arc and down to split another gibberkin's skull. He danced back from the two he had killed, helped one of our warriors back to his feet, then opened another gibberer's belly with a forehand slash.

Nay was no less magnificent. He caught a leaping gibberkin on his maul's spike, then dumped the belly-stuck creature onto two of its own kind as if a farmer pitchforking hay from one pile to the next. He parried a swordcut with his weapon's haft, then drove the steel butt-cap into a muzzle. An overhand blow crushed the gibberer's skull, then a sidelong slashing attack shattered ribs on another.

Of Leigh I could see nothing, but the nave had become a sea of chaos accompanied by a hellish chorus of screams and howls, bold laughter and hissed curses. I saw a knot of gibberkin break out to the right and feathered one before they disappeared beneath the priest's-walk. I realized they were headed for the stairs that I'd used to get up to the walk, so I drew my sword and ran to the archway.

I reached it a heartbeat before the first of many gibberers. A two-handed slash sent him reeling back, clutching his ruined face. Those following him battered him out of the way and came rushing out full on, longknives and clawed hands reaching for me.

I ducked back, letting one fly past. He sailed across the priest's-walk and caught the melted balustrade just below his knees. He somersaulted over it and lazily spun toward the floor below.

More came, howling, slashing at me with their weapons. I hacked at them, catching limbs, my blade sparking off longknives raised to parry. I caught one with a solid blow across the neck. He spun away, but not before a hot jet of blood spurted back into my face, blinding me. I inhaled some of it and started choking. I backed quickly, my feet finding minimal purchase on the blood-slicked floor.

I blinked my eyes to clear them and was rewarded with the vision of a wall of gibberers coming for me. I lashed out half-blind, stabbing here, cutting there. My armor turned strokes I never saw. My shoulders began to ache and one sharp blow to my left arm numbed it from the elbow down.

And on they yet came.

I tasted sour, salty blood on my lips and could smell it on my face. My stomach roiled, half from the scent and half from hurt. Gibberkin howls pounded me while anguished screams drilled into my soul. What had been a noble expedition and a chance to explore the world had deteriorated into a slaughter that dappled my moonmask with blood. Part of me was certain my own blood would soon be in the mix, and that part of me wanted to panic.

The tingle of returning sensation in my left hand gave me hope—not of survival, but hope that I'd take more of the gibberers with me. If Cooper's count had been right, we were outnumbered ten to one, and I'd not killed nearly my share yet. I was determined to do that and set my teeth in a fierce grimace as the gibberkin came for me.

My only hope was to play for time. I retreated along the priest's-walk, letting the gibberers string themselves out, so I could engage them one on one. A quick slash here opened one's belly, leaving him on his knees, madly stuffing ropy white entrails back into his open gut. His companions surged around him, undaunted.

I turned and ran the dozen yards to the end of the priest's-walk, then pivoted and cut to the left to continue my flight up the long side of the temple. I stopped quickly and lunged forward as a gibberkin rounded the corner. I'd have skewered him, but he allowed himself to career into the wall. He held his left arm wide, letting my blade pass between it and his rib cage.

He flashed fangs in a lupine grin of victory.

I slashed my blade up into his armpit. A wash of hot blood poured down the sword as I severed his brachial artery. My blade splashed his blood against the wall as I began to run again. He kept with me, his teeth snapping as if he wanted to bite me, then he faltered and slumped against the wall. His heart continued to pump the life out of him, gushing it into a lake that caused one of his followers to slip and crash into the wall. The other two leaped over it and came running.

I cut through a doorway into what had once been some priest's private chambers. Despite a little moonlight streaming in through open windows, the darkness lay thick enough on the room that I could discern all but nothing in the way of details. Almost immediately something caught me across the shins. My greaves absorbed the damage, but I spilled forward, head over heels. My sword went flying off into the darkness, clattering to rest somewhere. I picked myself up as I looked for it, but all I saw were the silhouettes of the gibberkin. I turned and leaped through one of the windows, praying the fall to the ground would not injure me.

My prayer was answered.

The window had not looked out on the street, but onto a courtyard garden built as an extension of the temple's second floor. I landed on a slick surface of melted and recongealed gravel, which sent me sliding along into the stony bulk of what had once been a wooden planter filled with rose bushes.

The pair of gibberkin that had chased me climbed through the window, and two more emerged after them. They spread out as they came for me, slowly, cautiously. Their shortswords dwarfed the dagger I brandished, drawing derisive hoots.

I moved around so the planter served as a breastwork. Straightening up, I waved them forward. "Which will it be?" I forced my voice to be firm and pitched it low. "The first of you to reach me will die. Which one of you wants that honor?"

That was the wrong question to ask. The four of them exchanged snaps and snarls. Then, apparently unwilling to let any one of them claim the honor, they came at me together.

CHAPTER 13

Their united front died seconds before they did. The two on my left pulled up short as if they'd hit an invisible wall. Silver moonlight flashed from circular shapes that whizzed through the air and *chunked* solidly into them, chest and throat respectively. Without more than a harsh cough from the one, the two of them collapsed into petrified rose bushes, crackling and popping them on the way down.

The third gibberer dove at me over the rose barricade, intent on stabbing me with his longknife. I twisted, letting his blade slide past harmlessly, then brought my dagger up. My thrust stabbed deep into his chest. A warm gush of blood covered my right hand as the blade's tip emerged from his back.

His dive continued, with his left shoulder catching me in the chest. It knocked me back on my heels and we went down together. We bounced once, hard, then I heaved, flinging his body off. He flew away and took my dagger with him. I heard his head smack wetly against an unseen planter, finishing what my knife had started.

I turned back to my left to face the last gibberkin. I saw it loom above me, then its upper body jerked forward. Its head hit its knees, then rebounded as the beast fell forward. It landed hard, muzzle-first on the ground. It stayed there for a second, balanced on knees and nose, then toppled to the side, its guts flooding out with a sigh.

Beyond where the gibberer had stood, I caught the first glimpse of my savior. Blood streamed from his sword's blade. Moonlight drained all the native color from his flesh, but painted the various tattoos on his bare arms in clear relief. He had sharpened ears, which were quite easy to see because his pale hair had been shaved away from the sides of his head and remained only in a narrow strip down the center. I thought from his profile and the shape of his ear that he must be an elf, but they were all supposed to be tall and slender. He was not. Tall, yes, very tall, but thickly muscled. He was easily larger than Nay.

As he knelt on one knee beside me, I gave him a grateful smile. "I'd like to th—"

He clapped a blood-slicked hand over my mouth and pressed me back down on the roof. "Silence!" His voice came in a harsh whisper colder than the north wind in winter.

I wiped blood from my mouth with the back of my left hand as he moved to the gibberer bodies. He bypassed the one he'd nearly cut in half with his sword and squatted beside the one I'd killed. He pulled down its lower lip, then snarled and moved on. He pulled the things that had killed the other two from their bodies, then checked their lower lips. Something about the second one, the one he'd hit in the chest with his missile, elicited a low chuckle.

The moonlight made it difficult to see what he did, but as nearly as I could make out, he jammed the tips of his thumbs into the creature's muzzle and pressed his fingers against its open eyes. He mumbled something with a sing-song melody and the shadows around his hands seemed to intensify. More sinisterly, a tattoo on his left forearm began to glow a deep dark blue. It reminded me of Fesyin sign, for it had the shape of the broken twig, yet had been embellished with sharply hooked thorns.

The gibberer's body shook. The elf pulled his hands free and the gibberkin lurched to its feet. Its lips curled back in a

feral snarl. The elf aped the grimace, then barked out an order
in a guttural tongue the very sound of which made my flesh
crawl. The gibberer turned, its arms hanging rather loosely,
and trotted back into the temple.

The elf turned back to me and the moon's light blazed
from his silver eyes. "Unhurt?"

I nodded.

"How many?"

"Gibberers? Two hundred."

"Vylaens? Temeryces?"

"Some, yes."

"Good." He waved me forward. "Come."

I rolled to my feet and bent to pull my dagger from the
gibberer, but a snapped command stayed my hand.

"Leave it." The elf extended to me the hilt of one of the
gibberer's longknives. "Better for killing, this."

I took it, then padded alongside him back to the window
I'd come through. "How did you . . . ?"

Again he covered my mouth with a hand. "Silence. Live
and I might explain."

He went through the window first, then snapped his fingers and I followed. I heard the scrape of metal on stone, then
felt the pommel of my sword poke me in the ribs. I took it and
nodded thanks. His crouched silhouette moved to the doorway, then into the hall, and I came hard at his heels.

The temple's nave was filled with bodies. Heslin's mage-
light still held, letting me see where my people had fallen back
to the entrance of a side room around which were arranged
overturned tables and other furniture to form a semicircle.
The breastwork limited the number of Aurolani forces who
could get at Lord Norrington and the others. The room allowed men to retire and rest as others stepped up to fight.

Lord Norrington and Nay stood behind the breastwork
dealing death and doing damage with an ease that belied the
sheer fatigue they had to be feeling. Norrington's silver blade
flashed, slicing paws from arms; gashing red, wet furrows in
flesh and cleaving skulls open. Nay's maul struck with viperish
speed. He shattered muzzles, scattering teeth; drove his spike
through chests, crushing ribs and piercing organs. The dead

and dying hung on the breastwork or were drawn back through the horde to be dumped on the stairs and slid down to where our horses shied from them.

The gibberer that the elf had magicked ran ahead of us on the priest's-walk, then hurled itself into the roiling mass of its fellows. It carried a half dozen of them to the ground, then heaved itself up and snapped its muzzle shut on the throat of a vylaen. The smaller Aurolani clawed at the gibberer. The gibberer whipped its head back and forth, cracking the vylaen's neck with the ease of a dog killing a rat.

As other gibberers hacked the assassin to pieces, the elf opened his arms and stalked across the priest's-walk. He barked in a loud voice and that quelled the gibberers chorus from below. Cruel hard words exploded from his mouth in a short, sharp cadence. I could not understand what he said, but he was nothing shy of magnificent. Standing there, wearing only a sleeveless leather jerkin, leather breeches, and tall boots fitted with greaves, he howled at the Aurolani forces.

A vylaen snarled orders at gibberers, and I noticed a bunch of them peel off from the rear of the pack to head toward both stairwells leading up to the priest's-walk.

The elf pointed at the opening I'd defended before. "None get past."

"Over my dead body."

My joke narrowed the elf's eyes, then he snorted and turned toward the doorway he would defend.

I darted through the opening and slashed at the first gibberer coming up the stairs. The stairs themselves helped me because the tight spiral meant the central spine was always on the right of anyone ascending. A right-handed swordsman couldn't bring his blade into play very easily, whereas I had plenty of room to make nice right to left slashes.

My first blow caught the gibberer on its raised forearm. I pulled my blade back, then raised my right hand to stab down over his forearm. My blade pierced him between neck and shoulder, going in a good handspan or so, then came out with a meaty, wet sucking sound. I used the gibberer knife in my left hand to parry his weak lunge at me, then I kicked out with my right foot, caught him in the muzzle, and sent him back into those bunched behind him.

As they peeled him off to the outside and continued up, I realized I'd made a mistake earlier by not defending the stairwell itself. The doorway was a great fallback position, but here I had them at a severe disadvantage. My strokes would fall on heads and shoulders, while they could only stab at my armored legs. My only vulnerability lay at my back, but I didn't think my savior was going to let anyone get past him.

On the gibberers came, heedless of how hopeless their situation was. A quick feint would bring an arm up in defense, then I would twist around to lunge past it and catch a throat. A low parry with the longknife would let me riposte to the chest or face. One gibberer did his best to swallow my sword, then he snorted blood and collapsed. A blow that went awry might only sever an ear or shatter an arm, but a second or third attack was usually enough to finish the gibberer and feed another into my killing range.

Finally the last gibberer flopped down, his neck open and gushing blood in rapidly decreasing spurts. He slid back, bumping limply over blood-drenched steps and other corpses, disappearing around the corner. Weak groans and pain-filled sighs greeted his passage downward.

I recoiled from the gory hole and looked back out into the temple itself. I could still hear the sounds of fighting, which made it tough for me to understand why no more gibberers had come for me. Across the way I saw the elf emerging from his stairwell, and below saw my comrades still at their defense.

Toward the rear of the temple I saw something new. It came from the direction of the initial temeryx wave. At first all I saw was a golden glow that I didn't think was that intense, yet it painted the shadows of the gibberers running toward it on the wall with sharp contrast. It continued forward. Gibbers reeled away from it and collapsed on the ground bleeding from hideous wounds.

Suddenly Leigh came into view wielding a golden sword. He lit into the gibberers with a cold ferocity I'd never seen in him before. The blade came up and around, decapitating one gibberer, then swept down to parry another. A quick, double-handed slash opened that one from hip to hip, then Leigh danced to the left and sliced open two gibberers that had moved to flank him.

I could recognize Leigh's style of fighting in each cut. He did nothing we had not been trained to do, yet now managed it with more speed and skill than he had ever exhibited before. Low sweeps sliced up into thighs and groins, opening arteries, careful parries directed blades past him by just enough, then the ripostes would pierce a heart, perforate a bowel, or cut a throat with the ease of slicing fruit.

A vylaen moved out and around with magickal energy gathering in its hands. The elf's left hand flashed forward. The vylaen's head snapped to the left, a silver star buried in its skull. It dropped to the ground, the spell it had failed to cast at Leigh igniting its paws.

The elf howled and crouched on the priest's-walk like a gargoyle. His inhuman scream and Leigh's golden harvest seemed to unnerve the gibberers. In retrospect I came to realize that the death of the vylaens had really broken the horde. Without their leadership exerting magickal influence over them, the gibberers' native cowardice flourished. The force pressed around the survivors' breastwork eroded and fled. I turned to the windows through which I'd originally shot at their horde and watched the gibberkin fade into Atval's shadows.

I looked over, but the elf was gone. I gingerly made my way down the stairs I'd defended. I passed a dozen bodies, ignoring feeble whimpers or bubbling of shallow breaths. The sheer stink of blood and gibberer and waste, where dying creatures lost all control of bladder and bowel, was enough to gag me. I swallowed my rising gorge back down, then started to slip in a pool of blood as I crossed the temple floor.

A strong hand caught me by the back of my mail and held me up. I glanced at the elf. "Thank you."

He nodded, then looked at the trail of bodies strewn on the stairs. "Good work."

"Work, yes. Butchery, not warfare."

The elf arched an eyebrow at me. "A butcher would have

died in the doorway. The warrior in you learned to defend the stairs."

"How did you know?"

"Read the sign. You defended the door at first and were chased off." He coughed into his left hand. "You did well. You will have my name first. I am Resolute."

I stared at him for a heartbeat, surprised by his name. The elves I'd heard of, in stories, in songs, all had names that were long and kind of curved around in the mouth. Rondelcyn or Arianvelle, Simsaran, and Winfellis. Resolute, given what little I knew of elves, just wasn't an elven name at all.

Resolute folded his arms over his broad breast. "You have a name?"

"Yes, sorry. Hawkins, Tarrant Hawkins. I—we—are from Valsina."

The elf reached out and flicked a finger against the temeryx feather I had tied to my moonmask. "Decoration?"

"I earned it."

"Indeed?"

"With my friends." I pointed off to where everyone was emerging from behind the breastwork. "Come on."

Walking over there I noticed several things. The first was that far fewer of our company had survived than I would have expected. Heslin's left arm dangled uselessly from his shoulder and all the bandaging in the world couldn't hide the funny angle of his forearm. Lord Norrington and Nay walked as if they were asleep on their feet. One of Heslin's apprentices had survived and four of the soldiers.

Leigh sat on the temple floor, his hands clutching the golden sword's crosshilt. He'd bowed his head forward so his crown touched the flat of the blade and his chest heaved. As I drew closer I could hear him sobbing, and the sound tightened my throat, too.

Lord Norrington crossed to Leigh and knelt beside him. They spoke in hushed tones and Leigh nodded once. His father patted him on the back of the head, then slowly stood and walked toward me. "You are unhurt?"

"Couple of bruises, nothing serious, my lord." I nodded

toward Resolute. "I'd have been a gibberer meal if not for him."

Lord Norrington pulled off a bloody gauntlet and extended his right hand. "Kenwick Norrington. Thanks for saving him."

Resolute took Lord Norrington's hand in his. "I once met a Marlborough Norrington of Oriosa."

"My father's elder brother."

"Dead now?"

"Ten years, at least."

The elf nodded slowly. "I am Resolute. Who is the boy with the sword?"

Lord Norrington half turned toward Leigh and smiled. "He's my son, Bosleigh."

"Oh." The elf's comment came flat and heavy.

I frowned. "Why, what's the matter?"

"Nothing, unless that blade is the one I think it is." Resolute shrugged. "If it is, well, it is a tragedy for someone to be the walking dead so young."

CHAPTER 14

I shuddered and suddenly felt the cold, sticky wetness of the blood soaking my clothes and spattered across my face. I stank of death and any euphoria that my survival might have sparked in me died with Resolute's statement. I looked around the temple and saw doom and death and pain. Somehow Leigh's tears struck me as the most appropriate reaction to all we'd been through.

I walked over to him, with Lord Norrington and Resolute following me. I stepped over a beheaded gibberer and reached out for Leigh. My right hand trembled even before it touched him, but his sobs flowed up my arm and tightened my chest. I dropped to my knees beside him, threw an arm over his shoulders, and touched my forehead to his left temple.

"We have survived this, Leigh. We will continue to survive it."

His helm grated against mine as he turned to look at me with one red-rimmed eye. "I know. Slay or be slain, and we slew."

"Lots and lots, yeah." I squeezed his shoulders. "We'll get through this. It's over, there's no need for tears."

Leigh chuckled once, his chest heaving with the effort. "You think I'm crying because of this slaughter?"

"Aren't you?"

"No." He twisted to face me and clutched the sword to his chest. "My tears come because, my dear friend, it was all so perfect. Each cut, each parry. I knew where their attacks were coming from and I had a legion of options open to me. It was magnificent, Hawkins, more than I could have imagined. More than I could have dreamed of and now it's over. I cry because I will never know that sort of perfection again."

"Oh. I see." I reared back onto my haunches, then stood. I didn't exactly hear glee in his voice, but close—and no regret at all. He sat there, Aurolani blood dripping from him, streaking his face, remembering, recapturing all he'd done. I felt a chill run up my spine, then reached down and hauled him to his feet.

Leigh looked at his bloody backtrail and nodded slowly. Without saying anything he turned at looked at his father as Lord Norrington and Resolute joined us.

The elf held a hand out. "The sword."

Leigh's eyes narrowed and he hugged the blade tighter. As he twisted away from Resolute, I got my first really good look at the weapon. The golden blade ran straight from a simple gold crosshilt for about two-thirds of its length. The last third of it tapered down into a very sharp point, though the point itself had been thickened to aid in punching through mail with a lunge. Worked along the blade were odd symbols that consisted mostly of loops, curves, coils, and hooks. The hilt itself had been wrapped in leather that had been dyed purple and the round pommel cap housed a purple stone that sparkled with a rainbow of colored specks at its heart.

"Bosleigh, let him see it. He does not want it, he merely wants to identify it."

"Yes, Father." Leigh turned back and extended the blade toward Resolute. "Do you know it?"

The elf studied it wordlessly. His silver eyes had no pupils, so it was difficult to tell where he was looking. He twisted his head this way and that, suggesting to me that he was reading the sigils right-side up then upside down. As he was doing this

I noted that one of the tattoos on his right forearm seemed to be written in a very similar script.

Resolute's head came up. "Where did you get it?"

Leigh pointed back down along the trail of bodies he'd left in his wake. "There."

"Show me."

Leigh started off and we followed. "I had gone back here looking for other entrances. I went down these stairs and along a passage I saw a symbol I recognized."

As Leigh pointed to the wall I saw the symbol used to mark a Fledgling's entrance to a Phoenix Knight meeting hall. Given how bricks had been set in the wall, cracks in the mortar precisely mimicked the symbol we'd been taught. I glanced over at Lord Norrington, fully expecting him to signal me to turn a blind eye, but he did not.

Resolute peered closely at the wall, then pulled out a small poniard and used the sharp blade to scrape away more mortar from a brick running beneath the horizontal line. His excavation outlined the brick completely. "You touched this brick?"

"Yes."

The elf pressed his hand against it. A little further down the passage a portion of wall withdrew into the ceiling. The three of us followed Resolute into a moderate-sized chamber. In it we found a stone bier that had the lid shifted around to lie across the foot of the enclosure housing a skeleton.

Leigh pointed to the lid. "I didn't touch it. It was this way when I found it. The skeleton was holding the sword against its chest. I just felt a need to pick it up. When I did, I knew what I had to do. I stalked from here and started killing gibberkin."

Resolute blew dust from the sarcophagus lid, then ran his fingertips over the runes incised into it. "A mystery ended."

Lord Norrington looked at the runes, but shook his head. "I can't read it. Would you care to explain?"

The elf pulled himself up to his full height, which meant his hair brushed the chamber's ceiling. "Behold Atval's last ruler. Baron Dordin Ore. He distinguished himself in battle because of a magickal sword of great antiquity. He believed himself invincible, believed he could slay dragons. He *did* get one . . ."

My jaw opened. "So he was the reason Atval refused to pay the tribute? He made the dragons destroy Atval?"

"He did, or that blade did." Resolute pointed to the sword. "The script, normally the sigils are bilaterally symmetrical—one side mirrors the other. Here they do not, allowing them to be read as one thing one way and another the other way. Ascending from the hilt it reads 'hero,' but descending it reads 'tragedy.' "

Leigh's lower lip quivered. "What does that mean?"

"This blade has a long history. It has various names—but Temmer is the most common one. It's said that, aeons ago, a mortal hero—an elf, an urZrethi, a man, it doesn't matter who—came to the *weirun* of a volcano and asked it to fashion a sword that would make the hero invincible in battle. The *weirun* cautioned that for such a blade to exist, a fearful price had to be paid. The hero said he would pay it, and the *weirun* created Temmer. When drawn, the wielder is invincible in combat."

Lord Norrington somehow kept his voice even. "And the price?"

"The sword consumes the wielder." Resolute's words came so matter-of-factly that it took a moment for me to understand the serious difficulty they implied. "He is as good as dead now."

Leigh's father brought his head up. "The blade will *kill* him? He'll die, absolutely? The legend says that?"

"That is one way the tales can be read. All agree, though, that the last battle will break the wielder. He will be destroyed. Physically, mentally, emotionally, it doesn't matter, he will be crushed. Your son will not survive his association with the blade." Resolute turned and pointed at the blade. "It is yours now, Bosleigh Norrington. You accepted it. You blooded it. It is yours until it destroys you."

Lord Norrington sighed heavily, his shoulders slumping a bit. I felt my stomach folding in on itself and looked at Leigh, expecting to see horror filling his expression.

Leigh smiled almost placidly, drew the sword he'd carried

from Valsina, and slid Temmer home in its place. Though I would have sworn Temmer was a good handspan longer than his other sword, it fit the scabbard perfectly. "There are Aurolani forces about in Oriosa. I think it is good this weapon is no longer hidden. The cost be damned."

I rested a hand on my friend's shoulder. "Leigh, didn't you hear what he said?"

Resolute watched Leigh closely. "If the tales are true, the others knew of the bargain they made before they accepted the blade. Perhaps your ignorance and innocence will shield you."

"Perhaps." Leigh shrugged carelessly, stroking the blade's hilt with his hand. He smiled, then headed back out of the chamber. "With Temmer in my hand, we'll exact a great blood toll from the Aurolani. Compared to that, the cost of using the sword is nothing."

The rest of us followed him in silence.

In the temple we freed our dead from the mounds of gibberkin. We sorted through everything, recovering what weapons and other useful items we could find. We would send the personal effects of each soldier back to his family, so we packaged them up separately. Once the bodies had been stripped, we piled them together and Heslin's one surviving apprentice, Shales, used a spell to burn them.

We also sorted through the Aurolani bodies. I tugged the throwing weapon Resolute had used on one vylaen from its skull. The device consisted of two-inch-long blade segments broken off Aurolani longknives, welded to a central hub. The blades were razor sharp, and the blood-grooves down their middle had been filled with a dark substance I took to be poison.

I carried it over to where he knelt among the gibberkin he'd slain. He looked up at me, his hands never pausing as he scalped a gibberer. "You needn't have."

"I thought you might want it."

He shook his head and moved to another body to scalp it. "I'll make more from the longknives here. Leave it. I want them to know Resolute was here."

"How did you come to be here?"

He shrugged. "I spend my time hunting in the Ghost Marches. I cut across sign of creatures heading south. I trailed them. Ambushed some, found others. A week ago the pace picked up, they started coming for Atval. I followed."

"Why the scalps? Collecting them for a bounty?"

"A bounty? No, I have no need for such." Resolute bent to his work, cutting across the brow and along over the ears. He ripped the scalp back, then trimmed it at the base of the skull with a single stroke. "I have use for them. You can take yours."

I glanced back at the pile I'd killed. "Maybe. I have a question for you."

"Another one?"

I looked at him and nodded. "What you did with that gibberer from the garden . . . the tattoo on your arm, it looked like Fesyin's Mark."

Resolute stabbed his poniard into a gibberer corpse to hold it, then touched the tattoo I mentioned. "Fesyin's Mark; yes, it is something like that. Your Fesyin, she's but a pale shadow of some things older and darker. I am from Vorquellyn, and without a homeland to pledge myself to, I have chosen other patrons."

His chin came up. "And what I did to that gibberer was magick. That gibberer, according to the clan tattoo on his lower lip, was born on Vorquellyn. He was bound to the island, which gave me a link into him. He was mine to use. I sent him after his leader."

"But you're a warrior. A warrior can't use magick."

"Perhaps not a *human* warrior. I am under no such restriction."

He waved me away with a flick of his left hand. "Go away, Hawkins. See to what you must so we can vacate this place. If dragons *are* coming, we want to be well away before they get here."

Despite being bone-weary and sore, we gathered our horses and led them out of Atval before the sun rose. Despite being greatly discomfited by his broken arm, Heslin agreed with Resolute's suggestion that the dragons' prohibition about allowing anything to take up residence in Atval meant people might have been able to spend at least a full day there before triggering reprisals. After all, allowing people to travel through the city and to see the destruction would go a long way to letting the story of the city spread far and wide.

Our band of twenty-one people had been cut in half, with our only advantage now that we had plenty of provisions and more than enough horses to carry us to Yslin. Resolute elected to travel with us, bringing his string of three horses along. He opted for riding at the rear of our formation to watch for signs of the Aurolani stragglers.

It took us just shy a week—eight days, to be precise—to reach Yslin. Traffic picked up along the border road heading southwest, but we kept to ourselves as much as possible. We did not find it very difficult to do that since, as bedraggled as we were, there were groups who probably figured us for bandits and so kept their distance. This suited us, of course, since any recounting of our experiences would have started rumors that could have resulted in a panic.

We had a discussion about that one night. I asked Lord Norrington if we shouldn't inform the Peacewards in the various villages about the potential for attacks by Aurolani forces. After all, my father was working in Valsina to guard against such things. Without a warning, various villages could have been overwhelmed by the kinds of bands we'd faced.

Lord Norrington ran a hand over his unshaven jaw. "Giving them warning might well save lives, but only if they put that knowledge to good use. To do that they need leadership, and since the leaders of Oriosa have yet to be told what is happening, there is no way to provide such leadership."

"But Peacewards in each town should be those leaders, shouldn't they?"

"Yes, Tarrant, they should." He gave me a gentle smile. "Your father, for example, is capable of being such a leader. He's the reason I'm confident that Valsina will be safe. Your father is a warrior, so he knows what to do in the case of an attack. What would he do if he heard that Beljoz were being raided?"

"That village isn't far from Valsina, so I suspect he'd raise a company of men and ride out to help."

"Exactly." Lord Norrington took a long pull on a water-skin. "Your father knows that stopping the Aurolani raiders there is better than stopping them at Valsina, but again, he's a warrior. The same is not true of most village Peacewards. They might gather a handful of men to defend their own village, but they'd not dare head out to save others. On the other hand, if the queen issues an edict that requires each county to raise a militia, house it in a central village, and dispatch it to any trouble spots, well, then, the sort of thing that has to happen to deal with this problem *will* happen."

Resolute snapped a stick in half and pitched the smaller piece into the fire. "You advocate the good of the many over the good of the few."

"In this case, yes."

"Yet it is the same idea which has left my homeland under Aurolani control."

Lord Norrington scratched at his cheek. "I disagree with how certain individuals have defined the good of the many in the case of Vorquellyn or the Ghost Marches or even the Black Marches. Too many see the presence of Fortress Draconis as a deterrent to an invasion, despite the fact that a century ago it did not stop Kree'chuc. A single Aurolani outpost south of the Boreal Mountains is an invitation to campaign over the rest of the world."

Reflection of golden flames danced in Resolute's eyes. "Have you influence over your leaders?"

"Can I get them to mount an expedition to liberate Vor-quellyn?" Lord Norrington slowly shook his head. "My past attempts have been futile, but never before have I come armed with the evidence I have now of Aurolani probing. That they could slip so far south without an alarm being raised is chilling."

"Peace is an illusion." Resolute opened his arms to take the entire company in. "We know the war is coming. We have fought the first battle. Yet our evidence will be denied."

"No, I won't let that happen." Norrington held up a hand. "I pledge to you that I will do all I can to get an expedition mounted to free Vorquellyn."

Resolute slowly shook his head. "The sincere pursuit of an impossible task does not guarantee victory."

"Yet he'll do it. We'll do it." I likewise raised a hand. "I give you my oath, Resolute, on my honor and life, and before all the gods in creation. I'll see Vorquellyn liberated in my lifetime."

The elf threw back his head and laughed. My cheeks burned with shame at what I took to be ridicule. As the elf looked at me again he must have read the pain on my face, because he cut his laughter off abruptly.

He glanced at Lord Norrington. "These youths you have with you, they are a valiant lot. They're also naive."

"I know what I said, Resolute, and I stand by it."

"Do you?" The elf stared at me with argent eyes. "When you make such an oath it not only binds you, but binds all you've sworn by. You have set great forces into motion, forces that will batter you, abuse you, and torture you. They will hate you for what you have done. They will do everything they can to crush you. And if they do, you fail."

I sat up straight. "Resolute, you lost your homeland back in the days of my great-grandfather, but you've not stopped fighting. Now the Aurolani threaten my home, threaten me with losing everything. Nothing in the oath I have given you could be worse than that. The only way we defeat them is to drive them back north of the mountains, and that I will do."

"I shall hope you are right, Tarrant Hawkins." The elf nodded to me solemnly. "But less for my sake than for your own."

CHAPTER 15

Riding as we did past isolated crofts and through tiny villages, I began to feel a bit sad for the people doomed to live in those places. After all, I came from the city of Valsina, and on this journey alone I'd seen more of the world than they ever would. I'd had all the cultural advantages of growing up in a city where theatre and art were available, and where the rise and setting of the sun did not dictate my schedule.

In short, as I saw their grubby faces—and that was the *whole* of their faces, since scant few of them had the right to take a mask—I thought myself sophisticated.

Then I saw the Alcidese capital, Yslin.

The first thing I noticed as we rode in from the northeast was that it was *big*. Three or four Valsinas could have fit inside the outer walls, and the city sprawled well beyond them. The whole festival had occupied a meadow to the south of the city, extending its boundaries even further. From miles out I could easily recognize three fortresses in the city that were the equivalent of Valsina's Old Town, and multiple temple districts as well as markets.

Huge mansions dotted the hillsides that gracefully sloped down to the sea. Each one of the mansions was large enough to make Lord Norrington's estate seem a carriage house. In the center of the city I saw buildings that rose three and four stories, and they weren't just temples and forts, but buildings owned by people, with shops on the ground floor and dwellings up above. And they even housed people who didn't work in the attached shops, but who worked elsewhere.

Yslin also had a seaport, which I'd not seen before, and the ocean was impressive as well. The day we arrived was somewhat overcast, with a breeze coming down from the north, so the surf was pounding the beach. The water looked all grey and angry, with hints of green and blue. In the distance I could see islands, but unlike the lakes near Valsina, I couldn't see the farther shore.

A lot of ships, large and small, bobbed in the bay. Long wharves allowed them to load and unload their cargoes into the warehouses located right on the shorefront. In that same area I could see miles of fishing nets hung up to dry, and a fish market that appeared to be very busy.

A hundred other curiosities caught my attention, but none as quickly as the beautifully colored spheres drifting above the city. They were captured in a net attached to a basket, and a line tethered the whole thing to the ground—Resolute claimed to have seen one of the contraptions before and called it a *balloon*. A couple of these balloons flew over the festival grounds. The regularity with which they rose and fell suggested someone was collecting money to provide rides.

Another fascination was the baskets hanging from cables strung between the fortresses and other towering buildings. The baskets, which appeared to carry people, moved along the cable from one point to another. They must have been on some sort of a loop because a basket heading one way would pass another at the same sedate rate of travel. The view from there had to be that of a bird on the wing, and traveling that way undoubtedly beat sloshing through the mud and manure in the streets below.

Lord Norrington led us around the city to the south. He and Leigh left us at the edge of the festival area and rode in to make inquiries at several pavilions flying the white-hawk-on-green-field flag of Oriosa. Within an hour they returned. Lord

Norrington gave Cooper directions concerning where our horses would be stabled, then led the rest of us into the city, to an inn called the One-legged Frog. We took our accommodations there, with Lord Norrington, Heslin, and Shales getting rooms; Leigh, Nay, and I shared a smaller one that did not have an overlarge bed.

Resolute left us then, despite Lord Norrington having offered to get him a room as well. Promising he would see us again, he headed deeper into the city. The inn's proprietor, Quint Severus, said Resolute would find a place with his own people in the Downs, which I took be a portion of the city catering to elves. I didn't ask if that assumption was true, though, not wanting to reveal my ignorance.

The toughest thing to get used to in Yslin, and all of Alcida for that matter, was that the folks didn't wear masks. Of course not everyone in Oriosa wore masks, but they were all latecomers and mostly peasants. They would defer to anyone in a mask, and we'd grown up knowing how to deal with the unmasked. Here in Yslin, however, a Count or Baron or Duke who outranked Lord Norrington would be as barefaced as a thief, so figuring how to deal with them was tough. On top of that, we were seen as curiosities, with folks pointing and murmuring behind their hands.

It might have seemed that dealing with Resolute's being maskless would have made the transition easier, but it didn't. While the elf didn't wear a mask, the tattoos on his body seemed to serve many of the same functions. Resolute himself seemed to be a mask dropped over an elf's outline, and while we did spend a lot of time with him, I never did feel I'd gotten anything close to a glimpse of who he really was.

Once in our room, in keeping with Lord Norrington's instructions, we ordered up a tub and enough hot water to bathe. The three of us drew lots and I was lucky enough to win the right to use the bath first. I scrubbed myself good and hard, leaving my skin all red and tingling. Getting out of the bath, I wrapped a towel around myself and brought one end of it up to form a hood that hid my bare face from the other two.

Carrying my moonmask in my right hand, I retreated to

the far corner of the room and sat with my back to Leigh and Nay. Using a small bowl, a little water, some saddle soap and a brush, I cleaned up my moonmask. I couldn't get all the blood off it, so a faint dappling remained. It kind of reminded me of the spots mottling a gibberer's pelt, so I didn't mind it too much. The temeryx feather shed the blood on it very easily and retained its raven-black color.

I tied the mask back on, being sure to catch a strand or two of hair in the knot. I dressed hurriedly in the least soiled of the road clothes I had, then went down to the inn's tavern. I ordered a tankard of a local ale that, I discovered, had a sharp, woody bite yet was sweet enough to avoid being bitter. I also got some bread, cheese, and a big bowl of chicken soup which made up for in vegetables what it lacked in actual bird flesh.

Nay and Leigh came down one after another. Nay had half-finished his meal when Leigh arrived, but before Leigh could order food, his father returned to the inn trailed by two masked servants wearing red-and-blue jerkins, marking them as being in service to the royal house. The two of them bore overstuffed sacks which they took up to our room. Lord Norrington bid us follow them and he brought up the rear. The servants deposited their burdens then departed, leaving the four of us alone in the room.

"I've been to see the queen." Lord Norrington turned from the door he'd just shut. "I wasn't able to speak with her, but I did have a conversation with her chamberlain, Duke Reed Larner. I told him our reasons for being here and he said he had heard rumors of similar sightings from other festival delegations. He believes that for the first time in a long time the festival meetings will have something important to discuss. Until that time comes, however, we are to say nothing of what we have seen or experienced."

I fingered my temeryx feather. "What if someone asks why we are wearing these feathers?"

"The 'War of the Ravens' tale worked well on the road. Give it life for a bit longer, boys." Lord Norrington's brown eyes hardened for a moment. "You know I'd not make that sort of request if it were not important. What we have done so far has been simple because we were facing an enemy who wanted to kill us, and we had to prevent that. It is my hope that the leaders of the world's nations will see that is what the Aurolani forces want to do to us. As I result I hope they will unite to fight them, but between where we are now and that goal is a slippery battlefield where politics is more valuable than swordsmanship. Until our queen can decide how and where to exert pressure to get others to go along with her plans—plans that will safeguard Oriosa while destroying the threat—she needs our information to be withheld."

"Well, that ruins my plans." Leigh snorted with exaggerated disgust. "Here I had decided to spend the evening earning drink and coin by reciting my opus, 'How to Vex a Temeryx.'"

His father laughed. "Well, I would hardly wish to spoil your fun, but just on the off chance that your poetry would cause the common folk here to riot, I have to inform you that you will not be free this evening. It turns out that we have arrived on the day that Oriosa hosts a feast. Protocol demands we attend."

Leigh's head came up and his eyes brightened. "If we must, I suppose we must."

Nay jerked his head toward me. "Hawkins and me, we'll wander about then and size up your competition among poets."

"While that would likely be more fun than this reception, that's not possible." Lord Norrington sighed. "Since we all have knowledge of what happened at Atval, Cooper and the others will be reporting to the barracks housing the queen's honor guard. Heslin and his apprentice are meeting with the Masters of Magick in the city's Arcanorium. Leigh and I will attend the feast, and you two will accompany us as our aides. Duke Larner said he couldn't imagine a Norrington being present without a Hawkins at his side and decided that Leigh could also not be present without an aide. The duke had servants rifle other nobles' baggage for suitable attire for us. Get dressed; they're sending a coach for us inside the hour. We'll go, you'll speak only when it is demanded of you and, if you can, enjoy yourselves."

•   •   •

To our surprise all of us managed to find clothing that fit pretty well. I ended up with a blue pair of trousers, a red silk shirt, and a black leather jerkin with blue trim. I got one of the innkeeper's boys to apply lampblack and wax to my boots, which made them shiny, and I ended up looking quite sharp. Nay received red pants, a blue shirt, and a black jerkin, and Leigh managed to dress in red from knees to throat and wrists.

In the coach on the way to the feast, which was being held in the Grand Hall of Fortress Gryps, we got a quick lesson in protocol. As far as Nay and I were concerned, we were outranked by everyone who would be present save the serving staff—and both of us knew better than to want to anger them by being presumptuous. Leigh bristled a bit when informed he only outranked us. Still, being of noble blood, he would be announced and would be expected to offer his good wishes for the festival.

Leigh sat back to figure out what he was going to say, and I could see the gleam in his eyes. I had no doubt he was trying to dream up some sort of rhyme, and I hoped it would be a good one. Somehow I didn't think he was getting the full import of where we were going or what we would be doing. I mean, I was just going to be standing around trying my best to be out of the way, and I was pretty sure that was well beyond my ability to handle.

We arrived rather quickly and were ushered into a side hall. Fortress Gryps, which was the nearest of the three to the docks, had a massive stone block construction that seemed to be scornful of anyone mounting an assault against it. Stout columns upheld vaulted ceilings which seemed to me to be the product of later renovations, since the stones used were different from those in the walls. Windows had been fitted with stained glass, which must have been magnificent in the daytime, but was hardly the sort of thing the original builders would have put into a fort. Fortress Gryps almost seemed to be an old warrior in the twilight of his life, now given to entertaining younger generations with stories of the past.

Slowly people started to file from the side hall on into the Grand Hall. As we got closer to the front, after nearly an hour of waiting, I could hear someone announcing each party. As we got to the point where we could see what was going on, it became apparent things happened exactly the way Lord Norrington said they would. He would be announced, I'd trail behind him, he'd drop to one knee before the queen, give her a greeting, and then move on.

Finally we reached the head of the line. The chamberlain, a maskless, skinny man with a few strands of black hair on his head and a handful more of teeth in his head, tapped a staff against the floor. "May I present Lord Kenwick Norrington of Valsina, from Oriosa."

Though Lord Norrington wore borrowed clothes like the rest of us, he had brought with him—as was his right and duty—the formal mask he was privileged to wear. It marked him as a grand warrior and stalwart leader of men. Though many of the guests arrived in finery the like of which I'd never seen before and would likely never see again, none of them looked as impressive as Lord Norrington.

The mask covered him from the corners of his mouth, back up over his head and flowed down into a full cape. It had been created from the skin of a temeryx he'd slain. The white feathers reflected a rainbow of lights with the delicacy of an oil-film on still water, always shifting as he moved. Battle ribbons had been eschewed and instead certain of the feathers at the crown had been stained the appropriate colors. A white-gold clasp held it closed at his throat and the entire cloak closed down around him as he sank to one knee before the queen and lowered his head.

"Majesty, it is an honor to be in your presence, as it is to be in your service. It is my hope that your festival will prove profitable and auger a future free of fear and full of prosperity."

Queen Lanivette, slender and elegant, regarded Lord Norrington with piercing blue eyes. Her white hair seemed a match for his cloak, and the smile slowly growing on her face a match for Lord Norrington's grace. She leaned forward and stroked the feathers hiding his left cheek.

"Kenwick, you are always one of my favorites. Seeing you is a pleasure, doubled when it is unexpected." Her words came low in tone and barely above a whisper, but somehow it seemed as if everyone knew she was pleased with him. "We will find time to speak more, later."

Lord Norrington stood, then moved to the right, and I followed in his shadow. I turned back to watch Leigh be announced and wondered at the poem he'd offer, but all I could see was some commotion. A tall figure eclipsed Leigh and stalked forward. He wore buckskins the color of mustard for boots, trousers, and a sleeveless jerkin that had only loosely been laced up the front. The tattoos on his arms and his shock of white hair confirmed that he was Resolute, and I wondered why I'd not identified him immediately.

A second's thought told me the answer because Resolute stalked forward in a patchwork furred cloak with no lining. It flapped back on itself, then snapped forward against his legs. It had been sewn together with rawhide strips, and as he drew close I realized the mottled fur came from the scalps he'd harvested from gibberers.

Resolute stopped on the spot where Lord Norrington had stopped, but did not lower himself to a knee. He pressed his right hand to his breastbone and looked about, taking in not only Queen Lanivette, her son, Scrainwood, and daughter, Ryhope, but all of the various royals and nobles who had been announced before us. He nodded once, slowly, then spoke.

"I am Resolute. I am Vorquelf. I have no rank or standing, yet I am here." He lowered his hand and allowed the gibberer cloak to close over him. "I am come to tell you all that Aurolani forces have ranged even into Oriosa, as far south as Atval, and I demand to know what you will do to end this scourge once and for all time."

CHAPTER 16

Queen Lanivette rose from her chair, restraining her son by pressing her right hand to his shoulder. A sapphire ring on one finger matched the huge sapphire hanging about her neck, and both complimented the blue satin gown that swished as she stood. She lifted her chin and smiled, though her eyes tightened beneath her mask.

She kept her voice even, but enough fire came through it to make me wince for Resolute's sake. "I am not unaware of what you allege. It is my intention to speak with my fellow rulers on this matter."

"Talk is all you have done, for three of your generations." Resolute thrust a finger toward Lord Norrington and me. "Ask them what good talk is against gibberers and vylaens and temeryces. A century ago I was unhomed, and in that century I have heard an eternity of words. I have never seen action."

Before the queen could respond, another elf slipped between courtiers and spoke rapidly to Resolute in a tongue that, while lyrical, had been sharpened with edges that were meant to cut. The male elf stood not quite as tall as Resolute, and likely weighed a third less than the well-muscled elf. The willowy slenderness of his form was repeated in the fineness of the long black hair that flowed over his shoulders and down the breasts of his dark blue satin coat. His clothes had been styled similarly to those Leigh had worn to the gala, though the lace shirt and the stockings were red, covering the elf in colors that honored the Oriosan royal house.

Most remarkable about him was that his eyes appeared to be very human. They had a pupil and the majority of the color had been locked into a tight band around it. While his eyes never approached true white because of the hint of gold still there, the vibrancy of the gold in his iris gave his stare a metallic intensity as harsh as a summer sun at noon. It sharpened his fair features and even seemed to make him taller.

Resolute barely turned his head toward him, almost like a dog casting a baleful glance at a cruel master. "In the common tongue, so they can understand."

The other elf pressed his left hand over his heart and bowed his head to the queen. "You will please forgive this Vorquelf. He has not learned restraint or proper conduct."

"I know exactly what proper conduct is—"

"Be silent, *nephew.*"

Resolute turned toward the other elf. "How dare you command me, *grandfather*? You are as guilty in this as they are."

The dark-haired elf again spoke to Resolute in what I took to be Elvish. Resolute replied in kind and a series of quick, sharp exchanges ensued. Resolute clearly intended his words to hurt, but the other elf remained unaffected by them. His replies, little by slowly, took temper out of Resolute's anger. The Vorquelf pointed a finger at his opponent, said something, then spun on his heel and stalked back out.

The remaining elf immediately dropped to a knee and bowed his head. "I beg your understanding, Queen Lanivette, and your forgiveness. There is no excuse for this, save that the Vorquelves lack maturity. They fail to see reason or to understand things."

The queen smiled indulgently at the elf. "It is of no consequence, good Jentellin. I, too, deal with those who know the impulsiveness of youth." She smiled at her son and daughter.

I was feeling very confused and turned to Lord Norrington. "I don't understand. The one elf called Resolute his nephew, but Resolute called him grandfather. And they're talking about Resolute like he's some child at least a handful of years from getting his moonmask."

"It's complicated, Hawkins, and I'm not certain of all of it myself." He smiled down at me. "Forgive me, Tarrant, for addressing you as I would your father."

I shrugged and smiled. "I don't mind. I hope I can serve you as well as he does."

"I'm sure you will. You'll serve me and serve Leigh as your father served my father before he served me. With a Hawkins to support him, a Norrington will not fail." Lord Norrington gave me a nod, then turned to address the elf approaching us. He placed his right hand over his heart as he greeted the elf. "My lord Jentellin, it is a pleasure."

Jentellin crossed his hands over his heart. "A pleasure as well, Lord Norrington. And this, your aide, would be a Hawkins?"

"Tarrant, yes. You met his father, I believe, twenty years ago or so?"

"When the festival was held in Jerana; yes, I remember. Please convey my greetings to your father when you see him next."

"I will, sir. I mean, my lord." I belatedly brought my hands over my heart, still surprised to know my father had met an elf. Granted, it was before I was born, but I would have thought he would mention it.

Jentellin smiled at me, then looked at Lord Norrington. "The Vorquelf indicated you had seen what he saw. Shall I take the temeryx feather on young Hawkins' moonmask to be proof of this?"

"Just proof of the beginning, but not of what we saw or did in Atval. I understand your anger with Resolute, but if not for him, we would likely have died at Atval."

"Yes, Resolute saved me, and if not for Leigh and his sword . . ." I stopped in midsentence as Lord Norrington touched a finger to his closed left eye.

The elf drew back and clasped his hands behind his back. "A sword, found in Atval? I would know more."

"And you shall, I imagine, sooner rather than later. A

question for a question? My aide asked about your treatment of Resolute."

The elf arched an eyebrow at me. "What do you wish to know?"

"You treated him as if he was a child."

"That's because he *is* a child."

I frowned. "But he's over a century old."

Lord Norrington laughed. "Age has nothing to do with maturity, Hawkins. Look around you and you'll see greyhairs aplenty acting as if they are boys and girls once again."

"Well, I guess that's true."

The elf chuckled quietly. "Resolute, being a Vorquelf who was not bound to his homeland, is very much a child according to our laws and traditions. Our binding to the land of our birth is much akin to your Moon Month. It is a time in which we realize and accept our responsibility. It grounds us, gives us a foundation, and Resolute has been robbed of that foundation. He is very much a child, impulsive and reckless.

"His eyes, you noticed them. They are a child's eyes. They would have changed to be like mine with his binding to Vorquellyn. Because he does not see through adult eyes, he sees things very simply." The elf smiled politely. "I am grateful he saved you at Atval, and I can easily comprehend your positive feelings for him."

Jentellin glanced at Lord Norrington. "This sword you found . . ."

"My son, Bosleigh, found it."

"Yes, your son. I take it the blade was remarkable?"

Lord Norrington slowly nodded. "The blade is possessed of serious magick. I've watched my son train with a sword and always dreamt he would master techniques, but I learned long ago that he would only ever be a fair swordsman. With this blade he becomes a master—every technique he knows he performed with a precision I've not seen in anyone before."

"Does the blade have a name?"

"Resolute said it was called Temmer."

The elf grew silent for a moment. "And your son blooded it?"

"Yes."

Jentellin's eyes closed and he mumbled something in Elvish. He reopened his eyes and gave Lord Norrington a slender smile. "I am certain Resolute told you horrible things about the blade. It is a rather fell thing. It has been lost for seven centuries, but when last I saw it being employed, it had the effect on the wielder you describe."

I did some quick mathematics in my head. "Then you are over . . . but you don't look . . . no grey . . . um, I mean, well, yes, Resolute would be a child to you."

The elf's smile broadened and rich laughter rolled from his throat. "Yes, young Hawkins, I am that old and yet older. Much older."

"Are you actually Resolute's grandfather?"

"No." Jentellin's long, black hair shifted on his shoulders as he shook his head. "In our tongue, the equivalent word is used as an honorific for elder males. My referring to him as nephew is because the same word in Elvish is used to address male youngers. Resolute is no blood relation of mine, though I do have a true nephew who is a Vorquelf, so I share Resolute's pain."

A captain in the Queen's Guards, if I read his mask right, came over and executed a crisp salute which Lord Norrington returned. "My lords, the queen will be retiring for a bit and has requested your company. If you will follow me."

"My pleasure." Lord Norrington turned to me and laid a hand on my shoulder. "Find my son and Nay. Keep them under control and tell them I have an audience with the queen. If I see you again before midnight we will return to the inn together, otherwise I will make my own way there. I will prepare orders for the morning as needed. Got it?"

I nodded, then folded my hands over my heart. "It was an honor meeting you, Lord Jentellin."

He covered his heart with his hands and replied with a nod, then the two of them departed with the soldier. I turned back toward the front of room, and after a moment's searching, saw Nay's red head above the crowd. I made for him and reached his side without difficulty.

He smiled when he saw me and offered me a goblet of wine. "Was for Leigh, but he's occupied."

I followed the line of Nay's gaze and saw Leigh seated in a chair, surrounded by a half-dozen young women. Two wore masks, the rest did not, but none seemed older than us by four years—save perhaps the elf. I had no idea how old she was, but she looked the flower of youth, and since she was very slender and soft and not decorated with tattoos, I assumed she was not a Vorquelf.

Leigh was flicking a finger against the temeryx feather hanging from his moonmask. "Oh, yes, our adventures have been quite exciting, and quite dangerous. I'd tell you all of them, but they are so horrifying I might make you faint dead away. I shudder to even think about some of the things I've seen."

My stomach roiled as the women began a sympathetic chorus of soothing remarks, which they followed quickly by fevered requests for details of his adventures. Leigh manfully resisted, allowing as how even thinking about thinking about what he had seen was enough to make him sweat. More sympathy gushed forth in response to that ploy, which Leigh lapped up like a kitten at cream.

"Well, my fair ladies, I would not want you to think me callous in resisting your entreaties. And I must say that I flatter myself to think myself a poet. I dabble in it, perhaps as a way to give me release from the horrible things I've seen." Leigh closed his eyes, lowered his head and massaged his forehead with his left hand. When the redhead on his right began to rub his right temple, he smiled wearily at her and reopened his eyes. "If you wish, I would share with you my latest. It is titled, 'How to Vex a Temeryx.'"

I drained the goblet at one gulp. Leigh was all set to violate his father's prohibition against speaking about our adventures. Granted, Resolute's outburst had destroyed any secrecy about what we'd been through. Even so, Leigh was headed for trouble and my realization of that fact left a sour taste in my mouth.

I quickly realized that the sour taste in my mouth was not entirely Leigh's fault. Nay's taste in wine was horrid. The vintage had burned on the way down, puckered the mouth, and seemed to be intent on bubbling its way back up. I glanced at Nay. "How can you drink this stuff? It's one step from vinegar."

Nay smiled. "Got that for Leigh." He raised his goblet. "Not the same thing in my cup."

"And you let me drink it?"

"Figured the edge would help you think of something to do with Leigh."

I nodded, handed him back the cup, and strode to Leigh's side. "My lord, are you going to spring your opus on them just like that?"

Leigh looked up, momentarily puzzled. "Well, I had thought . . ."

"It's a bit grim, isn't it?" I smiled at the ladies surrounding him. "Perhaps you would entertain them with something more witty. Name rhymes and the like."

My friend nodded and tapped a finger against his nose. I don't know if he thought I wanted him to elicit their names so I could ask them to dance later or what, but he warmed to the suggestion of twisting their names into rhymes like a dog lying before a roaring fire. His initial efforts brought titters and giggles, which kept him going, and Nay handed him a goblet of wine to keep his mouth from going dry.

I smiled at Nay. "A few more cups of wine and he won't remember enough of his opus to get himself into trouble."

"It's a plan." Nay rested a hand on my shoulder as we headed off to get more wine. "Saw you jawing with an elf."

"Lord Jentellin." I sighed and told Nay everything I'd heard. He took it all in stonefaced, offering only an occasional grunt by way of comment. "Leaves me feeling kind of sorry for Resolute."

"Yeah, though Jentellin wasn't the only one being high-handed here." Nay jerked his head back toward Leigh, whose cortege had expanded and resounded with giggles. "The spat made the doorman stop announcing folks, which riled Leigh, since he was deprived of his introduction. He got the way he does, ordered me to 'be a good aide and get me wine.' Shouldn't have given it to you."

"I just want to know how long I have before the poison takes effect."

We both shared a laugh over that, then began a search for a sweet wine that had a serious punch. Once we located one we returned to Leigh, who was now standing to recite his poems, and fed him goblet after goblet. Eventually he began to quiet down and restrict himself to spur of the moment, silly rhymes based on words his audience fed to him. By midnight he was asleep again, so we took him back to the inn, swaddled him in a blanket, and laid him on the floor.

I asked Nay if we should actually do that, since there seemed to be some new straw in the bed, so it was softer than it had been when I first laid down on it that afternoon. "If we leave him there, he'll wake up all stiff and sore."

Nay laughed. "Oh, he'll wake up a might worse than stiff and sore, but sleeping on the floor won't have anything to do with it. As long as he's going to be miserable, it might as well be on the floor. Don't need him sleeping with us because we'll need all the sleep we can get to deal with him tomorrow morning."

CHAPTER 17

Morning did come early, but not as early for us as it did for Leigh. He looked quite ashen-faced and held his head in both hands as if it were an overripe pumpkin perched precariously on his shoulders. I would have been inclined to tease him, but the low moan he uttered reminded me that Nay and I had as much as poured gallons of wine down his throat.

"Got a wineskull cure." Nay quickly pulled on clothes and headed down to the tavern's common room. "Back in an eyeblink."

Leigh crawled across the floor, leaving the blanket cocoon strung out behind him and slowly dragged himself up onto the bed. The way he was moving, even an eyeblink would be an eternity to him. He sagged facedown on the mattress, sweat pasting blond hair to his forehead. He turned and looked at me with his right eye.

"Did I make a total fool of myself?"

"You didn't vomit in the carriage."

"That's good. I meant at the feast."

I pulled myself up against the headboard and hugged my knees to my chest. "The ladies found you amusing—two especially. I think they were from Okrannel."

"Tall and blonde, like Nolda Disper?"

"That was them. I take it poetry is a novelty in Okrannel."

"Must be." Leigh closed his eye. "Feels like there's a horde of gibberers in my head trying to hammer their way free."

"Set yourself at ease, Leigh. You did nothing to embarrass your father or Oriosa."

"The queen didn't see me?"

"No, she was off meeting with your father."

"And the princess?"

I blinked and slapped him on the shoulder. "You took a liking to her? But Ryhope has dark hair, not blonde."

"Ah, but those eyes, those blue eyes. They're as blue as . . . as . . ."

"As blue as your eyes are red?" Nay returned and kicked the door to the room shut behind him. He tossed me a small leather pouch that clinked with coins when I caught it, then he extended a steaming mug in Leigh's direction. "Come on, your worship, your cure is here."

Leigh rolled over with the torpidity of a well-fed pig wallowing in slop and pulled himself up enough that his shoulders touched the headboard. He reached for the mug, then sniffed it and pulled his hand back. "That smells horrible."

"It's for drinking, not smelling." Nay shrugged and raised the mug toward his own lips. "Feel better or don't."

"No, no, no, give it to me, give it to me." The enthusiasm with which Leigh started his command petered out at the end of it, but his fingers twitched energetically enough in the mug's direction. Nay made sure Leigh had his fingers firmly wrapped around the mug's barrel, then reached down and pinched Leigh's nose shut.

"Have to drink it all, Leigh. One big drink. And chew the crunchy bits at the bottom."

Leigh blew on the steaming liquid for a moment. From my vantage point it looked a dark purple, with little flecks of white floating around the edges. Leigh shrugged, closed his eyes and drank. His throat-knob bobbed up and down, and I saw a tear crawl down from beneath his moonmask, but he drained the cup, chewed for a moment and swallowed one last time.

Nay released his nose and smiled. "There you go."

Leigh shook as if a snake had crawled up his pant's leg. "Gaaagh! That was *horrible*! My stomach feels on fire." He pointed a finger at Nay. "How does it work? Make my stomach feel so bad my head feels good in comparison?"

Nay took the mug from him, inspected the bottom of it, then nodded. "Just wine, garlic, willow bark, few other things. My mom does a brisk business in it after Mid-Summer's galas and the like."

I laughed as Leigh slumped back down on the bed and laid a forearm across his eyes. I opened the pouch and spilled a dozen silver coins into my lap. A folded piece of foolscap got stuck halfway, so I pulled it out and unfolded it. I read the message quickly, then tapped Leigh's hand.

"It's from your father."

"Read it aloud. Nay can't read it, I won't read it."

Nay frowned. "I can read. Some."

"It's pretty simple." I cleared my throat. " 'Gentlemen, the present situation has made demands on my time, so I will be unavailable until midafternoon. The money enclosed is for you to use to enjoy the festival. Return here no later than four hours past noon. Yours, KN.' "

Leigh's arm shifted and he looked at me with one bright blue eye. "He's going to let us play?"

"That's what it says."

Leigh laughed, sat up and swung his legs over the edge of the bed. "Well, then, no sense in wasting time, is there, lads?"

I arched an eyebrow at him. "I thought you were so close to dead we should be digging a grave."

Leigh stood, wobbled for a moment, then steadied himself against Nay. "That was before I learned the day was ours. Duty calls, lads. We have things to do." He glanced at the coins on the bed. "Ah, six silvers for me, three each for you; we'll have a grand time."

Nay frowned. "May not read good, but ciphering ain't hard. How do you get six?"

"Please, Nay, have you ever attended a festival with three silvers to spend? No? And did you ever lack for fun despite a lack of funds?"

Furrows gathered on Nay's brow. "No and no."

"Well, then, there you go. You'll have more than you've ever had, and I'll have considerably less. You'll be exultant and I'll be suffering, but I'll hold up, thanks a great deal to your cure." He slapped Nay on the back and staggered over to the wash basin to begin scrubbing up. "It will be fun, lads, you'll see. They'll remember the day we three came to the festival."

Harvest Festivals have changed rather a great deal since those days. As we strolled from the city we saw nary a face without a smile—even on the guardsmen who gave us a cursory inspection to make certain we were not carrying weapons. Merchants had arrived from all over the world, offering wares native to their own lands, and various prizes they'd traded for on the journey. Jugglers and acrobats staked out small parcels of ground, performing their dazzling feats in return for whatever coins or other offerings the crowd wished to give them. I saw one man who had a dancing bear on a leash, and another tent with banners proclaiming that within we would see voluptuous dancers from far Malca reveal the seductive secrets of their veiled dances. For those who could not read, the undulating form of one woman on a small stage near the entrance conveyed the message rather clearly.

Food was available, and drink, with winemakers offering their vintages by the mug, bucket, or barrel. Food varied from some rather potently spiced gruels to fresh breads and meats that had been braised, boiled, roasted, smoked, or dried. Fish was also offered very fresh. I recognized little of it, since most of it came from the depths of the Crescent Sea, so I was thinking I'd avoid it, then a shift in the wind swirled the scent past my nose and my mouth watered.

Leigh, as expected, took charge of our entertainment and directed us away from foodstuffs and toward the various games of chance and skill. The booths with games offered a variety of prizes for those who won. Most were trinkets, including a lot of charms fashioned after the signs of the godlings of luck or fate, and the goddess of love, Euris. Many places also offered garlands of ribbons woven with little dried flowers or interwoven with herb sprigs that smelled wonderful. The most interesting thing about the garlands was that while they could be worn, they also could be exchanged at some of the merchants for a big mug when you purchased a small, or two chicken legs for the price of one and a half.

As we strolled through the festival, people did notice us. The fact that Leigh was once again dressed knees to throat in bright red did make him stand out. Nay and I had returned to the cleanest of our road clothes, which by no means made us look like mendicants or bandits, but made for a sharp contrast with Leigh. Our moonmasks also attracted attention, and I was very aware of the temeryx feather fluttering against my left ear. I didn't know if those who looked and pointed and giggled behind their hands thought us just curious, or if they had heard some of what had happened the night before and were wondering at the significance of our feathers.

Leigh seemed oblivious to it all. He led us straight to a booth that offered prizes in exchange for shooting arrows into targets that seemed, at least to me, to be painfully close. We were offered ten arrows for a copper penny, which meant one of our silver coins would get us a thousand arrows. Five arrows in the target's heart would win a garland, which, at this range, was child's play.

Leigh smiled at me. "You're our archer, Hawkins. Care to try your luck?"

"Gladly." I produced my silver piece and snapped it down on the counter. "Goodman, I'll take ten arrows, please."

The man eyed the silver coin suspiciously, then produced ten arrows and handed me a bow. Nay moved around to watch him counting out my change while I stepped up to the line and looked at the selection of targets. "I will be shooting at the hart."

"Your pleasure, sir," the man grunted.

Child's play aptly describes the task I'd set for myself because the bow I'd been handed was the weak sort of thing a child might have been given. The bowstring hung limp and the bow's wood had little spring to it. I could throw arrows further than it would shoot them, but I assumed it would be able to get an arrow to the target.

The arrows themselves were little better than the bow.

Most were warped and all were poorly fletched. Their points had been blunted by use and not a few had split at the nocking point. It struck me that not only could we not bring weapons into the festival, but they didn't allow anyone to find them here either.

Leigh smiled at me. "A problem, Tarrant?"

"Not at all, my lord." I nocked an arrow, drew a bead on my target, then let fly.

The hart, which was made of grass-and-leaf-stuffed sacking tied around a frame to approximate the shape of a deer, had a big red heart painted behind its forward shoulder. My arrow started for it perfectly, but died before it could reach the target and instead stuck into the ground a good four feet in front of it.

Leigh coughed into his hand. "The wind, Hawkins?"

"Yes, the wind killed it. Must be that." I nocked another arrow, drew it back, sighted, raised my aimpoint and loosed it. The arrow wobbled a lot in flight, but struck the target in the ribs. Missed the heart by a handspan. "Lungstuck. Wouldn't have run far."

"True, Hawkins, but further than we'd have wanted to run after it, yes?" Leigh picked up an arrow and spun it around its central axis. "Perhaps this one will fly true."

"This hart's heart this time." I drew, sighted, and shot. The arrow did fly true as predicted and hit the painted heart squarely at its center.

Then, with a metallic clink, it bounced off.

Leigh's left eyebrow arched above his moonmask. "A rather stiff wind that time, eh, Hawkins?"

"Oh, yes, the wind."

"Perhaps," came a male voice from behind us, "it is the wind from so many brags about Oriosan archers and their skill."

The three of us turned to see who had insulted us, but immediately dropped to a knee. Leigh raised his head just a whit and smiled. "Your Highness, it is an honor."

Princess Ryhope smiled at us, and there was no denying she was beautiful. She was four years our senior and had sparkling eyes the shade of blue seen on distant mountains, or in a clear summer sky. Her long black hair had been gathered back into a braid and bound with ribbons that matched her eyes. A dusting of freckles graced her pale cheeks and the tip of her nose—a fawn-colored mask covered her cheekbones and forehead. She wore a simple dress of brown that was more suited to riding than it was to court, and carried a small fan in her right hand. A blue scarf had been fastened around her neck, the long ends of which rode a slight breeze to trail back over her right shoulder.

Courtiers surrounded her, but the man who had spoken had taken one step toward us. An inch or so shorter than me, and a mite leaner, he still had the look of a warrior about him. His black hair had been shorn close to his head, in keeping with Alcidese custom, and no mask hid his face or brown eyes. He'd grown a luxurious moustache, the ends of which curled back along his cheeks, and one gold earring hung from his left ear. His clothes, from boots and breeches to a simple tunic and jerkin, ran from dark brown to a light fawn, making him and Ryhope something of a pair.

Ryhope shut her fan and lightly tapped the man on the shoulder. "Prince Augustus, Oriosa does produce great archers; better than the bowyers and fletchers of Alcida, it would seem."

"But, Princess, from what your brother said, superior skill should overcome inferior equipment."

Leigh's head came up. "Please, Highness, do not rebuke Prince Augustus for having inferior equipment."

The Alcidese prince glanced at Leigh, turned away, then looked at him again. Leigh gave him a oh-yes-I-did-dare-say-that smile, and Princess Ryhope's reopened fan hid a smile. Titters came from the rest of the entourage, and I know I had a hard time keeping my laughter choked back.

Leigh rose to his feet and bowed deeply. "I am mortified, Highness, that my man's performance here has cast a pall over the reputation of Oriosan archers. I would make amends. I offer, here and now, to shoot one arrow and strike the hart in the heart."

Augustus barked a quick laugh. "Your man just did that."

"Yes, but I will do it blindfolded."

I looked at Leigh and he at me. "Are you still drunk, Leigh?" I whispered.

"Attend me and it will work, Hawkins." He smiled. "Highness, if I could trouble you for your scarf."

Ryhope handed her fan to one of her ladies in waiting, then unknotted the scarf. Augustus took it from her, then held it up and peered through it easily. "Faugh, this is no blindfold."

Leigh took it from him, then began folding it and refolding it into a strip an inch wide. "Folded it is impenetrable to sight." He held it up for Augustus to see and the Alcidese prince snorted. Leigh turned to me and placed it over my eyes. "Can you see through this, Hawkins?"

"No, my lord."

"Good." He turned and handed the bunched scarf to Nay. "Show it to those who would like to see it." As Nay carried it off, Leigh turned back to the counter where seven arrows remained. He chose one and showed it to me. As the others were distracted by Nay, Leigh's voice dropped into a whisper. "You will stand beside me, close, facing me across the bow. Point your right foot at the heart."

I nodded. "This arrow will fly straight, my lord."

"Good." He turned to those watching us and held the arrow up for inspection. "Nothing unusual about the arrow, yes?"

He got shakes and nods from all of them, then handed the arrow to me. He picked up the bow, tested its pull, then nodded. He assumed a heroic pose, legs spread properly, the bow gripped in his left hand, his body perpendicular to the target. Glancing back over his right shoulder, he beckoned Nay back with his right hand.

"Nay, if you will, the blindfold."

"No, that won't do." Prince Augustus snared the end of the blue scarf. "He's your confederate."

"I give you my word, Highness, even if I could, I would not look at the target." Leigh reached up and tugged his moonmask a little higher. "I'm half blinded by this moonmask as it is."

"Augustus has a point." Princess Ryhope took the scarf from Nay and stepped up behind. "I will blind him."

"Your beauty and grace already blind me, Highness."

Ryhope smiled and slipped the scarf over Leigh's eyes. The blue cloth settled neatly into the valley created by his moon-mask. She knotted the cloth securely, then patted Leigh on the shoulder. "Shoot well. Oriosa's honor is at stake."

Leigh brought the bow up. "The arrow, Hawkins. Help me nock it."

I settled the arrow atop his left hand and nocked it, then guided his right hand to the bowstring. As requested I pointed my right foot at the target. Leigh turned his head toward his left shoulder, brought his left arm up a bit, drew the arrow back and shot.

The arrow sped from the bow and flew straight. It was likely the best shot I'd ever seen Leigh get off. It arced down into the target and struck the hart in the heart, punctuating the rising chorus behind us with astonished gasps.

Then it bounced off, and the spectators sighed with disappointment.

Prince Augustus went from being shocked to triumphant in a heartbeat. "It did not stick."

Leigh turned calmly and faced him without taking off the blindfold. "I merely offered to hit the target in the heart, not stick the arrow there. What good is a killing shot on something that cannot be killed?"

Princess Ryhope touched Augustus' arm. "You wanted a display of skill, Highness, not dinner. I vouchsafe, however, give this Oriosan a good horse, a full quiver and a good bow, and there is nothing he could not slay to feed you."

Leigh bowed deeply. "You are too kind, Princess." He tugged off the blindfold and held it out to her. "Your scarf."

She shook her head. "Keep it, noble sir; you have earned it."

"I am Bosleigh Norrington, at your service and forever in your debt."

"And richer for that debt I shall be, I have no doubt." The princess smiled and turned away, walking off with her entourage in tow.

We watched her go, then Leigh laughed and handed the bow back to the booth's owner. "Well, my good men, that was an adventure."

Nay blinked slowly at Leigh, his jaw agape. He glanced from the target to Leigh and back again, measuring and re-measuring the shot he'd seen. His blinking, powered by complete disbelief, sped up. His voice came hushed and cautiously reverential. "The shot . . . How?"

Leigh looked around, saw the booth owner leaning close, so he pulled us away. "It was simple, Nay. As I set myself to be blindfolded, I did two things. First I positioned my feet so I was already aimed at the target. The shot was as good as in the beast at that point. I also tugged my moonmask up a bit, which let me look down past my nose at my feet, and Hawkins' feet. Hawkins had a toe pointed at the heart, which allowed me to double-check my aim. I moved my arm up at the angle he had to make his shot and let fly. I hit."

Nay shook his head in amazement. "Had the deed been unseen . . ."

I laughed. "Don't be too impressed yet, Nay. Tell me, Leigh, what had you planned to say when you missed?"

Leigh scratched at his chin. "A variety of things, mostly revolving around how a hart reminded me of Princess Ryhope and that how I could not shoot something as beautiful, graceful, and charming as she. I had variations worked on that theme."

I shook my head. "So the hart wasn't the only target you were aiming at?"

"No, and it looks as if I got two hits with one arrow." He held the scarf up to his nose and sniffed. "Two solid hits."

"Let's hope her heart isn't as armored as that of the target." My stomach growled. "Shall we eat?"

"Yes, I think so." Leigh unknotted the scarf, then slipped it around his own neck. "And after that, back into Yslin. For making that shot I need to thank Kedyn a great deal, and even cast some silver to Euris and Arel."

"Lots of it to Arel, because that shot was pure luck." Nay patted Leigh on the back. "And seems you'll be pressing your luck to pursue the princess, so you can have my silver as well."

CHAPTER 18

We found the Temple to Kedyn pretty easily—perhaps I should say we found the *nearest* Temple to Kedyn easily, since there were three scattered around Yslin. The one we entered was in the old imperial style, with tall columns and friezes depicting battles worked all around the upper reaches and even edging the priests'-walk. Massive bronze double doors, nearly black with age, stood open—though they didn't seem terribly inviting.

Inside, the temple's layout only varied in one significant way from the temple at Valsina—aside from having been constructed on a scale that dwarfed our temple. Back behind the statue of Kedyn, where we had a blank wall between the alcoves devoted to Fesyin and Gesric, the Alcidese had a long gallery extending a good distance deeper into the temple. After buying our incense and offering it, along with prayers, to Kedyn, we moved to explore the gallery.

I'd never quite seen anything like it. Row upon row of little statues, most no bigger than the dolls children play with, stood in various martial and mythical poses. Some showed warriors hacking off the heads of fallen foes, while others stabbed spears or swords into dragons and griffins, big snakes and howling beasts that looked a lot like gibberkin. Male and female statues were intermingled. Around the base of each a little moat of sand supported incense sticks and candles, the flickering flames of which cast haunting shadows up the walls and even onto the curve of the arched ceiling.

What had attracted us to the gallery was the sheer number of people, more young than old, who bypassed Kedyn and moved directly to these little statues. They stood before them, or knelt, their heads bowed and their hands in the appropriate position as if they were praying to Kedyn himself. None of the three of us could figure out what was going on, but I very much felt as if I'd fallen asleep and awakened in another world that was a step or two removed from my own.

We returned to the inn and did not find Lord Norrington there. Instead, a message that told us to go to a specific place in the city. Severus pointed us in the proper direction and we set off. We wove through crowds, then ascended a tower and took passage on one of the baskets strung between buildings. The basket swayed a bit as we went along, and Leigh had no interest in looking down.

Nay and I clutched the edges of the basket as the ferryman pulled us along to our destination. We passed from a newer section of the city into an older one, avoiding the tangled warren of streets below. Because we passed by only fifty feet or so above the ground, seeing things below in great detail was not a problem. We saw everything from washing hung out to dry to children playing, and what appeared to be a footchase between two city guardsmen and a sneak thief.

We arrived at the far tower and descended into the older section of the city. When we arrived at the corner of Fishmarket and Pearl Streets, we saw no one we recognized and no one approached us. I wasn't certain why we were there, then Nay spotted the Phoenix Fledgling sign near an alley mouth and we headed into it.

We located the sign in other places, carved into a lintel, scratched onto a post, and followed the signs as we might follow game. Finally we came to a closed doorway with a narrow, sealed peephole in it. I knocked on the door and the small window opened. Someone looked out and said, "Do you understand your business here?"

I touched my hand to my brow, then lowered it with my palm up and open.

The doorslit clicked shut, then the door itself opened. The three of us entered, then headed down a small corridor toward a robed man beckoning us onward. He led us to a small chamber where we were given brown cloaks, then he had us write our names in a massive visitor's tome. Leigh signed with a flourish, I didn't waste as much ink, and Nay drew the symbol he'd always stamped onto the weapons he'd made.

Our guide offered us a quick tour of the Yslin Phoenix Knights' Hall and the three of us followed in silence. The Grand Hall ran much deeper than the one in Valsina, with all the amphitheatre rows faced with white marble. The chamber's domed ceiling was upheld by two dozen marble pillars and had been painted with a huge mural depicting the life cycle of the Phoenix. The rebirth of the Phoenix took place over the area where new recruits would be brought in, or so I surmised.

Beyond that chamber lay a series of smaller rooms suited for meetings, and a dining hall that looked as if it could seat three hundred people at a time. A kitchen adjoined it, and then back behind the left side of the Grand Hall we ran through a complex of even smaller rooms that had been set up to house visiting Knights. Completing our circuit we moved over to the area behind the right side of the Grand Hall and found ourselves in a gallery very much like the one we'd seen in Kedyn's temple.

Here there were legions of statues, most very small, but a dozen or so life-sized and set in alcoves of their own. Candles flickered before all of them and incense burned by a few. Many of them looked like those in the temple, but I couldn't identify for certain any of the ones I'd seen before. Even so, the martial nature of the poses was the same.

I scratched at the back of my neck. "Forgive me . . ." I faltered for a name and decided to use an honorific that could not offend. ". . . Master, but we saw a gallery like this in Kedyn's temple and don't understand."

He held his hand up. "The reason you are here is to learn so you may understand." He led us back around to the meeting rooms and appropriated an empty one. He indicated we should sit in the blocky wooden chairs, then he dropped to the floor with his robe puddling around his folded legs.

"All three of you are aware that nearly two millennia ago, a vast conquering army swept out of the Wastes—which once included what are now the Black Marches—and conquered most of the known world. They established the Estine Empire, of which even Oriosa was a province. For many centuries the Estine Emperors ruled wisely and well, though a thousand years ago the Man–urZrethi War showed that the aristocracy was not capable of acquitting the duties they owed the Emperor. He swept the old order aside and rewarded the leaders who had led the fighting with title and land, creating a new nobility.

"Two and a half centuries later, Kirûn led his Aurolani horde down from the north, wielding the power given him by his DragonCrown, and laid waste to the Empire's central provinces, including your Oriosa. The people, aided by the elves and urZrethi, beat him back—but again the aristocracy had proven inept. Instead of sweeping them aside as his predecessor had done centuries before, the Emperor sent troops to put down the provincial revolts."

I nodded, being fairly familiar with the history of Oriosa from this point forward. It was during this time of unrest that Oriosans, Murosons, and Alosans—the people of the central provinces that had suffered the most—took the mask in what we call the Great Revolt. Imperial authority was overthrown and our nations declared themselves independent. They formed the Confederation, pledging themselves to defend each other, and that sort of unity survived to this day.

Our instructor continued. "The Emperor's brother, Valentine, saw disaster in what his brother was doing. He staged his own rebellion, ousting his brother. The Emperor, Balanicus, fled to Madasosa in Reimancia, claiming the eastern half of the Empire was the only legitimate government on the continent. Sebcia, Bilasia, Reimancia, and Viarca all consider themselves still to be the Estine Empire.

"Valentine, in turn, granted autonomy to the western provinces, but united them in the Valentine League. He ruled it until he died, and the League throne has never had a successor. The League's rulers maintain ambassadors in each other's capitals, with a Council sitting for a year in each of the capitals on a rotating basis. The Council is led by the local ruler, but only a Grand Council, one of all the rulers, could ever elect a new Valentine Emperor."

My understanding of the history of that time did not paint so beneficent a picture of Valentine, since his first effort at securing the League's borders involved trying to establish them somewhere north of Muroso and west of Reimancia, though his armies found moving through Oriosa rather difficult. As the story goes, his generals decided they thought the Oriosan countryside was beautiful, but they had no real desire to spend eternity there, so they returned to Saporcia and Alcida.

What Valentine had done, which was very important, was to shatter the DragonCrown and scatter the pieces. All the nations that had contributed armies to the effort to defeat Kirûn were rewarded for their efforts by being given a portion of the DragonCrown, if they wanted one. The remaining pieces were housed in Fortress Draconis, which Valentine established, built, and garrisoned. He used mostly League troops, but companies from all over the world have spent time there as part of the garrison.

"Many people came to see Valentine as a god for all he had done, but he refused that honor. He said he was but a man who might possess some godly attributes, but his true value was in showing men and women that the attainment of godly virtues merely required dedication, prayer, and works that brought one closer to the virtues themselves.

"Upon his death it was revealed that the gods themselves had smiled upon him and raised him to be more than a man. Not quite a godling, but certainly more than *weirun*, he became a patron for those who sought the virtues he represented. Likewise the gods accepted into his legion of followers those who attained virtuous status, and their representations are revered by families and the hopeful alike. These galleries are devoted to those individuals who have attained this exalted status. Those represented here were Phoenix Knights, and those in Kedyn's Temple were consecrated to him. The priests inform people—the families, usually—of the elevation of someone who has passed on when the gods themselves reveal this information to them."

I recall a chill running down my spine as our teacher told this story. Somewhat irrationally I began to wonder if the League had not gained special favor with the gods such that such great and miraculous things were revealed to their priests, but denied to ours. It was not until I was much older, and decidedly more cynical, that I wondered if the "revelations" were used as a means to bind wealthy families more closely to one temple than another, and to get them to spend money to guarantee the proper veneration of their dead ancestor would continue. Some families even went so far as to pay for the outfitting, training, and upkeep of army companies that fought beneath the banners of their ancestors, which took a great deal of pressure off local governments to maintain troops.

Later when I mentioned to Nay my wondering if Oriosans were doing something wrong, he just shook his head. "Leaguers need the extra help—the gods know we get it right from the start."

The chill running down my spine also started me thinking about whether or not I would ever be worthy of being elevated to such status. I needed barely a glance to tell that Leigh was long lost in that sort of musing. I knew his father would be worthy, and I thought my father would be as well, but the two of us? I could hope that what we had done so far would have pleased the gods enough to accept us. But if acceptance could be purchased that easily, perhaps the honor was not that great in the first place.

I should also point out that just because Oriosa does not have galleries featuring statues of our ancestors in every temple, it does not mean we do not revere the memories of those who have gone before. The masks our ancestors have worn are preserved and displayed on the anniversaries of their deaths.

We tell stories about them and hold them dear, but we don't treat them as godlets.

Our instructor told us more, including how the Knights of the Phoenix got their start in the aftermath of the Man–ur-Zrethi War, and came into its power with the Empire's dissolution. Valentine had been a Phoenix Knight, rising to the rank of Greater Eyre Master, which I gather is about as far as anyone can go in the society. He showed us a couple more hand signals, like the command to follow and the command to take something—including the overt and covert variations. He then took us back to the gallery, let us burn incense before the statue of Valentine—who was said to embody all of the Martial Virtues—then had us return the robes to him and sent us on our way.

Upon our return to the inn we met Leigh's father. He seemed a bit impatient, but allowed us to eat some bread and cheese and a little roasted pork before he headed us back to Fortress Gryps. "I have already heard of what you did this morning, at the festival and while I would have forbidden it had I been there, it turns out it was for the best. It transformed you from mere moonmasked youths into warriors of no mean ability, which provides some with a different picture of what we faced at Atval."

On our return to Fortress Gryps, we were again taken into the Grand Hall, but no longer was it arranged as a place for a celebration. A number of fairly plain tables had been arranged in a rather large circle around the center of the room. Each table had a banner hung behind it identifying the nation represented and the arms of the individuals seated there. Back behind each delegation more chairs were arranged. Very few were occupied, and they seemed mostly reserved for advisors to the royals seated at the tables themselves.

We were seated behind Queen Lanivette, her son, daughter, and Chamberlain. Princess Ryhope turned and looked at us as we sat. She gave Leigh a warm smile. He returned it, adding a wink, which brought a blush to her cheeks.

Her brother, Scrainwood, likewise watched us take our seats. Of him, by me, perhaps the less said is best, but I cannot omit him from this chronicle because of the major part he played in it. He was as handsome as his sister was beautiful, though they looked little alike. He was thirteen years older than she, making him a year shy of twice my age. Tall and lean, though not quite as tall as me, he had brown hair and hazel eyes which to me seemed a bit tight set together.

I didn't know that much about him at the time. He had married, I knew, as did anyone in Oriosa who had celebrated his wedding and the birth of his two sons. They were years yet from taking the mask, and remained with their mother in Meredo. She was a princess from Muroso and the marriage was political, though her acceptance of it was more gracious than his.

As I sat, my eyes met his for the first time—he'd not even wasted a glance at me the night before when I was attending Lord Norrington as his aide. I knew from that moment that he did not like me, nor I him. I don't know why this enmity sprang up at a glance, but a hateful fire had ignited in him the moment he recognized I existed.

Directly across from us sat the Alcidese delegation, with Prince Augustus attending his father, Penesius. Other delegations sat beneath the banners of the nations of the Valentine League, and around to the left Okrannel was represented. Reimancia represented the Estine Empire, Haorra the Ancient Union, and Jentellin sat beneath a scintillating banner with red Elvish lettering running down one edge.

King Penesius stood. "It appears, good Queen Lanivette, your marvelous young warriors have arrived."

The queen did not stir, but Duke Larner turned to us and indicated we should stand, which we did. Lord Norrington stood with us.

The Alcidese leader smiled. "We have heard from Lord Norrington of the deeds you have performed. We have been told that in the Black City of Atval you destroyed a force numbering over two hundred gibberkin. You must understand that we all agree your battle must have been horrible, and your surviving it speaks well of you, but it stretched credulity for many of us to believe that so few were able to stand against ten times their number and survive. Could what we have been told possibly be true?"

I had no idea how to answer that question, but Leigh did not shy from it in the least. "Your Majesties, I do not know what tale you have been told by my father, but because I know my father, I will assume he told it with undue modesty concerning his part in it, and his pride in us may have exaggerated our roles. Oriosa, as everyone knows, faced the urZrethi invasion, Kirûn's invasion, then a century ago, Kree'chuc's invasion. Our nation, by necessity, trains its warriors well and young to deal with Aurolani threats. Perhaps more remarkable than *our* survival, and that of some of our companions, is that eleven of the people who rode with us did not survive. Truth be told, we do not know how many enemies we faced. Our scouts' last count numbered them at two hundred, but there could have been more, or a few less. In a battle for survival, one does not have time to count the dead."

Nay and I just nodded as Leigh spoke.

King Penesius' brown eyes shrank. "Bravely spoken words, but they hardly answer my question. Is the threat you report credible?"

Leigh lifted his chin, which displayed Ryhope's scarf for all to see. "One or two or five or twenty or two hundred gibberkin does not matter. You all acknowledge that we fought them, but this question is akin to asking a man who says he was rained upon to guess at the number of raindrops that hit him. I can tell you, we were soaked in the blood of our enemies and our friends. It matters not how many gibberkin we fought, how many temeryces were slain, but that we fought them in Oriosa and on our way here. More importantly, the ones we met in Atval clearly were bent on stopping us from reaching Yslin. If you fail to interpret that sign correctly, then I predict it will rain, rain hard, and flood sufficiently that all of us will be washed away."

I was hard pressed to restrain a smile at Leigh's oratory, and Ryhope clearly abandoned her efforts. She smiled happily in his direction. The Duke nodded his thanks to us, then Prince Scrainwood stood. As he did so I saw his down-turned lips even out into a thin-lipped grimace.

"It is clear, Highnesses, that we need to undertake some serious discussions. These are not discussions for children, so these boys may be dismissed, but Bosleigh Norrington's words cannot be ignored." Scrainwood lifted his head and straightened his spine. "We face a crisis that has been in the offing for a century. Failure to address it now may mean we never have a chance to address it in the future."

Lord Norrington tapped Leigh on the shoulder, and Leigh led us from the chamber. Outside, after the doors closed behind us, he slumped against a wall and would have sunk to the floor but Nay and I held him up. His hands shook and he licked his lips. "I can't believe I said what I did."

"Pretty speech." Nay smiled. "The princess seemed impressed."

Leigh smiled. "I did notice that. Did you think I did well, Hawkins?"

I nodded. "You reported the right of it. Seems they wanted to deny what your father said so they didn't have to worry themselves about the future. You showed them that was wrong, and the prince picked up on it."

"He did, didn't he?" Some of the hopeful warmth leeched out of Leigh's voice as he straightened up. "Interesting man, he-who-will-be-our-king."

"Wanted us out of there fast enough."

I shivered. "I don't think he liked me at all."

"I don't think he liked us diverting attention from him." Leigh flicked a finger against his temeryx feather. "You saw his mask, all honorary ribbons from units. He's twice our age and hasn't done a thing, whereas provincials like us have slain temeryces and other Aurolani beasties before our Moon Month is up."

I frowned. "You're saying he's jealous of us?"

"Jealousy, envy; both are bad." Leigh tugged at the cuffs of his shirt and smiled. "He'll bear watching."

"I'd rather watch his sister."

Nay nodded. "My preference as well."

"Yes, lads, I'm sure that's true." Leigh slapped us both on our shoulders and guided us down the hallway toward the door. "So I'll have to see what I can do to secure that duty for myself."

CHAPTER 19

Lord Norrington remained involved in the Council of Kings for the next several days. The three of us kept ourselves busy wandering about town, visiting the festival, and going back to the Phoenix Knights' halls to learn more about the history of the organization. The lessons we learned there had a decided League slant to them, but our tutors didn't seem to have an anti-Oriosa bias. Instead they treated us as if we were from a backward province. We amazed them with our ability to learn fast, though, and devoured the materials Fledglings had to master before they could progress further in the organization.

The festival never again did rise to the level of excitement we'd seen on the first day, but there were a variety of reasons for that. Primary among them was Leigh's mood, which soured with each minute since he'd last seen Ryhope. I'd seen Leigh go through crushes before—Nolda Disper being the most recent of a spate of them. I was used to the pattern of his getting sulky when the woman of his dreams was not in sight, so I did my best to ignore him. Nay had a harder time of it and got a bit testy, which created new frictions among us.

I continued to see new and different things in Yslin, and began to recognize things my father had warned me about. I spotted a lot of swindlers playing tricks on festival-goers—often cheating them in games of chance through techniques my father had warned me about. Alley-bashers also preyed on those who drank too much, fake-cripples begged money, and cutpurses wandered through crowds not even bothering with artifice to take what they wanted.

There was one amusing note. The booth where Leigh had shot the arrow blindfolded into the heart was doing a lot of business. The proprietor had moved the hart back a good twenty feet and had adopted a mask of his own. He spent his time challenging passing individuals to match the blindfolded feat of archery that only an Oriosan could do. Attempts at salving national pride put a lot of copper in his pocket.

Either he didn't recognize us as we passed by, or chose not to recognize us, more like. Nay was of a mind to strip the mask off him and expose his fraud, but I held him back from violence. Leigh roused himself and agreed with me. "Think on it, Nay. He's doing more here to impress the world with our skills than any story of harvesting gibberers will ever manage."

One afternoon we all three split up and went our separate ways. It wasn't out of any disagreement, though the split probably did let us bleed off some frustration. Each of us wandered away to find suitable gifts for the others. We were coming down to the end of our Moon Months, when we would get our first adult masks, and it was customary for friends to present a gift to those who were getting their masks. The gifts were supposed to be something more than trivial, but not totally extravagant—though Prince Scrainwood was supposed to have been given a title and castle when he lost his moonmask.

Money for buying gifts would have been a problem, but Lord Norrington took care of that. He gave each of us three gold pieces and said they were from Queen Lanivette herself, by way of thanking us for our service to the nation. Fully funded by her generosity, we headed out.

I walked a meandering path that took me all over Yslin. I wanted to buy each of them something that would last a long time, and that would be useful and memorable and remind them of the time we'd spent together. While a lot of things fit that description, I saw very few of them in my travels. The festival wares seemed picked over and the clothes manufactured in Alcida seemed unfit for Oriosa. The bright colors weren't the problems; it was the lightness of the weave and the looseness of the cuts, which would mean a garment could only be worn for a couple weeks in the dead of summer.

Down in the docks area I found what I wanted. Sailors from the various ships that had docked had brought with them a few items from distant lands that they hoped to resell to make some money for themselves. One man, just arrived from Svarskya in Okrannel, had a sheepskin coat with black wool on the interior. I gathered from the quickening of the pace of those he offered it to that in Alcida natural black wool was not favored and might even be superstitiously avoided. The coat looked big enough for Nay, so I slowly circled the man and moved in when he seemed frustrated and desperate.

Now, having been to market with my mother many times, I knew how to bargain. I listened to his story of how he'd bought the coat for his dear father, but his father passed on while he was at sea, and now he needed money to give his father a proper burial and to make sacrifices at the Temple of Death in his father's name. I affected an attitude of horror at his plight and evidenced a desire to help him, which brought us to haggling over the price.

He started at four gold and I talked him down to one gold, five silver, which I raised to two gold if he'd also give me a carved malachite pendant of Arel, the godling of Luck. He agreed and we made the exchange. The jacket hung on me so loosely I wondered if the sheep hadn't been the size of a bear, and I made quick time back to the inn.

Once there I asked Severus to hide the jacket for me, which he agreed to do, albeit rather reluctantly. "In Alcida, young master, a black sheep is regarded as an ill omen."

"Oh, I know." I raised a hand to the luck pendant I now wore at my throat. "I only dared wear it this far because I had this amulet that makes me very lucky. Luckier than anyone here, I imagine."

That remark, which I made loudly, pricked up the ears of a greasy little man sitting in the back of the common room. "Lucky, are you?"

"I am."

The innkeeper shook his head to warn me off, but I flashed him a smile and touched the amulet again. "I was lucky to find that coat, and I'll be lucky again today, I can feel it."

"Perhaps you'd be willing to test your luck." The man beckoned me over to his table and set out three small cups and a wooden ball the size of a grape. He showed the ball to me, placed it beneath the center cup, then began to mix them up. He did the switching very slowly and obviously, letting me follow the cup with the ball very easily. He stopped the mixing and said, "There, find the ball."

I pointed to the cup on the right. He tipped it aside and there the ball was. "Very good. Try again."

I smiled and fingered the amulet. "I won't lose."

Again he mixed things up and again I chose the right cup. "Child's play."

"Well," he offered, "we could make it more interesting."

"How?"

"We could wager on it. I'll pay you three times what you wager if you are right."

I blinked my eyes. "But all I have is this gold coin."

He reached into his belt pouch, placed three gold coins on the table, then put mine on top of it. "Here we go, watch the ball." He placed it beneath the center cup and started mixing them up. His moves this time were much faster, much more smooth. I did my best to keep my eye on the appropriate cup, but I lost it. Looking up at me he must have seen my eyes flicker as I searched, for he slowed the mixing, then stopped.

"Which cup is it, good sir?"

I stroked the pendant with my right hand, then began to point with my left. "Is it this one, no, wait, I . . . I think it's this one, no, wait a moment." I squatted down to put my eyes level with the top of the table. "Just a moment. I know which it is!"

Rising, I brought both hands up and flipped over the two outside cups. They were empty. "There, I knew it, the middle one."

The man blanched and reached his right hand for the coins. I leaned forward and grabbed his left fist and pressed down with my weight on it, mashing it against the table. "I think, my friend, if I open your fist here, I'm going to find a ball in it, a little wooden ball. Wouldn't that be lucky?"

"Lucky, perhaps, but not for you." He glanced past me and nodded, which brought an immensely fat man up off a stool and waddling in my direction. "You've lost, boy. Go away while you can still walk away."

"No, no, no, my dear man, you have it all wrong, completely and utterly wrong." Leigh laughed as he sauntered toward the corner of the common room. "You've forgotten, my friend is very lucky."

The weasel snarled. "And my friend is very big."

"Indeed, he is, but not as ferocious as our friend." Leigh glanced back over his shoulder as Resolute ducked his head beneath a rafter and stalked into the common room. The fat man stopped dead in his tracks, though his body quaked a time or two. Resolute gave him a feral grin that set the man back a step.

Leigh reached over and pried the four gold coins from the weasel's hand, then reached up with his right hand and squeezed the man's cheeks together. "I think that my friend is not only lucky, but I think he's pretty much sucked all the luck out of you. While we're here, I think your luck is going to be much better elsewhere. You agree, don't you?"

Though Leigh started the man's head nodding up and down, it continued under its own power when Leigh released his grip. The weasel gathered his cups together and ran out, clutching them to his chest. Resolute's growl sped him on his way, and induced the behemoth to follow as quickly as he could manage.

Leigh handed me the coins. "Your winnings, Hawkins."

"Thanks very much." I nodded to Resolute. "Good to see you again."

"Resolute found me and we were looking for you and Nay. Is he here?"

"I haven't seen him."

Resolute frowned. "No time to wait. Come with me."

Leigh shrugged. "He won't tell me what it's about either."

We followed wordlessly as Resolute led us through Yslin.

We angled north, toward the docks, but broke off to the west before we got too close to the sea. We began to move into an older, worn-down section of town, where sewage gathered into stagnant puddles warred over by clouds of insects. Mildew clung to the walls and many buildings showed cracks in foundations and the walls.

This was the section of Yslin known as the Downs, and it was anything but the bucolic sort of place suggested by the name. This section of the city was sinking and would flood with extremely high tides. In another city or nation an attempt might have been made to reclaim it, but the Vorquelves had made it their home.

And, even now, I suspect Yslin does nothing to save it in the hopes the Vorquelves will finally quit the city.

The moist air penetrated my skin and carried a chill to my bones, though I must admit it wasn't just the moisture that did it. As we stalked through the streets, we saw all manner of individuals lurking about. All were elves and many retained the supple, lithe form of the other elves, though they seemed stunted, shorter, and not nearly as powerful as Jentellin. A few wore tattoos or had shaved their heads or wore their hair long in a myriad of braids. Their soiled clothes reeked of sweat, blood, and other things even less pleasant. All of them had pupilless eyes, with colors running from pure blind white through coal-black, and a few had metallic colors like Resolute.

Deeper into the Downs elven strumpets called to us and lifted their skirts to entice us. Bottles were passed between them, and elsewhere on the streets drunken elves slumped against walls or lay facedown in the mud. Some of the bodies twitched as they heaved up everything they'd drunk that day. Still others stumbled from smoky hovels with the acrid sweet scent of *morphium* clinging to them. Those lost souls drifted along oblivious to the world around them, heedless of the dangers of a dark alley or horse-drawn cart.

Many things were shouted at us, most of them in Elvish. The tone told me I didn't want to know what was being said, and Resolute offered neither translations nor warnings to those yelling at us. It struck me that the elves seemed as angry with him for bringing men into the Downs as they were with us for being there.

Finally Resolute led us down an alley and into a well-lit building that served as a tavern. Across the way a bartender— the only fat elf I'd ever seen—drew frothy mugs of ale and serving wenches brought them to customers. Rather unusually, though, most all the tables had been moved to the back of the common room and stacked there. The chairs had been arranged in rows and a clear space separated the chairs from a single table at the head of the room. Elves of various stripes filled the chairs, including one striking female, with black hair, gold eyes, and enough tattoos to give Resolute competition.

At the table sat four elves. From their eyes I guessed they were Vorquelves, yet these elves were well dressed, even fashionably so. They appeared to be clean, right down to their well-trimmed fingernails. They had parchment before them, quill pens and ink, so I guessed they were literate. They watched us enter and one of them, a red-haired male, directed us to a pair of open seats in the front row.

Resolute moved to one of two chairs set facing the bar. In the one to his right, between him and the table, sat a female elf whose white hair was a match for his. Her eyes were a copper color that seemed to shift a bit, as if currents moved through the molten metal trapped in her orbs. She did not turn her head toward Resolute, but dropped her hand on his after he sat.

The red-haired elf stood and spoke quickly in Elvish, before reverting to the common Mantongue for our benefit. "You have been brought here by Resolute because he is on trial. He has been charged with malicious conduct. Against this charge he maintains a defense of grave circumstance. In short, he claims what he did was not an offense because of the urgency of his mission.

"I am Amends. With my three companions we have brought this charge against him and will try it. Seated next to Resolute is our Truthteller, Oracle. She will determine the right of things here. If she offers no ruling, then we will decide what shall be done."

I frowned because it sounded that the people making the

charge would also be deciding whether or not Resolute was guilty of it. That hardly sounded fair. I glanced at him, but he just looked at Amends.

Amends glanced at the parchment in front of him. "You were present when Resolute had an exchange with Jentellin of Croquellyn."

I nodded. "I was, but I don't understand Elvish, so I don't know what they said."

"No matter. Was Resolute disrespectful?"

I scratched at my forehead. "He was angry, but with good cause. Disrespectful, I don't know."

The red-headed elf snorted sharply. "Is not a display of anger at a gathering such as that rude, and is not rudeness disrespectful?"

"Shouting 'fire' might be rude and disrespectful, but if the building was burning, it would be welcome." I pointed an open hand toward Resolute. "He'd seen what we saw at Atval. He saved my life, and he brought forward the fact that Aurolani creatures were in Oriosa. I make the two things the same."

Leigh smiled at me. "Well said."

"Thank you."

"If you please, men." Amends frowned at us. "It was not your impression Resolute's action disrupted things?"

I sighed. "We had been told that we were to discuss what happened at Atval with no one, so the politicians could work up to a discussion of things. Resolute forced the issue, which meant it couldn't be lost or forgotten. What he did might not have been desired by some, but it was the right thing to do."

Resolute nodded slightly, but Oracle remained still and silent.

Amends looked at Oracle, waiting in silence that was only broken by a drunk and a slattern laughing as they searched for something that apparently was lost within the folds of her skirts. The black-haired female hissed them to silence, but still Oracle said nothing.

Amends nodded. "Well, there apparently is no untruth in what we have been told. The whole of the truth has yet to be determined, so we shall retire to do that. Resolute, you will remain here until we return." The four of them got up and walked toward a back room.

Once the door to it had closed, Resolute slipped his hand from beneath Oracle's and crossed to the bar. Leigh and I walked over to him as he ordered three tankards of ale.

The bartender only drew one.

"I want three. One for me, and one each for these men."

The tallow candles imparted a golden glow to the bartender's bald pate and the tips of his pointed ears. "This ale isn't for the likes of them."

I held up a hand. "We appreciate it, Resolute, but it's not important."

"Likely it's sour and tastes of wormy-wood." Leigh sniffed indignantly. "I've already had more than my fill of bad ale in my lifetime."

The bartender narrowed his emerald eyes. "A man might fall for that trickery, but not me." He turned to other customers and ignored us.

"So, Resolute, what was all that about?"

The elf licked foam from his top lip, then leaned back on the bar and hooked his elbows on the edge. "Vorquelves tend to bunch in various groups. Amends and his type, they're the appeasers. They think that by being nice and polite, they will be able to influence men and elves into liberating Vorquellyn. Me, I'm just out for justice. I'll shame anyone I can into freeing my home. When I can't do that, I go out and kill things. Others, well, you saw them outside and back there. They've surrendered, they're the dissolute. They have no hope and have forever to wallow in self-pity."

He raised his chin and pointed at Oracle. "Then we have her and her kind. Mystics in the way I'm a warrior. They see things, bits and pieces of a puzzle, that tells us our home will be freed. Don't see it fast enough for me, though."

"Amends and his cabal have power over you?"

"No, Leigh, though they would like to think they do. All they really can manage is to turn me out of the Downs, or refuse to trade with me. They're angry because I spoke harshly to Jentellin, and they were hoping to enlist his aid."

"Resolute, take your friends home." A lean elf in stained

grey leathers stood in the middle of the tavern room and pointed a finger toward Leigh and me. "We don't need them here."

"Easy, friend." Leigh gave the elf a full smile. "We're just here helping a comrade."

"I'm not your friend, *man*." The way the elf said the word boosted anger through me. "Either you get out of here now, or there will be trouble."

Leigh's smile faded. "Oh, we leave here at your command, then you and your friends fall on us outside? Is that the plan?"

The elf clawed fingers back through matted brown hair. "I'll thrash you here."

I shook my head and stepped between him and Leigh. "No, you won't."

"I can handle him, Hawkins."

"I owe you from earlier, remember?" I turned and met the elf's sapphire gaze without flinching. "What's your name?"

"I am Predator." He gave me a crooked smile. "I lead the Grey Mist and we own the Downs."

"Good, then you can convey my message to all your people. If you or any of the Grey Misters touch a Norrington, I'll give you a lot of time and pain to think on why that was wrong."

"Nicely said, Hawkins. I appreciate it."

I turned back toward Leigh to nod at him, fully knowing what would happen. Leigh's widening eyes told me a punch was incoming, so I ducked my head and let Predator's right fist flash over my left shoulder. I stepped back quickly and jammed my left elbow in the elf's ribs. I got the *oof* I expected, but as I pivoted on my left foot and brought my right fist around to double him over, he slipped past my punch.

I sidestepped right, again cutting him off from Leigh. Predator's right hand flashed in again. It glanced off my left cheek and hurt, but wasn't anywhere near enough to put me down. My left arm came up and I got a handful of his slender arm. I pulled him forward, then pivoted to the left. I hit him with an open hand over the heart and dragged him over my right hip. Leigh danced back as the elf crashed down.

Predator scrambled back to his feet as Leigh appropriated

the chair Resolute had vacated. The elf came in more slowly now, more respectful, which was his mistake. I feinted with a low, slow left hand, then brought my right hand around and down in a big roundhouse right. I caught him in the side of the jaw and spun him around. His legs got all twisted up. He slammed against the bar and rebounded, hard, to the floor.

Two other grey-clad elves started after me, but a loud elven voice split the hoots, threats, and cheers. I spun and looked at Oracle. Her hand rested on Leigh's arm and she spoke in a clear firm voice. I couldn't understand her words, but the effect they had on the elves was nothing short of mind-numbing. Many sagged in chairs or against the bar and began to weep, while others stared at Leigh in amazement.

Amends and the others came out of the back room, their faces pure masks of astonishment. "Did you hear it all, anyone? Two verses?"

Resolute walked past me and knelt before Oracle, resting his scarred hands on her knees. "I heard it. It is burned into my memory." He repeated what she had said, but in hushed and reverential tones, then glanced back at me.

"My translation will lack something, for in Elvish what she has said is as lyrical as it is hopeful. In your tongue it is this:

A Norrington to lead them,
Immortal, washed in fire
Victorious, from sea to ice.

Power of the north he will shatter,
A scourge he will kill,
Then Vorquellyn will redeem."

My mouth went dry. "What does it mean?"

Resolute started to answer, but Amends cut him off. "It could mean much, and it could be nonsense. We will deliberate and decide. If this is meant to be heard outside elven councils, we will speak."

Resolute stood and gave Amends a wolfish grin. "Decide right, Amends. We all heard this and we know the justice of it. You speak, or I will, and I think you know I will be heard."

CHAPTER 20

The Vorquelf's prophecy conspired with other events to push the royals at the Harvest Festival to consider taking action. The strongest motivating factor came through a series of *arcanslata* messages sent to the Okrans delegation. They reflected a very serious situation developing in Okrannel.

Not being a magicker, my understanding of how an *arcanslata* works is decidedly simple, but here it is. Using a very powerful spell that, as I understand it, takes a long time to prepare and involves the use of fairly rare and expensive ingredients, a piece of slate is split down the middle to create two tablets. The tablets themselves are linked, such that what is written on the face of one appears in reverse on the other and vice versa. To read the message, the *arcanslata* is held up to a mirror. The transmission of the message is instantaneous and only goes from one of the paired slates to the other—no eavesdropping is possible. I have been told the magickal Law of Contagion is at play in the production and use of the slates, and the spells to send messages back and forth are not easy to wield.

The messages from Okrannel said Aurolani pirate activity from the Ghost Marches and Vorquellyn had increased, and that fortresses in the mountains were reporting increasing contact with Aurolani creatures. The city of Crozt on the tip of the Okrannel finger had been raided by pirates and some had even been seen in the Svarskya Gulf. The implication was that the Aurolani forces were making a push at Okrannel, and if nothing was done to help defend it, the lower half of the Crescent Sea and all the nations touching it would be vulnerable to attacks.

The reports from Okrannel told everyone what they had to do, and the elven prophecy provided them a focus around which to organize how they were going to do it. Already in Yslin there existed enough ships and elite troops—the royals' various Bodyguard units—to send a strong relief force to Okrannel. At the same time the nations of the east would send troops north toward Fortress Draconis and the western nations would launch their fleets to scour the Crescent Sea of Aurolani pirates.

The prophecy made it clear that Lord Kenwick Norrington would lead the expedition, and everyone knew a core of subleaders would be vital to the expedition's success. The various royals decided they would surround Lord Norrington with a circle of heroes who could lead. Though, to me, most royals seemed more interested in having their nation's representative forced into that circle. The honor would be in the going, not necessarily in the fighting itself.

Lord Norrington made certain Nay, Leigh, and I were present during the debates that determined the force's composition. From the questions he asked us after the various sessions I got the sense he was using us to figure out where the balance point was between politics and efficacy. Where politics undercut the ability of the force to fight, Lord Norrington would offer objections, or make requests that reestablished the balance.

For example, it was suggested by King Stefin of Okrannel that envoys should be sent to Gyrvirgul to enlist the aid of the Gyrkyme, but Jentellin objected strongly, claiming the Gyrkyme were nothing but beasts and should not be included. Now I would have thought the usefulness of creatures that are, in essence, winged elves, would have been obvious, but Jentellin said that elves will in no way have anything to do with a force that included Gyrkyme in it.

I guess I understood, then, the elven objection. Back when Kirûn ruled Aurolan, he captured a number of noble elven warriors and compelled them, through magick, to lie with *Araftii* as a husband lies with his wife. *Araftii* are savage, bestial creatures, with fully fledged human bodies, but wings instead of arms and legs that end in claws and talons. In some stories they are said to have comely faces, and in others are said to be hags, but all are female, and these *Araftii* laid several clutches of hybrid eggs that hatched and created the Gyrkyme. The elves consider the whole population of them nothing but rapeget, and no more accept them than I imagine men would accept the offspring of a sheep that had been covered by a shepherd.

Panqui were another species of creature that was deemed too bestial to be effective, so they were not included in the force. The Spritha were seen as being too small to be effective and too carefree to be suitably martial. And dragons, well, no one wanted to involve dragons no matter how much they might help. The question of dragons trusting men after Atval was an open one, but the reasons for leaving them out ran deeper than that.

It seemed obvious to everyone that one of the goals of the Aurolani forces moving at Okrannel had to be the recovery of the piece of Kirûn's DragonCrown that had been stored there. The DragonCrown had allowed Kirûn to control an army of dragons. A single piece would allow a powerful enough magician to control at least one dragon, so an ally could potentially be turned into an enemy in the blink of an eye.

Aside from men and elves, the only other species allowed into the force were the urZrethi. The urZrethi are small-statured creatures, proportioned as are human children. Their flesh takes on mineral colors, like the green and black of malachite, the black of coal, or the red of cinnabar. The one who joined the inner circle, a female named Faryaah-Tse Kimp, was a sulfurous yellow, with black hair and eyes that showed red where there should have been whites. Despite being slender, small, and very childlike, she had a weight to her that belied her form.

The urZrethi and elves usually did not get along well, but Jentellin welcomed them into the coalition primarily because they had a garrison company at Fortress Draconis. Without the urZrethi, the fortress would fall, because the urZrethi were builders and tunnelers, which suited them perfectly to fortifying the fortress and fighting against sappers from Aurolan. Faryaah-Tse would command that unit when we reached Fortress Draconis, and until then would serve as one of Lord Norrington's advisors.

The planning of the campaign took a long time, was punctuated by various arguments, and was full of boring details through which I began to sleep. I felt the most sorry for Nay because he had very little in the way of background for understanding all the details. Leigh and I could deal with it a bit more easily, but it still numbed us. Since meetings went late, then commenced again early in the morning, most of the sleep we got was in fits and starts, which left me tired and anxious.

The end of our Moon Month also sank me in melancholy. The end of the Moon Month was supposed to be a time of celebration with family and friends. By the time I received my first adult mask, my course in life should have been plotted. I should have already had an invitation from a military unit to join it, but I didn't. I had no doubt that being part of the Knights of the Phoenix would benefit me, but I had no idea how at that point. I'd done a lot in the first two-thirds of my Moon Month, but since then I'd done almost nothing.

I also realized I was homesick and missing my family. Just as I got my moonmask from my father, so I was supposed to get my harvestmask from him, or an older brother, or the oldest male relative available. That clearly wasn't going to happen for me. Even more depressing was my assumption that because I was not part of a military unit, I wasn't going to be part of the crusade against Aurolan. The only individuals being talked about for the crusade were heroes such as Lord Norrington, with Nay, Leigh, and myself going completely unmentioned in the Councils of Kings.

The events that began the night I got my moonmask were going to end, leaving me alone to wander back to Valsina and oblivion.

Leigh had no such worries. There seemed to be no question that he would accompany his father on the expedition. More important than that was the gold ring worked with the Norrington crest that Princess Ryhope gave him to celebrate the end of his Moon Month. It had a ruby set where a heart appeared in the crest and certainly must have cost a small fortune. I'd spent two gold pieces to buy him a silver gorget, which he actually wore, but he consistently admired the ring, polishing the stone against his jerkin, then holding his hand out to look at the light glinting from it.

Nay also seemed to be carefree as our Moon Month came to an end. When he and I chatted and exchanged gifts, I got a look at things from his perspective. "Only figured to be a soldier, and that will happen. All else—Atval, Yslin—that's a lifetime for me. If claimed by Death tomorrow, I'm further along than anyone would have ever suspected."

Nay did like his coat, and he gave me the small boot knife he'd carried with him from Valsina. "Wanted to get one for you here, but none were good enough. Made this one myself. Not the best, but it holds an edge good and won't fail you."

"Thanks." I slid it away in my right boot. "If the trip home is at all like the trip out here, it will be more than useful."

Leigh gave the both of us thick, black blankets woven in wool from Naliserro. The Nalisk workmanship was flawless, and even looking at the blanket I felt warm. Having seen what festival merchants wanted for them when I was looking at gifts, I knew Leigh had spent more than his father had given him. I also sensed he'd actually thought a lot about his choice, not just going with the first thing he saw. I felt as if he wanted us to have the blankets to keep us warm and comfortable on our trip home, which I appreciated.

It also drove me crazy because it underlined the fact that we'd be going back to Valsina while he was traveling the world and destroying the Aurolani threat. I had wandered down into the inn's common room and was sitting alone, sipping a bitter ale, thinking about all that when Severus' indolent son, Desid, came downstairs and found me.

"Beg pardon, master, but His Lordship asked for you."

I nodded, left the tankard of ale where it was, and slowly trudged up the stairs. With each step my heart sank, so that by the time I'd reached the top of the stairs, it felt as if my heart were back drowning in my ale. Despite feeling hollow inside, I straightened up and forced a smile on my face. I knocked on the door and entered when bidden.

Lord Norrington turned in his chair, setting a quill pen down on the desk beneath his right elbow. "Thank you for coming, Hawkins . . . Tarrant. Please, be seated."

I sat on the foot of the bed. "You wanted to see me?"

"Yes, I did." His voice came easy and he even sounded a bit pleased. "Today your Moon Month ends and you are to receive your harvestmask. Prince Scrainwood—at the urging of his sister, I suspect—asked if I would mind if *he* gave Bosleigh his mask. It was an honor I could not refuse, and I knew Leigh would make my life difficult if I did. He's off at Fortress Gryps now."

I blinked. "And you're not there? I mean, I would have thought . . ."

Lord Norrington raised a hand. "Leigh knows I am proud of him, but I want him to be the center of attention. After all, if I fall in this expedition, he'll be the Norrington who will have to fulfill the prophecy, right?"

I nodded.

"Duke Larner will be granting Naysmith his harvestmask. I gather that the bladesmith who taught Nay once forged a special sword for the Duke, hence the connection there." He smiled and opened the central drawer in the writing desk. "I know that the senior male relative wherever you are is supposed to grant you your harvestmask. As you know, my father died when I was very young, so your father trained me and very much was as a father to me. While my uncle—the man who would become my father-in-law, as well—granted me my harvestmask, I felt your father was the one who allowed me to earn it. And you and Leigh spent so much time together I often thought of you as brothers and I . . . well, I hope your father will not mind my usurping his role here."

From the drawer he drew a brown leather mask, not that much different from my moonmask, save that the brow portion had been nearly doubled in size. Above the eyeholes an inch-wide strip of gibberkin fur had been added, and two temeryx feathers, both black, dangled from either side of the mask. If I were to look at it today I would see it as very plain, but at that time it was the most beautiful thing I'd ever seen.

I reached up and unknotted the thongs holding my moonmask on. I remembered my father admonishing me not to bare my face for anyone save family, but I could not imagine him objecting to my showing it to Lord Norrington. Leigh's father glanced down toward the ground as I removed my mask, allowing me my modesty. I took my harvestmask from him and pressed its cool suede underside to my face. Lord Norrington moved around behind me and tied it securely.

"Now and forever," he said, "this mask will proclaim to others who and what you are. What once hid us from our enemies now reveals us to our friends. Wear it with pride and always honor the generations who have fought and died to provide you with the mask."

I nodded solemnly, then smiled as he returned to his desk. "Thank you, my lord."

"It was my pleasure, Tarrant." He smiled, then reached out and patted me on a knee. "Of course, I know the tradition of giving a gift to someone receiving his harvestmask, but I've had little time to consider what I should give you. If you have a suggestion, I would love to hear it."

Hope sparked in my chest and made my heart leap. "My lord, there is no *thing* I would have of you, but a chance, an opportunity; for me, and . . . and for Nay. Please, my lord, let us see to the finish what we started a month ago. Let us go on the Okrannel expedition. We won't be trouble, we'll do whatever you want, whatever you need."

Lord Norrington sat back. "I'm afraid I can't do that."

"But—"

He held up a hand. "Hear me out. You would let me acquit

my duty to you too easily. You and Nay will be going with Leigh and me—that was decided long ago."

"What? When? Why?"

"As I understand it, there are nuances to the elven language that are beyond my understanding. For example, the word translated as 'washed' in the phrase 'washed in flame' could also be 'born.' "

"That refers to your initiation into the Knights of the Phoenix, doesn't it?"

"Among those who know, that is what is believed, yes. In any event, part of the prophecy, when studied, is an allusion to an elven tale that involves three companions." He shrugged his shoulders easily. "Know you this, however: I would have demanded the three of you accompany me. I can't imagine a Norrington going off to do battle without a Hawkins at his side, and Naysmith is stalwart and sensible enough to keep you and Leigh out of trouble."

I nodded. "And there will be trouble aplenty." I narrowed my eyes. "Some people, like Prince Scrainwood and Prince Augustus, seem to think we'll be finished with this fight before the first winter snows fly."

"We can hope they are right, but I'm planning to dress warmly." Lord Norrington inked his quill and scratched a note onto the foolscap. "However, that matters not at the moment. You have yet to tell me what I can give you."

I shook my head as nothing I'd seen over the last weeks suggested itself to me. "I don't know, my lord. I guess, perhaps, maybe . . ." I drew in a deep breath, then let it out slowly and licked my lips. "I would like your trust, my lord. I would like you to know I will never fail you or betray you. If I could have your trust, that would be everything for me."

Lord Norrington sat stock still for a moment, then chewed on his lower lip. "Very well, you have it. I may yet decide there are things you are not to know, but that is not because I do not trust you with them, but that I wish you to have enough perspective to understand them. I will tell you nothing that will hurt you unless you need to know it."

"Thank you, my lord." I dropped to a knee before him, took his right hand in mine, and kissed the Norrington crest ring on his finger. "I will guard your trust as I will guard your life, unto my last breath, my last drop of blood, and my last thought."

He stood and pulled me to my feet. "Norrington and Hawkins heading north to face Chytrine and her Aurolani hordes. If only she knew what was coming, she'd already be running, and our glorious war would be over before brave blood flows."

CHAPTER 21

My joy at being included in the expedition knew no bounds, and kept me going throughout the next two weeks. A soothsayer could have come to me and predicted dire things, but I'd not have believed and wouldn't have cared. I was to be part of a grand crusade that would rid the world forever of a scourge—a scourge that cast a vast, cold shadow over all of us. What we would do would live on forever in history.

The two weeks we had to organize the expedition were full of chaos, joys, and disappointments. It was also full of discoveries for me. First was getting to see the ships of the fleet and actually stepping onto a seagoing vessel. Jerana, Alcida, and Saporcia supplied the vast majority of the ships for the fleet, including wallowing merchant craft and long, sleek war galleys. The merchantmen relied primarily on sail to move them, though they did have a couple of long sweeps that could maneuver them in port or when totally becalmed. The merchantmen were loaded with foodstuffs, wine, grain for the horses, and two were outfitted to carry heavy cavalry units from Jerana and Alcida. Prince Augustus commanded the latter company and shipped aboard the *Running Brook*, which was named after the estate that housed the Prince's Horse Guards.

The war galleys did have a single mast and could travel well on a wind, but relied on oarsmen to propel them in combat. Three men to an oar, twenty oars to a side, the ship could cruise at five knots an hour and hit bursts of twelve knots when closing with an enemy ship. Bow and aft towers allowed the ship's troops to shoot their crossbows down on the decks of any ships they were attacking. At the bow, an extension of the bowsprit formed a beak which, in close combat, could sheer off another galley's oars. More important, it could crush through the wall of shields on the ship's railing, and was wide enough to allow boarders to run across it and jump down onto the enemy deck.

Two pairs each of swivel-mounted grand crossbows were set fore and aft to shoot meter-long quarrels that could punch through shields and decking. Grapnels linked to stout line or steel chain were ready to catch hold of an enemy ship and keep it close. Two small mangonels on wheeled platforms could be moved about and used to toss canisters of *napthalm*, a pitch-like substance that burned fiercely, onto another ship, or scatter about small calthrops which would stick in the decking and tear up the feet of barefooted crewmen.

From the wharves it was difficult to gain a good perspective on the fleet, but I got a chance to ride in the basket slung beneath one of the balloons in Yslin. Our ascent was pretty easy and took me much higher than the other basket I'd ridden in. We rose swiftly, leaving me feeling as if I'd left my stomach somewhere back on the ground. Still, watching people shrink to the size of ants and watching buildings become as tiny as a child's playhouse was incredible. It struck me that Gyrkyme had the opportunity to see the world this way all the time, and I could only hope it always remained as magical for them as it was for me.

In addition to its crew of a hundred forty men, and a marine company of thirty, each of the galleys could take with it one additional company of thirty warriors. The Bodyguard units we were using were made up of roughly two companies, so a pair of galleys would be needed to move a single unit. A single merchantman carried supplies that would provide for ten galleys, so we only needed four in our convoy, but we doubled that number since we assumed supplies would be needed by people in Okrannel, or by ourselves if we became involved in an extended campaign there. That count of eight merchantmen did not include the two stable ships.

Forty-eight ships with multicolored hulls and sails lay at anchor in Yslin harbor, waiting for us to head out. We knew more ships from Loquellyn would join us, but we were not certain how many of the elven vessels would be sent to us. The urZrethi had no ships and, truth be told, Faryaah-Tse Kimp didn't look as if she wanted anything to do with the ocean. Still, the human component of the convoy would have twenty-four hundred combat troops and over double that number of sailors, who could be given swords and brought into combat if needed. It was a considerably large army and would be welcome relief to the defenders in Okrannel.

At least, that's what I thought, but rumors spreading through the expeditionary force suggested otherwise. People said that Chytrine, who was at once identified as Kirûn's daughter or consort or both, had raised a vast horde of creatures that was even now overrunning Okrannel. It was even suggested that the messages coming from Svarskya were false, that no troops still awaited attack there, but that Chytrine had people sending hopeful messages to lure us into a trap.

Lord Norrington dismissed that idea instantly. "It makes no sense for her to allow messages that warn us of her horde to be sent forth, since that would allow us to oppose her. And no one in Jerana is reporting an influx of refugees, which would be expected if Okrannel had collapsed. Moreover, as King Stefin has noted, the messages are coming from his son, Prince Kirill. He says that if Chytrine has been able to train someone to think and write like Kirill, she'd be capable of other very difficult tasks and we should all just lose heart now."

Lord Norrington did not play down other reports, though, of Chytrine having created an elite band of leaders for her troops, which she called the *sullanciri*. Men generally called them Dark Lancers and said they were renegade men, cunning vylaens, or some gibberkin magickally endowed with intelligence. There had been sightings of these malignant warriors in Okrannel, but details were vague. Rumor had it that Chytrine fed them their own shadows, which made them powerful and immortal, and that each had some special power it could use to defeat its foes.

"That rumor could well be true," Leigh's father admitted, "but to put too much stock in it is not good. Heslin will tell you that magick can always be countered or dispelled, and that spells are tricky things and can be quite literal. A spell that will blind fifty men might leave women with vision, or children, or elves. And in any event, a magicker with an arrow fixed in him is seldom good at casting spells."

Part of me shivered at the idea of facing magickally strengthened foes, but another part accepted it. After all, if Chytrine could create truly immortal warriors, she'd have come south and conquered everything ages ago. It could be that such magicks had only recently been invented or perfected, but if they existed she'd not have needed the scouting groups that had come down through Oriosa. No, I decided, her magicks might give some of her troops an edge, but there had to be a limit to even her power.

The preparations continued apace and without much in the way of upset until the eve of departure. The plan had been finalized earlier that day in the Kings' Council. Prince Scrainwood was given command of the whole expedition, though Lord Norrington was the warlord and would make all the decisions having to do with combat. He would be shipping aboard the Alcidese ship *Invictus*, while Prince Scrainwood traveled on the Jeranese ship *Venator*. That suited me fine, since the further he was from me, the better I liked it.

The expedition would head with all possible speed to Okrannel, intent on relieving Crozt. From there we would move down the coast to Svarskya and lift any Aurolani siege. After that, as determined by communications from Fortress Draconis, we would either sail east to bolster the fortress' garrison, or raid the Ghost Marches and shatter the pirate havens there.

On the eve of our departure, I traveled with Leigh, Nay,

Lord Norrington, and others to the largest of the Kedyn temples in Yslin. Night had already fallen as we made our way up the granite steps. I was running through in my mind the things I'd seen and the stories I'd heard, and trying to think what I would offer for a prayer when I bumped into someone. I bounced back down a step, smiled and offered a "Beg pardon," by reflex.

Resolute nodded quietly. "I should have expected your preoccupation."

I saw Nay turn back and look at me from the top of the stairs, but I waved him on. "Have you just come from making a sacrifice?"

"To Kedyn? No." The elf shook his head. "The god I know that fills Kedyn's niche in our pantheon does not suck incense and gather around him dead warriors the way old men gather pigeons when they spread stale bread about."

I tried to hid my reaction to the scorn in his voice, but I'm not sure I managed it at all well. "Why are you here, then?"

"I came to speak with you." He lifted his chin and bared his throat. "Jentellin informed Amends of the plans for your campaign."

"Yes, it's all very exciting, isn't it?"

"Exciting, I suppose, but that is not for me to discover."

"What?"

"I won't be going with you."

I rocked back a step and half-stumbled to the next level. "You won't be going? Why not? I mean, this is it, this is the chance to strike back at Chytrine. This is the chance to destroy her."

"I know." His silver eyes reflected the thin sliver of a new moon. "My goal has never been her death. My goal is the liberation of my homeland. As noble and good as your cause is, it is not *my* cause. I know you will acquit yourself well. Chytrine will regret her action, but Vorquellyn will still be under her control."

I shook my head. "But, don't you see? Once we break her army, we'll clean the pirates out of the Ghost Marches. Once we do that, we will isolate Vorquellyn and can take it back.

Doing this gets us one step closer to freeing Vorquellyn. You have to see that, Resolute."

"No, Hawkins, I don't have to see that. What I do see is that the same sort of success against her a century ago did not free Vorquellyn. If I go, if I agree, I am saying that a partial effort is sufficient, and I cannot say that. If I do, then Amends and Jentellin will know I've lost my resolve. I never will. I am Resolute; it is my name and it is *me*. As much as I want to go with you, I cannot until an expedition is sent to free my home."

I swallowed past the lump in my throat. "I understand what you are saying. I wish I could convince you otherwise. Having at least one Vorquelf with us would have frightened Chytrine so much she'd already be retreating."

"Vorquelves will travel with you, fight with you. I am seen as extreme by some of my own kind, but I'll accept that burden." He opened a pouch on his belt and withdrew a patch of fur. He handed it to me. "I took this from one of the gibberers you slew. Lord Norrington asked me for a strip of it for your mask. This piece I give to you for inside the temple, for your sacrifice."

I frowned. "I'll buy incense . . ."

"Listen to me, Tarrant Hawkins, listen well. Here Kedyn is shepherd to ghosts, and even in your land he is a proud guardian. You forget he embodies war. He is flesh and blood and bone—all the things we saw and did at Atval. He is the master of it all and offerings of incense are just too polite for him. Burn this, Hawkins, let the stink of it drift from you to him. He'll know that you know the truth of war. He will remember you. When Death hands him the roll of who will be called, he'll strike your name from the list. You'll be saved for great things, and terrible things."

I shivered, then looked him in the eye. "Is this how you survive?"

The elf laughed, and it was not a wholly pleasant sound. "One of the ways, yes." He slapped me on the arm. "Good luck, Hawkins—brave heart, clear eye, and sharp blade. Your name will be on everyone's lips when this expedition ends."

"Right. Then you and I go and liberate Vorquellyn."

"That we will." The elf tossed me a quick salute, then skipped off down the stairs.

I stroked my thumb across the mottled fur as I entered the temple. I paid for two charcoal shields and incense, then walked down to the statue of Kedyn. I knelt at the base, then looked up into the unseeing eyes set in a handsome face. The armored breastplate covering his torso had been carved with dozens of faces and it was easy to imagine they were matched by smaller statues in the long hall behind Kedyn. Looking between the statue's feet I could see warriors choking the gallery, burning incense and lighting candles.

My flesh puckered. Using my charcoal shields, I scraped several glowing coals together into a pile. I sprinkled a little incense on it, just to get Kedyn's attention, then I tossed the small patch of fur over them. The fur itself began to curl into little knots. The acrid scent of burning fur exploded up into my face as the fur caught fire. I coughed and my eyes watered, but I watched the column of smoke rise and caress the statue's face.

With my hands in their proper places, I bowed my head. "Kedyn, on this, the eve of a great expedition, I ask of you nothing that I have not asked before. Grant me the opportunity to prove myself to be brave and a boon companion to those who fight on my side. May I always see my duty and acquit it, without hesitation. If it is your will that I survive, in this I will be pleased. If I am to die, let me do so facing my enemy. Steady my hand, shield me from pain, and let all glory and honor be yours."

I looked back up, but saw no sign that my prayer had been heard. While Resolute could have been right, that offering that sacrifice would bring me favorable notice with Kedyn, part of me assumed that being ignored by the gods wasn't much worse than being noticed by them. Countless were the tragic tales in which the gods chose to make a man's life interesting. Heading off to war, I didn't need the help of the gods to make my life *more* interesting.

As it turned out, what I *needed* and what I *got* were two different things entirely.

CHAPTER 22

We sailed with the tide and it came early, so we were out on the open sea before the rising sun splashed bloody highlights over the calm water. The cries of seagulls, the dull booming of the stroke-drums and the crisp snap of canvas filled the dawn, but all played as accents over the consistent hiss of water against the hull. I stood on the forecastle of the *Invictus*, feeling the wind against my face.

We were off, at last, bound for a glorious war. You could read the enthusiasm on everyone's faces, including the sailors pulling at the oars. We were the select force that would make the world safe. Our mission was clear, it was simple and we would do it. Men dared boast of the creatures they would kill and talk about the riches they would win. By the time snow flew we'd all be home, warming ourselves before fires, spinning tale after tale for friends and family.

Even now, though, as I look back on that first morning, there were signs of trouble I should have seen. We almost didn't leave that morning because of a conflict among some of the captains. A number of them, from Jerana mostly, said our fleet should make an offering to the *weirun* of the sea, Tagothcha. Without such an offering he could turn the wind and water against us, stretching out what would be a week's journey into a month or more. A gallon of wine, a slain pig, a scattering of gold coins, any of those would have been enough to appease him.

The Alcidese captains countered that Tagothcha slept during the summer, and offers made to him during that time might wake him. The annual autumn storm season was pointed to as evidence that Tagothcha was not pleasant while still half-asleep. It was well known, they pointed out, that waves on the ocean were the furrows on Tagothcha's brow, and while he slept they were small. If he awakened angry, however, his frown could sink ships.

Lord Norrington, who knew little of Tagothcha's ways because our nation is landlocked, sided with the Alcidese contingent. None of us had any doubt the *weirun* existed and would be a nasty enemy if he opposed us, but leaving him alone seemed the wiser course. We sailed quietly, hoping the sea-spirit would think us nothing more than a dream.

The trip itself *did* have dreamlike qualities, though not for Leigh. Nay and I seemed to weather the ship's bobbing up and down at anchor, or the surge and crash of making headway against wavelets. Leigh turned a most unnatural shade of grey and spent much of his time at the wales, making his own offerings to Tagothcha, as the sailors put it. He looked miserable and said he felt worse. He managed to keep down some watered wine and porridge, though not much of either, and he started losing weight.

Late on the first day we sailed past Vilwan, the island magickers proclaimed as their own. While each nation, and even each town, had a magicker or two capable of teaching those who had the Spark how to work magicks, Vilwan was the place where the most talented came, to learn and create and teach. We did not venture close to it, and the rocky cliff-sides were not terribly inviting. Moreover, what should have been green hillsides in the island's interior were patched with yellow and red and purple and blue vegetation. Heslin, who said he'd gone to Vilwan once, when much younger, assured me there was nothing unusual about the odd-colored plants. I humored him, but still shivered when I glanced at the island.

A little ship did join us, sailing out from Vilwan. It had no oars and only a small sail, but caught up with us easily enough and maintained the fleet's pace. Twenty or so men and women, mostly all human, crewed the ship, with five of them taking a two-hour shift at a time. Everyone in the fleet soon realized they were moving their ship by magick, and when we translated the effort of our crew into what five of them were doing at any one time, well, we were suddenly happy to have them along as allies in the fight.

Early the second day I found our Vorquelf on the forecastle. Her long, black hair streamed behind her and her gold eyes burned with the light from the rising sun. She wore hunting leathers of a deep blue and had a gold earring dangling from her right earlobe. I'd recognized her from Resolute's trial and had been told her name was Seethe.

She smiled at me as I leaned against the rail next to her. "Good morning, Master Hawkins."

"And you, Mistress Seethe."

"Seethe is enough. Adult honorifics are denied Vorquelves."

I caught no anger or regret in her voice, just a calm recitation of facts. "Would you mind if I asked how you came to join us? I mean, from your name, it is so like Resolute's, that I would have thought you would have remained behind as he did."

She laughed lightly and pulled a lock of hair away from where the wind had strung it against her mouth. "I was told it was my destiny to go, much as you were. Oracle, the elf your friend touched, is my sister. She told me I would be accompanying you. The prospect seemed to no more please her than it did me, but prophecy is prophecy."

"I am glad you have come along." I picked at the railing with my thumbnail. "Oracle's name seems descriptive of what she is, and Resolute as well. How did you get your names? You don't seem that angry."

"You've not seen me when I am angry, but you will." Her eyes half closed as she smiled sidelong at me. "Some of us are given our names, some of us take them. You have to understand that when an elf is born in one of the homelands, she is tied to that homeland forever. When we are ritually bound to the homeland, we enter a pact with the land that provides us power but demands of us responsibility. The conquest of Vorquellyn barred those of us who were too young from ever becoming bonded to our homeland, isolating us from power."

She pointed off at the Vilwanese vessel. "Magick and magickal power are tricky things. Heslin will tell you that when he completed his training he was given another name, a secret name. Think of it as a key that unlocks a doorway to power. For him it is a small key and a small doorway, but that is enough for him. When we are bonded to our land, we, too, get a secret name that lets us access power. The names, of course, remain secret, because anyone who knows our secret name gains a certain amount of power over us.

"The Vorquelves who were bonded to the island were in great pain when they were driven from it. They headed west, always west. It is believed, among us, that there are many worlds and that when we move from this one we will find another where elves dwell. If that is the world meant for us, we will stay and flourish. If not, we will move on to the next world and the world beyond that, forever seeking our true home. Being unbonded, we were denied this ability to travel to these otherwheres. Since that is very much the essence of being an elf, we are not elves."

She sighed. "We have chosen names from the human common tongue, names that define us. We make these names known because taking that risk opens to us greater avenues of power than would a secret name. It is a dangerous game, of course, but our power offers us some protection."

"If you have that much power, why don't you just take Vorquellyn again?"

She stared out to sea and shook her head. "Different people use their power in different ways. Amends seeks conciliation and cooperation. Oracle peers into the future. Predator squanders his power in an effort to control an urban swamp. Resolute uses his to kill and kill and kill. And you are right, I'm not far removed from him, for my goal is to kill and kill and kill. But, the various directions we all take divides our power and does not let us direct it at the goal we all profess to cherish."

As we spoke the convoy slid past the thickly jungled fastness of Vael. Tall peaks rose along the narrow island's central spine, with their grey tips piercing the clouds that gathered around them. None of the mariners on the trip could tell us much about the island, save that it was home to dragons and panqui. Panqui were supposed to be hulking, semiintelligent beasts that were said to have been created by dragons as a parody of men. Panqui lived peacefully in the mountain fastnesses dragons stole from the urZrethi, or so the old tales went, with the panqui proving powerful enough on the defensive to make them too difficult for men to fight, thereby insulating dragons from human expeditions.

The stories sailors told of panqui pirates certainly did make them sound very fierce, but all the tales were at one remove, with none of the speakers ever having seen a panqui, much less having fought one. I really had no desire to see pirate galleys full of armed and armored monsters coming at us, especially when those same creatures were favored by dragons. Even so, I kept my eyes sweeping over Vael in the vain hopes I might spot something unusual.

I saw nothing and was disappointed, not realizing that in the days to come, seeing nothing would have been welcome indeed.

The third day at sea took us east of the island of Wruona. It was a well-known pirate haven with tricky shoals and hidden coves that made clearing it out very difficult. We slid past without incident, but Lord Norrington noted that if the Wruonin freebooters had reached an accommodation with Chytrine, chances were very good that they might use *arcanslata* to let her know we were on our way.

I took it as a good thing, then, that later that day, as the sun began to set, two silvery Loquellyn galleys moved to join us. The ships had been made of silverwood, a type of tree with silvery flesh that only grew in the elven homelands. Things made of it, like boxes or frames or chests or chairs were highly prized. They were seldom awarded to men, and only after the elves decided a man had performed a valuable service for them.

What I found most interesting about the Loquellyn ship was its form. Man-galleys resembled swans, after a fashion, in that they rode on the surface. The elven ship's form mimicked that of the sea creature known as a shark. The ship's prow sloped down into a broad ram that remained just below the water's surface. One fighting tower rose in the center, just forward of the mast, and another in the aft. It had no oars visible in the water, but rowers occupied their places in the ship, same as they did in ours, and they even pulled long handles. I later learned the oars they pulled were attached to gears and belts that drove massive hidden paddlewheels to speed the ship along.

Dawn of the last day showed us just coming around the Loquellyn headlands. We'd skirt the Okrans coast on the west, then head north to Crozt. We had one more day to go, as the breeze from the south had allowed us to make a steady five knots an hour. The same journey by horse would have taken two weeks, and that would have been only if we'd not had mountains, rivers or other obstacles to contend with.

In the early afternoon, dark clouds began to gather to the north and the wind died. With the oars the ships still made headway, but debate soon began as to whether or not we should make for the coast and seek shelter in a harbor. Before that decision could be made, however, the spotters in the crow's nests called down that they saw something else: Aurolani sails, full of wind, coming our way.

Orders were immediately given and everyone sprang into action. The merchantmen were dispatched with an escort of four galleys to head for a safe harbor. The rest of the fleet formed itself into a line and drove north to meet the approaching enemy. Buckets of water were drawn from the ocean and splashed over the decks to wet them down and make them less liable to burn if the enemy used *napthalm*. And, conversely, our Mastermarine started to boil up some of the flammable liquid.

All the warriors on board donned their armor, and I almost went without greaves and bracers or my mail because if I fell in the water, I'd sink like a stone. A passing sailor, who apparently read my concern on my face, laughed and said, "You'll not be swimming at all with a lopped arm or chopped leg, so gird yourself well." I followed his advice, then mounted the steps to the forecastle, arming myself with my bow.

Sailors hung steel shields along the wales and erected mantlets to ward them from enemy arrows. They armed themselves with shortswords and a couple had poleaxes, which they would use to chop through grappling lines from another ship. A squad of marines in heavy armor waited in the forecastle for our ship to ram into an Aurolani galley. Once the beak extended over the enemy deck, they'd boil forth and board the other ship. Then those of us atop the forecastle would cast grappling lines over and secure the ships together, allowing the rest of us to dash over and help the marines.

Crouched behind the tower wale, peeking out from between shields, I saw the enemy fleet looming closer. Their fleet consisted of some larger ships that would have seemed nothing more than buckets bobbing up and down, save that an evil red light glowed from within hatches and portholes, as if hellish fires burned in their bellies. Two dozen galleys made up the bulk of the fleet, twelve to a wing, and they spread out to try and flank our formation. Smaller boats, designed to be quick and highly maneuverable, occupied much of the center. Each of them seemed to have a ballista for shooting fiery missiles at us, a dozen archers, and twice that number of gibberers waiting to scramble up onto our ships and wreak havoc.

I glanced back at the aftdeck and saw Nay, all armored up and hefting his maul, standing with Lord Norrington. Of Leigh I saw nothing, but as sick as he'd been, it didn't surprise me. If he'd been able to dress himself I would have been astonished, and that exertion would have worn him out so much that he couldn't have lifted a sword.

Down below the captain bellowed orders. The sail was reefed, then drawn down completely. The speed-drums' pounding quickened to help us close the distance with the enemy fleet. Lord Norrington shouted another order, which the sergeant on the forecastle repeated, bringing us archers to our feet. We sighted and let fly.

The crossbowmen loosed their volley at one of the big brigs. Gibberers on the foredeck pitched and reeled away. One creature near a ballista—a vylaen, I think—fell back, and his weight yanked the lanyard wrapped around his hand. The siege machine's arm came up, hurling a stone in the air and, in a shorter, more shallow arc, the flailing form of the gibberer that had been loading the stone into the ballista likewise flew.

Since my bow did not have the range of the crossbows, I picked a closer target. I sank an arrow into the belly of a small boat's helmsbeast. He stumbled back over the aft wale, grabbing at the tiller as he did so. His small ship swung quickly to the left, bringing it broadside to our surging line. The gibberer crew looked back to see what had happened, but before any of them could do anything to regain control of the ship, one of the elven galleys hit it amidships. The silverwood ship stove in the smaller ship's side, snapped its keel, and scattered shattered pieces of flotsam in its wake.

The speed-drums quickened their booming pace again, hurling our ship forward at ramming speed. I loosed another arrow, this time hitting a brig crewman. I ducked back quickly as a return volley from the brig arced up at the forecastle, then nocked another arrow, stood, and shot. We were so close I saw black blood splash on a white oak deck as the arrow pierced a gibberer's neck.

Then the *Invictus* slammed full on into the brig, throwing me forward against the rail. Our beak snapped the brig's wales, crushing one gibberer and battering others aside with wooden shrapnel. Below us marines screamed inhuman war cries and boiled out along the beak, leaping down to the enemy deck. Weapons drawn they began dealing death, with the rest of us shooting as fast as we could.

The Battle of the Crescent Sea had been joined.

CHAPTER 23

I could tell you that arrows flew so thick that they blackened the sky, but the fast-approaching clouds did an admirable job of that all by themselves. Arrows and quarrels instead zipped about like lightning, striking a man here or there. Black shafts covered the forecastle like quills on a stickle-hog. An arrow clanged off my helm, dropping me to the deck. A man landed next to me, two arrows quivering in his chest, and another reeled away with an arrow in his eye and fell over the railing to the deck.

It took a moment or two for me to shake my head and clear it. In that time I managed to look west along our line. Ships burned in the distance, and I could not make out if they were ours or those of the enemy. Closer I saw the smaller Aurolani ships closing with our galleys, launching grappling hooks up over the wales. Sailors on the *Invictus* hacked at the lines attached to them with poleaxes, but the grapnels fixed with stout chain did not break, and gibberers began to swarm up over the deck.

Lord Norrington and Nay descended from the aftcastle and attacked the boarders savagely. Lord Norrington's silvery blade flashed left and right, cleaving ribs and flesh, laying open bellies and slicing through fanged muzzles. Blood sprayed from his blade in a wide arc. Wounded and dying gibberers clawed at severed limbs and clutched tightly at gaping holes in their flesh.

Nay laid about with his maul, employing all the power he might have used to hammer hot steel. A lunge would impale a gibberer on his spike, then he'd rip it free, parry a sword cut with the weapon's haft, then snap the head down hard, crushing a shoulder or ribs. When he swept the blade low, knees twisted and popped, legs snapped like oars trapped between ships. War cries became painful howls as he crushed muzzles at a stroke.

I drew myself up on one knee and fitted arrow to bow, shooting into the swarms of gibberers pouring over the wales. Clear shots were not easy to find as the deck became choked with combatants. A quick twist between two wrestling fighters, and an arrow meant for a gibberer's back might strike a sailor. I sought my targets among those just boarding the ship, or those seeking to slip behind my friends. The good thing was that I shot well, but the bad was that targets outnumbered my arrows.

I was about to draw my sword and leap down to the deck when I felt a wave of heat wash up over my back. I turned, fearing a bucket of flaming *napthalm* had been splashed on the forecastle, but I saw no bright flames. Though the warmth built sharply, what I saw sank a chill into me.

A massively huge man-thing emerged from the brig's hold, locking a colossal hand around the mast. The wood charred beneath its grip. It appeared to be a man—Nay's size and then some—but its flesh was as black as cast iron. A shock of long red hair and a long red beard flowed from its head. All other color, from the burning intensity of its eyes to the places where shadows outlined the muscles of its bare arms, legs, and torso, was a purple so vibrant and deep it hurt to look at the thing.

One of our marines raced at it with sword held high. As he brought the steel blade down, the creature brought its right arm up and took the cut on its forearm. The blade bit into the creature's flesh, but not deeply, and the impact rang loudly with the peal of metal on metal. The marine bounced back, glanced at his notched blade, then the creature clapped its metal hands, flattening the man's helm to the width of a dinner plate.

The blood and brains that spattered it sizzled like fat in a hot skillet. Greasy smoke washed up into its beard and hair. The creature threw its head back as if to laugh, though no sound issued from its throat. It paused for a moment, then stalked across the deck.

This was a *sullanciri*, a Dark Lancer. Its metal flesh moved as the muscles beneath it flexed and stretched. The unarmed figure stalked the brig's deck as quarrels flicked out, striking sparks as they hit, then bouncing away. Someone on another galley shot at him with a grand crossbow, but the creature snatched the yard-long shaft from the air and used it to pin a marine to the deck.

The fearful shouts from our marines was suddenly matched by screeching from the gibberers on board the *Invictus*. Back by the aftcastle, Leigh had emerged from below decks. Stripped to the waist, wearing only mask, boots, and black leather breeches, he swung Temmer in a golden circle. Though I still saw the dark marks of fatigue beneath his eyes, he moved with a vitality I'd not seen in him in days. Swinging through a forehanded blow, he opened a gibberer from hip to spine, then lunged to the left, punching through the breastbone to the heart of another. His blade came around in a parry, then whipped back up as if his arm was a spring. He laid his foe open from hip to hip, then glided forward, slicing here, stabbing there, hacking off a limb beyond.

A man behind me screamed. I whirled, then fell back on my buttocks as the *sullanciri* came flying through the air toward the forecastle. It hit the tower hard, shaking it, and bouncing me across the deck. Its hands closed over the railing. The shields mounted there screamed as its grip bent them backwards. The Dark Lancer hauled itself up to the forecastle deck, then reached out and closed a hand over a paralyzed man's head.

The sound of sizzling flesh overrode the man's muffled scream. A sharp crack exploded and sticky wetness covered me. The man's body dropped away. The *sullanciri* opened its fist, looked at the crumpled ball of metal that had been a helmet, then cast it aside with the contempt of a child discarding an ugly rock.

The creature slammed one metal fist against its chest and the peal cut through the din of battle. The gibberers looked up to the forecastle and howled. Leigh raised his bloody sword skyward in a challenge. The Dark Lancer waved Leigh forward, but my friend laughed contemptuously. Without looking, he flicked his blade out in a backhanded cut, decapitated a gibberer sneaking up on him, then pointed to the main deck.

The *sullanciri* leaped down from the forecastle, crushing oak decking and scattering several gibberers. It stalked forward. A terrible glee lit Leigh's face as he stepped over bodies in his approach to the *sullanciri*. I rose to my feet as Leigh brought Temmer up into a guard and I noticed, for the first time, that the gold blade's purple runes burned as intensely as the Dark Lancer's eyes.

Quick enough to be little more than a blur, Leigh struck. The Dark Lancer's right arm came up to block. The gold blade's arc slashed partway through the iron warrior's flesh, half severing the limb above the wrist. The *sullanciri* recoiled, its left hand clutching right forearm. Purple fire oozed from between its fingers, dripping free, to splatter the deck with tiny flames.

Leigh laughed aloud and snapped his blade toward a knot of gibberers. The purple gore sprayed out, igniting fur. Leigh used his free hand to wave the Dark Lancer forward. "You've met your match. Come and die."

The *sullanciri*, while speechless, was not stupid. It stamped its right foot down, springing up several deck planks. One caught Leigh in the right knee, the other came up beneath his left foot, catapulting him into the air. When he came down, Leigh hit hard, landing with his back on a helmet. He bounced once, and Temmer twisted out of his grasp. Its gold glow faded, and a palsy shook Leigh.

I stooped and snatched up a pair of grapnels, one in each hand. Whirling the one in my right hand by the chain, I arced it at the Dark Lancer. The grapnel arced out over the *sul-*

lanciri's right shoulder, then the chain attached to it began to wrap around his torso. The metal links clattered across its chest, then the grapnel swung up past the *sullanciri*'s left hip and entangled its three tines on the chain.

I gave the chain one violent jerk, rattling the bulk of it against the monster's chin. "My turn, now."

The *sullanciri* turned within the chain's embrace, then reached out and wrapped the slack around its injured forearm. It gave the chain a little tug, which carried me to the forecastle rail. I let more of the chain slip between my fingers, stopping it from hauling me to the deck below. It smiled, then jiggled the chain again.

I nodded and slid over the railing, then dropped to the deck in the forecastle's shadow. Chains from both grapnels pooled at my feet. Beyond the Dark Lancer I could see Leigh crawling over the deck, his right hand reaching for Temmer's hilt. Only Leigh and his sword could destroy this thing—of that I felt certain—but I didn't know how long it would take Leigh to recover.

I just had to buy him the time.

I dropped to one knee and raked the grapnel in my left hand through the links of the other chain, and then through the anchor chain. I lashed out with my right hand, snapping the catch off the windlass, then launched myself in a forward somersault over the flailing chains. The anchor's weight whipped the chains out through the little port, taking up all the slack in the chain I'd hung on the *sullanciri*.

For a heartbeat it looked as if my tactic might succeed. The chain's tugging warped the *sullanciri*'s right forearm, allowing more of the fiery blood to gush from it. The Dark Lancer stumbled a couple of steps toward the bow. I rolled to the left to avoid being trampled, but Chytrine's creature hunched its shoulders, bent its powerful legs, and dug its heels into the deck. Yellow curls of wood gathered beneath the creature's heels as it hauled back, then twisted, catching the chain on its right shoulder and hauling its burden back toward midships.

When it turned, it turned straight into Leigh.

Leigh's double-handed blow cleaved Temmer straight through the *sullanciri*'s left knee. In falling over, the severed limb shook the deck and cracked planks. Purple fire pulsed from the stump in gouts that crisped wood and ignited gibberkin corpses. The anchor's weight tugged at the unbalanced figure, dragging it off its one good leg. The *sullanciri* flopped onto its back, purple fire trailing in its wake as the anchor dragged it toward the wales. Leigh leaped through the jetting flames, raising his sword high as he flew. He hurtled through the air, all gold with purple highlights, as if he were some heroic statue in a temple to Kedyn. He stabbed Temmer down, driving it with all his strength through the monster's breast. The blade sank in to the hilt, with purple flames licking up around it, anchoring the *sullanciri* to the deck.

Leigh, one knee on the monster's chest, screamed triumphantly. The golden glow and purple fire cast his face in a mask of martial fury. His expression was enough to send a half-dozen gibberers diving overboard. Laughing boldly, he raised his fists in victory.

This broke his connection to the sword.

He wavered, then slumped to the left and fell into my arms.

CHAPTER 24

I let Leigh slip to the deck, then drew my sword and bisected the first gibberer leaping at me over the *sullanciri*'s body. He flew past on my left, curling himself around his rent belly, then slammed into the forecastle's wall and sagged to the deck. A sailor's poleax split the skull of the next one, then Nay blasted through the wall of gibberers headed in my direction. Side by side, we shielded Leigh from their attacks.

The *sullanciri*'s death had broken the spirit of many of the gibberers. A few remained to oppose us, but even they dove for their small boats as their support evaporated. We threw off their grapnels, happy to let them go, then laughed as someone shooting the grand crossbow drove a shaft through a hull and water geysered up.

The black storm clouds broke over us and brought with them a bone-chilling rain. Thunder cracked, and the ship's deck rocked. The howling wind drove sheets of rain at us and scoured the ships of blood. The only advantage was that it put out the few fires burning on our decks.

The onslaught of the weather was as fearsome as it was sudden, and gave Lord Norrington no choice but to order the fleet to retreat to the harbor town where the merchantmen were waiting. He did send a prize crew onto the brig and had them sail the Aurolani ship after us. Our fleet captured a few other enemy ships, including two of their galleys. A couple of our galleys dragged the smaller ships back with them, not having the crew or time necessary to cast them off.

We ran before the wind, making for Mirvostok. We came around a small headland and entered a narrow bay that was fed by a small river. The storm still raged over the landscape, but the ocean became far more calm within the harbor. Small fishing boats headed out toward us and guided us to safe moorings. Since the *Invictus'* anchor had been fouled, we moored the ship to the *Venator*. Most folks thought we should have just cut the old anchor away and used the dead *sullanciri* in its place.

Once in port, we moved Leigh to an inn, got him a hot bath, some soup, and a little ale. Nay and I stayed with him as he began to come around. His color improved, a little pink brightening the grey of his flesh. Despite strict orders from his father to remain in bed, Leigh dressed warmly and went out to the *Invictus* to recover his sword. He drew it from the *sullanciri* as if it had been sheathed in straw, then slid it home in its scabbard and returned with us to the inn.

Up in the room he collapsed on the bed. Nay pulled Leigh's boots off, then Leigh crawled beneath a down comforter. He propped himself up on the pillows and nodded at Temmer, which hung by his sword belt over the nearest bedpost. "Let me have it, please, Hawkins." He patted the bed beside him and I laid the blade there.

He rested his hand on it and closed his eyes for a second. A look of serenity passed over his face. "Thank you, my friend."

"My pleasure."

He opened his eyes. His hand stroked Temmer's hilt. "Yes, you too, Hawkins. If not for your quick thinking, things would have been much more difficult."

Nay frowned. "If not for Hawkins, the Iron Prince would have had you gushing up between his toes."

Leigh laughed. "Ah, such a jest. I had Temmer back in hand quickly enough."

"Your quickly looked like sloth to me. If Hawkins hadn't dropped a chain on Wresak, you'd have been done for. We all would have."

Leigh blinked his eyes. "Wresak . . . Yes, that was Wresak."

I glanced at Nay. "You know the *sullanciri*'s name? How?"

"Tale told to armorers. King of Noriva had an ailing son named Wresak. The king got the idea that the artisans could create a metal body for his son. It would do for him what Temmer does for Leigh. The Prince, though, he didn't like how it felt in it. He got himself out and never used it again. It stayed in Noriva's palace until Kree'chuc attacked. Wresak's youngest great-grandson, also named Wresak, decided the Iron Prince could be used to defeat the Aurolani Horde. He fought against them initially, then his lust for power took over and he became Chytrine's plaything. He destroyed his brothers, destroyed his nation."

Leigh slowly nodded. "I knew that story, but thought I'd dreamed it. Perhaps I did dream it, with Temmer in hand."

Nay frowned at Leigh's musing, then shrugged. "At least, I think that's who that was. If not, there's another one out there."

Leigh's eyes brightened. "Bring him on. I'll carve him up as easily as I did this one."

I exchanged a quick glance with Nay, then patted Leigh on the leg. "Get some sleep." I looked past him and out the window at the rain pouring down. "We'll be here for a while."

I got something to eat with Nay, then we went in search of Lord Norrington. We found him at another inn, in the company of Princes Augustus and Scrainwood, as well as a number of other advisors. Prince Scrainwood objected to our presence, but Lord Norrington waved that objection away. "If not for them, I'd not be here. They stay."

The expedition's leaders worried over charts showing the coast of Okrannel. Mirvostok was located on the eastern shore roughly thirty to forty miles from Crozt. The coast road running up to Crozt and then down around to Svarskya would be the fastest overland route to the Okrannel capital. Going directly inland would require us to travel over some of the highest mountains in Okrannel, and we had no passes to speed us on our way. Heading up the coast road would present no problem, save that the Dnivep River cut deeply across the base of the Crozt peninsula, all but severing it. The Radooya Bridge spanned the river gorge on the coast road, and a company could hold that bridge against an army.

But sailing out and around Crozt to get to Svarskya likewise presented a problem. The locals told us the sea only acted the way it was when Tagothcha was awake, and it didn't take much imagination to figure out that Chytrine's forces had awakened the sea's *weirun*. They assumed she'd bribed it with fabulous gifts, inspiring it to work against us. While the harbor's *weirun* was able to keep us safe and the water calm—thanks to gifts the locals made—Tagothcha's anger meant we were bottled up here until such time as he got bored and let us go.

To make matters worse, refugees from Crozt had already passed down the coast road and gathered in Mirvostok. The stories they told were not pretty, nor were they likely exaggerated. Chances seemed excellent that part of the force that had been landed at Crozt would be headed down to Mirvostok. The town's landward defenses weren't bad, but they were not up to holding off a determined Aurolani horde. Taking the town wasn't necessary, they just had to keep us here defending it. That would give Chytrine's troops plenty of time to lay siege to Svarskya.

Prince Scrainwood stabbed a finger at the bridge on the map. "I propose we send troops forward to defend the bridge. A small number of us can hold the bridge against the forces chasing refugees. Prince Augustus's cavalry and the Oriosan Guards should do the trick. This will free the rest of you to swing around and relieve Svarskya."

Prince Augustus smiled. "We can do it, I'm certain. It will take us no time at all to reach the bridge."

The grim smiles and nods of the others gathered in the room seemed to show approval for the plan, but Lord Norrington still stared at the map. He pressed his left hand over his mouth and let his right hand ride the dagger hilt at his right hip. I wondered what he was looking for, and suddenly I thought I saw it.

"Of course." I smiled, then raised my hands to apologize for my whispered comment. "Forgive me."

"No, no, Hawkins, no apology needed." Lord Norrington pointed his left hand at the map. "Tell me what you see."

I squeezed my way through the ranks to the table. "A couple of things. The fleet that met us probably came down from Crozt, which meant they were sailing for a good eight hours before the battle was joined. That would mean that spies on Wruona probably used *arcanslata* to inform the Aurolani we were coming. Attacking us where they did, and using the Crescent Sea against us, they pretty much made Mirvostok the only harbor we could hide in. Given that the fleet had at least eight hours of warning, we have to assume land troops did as well. Chances are they've already reached the Radooya Bridge and may even be on this side of it."

Lord Norrington looked up at Prince Scrainwood. "I think Hawkins has the right of it. If I let you two go, you could well run into a large force already on the road."

Scrainwood curled a lip in my direction, then nodded to Lord Norrington. "I realize the potential risk, but have we another course?" Sarcasm dripped through his words as he asked, "Perhaps you have another plan, Hawkins?"

I shouldn't have risen to the bait, but I did. "Well, if we were able to land a force *north* of the bridge and hold it or destroy it, that would cut off the force that's moving against us now. That would lessen the troops we'll face at Crozt or Svarskya."

Scrainwood traced his finger along the coast near the bridge. "It's all impassable; says so here on the map. Nearest you could land would be twenty miles north of the bridge."

"Begging your pardon, Highness, that's not 'zactly so." A grizzled old native fisherman scratched at his throat. "This map here, it's by royal warrant. Smugglers here about, so I'm told, know of places where a ship can land to the north. The cliffs there is fierce, but birds nest on 'em and sheep get stuck on them, so they're not impossible to climb. Or so smugglers brag."

Prince Augustus laughed lightly while Scrainwood reddened. "Well, Hawkins, it seems your plan has merit. Problem is that shipping a force to your cliffs is impossible, given the state of the sea. Or do you have a solution to that?"

I shrugged uneasily. "How is it that Tagothcha knows which ships have offered him something for safe passage?"

The fisherman smiled, revealing a half-dozen yellowed teeth scattered in his jaws. "We offer wine. Tagothcha isn't terrible particular for vintage and isn't hard to trick. Vinegar serves some times, in bad years. We let it pour down the sides of the ship. He knows by feel which ships have been touched."

"Doesn't matter who crews them?"

"It's the ships not the men, near as I can figure."

I clapped my hands. "Perfect. Heslin was trying to explain *arcanslata* to me, and he said there was a magick Law of Contagion—things that touched other things bore some of their essence. I know we have some small ships that we can use to send a force north to destroy the bridge. The rest of our ships, though, ought to get through if we trick Tagothcha. If we take apart some of the captured boats and nail some of the planking to our hulls, that contagion thing should make all our ships seem right for passage."

Lord Norrington's eyes narrowed as he regarded me. "Do you mean to suggest you understand that much about magick, Hawkins?"

"No, my lord. You'll be wanting to check with Heslin on all this."

"Then how . . . ?"

I blushed. "It's just camouflage, my lord. If we look like an Aurolani fleet, we'll be safe. By the time the mistake is spotted, we'll be in Svarskya, or better yet, Chytrine will be angry enough to stop sacrificing to Tagothcha, giving us a chance to win him over."

"Ah, I see it clearly now. Thank you."

Prince Augustus frowned. "The key problem I see with this plan is that if we succeed, we'll leave an Aurolani army trapped here in the south, bound for Mirvostok."

"I agree, which means we'll have to evacuate the town. We'll organize that effort while our force heads north." Lord

Norrington nodded, then pointed to Prince Augustus. "You won't be able to take horses, but I would have you lead the taskforce going north. Prince Scrainwood will be your second. I suggest you pick people who climb well."

"I will. I'd also like people who see clearly." The prince nodded to me. "If I might, Lord Norrington, I would take your aide, your son, and even Master Carver with me."

Scrainwood frowned. "They're mere boys, Augustus."

"As mere boys they were at Atval, Scrainwood. As men they slew a *sullanciri*. Don't question why I want them with us, question why I would not."

Lord Norrington looked at Nay and me, then nodded. "If you were yet boys, I'd keep you here; but none of us are safe on this expedition. Go with the blessings of Kedyn."

CHAPTER 25

As the sun died the next day, we made our move. Two of the small boats we'd captured from the enemy fleet hauled anchor and spread sail. Rain still lashed us, and lightning still flashed. Ballistae on the other ships shot flaming balls of pitch high through the sky, but our little ships evaded them. Cries went up about the escape of prisoners, but we quickly left the chase ships behind and slipped around the headland into the Crescent Sea.

As we came into the open ocean, the waves increased, pounding the headland mercilessly. One of the galleys pursuing us came into view and the waves battered it. The ship turned about, barely avoiding being grounded on the far side of the harbor's mouth.

For us it was clear sailing, though all of us felt miserable. The rain still soaked us, and our new cloaks did not help much. We'd spend most of the day dressing out dead gibberers and pulling their flesh on over our leather armor. Heslin couldn't be certain if disguising ourselves as gibberers would help deceive Tagothcha, but he knew it wouldn't hurt. Fortunately for us, the lack of sun and general coolness meant the skins had not begun to stink too badly.

On each boat we had thirty-six individuals. Twelve of us rowed at any one time. All the crew were volunteers and representative of all parts of the force. Princes Augustus and Scrainwood led, but each ship had a dozen Loquelves in addition to men. Our ship also had Seethe and the urZrethi, Faryaah-Tse Kimp, aboard.

The inclusion of the urZrethi surprised me. I know it was because of her size—it seemed to me that someone so childlike couldn't possibly scale a three-hundred-foot cliff, much less scale one that was supposed to be impassable. Doing it while carrying over a hundred yard of line looped over her body just didn't seem possible.

Once, standing in the bow of the ship I smiled at my sulfur-colored companion. "Are you sure you can make the climb?"

"I am from Tsagul. I have spent my whole life in the mountains."

"I know, but I thought the urZrethi spent their time *in* the mountains, not climbing around on the outside of them."

"Even the interiors can require climbing skill, Hawkins." She brushed her left hand against the bow wale, then tapped a finger on a board that had warped up away from the one beneath it. "This is why I will climb first."

She stiffened the fingers of her left hand. More quickly than slow, her fingers and thumb merged. The whole hand assumed a sharp wedge shape, which she shoved into the gap. I heard a cracking sound, and a piece of the board splintered and came up. She pulled it away with her right hand. The tip of her left hand had expanded into a block, which had broken the wood. As she pulled her hand free, the wedge flexed. In a heartbeat she waggled her fingers at me.

My jaw worked, but I had nothing to say.

Faryaah-Tse grinned broadly. "UrZrethi have a certain flexibility to our form. We find it . . . useful."

"I can see that." I shrugged uneasily. "And you wear no weapons or armor because . . ."

In an eyeblink her left hand lengthened and tightened into a stout shortsword blade. "Why chance losing something you don't need? I cannot shoot bits of myself as arrows, but most of my fighting is done well inside an archer's range."

"But doesn't it hurt when you get hit?"

Faryaah-Tse shrugged as her hand returned to normal. "Does it ever *not* hurt?"

"Good point."

Our trip north took just under three hours. We located the tiny smuggler's cove and beached our ships. We made them fast with lines to the rocks, since the tide was running low and they'd be afloat by the time we returned. We armed ourselves. I went with only a sword and gibberer longknife. Archery we were leaving to the Loquelves.

Faryaah-Tse scrambled up the cliff as easily as I might scuttle across the beach on hands and feet. I couldn't see her much past a hundred feet up, but in no time at all her coil of rope unwound down the cliff. Nay went up next, carrying two more coils, then a couple of Alcidese warriors from the west made the climb. Once all five lines had been secured at the top of the cliff, the rest of us began our ascent. Those who could climb did and those who could not—like Heslin—would be hauled up last.

Three hundred feet doesn't sound like much, but when the rocks are rain-slicked, your fingers are cold, and everything you're wearing is water-logged, the distance seems likely never to end. My feet slipped a couple of times, raking my legs against the rocks. I might have fallen once, but an outcropping caught my belt and held me long enough to find my footholds again. By the time I neared the top, my shoulders and back burned and my legs quivered.

Nay grabbed the scruff of my gibberskin neck and hauled me onto the flat at the top of the cliff. Ahead, I saw the outlines of a couple of the Loquelves crouched on a hill that would take us to the main plateau. The coast road, if the charts had been at all right, would be two dozen yards past the crest of the hill.

Beyond them, limned in the weak grey light the moon projected through occasional breaks in the clouds, I saw the Radooya Bridge. The stone span arched regally over the

Dnivep River. Four stone pillars rose from the river's mist to support the bridge. Little obelisks added spikes to the bridge's curve, and fires guttered at their peaks.

The sheer size of the bridge did not register until I realized I still had a mile's worth of march to reach it. The bridge had to be five hundred yards long. The only consolation I got was the confirmation that the obelisks were too small to house any sort of a garrison.

By midnight we'd all gathered at the top of the cliff. The Loquelves went forward, moving through the forest on the north side of the gorge while the rest of us shambled down the road. We all assumed the gibberers and vylaens left to hold the bridge would have good night vision, but just how much detail they could pick out we couldn't guess. We hoped we'd look like a relief unit, so Faryaah-Tse, wearing the skin of a vylaen, marched in front of us.

Seethe returned from scouting with the Loquelves and found us before we made the final turn in the road to the bridge. "Twenty gibberers at this end and an estimate of the same at the far end. The bridge's arc prevents us from seeing them, though two vylaens are stationed in the middle to watch both ends."

Prince Augustus nodded at her report. "Can the archers kill the vylaens?"

Scrainwood snorted. "Two hundred fifty yards or more for a shot? At night, in the rain? Very difficult."

Leigh shook his head violently enough for his gibberer-flesh hood to fall back. "Doesn't matter. Have them shoot the near garrison. We'll be on them and through and get the vy-laens."

"Workable plan." Prince Augustus dispatched Seethe back to the Loquelves with their assignments. Leigh grabbed Nay and me and hauled us to one side.

"Listen, stay with me. Speed's the key here." He smiled and rested his hand on Temmer's hilt. "First, fast, victorious."

At Prince Augustus' order we moved out, marching quickly along the road. As we came within sight of the bridge, I noticed two things. The first was that the garrison of gibberers was mostly lying down on the bridge, sleeping. A handful of them paced at the foot or leaned against the obelisks at the near end. The guttering flames highlighted the wetness of their fur, while the pitter-pat of raindrops on our disguises drowned out anything they might have been grumbling.

We closed to thirty yards before the sentries seemed to take any notice of us. Two started toward us, walking casually, and one raised a hand. He howled something, not loudly, but clearly expected a response.

Before we could have answered him, and before Prince Augustus gave any order, Leigh drew Temmer and started to sprint at the bridge. Each footfall splashed muddy water from the road's wagon-wheel ruts. There was a madness in his dash that infected me, for I ran a step behind him. I held my sword aloft the same as he did, and I heard Nay bellowing behind me. Raindrops danced hard on the roadway and bridge and all sound save the hoarse thunder of my own breath seemed dulled.

Ahead, gibberers stirred and threw back sodden blankets. Then their movements became jerky as arrows fell among them. One gibberer, with both hands clutching the arrow in his throat, splashed facedown in a puddle. Other figures spun, smacking into the bridge's posts or walls before they fell. Two seeking to rise crashed back to the bridge's cobbled surface and yet another curled up around the arrow in his belly.

I remember with crystal clarity the shocked look on the face of one slow riser. An arrow hit inches in front of his muzzle. The arrow bounced straight back up in the air, much as the gibberer sat bolt upright in surprise.

And that astonished look remained on his face as Leigh's blade swept through his neck. The gibberer's head began a lazy tumble through the air. Dripping blood merged with the black rain, and the body sagged to the ground.

My two-handed swordcut caught a gibberer over his right hip. I opened him up cleanly and spun him away. He flew into the bridge's wall, then landed hard on his cut flank. I saw him struggle to rise, but his feet found no purchase on wet stone. He convulsed once, then flopped forward onto his face.

In an eyeblink we were through the gibberer line and racing toward the vylaens in the center of the bridge. One faced away from us and raised a hand. A gout of green flame shot up from his palm. He waved his arm in our direction and I assumed he was summoning help from the bridge's far end. The other one moved toward us and set himself, undaunted by the taunts Leigh shrieked.

That this creature was waiting for us made no sense. I couldn't figure out why it wasn't doing anything as we closed. I thought for a second that perhaps our disguises had confused it, but then I saw a glint in its dark eyes and I knew why it waited.

We weren't yet in range.

Leigh ran a step or two in front of me and I knew he had to be the vylaen's target. The gold glow from Temmer, the shrieking, all of it made Leigh the greatest threat. And, as powerful as Leigh's sword might be, could it save him from a spell?

He was running into a trap and didn't know it. I put my head down and picked up my speed. Leigh had never before beaten me in a footrace. Magick sword and a head start or no, if I let him beat me now, I'd be killing him.

It didn't occur to me until I'd shoved him aside and seen the spark blossom in the vylaen's right palm that by removing him as a target, I'd pretty much transferred that honor to myself. Leigh started to go down. I twisted to the right and leaped to avoid his sword, but the hilt still caught me in the ankle, spinning me more and exposing my back to the vylaen.

I caught a quick glimpse of those running behind me. Nay was leaping over Leigh's fallen form. Back a half-dozen paces came Faryaah-Tse, Prince Augustus, and a knot of Alcidese warriors. Then a wall of heat hit me and green flames eclipsed my view. The thick scent of burning fur choked me. I landed heavily on my back, flinging my heels up over my head. I somersaulted over and landed in a kneeling position.

I heard a meaty wet *thwack* from behind me and came up on one knee as I turned toward the sound. A vylaen with a serious concavity on the right side of his chest—so serious it looked as if his shoulder started where ribs normally end—bounced off the cobbles. On my right Faryaah-Tse flashed past to shove a handblade through the chest of the other vylaen.

All about me hung tattered, charred and smoking bits of gibberer flesh. I felt a stinging burn radiate out from between my shoulders, which was where I guessed the spell had hit me. The disguise, though far from fooling the vylaen, had burned off the virulence in the spell, leaving me alive and relatively unscathed.

Leigh lunged to his feet with an insane fire in his eyes. He started in my direction, his blade coming back for a stroke, then the howls of charging gibberers snapped his head to the left. He answered them in kind and started running toward the enemy.

The rest of us ran after him. *We* knew he wasn't invulnerable, but he didn't seem to have a clue about that. Leigh's charge, had he been mounted on a warhorse and at the head of a heavy cavalry unit, might well have carried him clean through the score of gibberers coming at us. On foot, however, armed with only a sword and as small as he was, he might as well have hurled himself against a wall.

The charging gibberers, on the other hand, seemed impressed with the little golden tongues of flame playing over Temmer's edges. They'd also seen two vylaens die and me engulfed in flame, yet keep on coming. As Leigh screamed at them and whirled his blade in a circle above his head, they slowed, then some at the edges turned. The gibberer line collapsed.

Leigh sailed into them, Temmer describing golden disks that sliced through arms and legs, spines and heads. His first victim still twitched on the ground before I reached the pack. With a quick slash I hamstrung one, then brought my blade up and around in a two-handed cut that split another from shoulder to the small of its back.

Our charge carried us through their pack and we turned to face them. The gibberers at the edge sidled away, but Augustus and his men fell on them. Nay's maul pulped skulls. Faryaah-Tse clawed her hands and raked them through bellies and throats. Warm blood chased away the rain's chill as I slashed a gibberer's throat.

Throughout the slaughter, Leigh's battle cries rose above the whimpers and groans of the dying. I shivered to hear him, though not because my friend sounded insane. What made me shiver was that some part of me shared that madness. We stood there with rainwater washing blood over our feet and I was happy, I was proud.

I felt as if all I was ever meant for was killing.

I shivered again, then began the long trudge back to the bridge's north side. As we came over the crest, a crouched man rose from beside one of the gibberer bodies and walked toward us. I could tell it was Scrainwood from the way his long locks hung limp in the rain. His right hand ended in a poniard and his sword remained in its scabbard. In his left hand he held a gibberer scalp.

Scrainwood brandished the dagger. "They're all dead. I've made certain of that."

Augustus pointed back toward the bridge's far side. "The garrison there is dead, too, or soon will be."

The Prince of Oriosa twirled his blade between his fingers. "I'll make sure."

I held up a hand. "They're dead."

Scrainwood went to say something to me, but Heslin cut him off. "There's no time to be about silliness. Get over here. We need to get this bridge down now."

As we left the bridge, Seethe and the elven archers joined us. Aside from a couple of men who had taken some fairly superficial cuts—in one case a warrior had gashed his own leg when he missed with an ax stroke—we'd come away unhurt. The battle's result was nothing short of miraculous, and had to be attributed to planning, surprise, and Leigh's magickal sword.

The magicker dropped on one knee and pressed his good hand to the bridge's base. "This first spell will loosen the mortar. You can remove the paving stones, then we get down to the supports. If they're wood, we can burn them. Otherwise I'll have to use some other magicks."

A white-blue glow brightened beneath his palm, then little sparks shot out like bugs, racing along the lines of mortar. They jigged and jagged, left and right, curving around some stones, angling between others. Had the bridge been ice and they cracks, the structure would have fallen apart in a heartbeat. As it was, the sparks played out maybe six feet from where Heslin touched the bridge.

The mage sat back and shook the gibberer-flesh hood free of his head. "That is odd."

Prince Augustus frowned. "What's the matter?"

"That spell should have shattered the mortar, and it should have extended all the way across it."

"Why didn't it?"

Heslin shrugged, then stood. "I think the bridge is alive."

Scrainwood's jaw dropped open. "What insanity is this? How can a bridge be alive?"

The magicker turned and coldly regarded the prince. "It has a *weirun*."

"Not possible. It's man-made." Scrainwood waved the suggestion away with both hands. "Destroy the bridge and be quick about it."

Heslin's voice took on an edge. "I am a man. My magicks work well on inanimate objects. Were I older, more learned, I might be able to destroy it with a spell."

"Older?" Scrainwood turned to the elves. "What about you, have you magick talent? You're all older."

The Loquelves looked at Scrainwood with expressions running from mild amusement to cold contempt. Seethe just shook her head.

Faryaah-Tse Kimp pointed a yellow finger at the bridge. "Look."

It took me a moment to see it and, at first, I mistook it for a little wave of water washing down the stones and distorting them. Then I realized that the distortion came from the stones themselves. Something was moving toward us as if it had burrowed beneath the stone's flesh. When it neared our end of the bridge, it slowed and gently prodded the gibberers' bodies. It sank back into the stone for a moment, then reappeared.

As the bump grew, it took on a vaguely humanoid form. It had a head—sort of a misshapen lump that sat directly on broad shoulders. The arms had a sweeping curve that roughly mirrored the bridge's arc. A perfectly shaped keystone about the size of my fist lay centered in its chest. The shoulders tapered down into a narrow waist, then broadened back out into powerful thighs and legs with broad stable feet.

The bridge's *weirun* appeared to be made exactly like the bridge, with all the stones composing it fitted together and then joined with mortar. Natural depressions in the face served as eye sockets, but only shadows resided there. The spirit shifted its shoulders to look at us, then reached down with a hand to prod one of the dead gibberers.

"Why do they not wake up?" Its voice grated harshly, while resembling the whine of the wind through the pillars and obelisks. Despite the inhuman nature of its voice, the question came with a childlike innocence. "Why do they leak?"

Heslin canted his head toward the *weirun*. "You see, Prince Scrainwood, the bridge *is* alive."

Scrainwood said nothing, but Augustus frowned. "How can this be, Heslin? This bridge, it's all of five hundred years old. How can it have a *weirun*?"

The mage shrugged. "Perhaps the ghosts of men who died building it imbued the bridge with their essence. Perhaps the bridge is so important that the very fact of its existence demanded a spirit inhabit it. I don't know."

The urZrethi bowed her head to the *weirun*. "Forgive the rudeness. They will not wake because they are dead. They leak because we have killed them."

The *weirun* slammed its hands together, striking sparks. All of us save the urZrethi leaped back, and Scrainwood a bit more than most. "They guarded me. Why kill them?"

Faryaah-Tse gentled her voice. "They were not guarding you; they made you into a trap."

"No, no, not a trap." The *weirun* stamped a foot. "They guaranteed safe passage."

"For their kind."

"They guaranteed safe passage!"

Scrainwood snorted. "It's an imbecile and it's working for Chytrine."

Seethe narrowed her golden eyes at Scrainwood. "If it is an imbecile, as you suggest, can it be responsible for its conduct?"

"Immaterial and irrelevant, Seethe." The prince sneered at

her. "We need the bridge down, alive or not. It's mentally unsound. It is a retard." He flicked a hand at Leigh. "You have a magick sword. Kill it. That will destroy the bridge, won't it?"

I reached out to stay Leigh's hand, but he made no move to draw Temmer.

"No!" Nay stepped between Leigh and the *weirun* and stabbed his spike into the earth, almost pinning one of Scrainwood's feet to the ground. "Don't matter if it's dull or not. No killing."

"But we need the bridge down."

Nay growled and poked Scrainwood in the nose with his index finger. "My way or not at all."

Heslin nodded. "Please, Master Carver."

With his hands open, Nay walked over to the *weirun*. "The killing had to be done. You remember, before they came, there were others."

"I remember."

Nay kept his voice soft, using the same tones I had heard my parents use when speaking to a child. While the *weirun* might have been born with the bridge, it was but a child as far as spirits, gods, and godlings were concerned.

Nay smiled tentatively. "And you remember they were scared, very scared."

The *weirun* drew a stony hand across his cheek. "Their eyes rained on me."

"Because they were afraid, very afraid. They were being chased." Nay spoke slowly, as if telling a story to a child. He'd clearly figured out that this *weirun* was childlike, not slow, the way Scrainwood described him. *It is slow, but only slow in the way a river cuts a gorge. Nay's dealing with this* weirun *the only way possible.*

Nay sat down, crossing his legs in front of himself, and the *weirun* likewise sat. "The friends of these dead ones were chasing the frightened people. They are gone from here. For now. But they will return. Up the road are more who are scared. When the bad ones return, the scared people will run, or will leak and be dead."

"Leak and be dead." The *weirun* reached out and stroked

one of the gibberer corpses as if it were a dead kitten. "Dead is bad."

"You always help people. You are strong for them. You carry them across the river. You protect them." Nay smiled. "You protect them very well."

The *weirun* nodded slowly. "I protect them."

"But now, the bad ones will be returning. They will use your strength to hurt the others. You will help the bad ones. You will help them make others leak and be dead." A tremble entered Nay's voice. "More people will die because you help the bad ones."

"Dead is bad."

"Dead is very bad." A distant rumble of thunder underscored Nay's words. "If you want, you can help us stop the bad ones."

"Yes, help."

"The cost will be great. It will be everything. But, it will be less than the pain of knowing that you hurt others. Do you understand?"

The *weirun*'s head flowed around in a circle to survey the bridge. "If I am here, others will be dead."

"Yes."

"If I am not here, I will be dead."

Nay's lower lip quivered and he nodded wordlessly. "You will live in our memories for this bold act."

"It is not enough."

"What?"

"I was bad. I will be no more. No more pain from me, but I know pain." The *weirun* extended a hand and touched Nay over his heart. "You will help me. Help me atone for the pain."

"I will."

"You will promise me."

Nay's reply came in a hoarse whisper. "I promise."

The *weirun* flowed back to his feet and pulled Nay to his with one hand. The spirit's hand then touched his own chest and pulled free the keystone there. It glowed and sparkled with internal fire, in an instant transformed from lifeless stone to an opalescent gem. The *weirun* reached out and pressed the stone into Nay's hands, then gave him a little shove that propelled him back off the bridge.

Bit by bit, stone by stone, the *weirun* began to crumble. Behind it, starting at the highest point of the arch, the bridge came apart. Obelisks teetered and toppled, streaking fire as they fell. Whole chunks of the roadbed sank from sight. The crackling thunder of mortar parting and stones splitting filled the air. Faster and faster the collapse came, gobbling up pieces of the roadway. Stones cascaded down into the dark valley below, bouncing and spinning off each other.

Finally the last of it went, taking with it the bodies of the gibberers and the gravel traces that had been the *weirun*. Even the massive stone footings ripped free of the earth, splashing mud and bits of sod over us. As they tumbled into the gorge, they rebounded from the stone sides and careened into the bridge's support pillars. The footstones snapped the pillars in half, scattering stones like seed from a farmer's hand.

Scrainwood snorted. "Well, at least that's done."

I stepped past the prince and knelt beside Nay. He clutched the glowing keystone to his chest, seemingly oblivious to the puddle in which he lay. "Are you hurt?"

"His name, it was, it *is* Tsamoc." As Nay spoke the name, the light in the stone dulled a bit. Nay smiled and nodded, as if he could hear words I could not, then his eyes focused on mine. "Bit wet, bit hollow. That's it."

I took one arm and Leigh took the other. We tugged him to his feet. I gave him a weak smile. "I understand the hollow bit. Feel hollow myself."

Prince Augustus came over and laid his right hand on Nay's shoulder. "Just remember, what you did saved a lot of lives."

"What *he* did saved lives." Nay's nostrils flared. "When this war is all done, you'll get credit for winning it. Just remember who made the sacrifices to let you win."

Prince Augustus nodded and began to trudge back to the cove in silence. He wore an expression that told me he'd taken Nay's words to heart. Behind him came Scrainwood, and though a mask hid most of his face, his grin and the way he hung on to the gibberer's scalp told me that even *if* he'd heard Nay's words, he didn't understand them.

Only later would I realize how painful a failing on his part that would be.

CHAPTER 26

The return to our ships was much easier than the journey to the bridge, largely because sliding down ropes is easier than climbing up slippery cliffs. We didn't say much heading back. I found myself shivering and huddled against the bow wales as we set off. I knew my shivering wasn't because of the cold or the rain.

I found it very curious that there was no question in my mind we had done the right thing. The Aurolani warriors had to be destroyed. The bridge had to be destroyed. Doing what we had done was the only way we could help save the people in Crozt and Svarskya. Acting when and how we did saved countless lives—lives the Aurolani host would gladly have taken.

Even so, the elation I'd felt in the killing, the sense of power—that was wrong. Certainly, every story I'd ever heard about heroes had them celebrating their triumphs—but that impression came solely from songs and stories created by people who probably never knew the hero whose exploits they . . . well, exploited. Heroic stories and songs imparted motives and feelings to figures who had become *more* than they ever were in life.

Leigh slumped down against the bulwark next to me, his sheathed sword held loosely between his knees. The hilt touched the top of his head, the tip pressed against a bit of uneven planking. His hands clung to the crossguard. His flesh had again taken on its grey pallor. The only color remaining was little bits of blood that had not yet been washed away by the rain.

"I bet you've already composed a poem about the Battle of Radooya Bridge."

"Did you ever try to find a rhyme for bridge?"

"No."

"It's even tougher than the battle." He rubbed his right hand over his forehead. "Hawkins, there, on the bridge, you . . ."

"Don't mention it."

"No, I have to, I have to." Leigh's voice trailed off as if he had run out of strength. "You saved my life. You nearly died for it."

I shifted my shoulders. "It aches a little, but my leather saved me."

"Just listen, Hawkins, please." He took a deep breath. "When you shoved me down, I knew what you had done, but part of me didn't. Part of me saw that as an attack. You hurt me. You betrayed me. No, wait, let me finish. And when I got up, part of me wanted to make you pay. I wanted to punish you. Then the gibberers howled and I saw they were the threat. I went for them."

The dark color of his mask contrasted sharply with the bright blue of his eyes. "Temmer, it lets me do things. It makes me faster. It makes me more sure. It makes me into a hero."

I bumped him with my left shoulder. "You were a hero before that, Leigh. You got help for us in Westwood. You faced down a temeryx and saved Nay's life."

"I hear what you're saying, but I never felt like a hero in my heart. I was willing to run to get help because I was afraid to stay. And I ran to help Nay because I was afraid what people would say if he died there and I didn't help him." Leigh leaned his head back against the wooden wales. "It wasn't about me being brave, it was about me being afraid. With Temmer, that goes away. Mostly."

"What do you mean mostly?"

Leigh patted Temmer. "Don't you remember? I'll be broken in my last battle."

"Sure, but that last battle will be when you're old and your great-grandchildren are fighting over who gets to sit in your lap for a story."

Leigh laughed, but perhaps more than he should have. "Would that such a thing would happen, Hawkins, but it won't. The blade, you see, my good man, it gets into my head. It eats away at me. In Atval I saved everyone, but now, now it makes me wonder. At Atval I slew ten gibberers, but I wonder if a true hero would slay a dozen or even more. Will I eclipse my father or the heroes of the Great Revolt? It pushes me onward, makes me more daring. Makes me more reckless."

I turned toward him. "Then throw it away."

"No, can't do that."

"Yes, you can."

"No!" His eyes narrowed and he caressed the blade's hilt. "Without it I would be nothing."

"You'd still be my friend."

Leigh's expression eased. "Well, that would be *something*, anyway. But there is a more practical matter at stake here, too, Hawkins. If I pitch the sword away now, someone else will end up with it. If that person is an ally, he will be destroyed."

"You could give it to Scrainwood, but I don't think he'd draw it."

"Oh, very astute and nasty. I like it." Leigh laughed again, this time with more life. "If one of Chytrine's creatures gets it, another of the *sullanciri*, for example, we're all dead."

"There has to be a way to get you out of this trap, Leigh. You didn't know what you were doing when you took the sword."

"Maybe I did, Hawkins, maybe I did." He sighed. "The only thing of value left in a dragon-melted city, where merely trespassing invited death? I knew it was special and powerful and probably dangerous, to judge by the guardians set over it.

But then, if dragons feared its being in someone's hands, well, just the thing for me, eh?"

"Just like you dancing with Nolda—always overreaching yourself."

"True." His eyes twinkled for a moment. "But Nolda is a memory. How do you think Ryhope would look on my arm?"

The note of hope in his voice gave birth to my lie. "Only a hero like you could win a princess like her."

Leigh clapped me on the right shoulder and closed his eyes. "Let's hope she thinks the same. If she does, Hawkins, I promise you this. In all the tales of Leigh Norrington, hero, I will make sure it is well known that you, Tarrant Hawkins, were always the best friend a man could ever have."

We met up with the rest of the fleet an hour after dawn. We knew it was dawn because the storm had moved south, allowing us to actually see the sun. Part of the fleet, hauling refugees, fled south, while the rest sailed up to meet us. A flagman communicated to the *Invictus* details of our victory and Lord Norrington sent back his congratulations.

As good as that should have made us feel, the black stain in the sky rising from where Crozt should have been shrank our hearts. I'd not seen Crozt before, but from the fire-blackened ruins I could tell it had been a marvelous city. Tall towers, now shattered or belching smoke and flame, dominated the landscape. Some of the arched walkways linking them yet remained, while others reached toward each other across a gulf they could never narrow. White walls had tumbled down at points, and warehouses burned at the docks.

Even under the harsh glare of the noon sun, the city had a taint of night about it—and seemed to radiate cold. We did not make landfall there, skirting the harbor by a wide margin despite its being empty. All I could see on shore were slinking curs and ravens looking for carrion. Judging from the size of the flocks and the packs roaming the city, the search for food must not have been difficult.

We sailed into the Svarskya Gulf and headed southwest toward Okrannel's capital. As dusk fell, we came across debris from what must have been a hideous sea battle. I could pick out bits and pieces of burned hulks amid which floated the bodies of gibberers and men alike. Small fish nibbled at them while some larger fish—sharks and others—went at them with abandon. A corpse would bob for a moment, then sink from sight. Water would froth where it had been, then it would pop back to the surface again. An arm or a leg would be gone, or sometimes the head. Or just a big bite out of the middle, leaving it to trail intestines behind as if it were the thread needed to sew the wound shut again.

We did find a couple of survivors clinging to debris. Both men were in wretched shape. Their lips were cracked, their skin blistered, and they were half blind. After we got some water into them, they told a story of how the Okrans fleet sailed out from Svarskya and defeated the ships coming from the sack of Crozt. While an Aurolani army had successfully laid siege to the city from the landward side, the harbor remained in Okrans hands. Both men said the southern and western gates had not yet been breached, but they weren't certain that would be the case when we reached the city.

That night, looking southwest, we could see a distant glow. We knew at least part of the city was burning, and around midnight we came across a convoy of ships fleeing from the city itself. We arranged the transfer of a couple of harbor pilots to our boats, to enable us to travel into Svarskya's harbor safely. That these men and women were willing to go back with us spoke well of the nobility of the Okrans people.

The pilots were willing to return in no small part due to Prince Kirill's leadership, and the bravery of his family. When he had ordered the evacuation, he sent his entire family away, save his infant daughter Alexia. As the story went, Prince Kirill said to his Gyrkyme companion, Preyknosery, "I'll have no daughter of mine die in this city."

The Gyrkyme was said to reply, "My pledge she will not. Still, she is your daughter. She will remain here, to love this city as you do. She will weep as you do. Someday she will return and make it free again."

The prince accepted this statement and the defenders pledged themselves to buy the young princess every moment in the city that they could. Though the outer walls had been breached, the inner walls still held, and the defenders were forcing Chytrine to pay a fearful price for her aggression.

We arrived in Svarskya in the wee hours of the morning, just as the sun began to peek over the Crozt headland. In the inner reaches of Svarskya we could still see the tall, proud towers that marked Okrans architecture. What struck me as special about them were the bright colors they were painted, and the way tiles had been inset around windows and doors. The ornate carvings I had seen in Yslin had given way to something more subtle, and something less likely to weather in the brutal northern winters. Here the covered walkways linking buildings made perfect sense and would allow people to move about even if a blizzard blanketed them with deep snow.

The city's defenders greeted us loudly and warmly. We rotated the galleys through berthing and off-loaded our troops as quickly as we could. Leigh, Nay, and I rejoined Lord Norrington and, along with the two princes, Seethe and Faryaah-Tse Kimp, wended our way through debris-strewn streets to find Prince Kirill. Garrison forces rested in a variety of buildings and pointed us further and further into the city.

As we worked our way from the harbor to the inner city walls, it became apparent to me that the debris had been laid out specifically to hamper Aurolani forces when they broke through. If the harbor was the hub of a wheel, the streets shot out like spokes from it. Cross streets linked the spokes, making the roadway layout something akin to a cobweb. The streets had been offset so no spoke ran directly from the inner city gates directly out to the outer gates, which meant the sieging force had to use roads that paralleled the walls, letting the defenders abuse them mightily before they could reach the gates.

We found Prince Kirill easily enough and I took an instant liking to him. He stood tall and smiled broadly. His curly black hair was complemented by his moustache and goatee, and his eyes were that deep green color of pine needles. He wore a black surcoat over a full suit of mail; a winged horse rampant in white decorated the surcoat's breast, though blood did color it. That same crest graced every flag flying over the inner city's towers.

He greeted Lord Norrington as if he were a long-lost comrade. "Welcome to my city, Lord Norrington. Your arrival is much anticipated. I regret not holding more of Svarskya for you."

"You've done well to hold what you have."

Just looking out over the ramparts made it easy to tell Lord Norrington was not lying. As much as the inner city was still brightly colored and strong, the outer ring looked as if a blight had settled on it. Red-tiled roofs were holed, revealing charred rafters. Towers were stained with blood and many had the former inhabitants—or portions of them—hanging from windows or mounted on spikes on balconies or rooftops. Shadows seemed deeper down there, and gibberers and vylaens and other things moved through alleys and along roadways choked with carcasses of everything from horses and dogs to small children.

Beyond all that flew Aurolani flags. Whereas the civilized world tends toward standards that have noble creatures and other uplifting representations on them, the northern host chooses other sources of inspiration. I saw a nine-skull banner flying from one tower, and a green flag with a red quartered body on it at another. One banner was nothing more than red silk that had been slashed by a temeryx; another had been raised on a pole decorated with scalps.

Prince Kirill laughed openly. "I am flattered that Chytrine saw fit to send two of her armies after me. Most of one litters the streets out there. I have a pair of knuckle bones I roll to choose between plans, so they never know exactly where I attack. The loss of the city is foregone and I would have evacuated everyone, but there remains a problem."

Lord Norrington folded his arms over his chest. "And that is?"

Kirill pointed at one of the older towers near the harbor. "That tower was home to the fragment of the DragonCrown which we had. It is clear this is their target, and we wish to deny them the fragment."

"And the problem is?"

Prince Kirill turned around and pointed at a green tower only three blocks from where we stood. "That tower is home to the Vilwanese consulate. A year ago a number of magickers wanted to study the fragment and it was agreed to lend it to them very quietly. No one knew the fragment had been shifted there, not even my father. His sorcerer agreed to the loan in my father's name, assuming things arcane should handle themselves. My father does not know, even now, and I only know because his advisor used an *arcanslata* to communicate these facts to me."

Lord Norrington swiped his hand across his mouth. "You mean to tell me that the Aurolani forces have already taken the building holding the DragonCrown fragment?"

"Yes. Enchantments on it have proved too difficult for them to breach, but they will. I am planning a foray to the building to take back the piece of the crown."

Lord Norrington slowly shook his head. "Reckless and dangerous."

Prince Kirill arched an eyebrow. "You will help me?"

"If we can come up with a plan that will work, yes." Lord Norrington smiled. "Given that we know more than they do, chances are such a plan exists. Let's map it out and then we go."

CHAPTER 27

The plan which Prince Kirill and Lord Norrington drew up—with suitable input from Princes Augustus and Scrainwood—took advantage of what we knew about the tactical situation in Okrannel. Prince Kirill reported that the Iron Prince was the only one of Chytrine's *sullanciri* that had been spotted as part of the invading force. As nearly as Kirill knew, Chytrine only had four *sullanciri* in her entire force, so the Iron Prince's death had to be quite a blow to her plans for conquest. Still, since a *sullanciri* was supposed to command each of her armies, and two armies had been sent to take Okrannel, we could not discount the possibility that another Dark Lancer would be directing the opposition.

We did know, however, that even a *sullanciri* would find himself at a disadvantage here at Svarskya.

Because we had destroyed the Radooya Bridge, we knew the portion of the army that had gone south would require at least a week to reach Okrannel. We also assumed that if Chytrine was using Tagothcha to keep our fleet bottled up, the *weirun* would still be reporting that we'd not left the Mirvostok harbor. Even if the Aurolani troops heading south reached Mirvostok and reported we were missing—*and* Chytrine successfully guessed we were at Svarskya—her ability to blunt what we were going to do in the next day would be limited to communicating orders via *arcanslata*.

And, if her abilities weren't that limited, I really didn't want to see what she would do.

The plan developed so simply and easily that it could be seen as desperate. It certainly was. It began with trumpets blowing retreats all across the Okrans line. Men began disappearing from walls and towers, especially to the west, on the line that would take the Aurolani troops to the Crown Tower the fastest. Since Aurolani forces undoubtedly had seen our fleet arrive, and since the Okrans forces had evacuated a lot of folks by fleet before, the easiest assumption was that the troops were going to run.

And since the fleeing troops would never abandon the DragonCrown fragment, it became paramount for the Aurolani troops to break through and take the tower. The speed requirement meant that finesse was out—they'd need a full-force assault, which would mean stripping the rest of the city of troops so their drive would have serious weight of numbers to it.

Once we gave way to their attack and allowed them into the Crown Tower section of town, we'd counterattack their flank. Okrans defenders would slow their drive, then our taskforce's troops would hit from the flanks. As that distracted them, a small force would make their way to the Vilwanese consulate and recover the DragonCrown fragment. If things went well, we'd be back in time for a general retreat and evacuation. By the time the Aurolani host knew it had been hoodwinked, we'd be away.

Prince Augustus was left in command of the Crown Tower defense, and he requested Scrainwood help him. Lord Norrington must have realized that what little in the way of fellowship Leigh, Nay, and I had with Scrainwood had soured at the bridge, so he pulled us into the Thief Company. Seethe, Heslin, Faryaah-Tse Kimp, and a handful of elven warriors became thieves as well. We fitted out the rest of the force with an even mix of Okrans and taskforce warriors, stalwart men and women all. Twenty-four of us would move on the ground and another six, Gyrkyme, would move through the air to the tower, but only after we'd broken through and secured it. They'd be able to carry the fragment away while we fought our way back to safety.

The elves wanted nothing to do with the Gyrkyme and almost balked at the mission, but they knew how vital success was. Prince Kirill gave them a way to preserve their honor by noting that the elves were tasked with getting to the tower, in and back out. Their responsibility ended there. The Gyrkyme were merely tasked with getting the fragment away, so their job was not in any way involved with what the elves were doing. Though the ruse was transparent, it was a sufficient blind to let the elves participate.

I'd never seen a Gyrkyme in person before. Overall they looked to be elven, with pointed ears, sharpened facial features and long, wiry bodies. A down covered them all over, and they wore little in the way of clothes—save light jewelry or daggers strapped to arm or thigh. Longer feathers covered their wings, back, head, and neck, with the head feathers often forming a crest that rose as a Gyrkyme became excited. The furled wings towered above the Gyrkyme's heads and easily measured twenty-eight feet from tip to tip. Their coloration varied, with some almost completely white, others raven black, and Preyknosery—their leader—was colored very like a kestrel, with brown over his back, and white on his front and face, save for the distinctive dark coloring around the eyes and down by his nose.

The Gyrkyme only had four fingers and toes. The foot seemed very like a man's, save the toes were a bit elongated and might be suitable for grasping. Each toe ended in a nasty talon that I imagined could be as devastating as those of a temeryx. Their fingers likewise ended in talons, but the Gyrkyme trimmed those on their thumbs and index fingers back to where they were nothing but nubs. Those who were archers even trimmed the second finger's talon, so they could draw a bow and release it without slicing the bowstring in half.

Preyknosery had big amber eyes and swiveled his head to regard me as I entered Prince Kirill's quarters with a message from Lord Norrington. The Gyrkyme said nothing, but blinked his eyes once, slowly, then turned his head back toward Kirill. The prince smiled and looked up at him, then over at me.

"Is it time?"

"Soon."

The prince nodded, then returned his attention to the squirming bundle in his arms. "Hawkins, you've not met my daughter, have you?"

"No, Highness."

He sat her up on his left hand, supporting her head and back with his right hand. "This is Alexia, my daughter and heir." The infant tugged at a bracelet braided of pale hair that encircled the Prince's right wrist. "Her hair she gets from her mother—may the gods keep her soul. She's a happy child. She is my heart."

As difficult as it is to judge the final shape of a tree by looking at a seedling, I have trouble reading the future in the face of any infant. Comparing Alexia to what I remembered of nieces and nephews, I assumed she was half a year old at best. Her hair had come in very light, almost white, and she had two Gyrkyme feathers lashed to a small braid hanging from her left temple. The child had the most brilliant violet eyes I'd ever seen before and a big, giggling, gurgling smile.

"I can see why you are proud of her."

"She is all I have." He cradled her again in his arms, letting her little hand tug at his goatee. He laughed, then kissed her on the forehead and held her out to Preyknosery. "It is time I entrust her to you."

"There is time for that later, friend Kirill." His voice surprised me because I had expected a high and harsh sound from the Gyrkyme, but instead found his voice to be deep and resonant. "I will board a ship with you and we will sail from here."

Kirill shook his head. "No, my friend, I want you and your wing to leave here the instant the attacks begin. Your chances of escape will be highest then. Take Alexia to your home. I will come for her there."

The Gyrkyme took the child in his arms and Kirill reached out to stroke her head. "Poor child. You were robbed of your mother at birth, and your city when less than a year old. Your lifetrek begins at the base of a mighty mountain, but scale it you will." He kissed her again, then turned away.

"Go, friend Preyknosery. She is your daughter now. Go while Svarskya is still ours. Always remind her it belongs to her."

The Gyrkyme bobbed his head at the prince's back, then swept from the room. Kirill did not watch him go, but instead strapped on his sword and picked up his helmet. Turning to me, he smiled. "Come, friend Hawkins. Chytrine wants my city. The lease price has gone up again, and it is time to draw from her a very bloody payment."

Everyone in Thief Company mounted a horse save for Faryaah-Tse Kimp. She merely shifted her legs from normal into the heavy haunches of a temeryx. The change gave her a weird sort of hopping gait and allowed her prodigious leaps. Having seen temeryces in action, I had no doubt she could move fast, and the sight of her was odd enough that she might give an enemy pause before striking.

From the west we heard the sound of the gates finally giving way. The sharp crack was chased by a victorious howl. Buildings broke the sound up, but I had no trouble imagining a flood of vylaens and gibberers pouring through the gate. They'd find themselves channeled along a wide boulevard because of the debris choking alleys and cross streets, but with the Crown Tower in front of them, their concern wouldn't be with their flanks.

Archers on the wall above the south gate rose and loosed shot after shot at the nearest troops. Warriors drew the massive beam that served to bar the gates and swung them open. We poured out at full gallop, swords drawn, with Kirill and Lord Norrington in the lead, Leigh on the left flank, and Nay and me on the right with Seethe. Faryaah-Tse came up the middle, hopping and bouncing along, and the rest of our troops rode in behind the wedge we formed.

The sheer devastating force of a mounted charge against infantry cannot be underestimated. To some, including bards who have gotten no closer to combat than the occasional bar-room brawl, a horse and rider seem quite vulnerable to a man on foot. After all, a quick dodge to the rider's shield side means his swordcut will go awry, then the footman can slash at the horse and bring it down. The rider is tumbled and the footman can fall on him before he recovers.

The problem is, of course, that dodging a wall of charging horsemen is impossible. Moreover, the sheer weight of the charging horse is such that, when it catches a footman with even a glancing blow, it can shatter bones. It will, at the very least, knock the footman flying—if not kill him outright. And while a downed man becomes an obstacle that most horses would rather leap than step on, the broken footman has no way of giving chase to the cavalry. If he struggles to his feet at all, he probably will just make himself a target for their return charge.

Leigh and Nay relied on Temmer and maul respectively, but I'd armed myself with a horsebow and let fly as fast as I could find a target. I sank an arrow into one gibberer a heartbeat before Lord Norrington's charger clipped the beast with a shoulder. The gibberer spun limp-limbed through the air and snapped its back on the corner of a building.

Seethe wielded a heavy-bladed sword with the slightest of curves to it—one almost identical to the sword Resolute had used. The blade actually broadened two-thirds of the way from the hilt, then tapered back down into a sharp point suitable for lunging or spearing things. The whole of one edge had been sharpened, as well as a full third of the other edge, allowing her to slash both forehand and back. It had a simple crosshilt and a slightly curved, hardwood hilt, but otherwise appeared unadorned.

A tattooed rune on her forearm glowed with an iridescent red that spread to encompass her whole right arm. She beat aside the haft of a spear and rotated her wrist, flicking the blade with such speed that I couldn't see it. Only the blood tipping her sword and a gibberer reeling away with his severed head lolling back gave evidence of what she had done.

A volley of arrows from the wall finished the gibberer force we'd ridden through. Our hoofbeats thundered through the town as we raced for the Vilwanese tower. We reached it and the broken gate in the simple wall surrounding it. I ducked as I rode beneath the arch, then shot a vylaen that had been in the process of scaling one of the garden trellises which rose against the tower. Others of our force leaped from their saddles, laying about with sword, ax, and club. Faryaah-Tse sailed over the garden wall, crushing another vylaen beneath her feet, then lashed out and disemboweled a gibberer with a single stroke of the twin hooked blades that had replaced her right hand.

A number of vylaen corpses littered the tower's little garden, and most of them had died long before we arrived. One, burnt to a crisp, clung to the trellis and a low balcony. Burn marks around the doorway indicated where others had died trying to break into the tower. The door itself appeared to be a solid piece of obsidian, with no knob or other indication of how one was to open it, though burned and splintered remnants of roofing beams showed that a ram wouldn't work.

Heslin mounted the steps to the tower's door and passed a hand through the air before it. In the wake of his hand I saw what appeared to be strands of a web glowing a milky jade green, though the lines wavered and twisted as if I were viewing them through rippling water. The mage studied the web's shape for a moment, then he reached out and touched the door. A purple light pulsed from beneath his palm, then the stone door evaporated.

Heslin led the way. I moved into the tower behind the prince and Lord Norrington. The Archmage strode into the tower with a confident ease and strength he'd lacked since his wounding at Atval. It almost seemed as if he drew power from the building itself, which did not surprise me, since I found the place very odd.

The tower, though round, appeared to have all manner of angles to it. The place definitely seemed larger on the interior than it did on the exterior, which I found disturbing. Even more so was the fact that, as Heslin led us deeper into it, the features I saw—such as stairwells and windows, fireplaces and arches—vanished to be replaced by things just as utilitarian, but different in locations.

I pondered that for a moment, then Seethe hissed from my

right. "This place stinks of illusion. Can't you do something about that, Heslin?"

The mage snorted and glanced at her over his shoulder. "Destroying the enchantments would take more time than does warping them. Besides, the traps here will kill more Aurolani when they come to see why we entered the tower."

"Good reason, then, to keep things as they are."

"I'm so glad you approve." Heslin smiled at her. "It's probably worse for you than others since you are so open to magick."

The Vorquelf shrugged. "It's worth the trouble."

Heslin led us up through a circular stairway that had been cored in one wall. We went up past two landings and came out near the top of the tower. The room up there occupied the whole level. Windows and a doorway leading to a balcony ringed the tower. The floor had been made of blond oak planking, fitted well enough that walking on it elicited no creaking.

Hanging in the air at the center of the room was the DragonCrown fragment. The metal holding the single, fist-sized stone appeared to be gold. It looked so smooth I wondered if it weren't still fluid and if, somehow, I couldn't feel the heat from it. The stone it encircled shone with the same sort of starlight found in a sapphire, but the stone itself was a deep, rich green with hints of gold. In addition to its being breathtakingly beautiful, palpable power radiated from it.

Tables with glassware, odd tools, colorful concoctions, and dried pieces of creatures I'd never have been able to identify had been arranged around the crown in a circle that had only three breaks in it. Heslin held up a hand to restrain us in the doorway, then slowly approached the circle of tables. He paused in one opening, then waved his hand through the air much as he had before the door below.

More ethereal webwork made itself visible. Three spheres—blue, red, and yellow—surrounded the fragment, one inside the other. They slowly spun, the blue to the right, red to the left, and yellow down. While it might have been possible to reach through the webwork and grasp the fragment, the spinning webs would catch the arm. I recalled what had happened to the vylaens trying to enter the tower and could only imagine the trouble these spells could cause.

"Smart folk, my brethren, but only by half." Heslin reached out and grabbed the blue sphere. He stopped its spinning easily enough, but the other two globes sped up. "A nice trap, this."

Kirill frowned. "What do you mean smart by half?"

"Well, if they were fully intelligent, they would have taken the fragment with them when they fled instead of leaving it here. As it is, this spell would ward it well, for one person cannot steal it all by himself. Seethe, if you would not mind . . ."

The elf sheathed her sword and stalked forward. "I am not schooled in magicks. I merely use those burned into my flesh."

"No matter; you are open to power." He took her right hand in his left and brought it to where he held the blue globe. "Just grasp it here and keep it still."

She nodded and curled her hand over the glowing blue strand of light. Heslin released his grip and the elf gasped. The blue sphere started to shift and seemed as if it would drag her off the ground, but she pulled back and the blue sphere stopped moving. "Be quick about your task, wizard."

Heslin smiled and moved to a different part of the table circle. From one of the tables he grasped a silver device with twin hooks on each end. He reached through the still blue sphere and snagged the red sphere. He quickly attached it to the blue one, stopping its spinning, but pulling a grunt from Seethe. She redoubled her effort to hold the spheres motionless and the yellow one spun yet faster.

Heslin quickly moved around the circle of tables again and laughed aloud. Though the yellow sphere somersaulted with enough speed to form a yellow curtain between the doorway and the crown fragment, he came at it from one of the poles of the axis around which the sphere rotated. He reached through the blue and red spheres, then pushed his right hand into the polar opening and grabbed the green stone. He pulled it free, then nodded at Seethe. She released her grip, starting the spheres spinning.

I ducked as the silver implement Heslin had used came whirling toward the doorway. Seethe staggered back toward me as Heslin and the prince went out onto the balcony. Kirill waved his arms, and inside a minute one of the Gyrkyme landed and slipped the piece of the DragonCrown into a pouch strapped to his right thigh. Three other Gyrkyme, armed with bows, circled near him. The four of them departed for the inner city and the ships that would carry us all away.

A great cry arose from outside the tower and we all hurried back down the stairs and out. A force of gibberers had formed and attacked the gate. A few tried to come up over the walls, but on the left Locquelf arrows pitched them back into the street, and on the right, Leigh danced along the wall top, Temmer blazing with gold fire. He twisted and dodged arrows, rocks, and spears, then slashed through arms and faces as gibberers sought to climb the walls.

Faryaah-Tse cleared the wall in one leap again, this time descending on the group gathered in the street. I shot above and around Nay's form as he stood in the gateway and bashed away at the gibberers. He finally spun away, his left thigh opened by a longknife slash. Seethe dashed forward, filling the gap he left, then Leigh dropped over into the street. Kirill, lodged firmly on his horse, ordered the gate cleared.

Lord Norrington followed on his horse, checking the surge of gibberers that would have closed around Kirill and dragged him from the saddle. Abandoning my bow, I drew my sword and rushed forward, attacking the gibberer flank as they turned to go after the horsemen. Kirill and Lord Norrington slashed left and right with their blades, splitting muzzles and shattering arms raised to ward off blows. Seethe moved into their wake. Her blade darted snake-tongue quick, puncturing a belly, opening the inside of a thigh, or slipping beneath a buckler to skewer a heart.

Compared to her delicate swordwork, I was a forester hewing at trees with a dull ax. I blocked a cut at my head, then shifted my grip and smashed my pommel into the gibberer's muzzle. As it fell back, I slashed down, cutting it deeply across the chest. I cried out as a gibberer's longknife stroked me across the left side of my chest, but he cut more leather than he did flesh. I lashed out with my left fist, catching him in the throat with a mailed punch. He staggered back, caught his heels on a dying comrade, and went down. One of the Okrans soldiers gutted him with a sword thrust.

The gibberers broke, and of our company, I saw eight down. Faryaah-Tse was helping another to his feet, and Nay came limping back. Prince Kirill had slashes opened on his boots and his horse bled from a cut on the right shoulder. Blood stained Lord Norrington's left sleeve, and even Seethe dripped from a cut high on her right arm. In fact, not a one of us save Leigh seemed to have escaped without injury.

We turned toward the inner city to retrace our path to the tower and saw a sight that sent a chill through us all. A Gyrkyme lay in the roadway, his wings unfurled and back arched unnaturally because of the black arrow that transfixed him. A white temeryx clawed at the Gyrkyme's right thigh with its forepaws and hooked the pouch that contained the DragonCrown fragment. The beast tore it free, then began to scamper off to the east.

Kirill spurred his horse forward and galloped down the road. I sprinted after it, as did Leigh, Faryaah-Tse, and Seethe, each of them making better time than me. As Kirill reached the intersection where the Gyrkyme lay, a black shaft flew from the east and struck his horse through the forequarter. The horse went down, spilling Kirill onto the dead Gyrkyme. The prince tried to get back up, but his foot slipped in blood and he fell again.

Another arrow passed just above him and shattered brick in the building on the other side of the street.

I reached the intersection a second or two after Leigh, Seethe, and the urZrethi. Off to the east ran a knot of four temeryces; on one rode a vylaen holding the pouch. Faryaah-Tse started after them, but a dark figure, tall and slender, stepped from an alleyway a hundred yards down the street. Between him and us lay the temeryx-slashed bodies of the other Gyrkyme warriors.

The figure looked elven, no doubt about it—an impression reinforced by the shape of the bow he bore. Unlike the Loc-quellyn silverwood bows, however, his appeared to be black and flecked with gold. Out behind him billowed a cloak that seemed to float on a breeze I could not feel. More unsettling than that was the frequency at which wisps of it would curl up like flames and then leap free, evaporating into nothingness.

His hair matched the midnight hues of his cloak and clothes, while his eyes glowed with the same purple light that had lit the Iron Prince's gaze. There was no denying that another *sullanciri* had indeed been part of the Aurolani host. And this one, being able to fight at range, could kill us all before Leigh could get close with his magick sword.

The Dark Lancer nocked another arrow and let fly. I saw the black shaft coming straight for me and I could do nothing to evade it. I watched it grow larger and larger, knowing it would split my breastbone and burst my heart. I wanted to shift my body, pull one of my shoulders back in the hopes that it might miss me, but I knew with uncanny certainty that the arrow would not miss its target.

Then the arrow twisted in flight, turned the street corner, and flew on down toward the Vilwanese tower. Heslin's head came up as the black shaft veered toward him. The arrow took the wizard high in the chest, just to the right of center, and spun him to the ground.

"Leigh, go! At him!"

Leigh looked up as I yelled, then glanced at his sword and turned down the street. He began to run down the right side and Faryaah-Tse started her sprint down the left. I dove for one of the Gyrkyme bodies and snatched up one of their bows. That it was longer than my horsebow and had a heavier draw didn't matter to me. I nocked an arrow, drew it as far back as I could, and let fly.

My arrow, a golden wood shaft with bright red fletching, tore through the Dark Lancer's cloak. I could have sworn it also passed through his flank, but the figure gave no indication of any injury. I snarled in frustration, realizing it would take a magickal weapon to hurt him. I dipped my next arrow in Gyrkyme blood, hoping that might enchant it, but that shot passed through him without drawing so much as a glance in my direction.

The *sullanciri* drew and shot at Faryaah-Tse. She leaped up to evade the shot. The arrow jerked in flight, shifting sharply. It pierced her left thigh, then shot through to the right. She spun in the air and flopped onto her back, screaming in pain.

Leigh had halved the distance to the Dark Lancer. Gold flames whirled around Temmer as if the sword were a torch in a windstorm. Leigh shouted at the *sullanciri* in words I did not understand and kept driving at him, not shifting or dodging or evading.

The Dark Lancer loosed an arrow at Leigh and somehow it missed. I didn't know how or why it missed him, when the shots so clearly were magicked to hit their target. Faryaah-Tse's leap couldn't have been anticipated, yet the arrow was drawn to her. *And the shot that missed Kirill missed because he slipped, something he did not anticipate.* All of a sudden I realized the arrows somehow knew the mind of the target.

Regardless of that, Leigh's charge had brought him so close that no enchantment would be needed to hit him. The Dark Lancer drew his arrow, laying his hand beside his cheek, and waited for Leigh to close even further. None of us could hurt him or kill him, and that meant he was free to kill Leigh at his leisure.

I refused to let Leigh die. I don't know where the idea came from, but as I nocked and drew a third arrow, I knew exactly what I had to do. I aimed, breathed a quick prayer to Kedyn, then let fly. As my arrow sped to its target, the Dark Lancer loosed his shaft.

My arrow struck the broad face of the *sullanciri*'s bow up by the elf's ear. The impact tipped the bow up a bit. Not much, but just enough to launch the dark lancer's shot high, so it passed above the level of Leigh's left shoulder. The arrow did slash at his left cheek and split his earlobe, but Leigh never seemed to notice.

Temmer arced. An unearthly scream split the air as the fiery blade swept through the *sullanciri*'s middle. Golden fire burst up into the Dark Lancer's eyes, then poured out like molten tears. He snorted gold flames, then bent forward to vomit more of the same. The figure then fell toward the ground, smacking his face against the cobbles. A gold pillar of fire shot into the sky, then collapsed into a greasy black column of smoke.

Of the Dark Lancer itself there was no trace, though his bow lay on the ground. Leigh dropped to one knee beside it and held himself up on his sword. Nay ran to Faryaah-Tse and Seethe ran to help Leigh. Lord Norrington pulled Kirill into the saddle behind him, and the others from our party came running up.

I stood, looking for Heslin. "The mage, where is he?"

One of the Loquelves shook his head. "Heslin said he was dying and there was no saving him. He said to leave him in the tower and he would see to it that the Aurolani paid dearly to take it."

Lord Norrington pressed his lips together in a grim line. "Help with the wounded. Get everyone back to the inner city."

I looked up at him. "What about the DragonCrown fragment?"

He shook his head. "We haven't the people or the time to mount a search for it. Chytrine has lost two *sullanciri* here in Okrannel. It's not a trade I like because she's got the better of the deal, but there is no going back and fixing things now. Besides, it's not in her hands yet, so we might be able to get it back again."

I heard what he was saying and understood it, but somewhere in my heart a sense of doom had begun to take hold. Faryaah-Tse struggled against pain in Nay's arms, Leigh leaned heavily on Seethe, Heslin and others were dead or dying at the tower, and my ribs ached. The grand expedition which had traveled so far to save Okrannel had failed, and even then I knew that was a fell omen.

CHAPTER 28

Upon our return to the inner city, trumpets blared loudly, signaling a general retreat. Our troops filtered back through the city slowly, grudgingly. Though most were wounded and all of the archers' arrows had been spent, the warriors were jubilant. They struggled against the recall the way hounds fight the leash. Each one of them knew he had the enemy on the verge of breaking, and only the recall prevented a total victory.

They managed to transform even our loss into a cause for celebration. I couldn't fault them there, for the death of a *sullanciri* was certainly good for our cause. The significance of the DragonCrown fragment was not truly understood—perhaps because men did not want to comprehend the vast horror of its being in the hands of the enemy. For now, though, Leigh was a hero, having slain two *sullanciri*. Soldiers marching to their boats hailed him and cheered him as he sat on the *Invictus'* forecastle getting his face sewn shut.

Many remarked how stoic he was, not wincing, not reacting as the needle Seethe wielded pierced his flesh and pulled the seams tight. The arrow had slashed along his left cheek, slicing through his mask and all but severing his earlobe.

Seethe had deftly sewn the lobe back on as well, apologizing for the scar.

Leigh shook his head lethargically. "Your magickers have enough to do saving those who are truly wounded. My mask will hide the scar well enough."

Wounded there were, and many of them gravely hurt, so the eleven magickers among the Vilwanese crew and the Locquellyn ships, as well as Winfellis, the Croquelf who had been with us from the start, had much too much work to do. The wounded were divided into three groups: those who would die, those who might die, and those, like Leigh, Nay, and myself, who had minor wounds. The elven magickers worked on the middle group, then sought people from the first group. The rest of us were left to needle, thread, and healing poultices.

The human magickers were put to the task of making poultices or working to make the ships ready for the open ocean. As it's been explained to me, spells that have an effect on living things are difficult to master, so human magickers deal mostly with inanimate objects. Elves, because they live much longer, have a greater chance for the study of and mastery of greater magicks. They were careful to note to those they treated that while they might speed the healing process, it would be the body doing the healing. Those who had been spelled back to health required a lot of rest and food, to keep up the strength their bodies needed to repair the damage.

Seethe leaned close to Leigh's cheek and nipped off the end of the knotted thread. "That should do you, Master Norrington."

"Thanks."

She next turned to me. "Strip yourself out of your armor and let me sew you up."

I unfastened the ties holding my jerkin closed, slipped my left arm from the sleeve, and peeled the jerkin back. I raised my arm so she could get a good look at the cut, which had bled not too seriously. She knelt at my left, washed blood away with a damp rag, and began to work on me. I looked to my right to avoid watching her, thinking that might dull the needle-pricks and thread-tugs a bit.

Leigh fingered his torn cheek with trembling fingers. "He would have killed me."

My quick laugh died in a hiss as Seethe jabbed me. "Ouch. Leigh, he was a bad shot. He needed magick to hit his targets."

Leigh's eyes narrowed as he turned to face me. Anger contorted his features. "Don't do that, Hawkins, don't make fun. I know what you did. I felt your arrow come past me. I saw it hit his bow. If not for you, I'd be dead."

"If not for you, Leigh, we'd all be dead."

His shoulders slumped forward a bit, then he seemed to half rouse himself with a barked laugh. "Vathendir Krithron would have killed me and taken Temmer."

"Who?"

"The *sullanciri,* that was his name, Vathendir Krithron."

"How do you know that?"

Leigh closed his eyes and shook his head. "I don't know. From Temmer, I guess, just like with the Iron Prince. I just know that as I closed with him, I learned about him. It was as if with each step I could hear a bard telling the story of his life. He'd started out noble, from Harquellyn. He embraced the Vorquelf cause and mounted a peaceful expedition to get Chytrine to cede back Vorquellyn. She negotiated with him, gave him hope, showed him wonders and seduced him with offers of power. She found his weakness—a hatred for Gyrkyme—and she exploited it. He accepted her invitation to become a Dark Lancer.

"It was him or me there, the dark against the light. I had to kill him else all would have been lost." Leigh's eyes focused distantly and I noticed his left hand had fallen to stroke Temmer's hilt. The palsy that shook it before had vanished. "It was an almost thing, my death. I would have been defeated in my final battle."

Leigh blinked his eyes and looked at me. He gave me a smile, then leaned to the right and came up with the Dark Lancer's bow in his hand. "You lost your bow back there. I want you to have this one."

I held my hands up. "You killed him, it's yours by right."

"No, Hawkins, *we* killed him, and this bit of plunder is

yours. It's enchanted. With it you can kill the next *sullanciri* we see."

"Truth be told, Leigh, I'd rather have magick arrows; and missed my chance to gather them in the streets."

Leigh raised an eyebrow at me. "You were a bit busy there."

"You noticed?"

"Yes, and if you need a magick arrow, there's always the one in Faryaah-Tse." He shoved the bow toward me. "Take it. Use it."

I took the bow from him, and as I wrapped my left hand around the grip, I did feel a tingle run over me. I looked past Seethe toward the city and picked out a window as a target. From the bow I got a vague sense of the distance to it, and felt an urging to raise my left arm to get the proper elevation to send an arrow through the window. I didn't get the information in rods, yards, feet, or inches and fractions thereof; it was more like the sort of hunch I'd come to rely on when making quick shots.

The value of such a weapon immediately hit me, but a little chill ran through me. If I came to rely on its magick, my innate sense of making a shot might be lost. Still, in as desperate a situation as we found ourselves, could I abandon so powerful a tool? Would allowing an erosion of my own skills in the name of our greater cause be good or bad?

I didn't have an answer, but I nodded and accepted the weapon anyway. "Thank you, Leigh."

He nodded as if he'd only half heard me, then tore the hanging strip of leather from the left cheek of his mask. He pulled the mask back on and tied it in place. "I'm going to go get some sleep."

"Good idea."

He staggered toward the steps down to the main deck and leaned heavily on the railing with both hands. He would have slipped and fallen, but Nay caught him and steadied him as he mounted the steps himself. I could see the top of his flame-haired head as he guided Leigh to the forward companionway, then Nay returned and limped his way up the steps.

He plunked himself down on the cask Leigh had been

using as a seat and extended his left leg. Through the rent in his leather trousers I could see the stitching that had been done on him. He sighed wearily and scratched up under his mask at the corner of his right eye.

"Faryaah-Tse will heal."

"That's good to know."

Nay nodded. "Pain from the arrow was fierce. She concentrated and shifted a bit. They only cut skin to get it out."

I frowned. "Why didn't they just break the arrow, pull one end out, and push the other through?"

"Couldn't. Don't know what it's made of. A fell thing, by the touch of it."

"Leigh and I were just talking about those arrows. I'd be interested to have a look at it. Might be a match for this bow." I winced as Seethe tugged on the thread to tighten a knot. "How's your leg?"

"No more serious than your ribs." Nay gave me a wry grin. "The three of us have been lucky. Just cuts. Heslin is dead. Faryaah-Tse is shot through. Prince Kirill's shoulder is hurt from his fall. He's heartsick with the idea that his daughter might be dead, too."

"No surprise there, but she's alive. The Dark Lancer was hunting the DragonCrown, not an infant."

Seethe glanced up at me. "How can you be so certain?"

I shuddered. "If Preyknosery had been downed, the *sullanciri* would have traded Alexia for the DragonCrown fragment. Traded her or her corpse, whichever would have caused Kirill more pain."

The Vorquelf thought for a moment silently, then nodded. She leaned in and nipped off the thread with which she'd closed my wound. Her lips brushed my flesh as she did so. I felt a thrill run through me as that happened. I reached down with my left hand to pat her on the shoulder in thanks, but my hand stroked her dark hair and fair cheek in its descent. She looked up and our gazes met, redoubling the thrill.

Seethe stood slowly, then nodded. "There are others I must tend to."

"Thank you, Seethe." I hesitated. "If there is anything I can do to repay you . . ."

She laughed lightly. "I shall think on that, Master Hawkins, and may accept your kind offer at another time."

I nodded, then looked at Nay to see if he'd noticed what had passed between Seethe and me. I think I was less worried that he had and would tease me about it than that he hadn't noticed and I would have no way to double-check my impressions.

Fortunately, or unfortunately, his eyelids had grown heavy and he swayed on top of the cask. I caught him by the shoulder and eased him to the deck. He curled himself up against the bulwark and began to snore. I almost poked him, for the sound seemed grossly out of place as our fleet readied itself for retreat. Then it occurred to me that his snores were something natural in a most unnatural setting and, for that reason, I left him alone.

I cast about for something to do, but I just seemed to get in the way, so I sought out Lord Norrington to see if I could be of service to him. I found him out on the breakwater that separated the harbor from the gulf. Massive stones had been placed together to create the breakwater, which stood a good six feet above the calm harbor water level and had an expanse of twice that across the top. He was speaking with the three princes, and though it might be unkind of me to note it, only Scrainwood had managed to come away from the battle without need of stitch or bandage. The fifth man with them I recognized as one of the harbor pilots we'd taken on board as we were coming into Svarskya harbor.

The pilot pointed out into the gulf. Black clouds gathered there, and slowly drifted in our direction, with lightning flashing within them from top to bottom. Waves crashed into the breakwater itself, sending spray to dapple the calmer harbor waters and drench us. "Tagothcha seems a mite upset at you for fooling him before."

Lord Norrington nodded. "Chytrine doubtlessly knows we tricked the *weirun* and she's making sure we don't get to sail to Fortress Draconis."

Scrainwood flung his arms wide open. "We can't stay here. Even if we gather the ships in the harbor, fire arrows and fireships can destroy us."

Augustus, whose head was crowned with white bandages that were reddening in some spots, rested a hand on Scrainwood's shoulder. "No one is suggesting we remain here. We've got to be going, but the question is one of whether or not we can win the *weirun* over to our side."

Scrainwood knitted his fingers together and hooked his thumbs in his sword belt. "Offerings will do it, won't they? What will the *weirun* demand?"

Kirill frowned. "I've not seen Tagothcha this irritated before, at least, not this early in the month of Leaffall."

Seethe appeared at my left shoulder. "The *weirun* have always been subject to tantrums."

Lord Norrington looked at her. "We were discussing possible offerings for Tagothcha. Have you an idea? It should be something special."

Seethe laughed, then turned and spat into the gulf. "There, I offer Tagothcha what he is worth: nothing. On his back were borne the ships that brought death to Vorquellyn. He will have nothing from me but venom."

A wave hurled itself against the breakwater and gallons of brine splashed over her. The wave's power staggered her, but I caught her and stopped her from falling into the harbor.

Lord Norrington scratched at his chin. "Interesting offer, but one that was counterproductive. Other suggestions?"

I stepped toward the gulf side of the breakwater and unslung the *sullanciri*'s bow. Again I got a sense of target, one deep within the roiling black waters. I knew if I fitted an arrow to the bow and drew it back, I could drive the arrow through the *weirun* who watched us from below. I let my hand slip down from the grip and dipped the bow's tip in spray from the next wave.

"Here, Tagothcha, I offer you a magickal weapon. With it I probably could not slay you, but I could hurt you. Anyone could, but I give it to you to keep you safe. In return, I ask you do the same: keep us safe."

"No!" cried Scrainwood from behind me.

I flung the bow as far out as I could. A wave rose to snatch the bow from the air. It sank without a sound or ripple.

The sea calmed, ever so slightly.

Smiling, I turned to face the others. "That seems to have worked."

Fury burned in Scrainwood's eyes. "That was a waste of a valuable tool. If you did not want it, you should have given it to me."

"Oh, I did want it, which is why it made a very suitable sacrifice."

"You're a fool, Hawkins. That bow might have won us the war."

"If that bow could defeat Chytrine, she never would have placed it in the hands of a *sullanciri*." Seethe wrung water out of her long hair. "And a weapon like that does not a warrior make."

Scrainwood's nostrils flared. "Meaning?"

"Meaning," offered Lord Norrington, "Hawkins had good reason to offer the bow up, didn't you, Hawkins?"

"I think so, my lord." I opened my hands. "The magick in it would have made each shot more certain, if I chose to rely on the bow. The problem is that I would have stopped trusting my judgment. It would have destroyed me, in little bits and pieces. It wasn't a thing meant for mortal hands, and now it is no longer in them."

Kirill smiled slowly. "Personal gifts, things that have meaning for us, that are hard to give up . . . these are the things Tagothcha treasures. Selflessly given—which we know Chytrine's gifts could never be." From his right wrist he tugged the braided bracelet woven of his dead wife's hair. He grimaced as he pulled it off—less because of the pain in that shoulder, I think, than the pain of losing the bracelet.

He lofted it into the sea. "There, that is all I have of my wife, save memories and my daughter."

Tagothcha accepted his gift and the sea calmed a bit more.

Prince Augustus stared hard at the obsidian water, then nodded. "Listen to me, Tagothcha. You know me, Augustus of Alcida. You have my word that my gift to you will be special indeed. I am sending an order, as fast as I am able, for my grooms back in Yslin to drive my favorite horse, Cursus, a horse I raised from a foal, into your depths."

Augustus' voice trailed off and the seas lessened their

pounding on the breakwater. He nodded, then begged our pardon and marched off in search of the *arcanslata* that would relay his order to Yslin.

We all looked at Scrainwood. He ran a hand over his mouth and in his narrowed eyes I could read all the calculations his mind was going through. His gaze flicked from me to Seethe, to Prince Kirill, and then Lord Norrington. He closed his eyes for a moment, then twisted his gold wedding band from his left hand.

"Here, take this, the symbol of my undying love for my wife and the mother of my children."

The waves accepted his gift and perhaps they did abandon some of their restlessness.

A wry grin twisted Lord Norrington's features. He dropped to one knee and scooped up seawater from a puddle in his cupped hands. He lowered his face into it and bubbles sprang up to pop around his ears. He raised his face again, with crystal drops running from his chin, and poured the water from his hands back into the ocean from which it had come.

The ripples from the water spread out far and fast, rolling over waves and leaving a placid surface in their wake. I gasped to see it and Kirill's jaw dropped open. Seethe kept her face expressionless, but Scrainwood's eyes widened enough to account for her shock and his all at once.

Kirill grasped Lord Norrington's left forearm. "What did you do, my friend?"

"I gave it a sacrifice of the thing I hold most dear." Lord Norrington smiled slowly and wiped his chin with the back of his left hand. "I gave Tagothcha my real name."

Seethe bowed deeply to Lord Norrington. "As one who has made a similar sacrifice for a cause I hold above all others, I salute you." As she came up, an edge crept into her voice. "You know what you have done, don't you?"

He slowly nodded. "Does it matter when we're faced with the need to get to Fortress Draconis?"

"Perhaps not."

I shook my head. "Real name? What are you talking about?"

Lord Norrington laughed and, walking past me, tousled

my hair with a playful flick of his right hand. "What you know of the world, Hawkins, is admirable, but it is not all there is to know. You have my trust, as per your wish, and someday you will have this secret. When you are ready for it."

He looked out at the sea. "The *weirun* is ready to receive us. Let's move."

CHAPTER 29

We left Svarskya in flames behind us. Dusk fell as we sailed, and I recall seeing Prince Kirill standing there on the aftdeck, limned by the fires. At water's edge gibberers and vylaens danced and cavorted, though whether they were joyous at their victory or outraged at our escape, I could not tell. One company of gibberers did run out along the breakwater to harry us, giving the Okrans archers who formed the Prince's Honor Guard one last chance at revenge. The Okrans archers feathered the lot of them, casting one more sacrifice into Tagothcha's fluid grasp.

The winds blew in our favor, allowing us to travel as swiftly as we could toward Fortress Draconis. Tagothcha smoothed the way enough so that even Leigh no longer felt seasick. He still seemed weak, and used Temmer as a crutch, but some of his wit was back. He amused the Okrans soldiery amidships with his temeryx poem, and even offered some quick rhymes on their names.

Dusk of the second day brought us very close to Vorquellyn. Though Lord Norrington ordered the ships to steer well north of it, keeping us safe from any Aurolani forces that might ship from the island's harbors, Tagothcha swirled cur-

rents so we skimmed through the breakers crashing on Vorquellyn's beaches. He would let us get no closer than that,
though, so we had no chance to set foot on the island.

I knew, as did everyone else in the fleet, that landing
troops in Vorquellyn was folly. Not only had we no clue as to
the number and type of forces that would oppose us there, but
liberating the island would not lift the siege of Fortress
Draconis. Any action on the island, even if it were complete
and overwhelming, would be a hollow victory.

Even with that realization, I very much wanted to venture
forth. I felt it would be keeping faith with my pledge to Resolute, though I knew I could do nothing alone. Others looked
longingly at the island, and yet others fearfully, but none with
the anguish that Seethe did.

"Tagothcha does this to torture me." Seethe rested against
the *Invictus*' masthead, with her black hair blowing back past
her shoulders. "I showed him contempt and now he tries to
break my heart."

Standing beside her, with the cool breeze puckering my
flesh, I studied the island that once had been her home. Trying
to describe it is difficult because much of what I saw was
colored by the sad tone of her voice, or the distant longing in
her gaze. In both I could imagine a land that was greatly
desirable, down on a level that shot past conscious valuations
of yield per acre, or how much lumber could be harvested, or
how much water was to be had. She needed Vorquellyn and
needed it the way I needed air to breathe and water to drink.

The island itself was such that it seemed to be a shadow of
what she must have remembered. It was black, the whole of it,
like a hillside after a wildfire. Trees had been stripped of foliage, leaving brittle black limbs to claw at the sky. Vales folded
in on themselves, black on black, hillsides seeming to cast
shadows that became mountains behind them. Streams that
ran to the sea poured water blacker than bilge down dark
cliffsides.

Throughout the time the sun illuminated Vorquellyn I saw
no life, but with night the island came alive. Red lights, mil-
lions of them, began to glow all over, as if the dead trees had
red embers still burning in their heartwood. I held my hands

out to see if I could feel any warmth, but instead my hands grew colder. Things moved within the landscape, shadows blotting out the red lights from time to time. Terrible shrieking rang from the hills, and snarling growls accompanied them, but I heard nothing of the noble howls of predators, or proud roaring of a triumphant killer standing over prey. Instead all the sounds were born of fear—fear of being consumed, fear of having a kill stolen.

Vorquellyn had become a dead land where brutish cruelty held sway.

I stroked Seethe's back with my left hand. "I am so sorry for your loss."

She chewed her lower lip for a moment, then looked at me with a single tear rolling down her left cheek. "When they came, I was three years younger than you are now. I was days from my bonding to the land. At first we were told not to worry, that our warriors would hold, but that was because no one could believe Kree'chuc could sustain his attack. But the ships still came, and they landed north and south, and in the west. We had counted on the sea as our fortress and Tagothcha betrayed us.

"My sister and young brother were given to my care and I kept us together. We escaped in the great flotilla. Sebcia, Saporcia, Muroso, merchant fleets from all the states came to carry us to safety. Fisherfolk, too—men and women who had forever stayed away from Vorquellyn because of wild tales of what we would do if they were found fishing in our waters—they came to help."

She sniffed and another tear crawled from her left eye. I reached over and brushed it away. "And Loquellyn, did they send ships?"

"Some, I've been told, though the Loquelves maintain they were engaged crushing the Aurolani fleet. That may be true, they may have prevented Kree'chuc from reinforcing his army on Vorquellyn, but by that time it was too late. Our homeland had been overrun and the desecration began."

Seethe gave me a half smile. "You want to know why Vorquelves, for the most part, endure conditions in Mantowns like the Downs? Why we have adopted Man-words for our names? It is the brave kindness men showed in saving us. We honor that, and we honor your sense of urgency."

"I don't understand."

She reached up and stroked my cheek in turn. "The leisure of a long life allows elves to view things in cycles, as if time and relations ebbed and flowed like the tides. We wait until the time for something is optimal, instead of merely possible. Men work when work is to be done, rejoicing at how easy it might be at the right time, but not shying from it if the timing is not perfect. The Vorquelves cannot wait for the best time to take Vorquellyn back. Elves tell us the time is not right, and men, well, the benefit of shedding their blood to free a land to which they have no claim is hard to see. Resolute's hope for a campaign to free Vorquellyn is a slender one. I hope, by joining this expedition, by fighting with you to save men, I will inspire others to help us."

I nodded solemnly. "I gave Resolute my pledge that I will see Vorquellyn liberated before I die. I make that same pledge to you."

Seethe watched me in silence, her golden eyes unmoving. Then her smile broadened, but her brows furrowed, giving her a puzzled expression. "You are a curious man, Tarrant Hawkins. You are young, yet very old; wise, but terribly foolish. You see things with clarity, but you do not see far enough. Even so, you commit yourself to your friends and your ideals, and you do not waver from them."

I swallowed hard. "I don't know what to say to that."

"And yet you admit it." She laughed a little. "That's one of your more endearing qualities."

I almost mouthed one of the quick, glib remarks that Leigh would have once made, but I swallowed it instead. "Thank you."

"You are more than welcome, Tarrant, more than welcome." She turned forward again, resting her elbows on the wale and studied the red lights on her homeland. "I know you will be true to your pledge, and I look forward to standing with you in the heart of a Vorquellyn renewed."

It took us a full day to sail past Vorquellyn. I stayed with Seethe all that time. I wrapped her in the blanket Leigh had given me and slumbered with her against the bulwark. I got us food and water. We did not talk much. We didn't feel the need to talk. An occasional touch, feeling her lean against me, that was all we needed. Having relied on men to save her from Vorquellyn, and relying on a man to support her as she sailed past, I think these things felt right and natural to her.

Once past Vorquellyn, it was decided we would put in at some of the various coves and harbors that dotted the Ghost Marches coast. We would land small scouting parties to see what we could learn about the Aurolani forces in the area. *Arcanslata* communications with Fortress Draconis indicated that the Aurolani forces—two large armies worth—had cut off the landward edge of the peninsula. This was not unexpected since Chytrine could not afford to leave Fortress Dragonis behind her advance where the troops could disrupt lines of supply and sally forth to attack her armies from the rear.

A fleet blockaded the harbor at Fortress Draconis, and while it was deemed likely that we could win through it, our doing so would not lift the siege. It was thought we might be able to accomplish that task by landing a force to the west and coming overland while our fleet engaged the Aurolani fleet. Chytrine's ground forces might assume our entire force had been fed into Fortress Draconis at that point, leaving them vulnerable to an attack from their rear.

Before we could do that, however, we needed to guarantee that no Aurolani troops ranged through the Ghost Marches to fall on us from behind. Each ship in the fleet filled a long boat with a dozen warriors and dropped us off at various points. We were to look around, see what we could find out, and report back after a day of scouting.

Leigh, Nay, Seethe, and I made up a third of the *Invictus'* scouting party. Lord Norrington wanted to come along, but his position made that impossible, just as Prince Kirill's injuries kept him aboard ship. We did have with us two Gyrkyme, toward whom Seethe acted somewhat coldly, but she agreed to travel with them nonetheless. The Loquelf scouts refused to have Gyrkyme with them, despite the ease with which the Gyrkyme could fly out to a ship and report findings—much less the ease with which they could fly around and see much more than we could on the ground.

The Loquelves were not completely unsympathetic, however. Word had gotten around about my giving the *sullanciri* bow to Tagothcha despite having lost my bow in Svarskya. One of the elven bowyers took a silverwood blank and carved it into a close match for the sort of horsebow I was accustomed to using. He likewise cut down two dozen arrows to match my bow's shorter draw. He fletched them in green and white, the Oriosan colors, and sent them with compliments.

I didn't know how to react to such kindness and the notoriety I'd gained. I suppose, in looking at the whole of what Nay and Leigh and I had done, we had done a lot, but I had no perspective on it. We slew temeryces in Westwood because we had no choice; likewise fighting as we did at Atval. And Leigh's blind bowshot at the festival on Yslin had become a thing of legend, yet I knew, as did Nay and Leigh, that blind luck had been more at play than skill. Our actions at the bridge and the killing of two *sullanciri,* these *were* momentous things, but they were also things about which we had no choice. By virtue of our innocence we had embarked on an adventure that wiser, more experienced folk would have rejected.

Nay handled it with silence or blushed smiles. Leigh, as he recovered, accepted praise with wit and bluster, belittling what he had done by exaggerating the circumstances, entertaining all and impressing them with his rakehell indifference to what he had endured. I felt very uneasy with it all, but also very proud of what we'd done. I thanked well-wishers and tried to escape, but I'll admit to enjoying seeing eyes widen as I related some of our adventures. Hearing the praises of others can be seductive, and while I didn't seek them out, I didn't shrink overmuch from them when they were offered.

The half-dozen men in our boat, drawn in pairs from Oriosan, Alcidese, and Okrans soldiery, foolishly looked to Leigh and me for leadership. I deferred to Şeethe and convinced Leigh to do so as well, since she had a century of experience over either of us. Leigh raised an eyebrow at my suggestion, then nodded and winked, clearly assuming I wanted to impress Seethe with my trust in her judgment because I was sweet on her.

We landed in the early evening in a small sandy cove that had a well-worn trail leading back into a forest that all but reached the water's edge. Up over a small ridge, we came down into a marsh strewn with cattails, sawgrass, and fallen trees. We tried to skirt it, and one of the Gyrkyme flew out to see if she could find a path for us to cross. We were eventually able to get to the other side by moving along logs to little islands, leaping boggy puddles, and wading through reeking water.

Heading a bit west we did find signs of a path that would take us back through the swamp without getting us too wet. It matched up with a meandering path that passed below the ridge of the hills. We likely would have headed out along it save that Nay saw a small cluster of *metholanth* trees and decided to harvest some leaves. He found leaves stripped from a couple of other branches and a footprint leading further west, which brought him to a narrow game trail that shadowed the larger footpath, but on the other slope of the hill.

We took the game trail and headed north. We moved quietly, with Seethe in the front, since she could see in the dark. Leigh came behind her, then me and Nay, with the other men strung out behind and the Gyrkyme at the back. While the dense foliage prevented them from taking to the air, they likewise could see in the dark, and having that in a rearguard is rather nice at night.

Suddenly, ahead of us, something sounded with a faint pop, then Seethe spun and went down with an arrow quivering in her. Temmer swept from Leigh's hilt. The blade blazed like a torch as he dashed forward. He leaped over Seethe, then swung his sword down and around in a great arc that sliced through a sapling's bole as if it were nothing more than a jackstraw. The tree crashed and something struggled in its branches. Leigh's blade rose and fell again, and the struggling ceased while he sped on.

I dropped to a knee beside Seethe. The arrow had taken her through the meat of her upper left arm. She hissed in pain, but grabbed my jerkin and propelled me in Leigh's direction. "Go after him. Go! All of you, go!"

I upped and sprinted after him, passing close on Nay's heels. Cloven branches and dying men littered Leigh's trail. A couple of the men had their faces or stomachs slashed, but more and more of them were facedown with split spines or crushed skulls. That they had been struck down while running didn't wring any sympathy from me. They laid an ambush for us and it went wrong, so they got all they deserved.

Over a ridge and down a thickly forested hillside we raced. I smelled smoke well before I saw fire. Running full out I clipped a tree with my shoulder. That spun me about and sent me crashing through a bush which caught at my ankles. I flopped on my face at the edge of a clearing. At its center burned a bonfire and in its light I could see Leigh.

Temmer's blaze rivaled that of the fire, splashing tall shadows against tent and tree, then hacking them in twain. Leigh was magnificent, his body taut, his every move precise and exact. He'd parry a lunge low, then come up with a cut that opened a man from groin to breastbone. A quick sidestep would dodge an overhand blow, then he'd draw Temmer along the man's belly. Sliding it free, he'd spin, duck a head-high slash, then hamstring the man rushing past. As pain arched the man's back, Temmer would cleave head from shoulders.

Leigh spun once again, his shining blade raised high, the light in his eyes flickering with the fire.

"Leigh, no!" I scrambled to my feet and ran at him. "No, Leigh!"

Temmer fell quickly, as if sped by my shout. No hesitation, no shifting of its deadly arc. It fell true and straight and strong, chopping effortlessly through collarbone and breast, with a wounded heart pulsing blood up over the golden blade's length.

A terrified child, whose mother now lay dying before her, looked up at Leigh with huge eyes and began to cry.

Temmer came up again, which was when my diving tackle caught Leigh at the knees. I gathered his ankles to my chest, but lost my grip as we hit the ground. Leigh spun to his feet and leveled Temmer at me. Fury contorted his face and he snarled at me in a tongue so ancient it made my flesh crawl. Temmer aimed itself at my eyes and Leigh began a lunge.

Nay dropped his maul over Leigh's head and shoulders, then hauled back and crushed the smaller man against his broad chest. Nay arched his back, hauling Leigh from his feet. Leigh tried to kick both heels back into Nay's legs, but Nay had spread them. Closing his legs again, he caught Leigh's ankles, then twisted and fell on his side. Nay rolled right, pinning Leigh beneath him and I stepped on Leigh's right wrist, trapping Temmer.

Leigh's hand opened and the sword rolled from his grip. Nay waited a moment or two, then relaxed his grip and kicked the sword away. "What did he . . . Why?"

One of the Okrans soldiers toed the woman's body onto her back. "She had a knife."

He told it truly, she did have a knife. A short-bladed, dull knife that still had a bit of a dirty peel from a forest tuber caught near the wooden grip. A short ways away lay a pile of peels, a pot, and more roots to be prepared for boiling. Judging from the state of the tubers she'd already tossed in the pot, her knife couldn't have so much as creased Leigh's leathers, much less hurt him.

I looked from Leigh's unconscious form to Nay seated on Leigh's back. "She had a knife. She was the enemy."

Nay shook his head. "Leigh couldn't have seen her as a threat."

"No, Leigh couldn't." I toed Temmer. "But the man who wields this blade isn't Leigh. I don't know who or what he is, but I hope to all the gods he's not destroyed our friend."

CHAPTER 30

What we learned from our scouting mission matched what the other parties found out. Chytrine's armies had come south through the pass in the Boreal Mountains making straight for Fortress Draconis. More troops filtered through the pass on a daily basis and some of them got turned around. The men who had attacked us preyed on anyone moving through the area—Aurolani, men, it didn't matter to them what they hit.

The band we'd captured were mostly women and children. While Leigh's attack on that woman was enough to cow anyone, most of them didn't give any sign they cared. What they'd seen, the sort of existence they lived, had long since snuffed any sense of life. They seemed genuinely surprised that we buried the dead; I had the impression that had we left them alone, meat would have joined the roots in their pots.

The rumors our scouts picked up did paint a nasty picture of the forces besieging Fortress Draconis. The armies that had headed west and hit Okrannel were composed mostly of vylaens, gibberers, a handful of renegade elves, and a few temeryces. The emphasis seemed to be on mobility and speed. While plenty of vylaens and gibberers filled the armies travel-

ing south, drearbeasts, hoargouns, and enslaved men supple-
mented those armies.

Drearbeasts and hoargouns I only knew from legend.
Drearbeasts most resembled bears and lived on the icefields
north of the Boreal Mountains. They were supposed to be
huge, have long, saberlike fangs and white coats decorated
with light blue striping. One rumor had an urZrethi *sullanciri*
riding in a war chariot drawn by drearbeasts, but I doubted
that since they didn't sound like draft animals to me. Still it
did sound as if these creatures made up for in strength what
they lacked in speed, and it didn't make me at all confident to
hear that they preyed on temeryces by preference.

Hoargoun is the word in the Aurolani tongue applied to
glacier giants. Some folks said they were made of ice, but I
gathered they said that because the hulking creatures had
white hair and beards and pale skin. They stood two or three
times as tall as a man and had massive feet to allow them to
walk across snow without sinking. They were said to favor
clubs, much as Nay did, which left me with an image of a
creature towering up over me, wielding the iron-bound trunk
of an oak tree.

Not an image that lets one sleep without shivering awake
in the wee hours of the night.

To make things worse, one of the hoargoun was supposed
to be a *sullanciri*. Those who saw it said they knew what it was
because its flesh was black, though beard, hair, and eyes still
remained white. Even now, years later, the very thought of a
giant *sullanciri* sends shivers down my spine.

Arcanslata consultation with Dothan Cavarre, Draconis
Baron, produced a simple plan that our scouting runs indicated we should be able to accomplish to great effect—and
with little risk to ourselves. We grounded our main force
northwest of the peninsula, about ten miles west of the Dûrgrue River. Aurolani troops heading south tended to pass east
of it, moving in long columns through the forests that led to
the plains surrounding Fortress Draconis. According to the
scouts Cavarre had operating in the area, the columns moved
through the forests without fear and were ripe for an attack.

The other bit of trouble he had planned for the Aurolani

host was something he'd been saving for the right time. The Dûrgrue River had once flowed into a saltmarsh to the northwest of Fortress Draconis, but after the last invasion from the north, the marsh had been drained and dikes had been raised to hold back both the sea and river floods. He already had urZrethi sappers in place and they'd prepared deep tunnels that would flood the reclaimed land by diverting the river into it. Our attack would force the Aurolani generals to shift troops to the lowlands to cut us off from the fortress, then he'd be able to flood it and catch them.

We landed 3,500 troops at the appointed place and hooked up with the Draconis scouts—elves from Croquellyn and Harquellyn—while our ships sailed south to harry the blockade. We only had a hundred and twenty cavalry, which Prince Augustus formed up into two battalions and used as a screening force for our northern flank. Though the elves—both those who had been with us and the new ones—refused to even acknowledge their existence, the half-dozen Gyrkyme scouted ahead for us. The rest of the force divided itself up into companies based on nationality, with the remnants like Leigh, Nay, Seethe, Faryaah-Tse Kimp, and myself serving in Lord Norrington's command company.

In my comments about the ambush laid for us by the Ghost Marcher bandits, I may have implied that an ambush is a craven act. I think, in their case, it was—because they were only concerned with banditry. Their objective was to slaughter us for their personal gain. They attacked us with the zeal a prospector might employ to attack the earth when he hopes to uncover gold or gems.

The ambush we laid for the Aurolani was far from an act of cowardice, though, and I don't think I'm being hypocritical in saying that. Our aim was to destroy a force that was going to slaughter our comrades in Fortress Draconis. We meant for the Aurolani troops to disappear in a manner that would sow consternation among those in the siege force. What we would do could never be considered honorable in any mythic sense—bards would not sing of details, but of our results.

What we would do was what was required of us.

For the ambush we selected a stretch of road that ran fairly level through the forest. Our site came just beyond a valley which would have been a perfect location for an ambush, and which would have had the Aurolani troops on edge. Their relief on passing that point without an attack would make them relax, and prime them for our attack. The hills making up the western side of the valley still crowded the road on one side, but on the other the trickle of a stream ran through a shallow ravine with a hill further on, maybe twenty yards from the road. The trees in the area were such that only the first ten yards of that hill could be seen from the roadway, so anyone waiting on the crest would be invisible.

Lord Norrington arrayed his forces beautifully. The Okrans guards he placed on the hilltop, armed with spear, ax, and sword. To the south on either side he hid Oriosan and Alcidese warriors. On the western hill he placed his archers, so they could shoot down on the Aurolani troops. Prince Augustus kept his horsemen back from the road in a clearing to the west. When the ambush happened they would swing around and down to charge through any Aurolani forces that sought to retreat to the north. Other companies would cut the road to the north and prevent any other forces from catching up with the stricken group.

I had my place with the archers and crossbowmen, which kept me close to Lord Norrington since his signal to us would begin the ambush. Leigh and Nay and Seethe, along with a company of Oriosans, stood with us to keep the Aurolani forces away from the archers. It wasn't that we couldn't fight in our own right, but our shots picking out targets on the road would be more useful than our trading swordstrokes with gibberers on the hillside.

Seethe stood near me, her sword in hand. The arrow she'd taken the day before had been pulled from her muscles easily enough and I'd returned the favor of stitching her flesh shut. I wasn't as skilled at it as she was, but I did my best because I didn't want scars marring her smooth skin.

Nay stood near Leigh, his maul resting on his right shoulder. Leigh had not yet drawn Temmer; instead, a crossbow hung from his right hand. Still, his left hand did rest on the sword's hilt. Back on board the *Invictus*, Leigh had apologized to me and thanked both Nay and me for holding him back. He stared into space, reaching a hand out, as if he could brush away the tears on the little girl's face. "What I almost did . . ." he breathed over and over. "Never again."

Looking at him, now, waiting to fight again, he looked determined. I think he knew the sword had gotten the better of him in the chaos of the ambush. He was set against it doing that again. On his face I read the same sort of resolution I had seen countless times as my father put us through our paces. It felt good to see him wear that expression again.

The Aurolani host came marching down the road with an ease that suggested they were parading through a village, not making their way through hostile territory. I guess it would have been a battalion—eight companies of thirty individuals, with a double-handful of vylaens to lead them and several younger gibberkin bearing the unit banners. Behind them came several makeshift wagons, laden with arms, armor, food, and the other necessities of an army on the road. A final company came in the rear with a shambling hoargoun dragging a massive club behind him.

We'd been assigned our targets beforehand, so when the middle of their column reached us, with each company arrayed five deep in six rows, we stood up at Lord Norrington's hand signal. With the first blast of a horn we shot, bows twanging, crossbows thrumming. Arrows and bolts hissed through the air, striking targets with wet sucking sounds, hard cracks, or loud clanks. The lead company crumpled as if they were toy soldiers flattened by the swat of an angry child's hand.

I shot at the middle company and found my elven bow a joy. I could draw it easily and it sped my arrow to its mark. I hit a vylaen, spinning him around before he dropped to the ground. His command baton flew through the air as his hand slackened, then a gibberer shot through the head flopped down over him.

Again I shot and again, sending an arrow into a gut-shot gibberer. I caught another scrambling up the hill toward us and sent an arrow through his paw, pinning it to a tree he was using to help himself up. Two more arrows crossed in his chest, leaving him dangling there for a moment until his weight tore his flesh free.

On the roadway, pandemonium reigned. The horses drawing the carts bolted when arrows stung their flanks. The wagons careened off the roadway and overturned, breaking apart. Armor and provisions crashed and clanked into an avalanche that buried fleeing gibberers. I saw at least one carter leap free of his doomed wagon, though by the time he struck the ground, a half-dozen quivering shafts had transfixed him.

Gibberers poured down over the edge of the road and splashed across the stream to get away from us. On all fours they fled, looking so very bestial in their panic. Because of the trees, they disappeared from my sight quickly, but a trumpet blast from that side of the road split the night, followed by war cries shouted from human throats. Gibberers shrieked and moaned, stumbling back down the hillside clutching split heads. Others ran as if being chased by arms that dangled from shoulders on sinewy cords.

Others came up at us, so Leigh cast aside his crossbow and moved into the thick of them. Temmer burned brightly as Leigh stalked the hillside with a cold, deliberate tread. A gibberer drove at him, lunging with a longknife. Leigh backed half a step, whirled Temmer around in circle that took the sword-arm off at the elbow, then continued up and around and back down to decapitate the creature. Its head bounced its way down to the feet of other gibberers who stared in horror at it and Leigh. My friend feinted with his head, leaning toward them, leering at them, daring them to come against him.

The rearguard, save the hoargoun, fled north, right into the teeth of Augustus' charge. The infantry broke on the horses' breasts. The cavalry slashed with their swords, striking down those who sought to run from them. They passed from company to company, blasting through ranks, scattering gibberers and chasing more along the roadway.

The hoargoun leaped from the roadway and began to crash his way up the hill toward us. His free hand battered aside saplings, and his broad feet smashed bushes and dead gibberers. Arrows flew at him, stinging his face, chest, gut, and legs, but on he came as if they were of no consequence. His feet churned the earth and his advance split the gibberers facing Leigh. The hoargoun's club rose, sweeping through branches, and trembled as he came within striking distance of the man with the golden sword.

Leigh stared up at him, brandishing the blade.

Defiant.

Terrified.

Ready to die.

The giant's ponderous club started down, but before it could strike, Nay flew from the hilltop and swung his own club in a flat arc. The club slammed into the giant's left knee from the side, shattering bone, popping sinew. The hoargoun roared with pain and his club pounded the ground, filling the gap between Leigh and Nay. The blow shook the earth, pitching Leigh into a roll across the face of the hill.

Nay kept his feet and danced to his right, whirling his club in an upward stroke. It caught the giant's left elbow, shattering it with the sound of a ship's mast snapping. As the giant tried to catch himself on his left hand, he crashed to the ground. His chin dug a furrow in the leafy loam, and a stout oak's trunk stopped the giant's roll to the left.

Nay's last blow landed hard on the giant's right temple. A wet sound dulled the sharp crack of bone, but there was no mistaking the dent he left in the hoargoun's head. The giant's body shook and his last shuddered breath blew a blanket of leaves over Leigh.

More arrows flew, more gibberers screamed, and more blood flowed, but within minutes we had wiped out an Aurolani battalion. Our ambush had been swift and deadly. We suffered a few casualties, but nothing splints and thread would not cure. In less than a quarter of an hour we'd slaughtered an enemy force. We rejoiced in what we had done yet all of us knew this was only the beginning.

What we did next has been said to have taken the heart out of Chytrine's army. I'm not certain that her force ever had a heart to start with. It certainly *did* show her and us the depths to which we could and would go in our war. Somehow I had never doubted we would do what must be done, but being shown so graphically that which we were capable of, it was the sort of thing that still fuels nightmares.

Prince Scrainwood engineered the whole thing. Orchestrated would be a better word. At Scrainwood's direction we moved the hoargoun around and propped him up against some trees, as if he had just stepped off the road and seated himself for a time. His club rested across his knees and his arms were folded over it. His head lolled against a tree, hiding the crushed portion of his skull, making him appear as if he had just fallen asleep.

Of course, chances are that no one who looked at the tableau below him could ever sleep, then or ever.

We hacked the heads from each and every one of the gibberers and vylaens, then placed them, row upon row, back in the formations they'd had as they marched along. The units' banners were dug in, so each company could easily be identified. We salvaged two of their wagons and filled them with arms and armor and other relics. Scrainwood insisted that we tear strips of gibberer hide from the bodies: one for each of us and some left over for the kings and queens who ruled over us. The bodies were then hauled away to a ravine and dumped.

As we marched away, with dusk slowly stealing through the trees, I looked back at what we had done. With distance and fading light, it almost looked as if the Aurolani host had somehow sunk to their necks in mud. The scene looked terribly peaceful, which I knew wasn't right.

Then again, at the time, I couldn't think what was wrong with it.

Seethe reached out and took my left hand in her right, tugging me along. "It's best to be away from here."

"Afraid of ghosts, Seethe?"

"No, Tarrant, not afraid of ghosts." She looked back at the ranks of heads and I felt a tremble run through her. "Just afraid of being haunted."

CHAPTER 31

It took us a day and a half to reach Fortress Draconis. We moved down the river road, making good time. Prince Augustus' cavalry forded the river about a mile north of where the infantry would cross a bridge. When Gyrkyme scouts returned to tell us they were in position, we moved in, hitting the ford garrison from both east and west. They died quickly enough, and after we got ourselves across, we destroyed the bridge.

Being less than a century old, it had no *weirun* and came apart easily as magicks eroded the mortar.

The day remained cool and low fog lingered on the land until noon, which was when we reached the mile-long stretch of rolling plains that separated the upland forests from the peninsula at the western shore. To the east the plains broadened in a wide semicircle, covering the land from northwest to southeast, completely cutting the Draconis Peninsula off. Encamped there, from the edges of the forest down to the lowlands nearest the fortress, Aurolani hordes stretched as far as I could see. Their tents dotted the landscape like fungus, and knots of gibberers moved between them like ants, scurrying from home to food and back.

Between the enemy camps and the low walls of Fortress Draconis' outer city lay a series of trenches. The Aurolani trenches paralleled the walls, with offshoots moving closer. Their aim was to move their siege machinery close enough to shoot at the fortress's walls, and to get their sappers close enough to tunnel beneath them, to undermine them and pull them down. The trenches nearest the fortress worked out toward the Aurolani trenches, both to break up any avenue that would allow a charge and to let *our* sappers locate enemy tunnels and collapse them.

The only area where no trenches existed was the area we were coming through. The Aurolani troops had not spread themselves to cover this approach yet, and with good reason. If Dothan Cavarre decided to evacuate the fortress, they'd only allow him to go north, which would not help him at all. The Aurolani forces had concentrated themselves to the south and east, preventing escape and cutting off landward reinforcement. When more of their forces arrived, they could complete their encirclement of the fortress and the siege could begin in earnest.

The siege would not be easy—just a glance at Fortress Draconis would tell anyone that. I apologize for not describing it first, since it was definitely the dominant feature on the plain, but to present its majesty first would make it seem impossible that the Aurolani forces presented any threat to it at all. When I looked at it I felt my spirits soar—and even Leigh, as lethargic as he had been since his close brush with death, mustered a smile. Had we not been ordered to keep silent, a cry would have risen from our company.

Fortress Draconis had been started seven centuries before and constantly expanded since then. The fortress sat astride a peninsula that jutted into the Crescent Sea and rose to a height of a hundred yards above sea level at the highest point. The northwest side had a natural harbor to which had been added a causeway that served as a breakwater. At its western end rose a massive tower which commanded the approach to the harbor.

A low, thick wall with towers every two hundred yards along it sealed the landward end of the peninsula. The rocky nature of the peninsula itself served as walls on the seaward sides, but towers had been raised along the shore to allow defenders to repel attackers. Elevated causeways linked these towers and made the open spaces between them seem inviting. Anyone scaling the cliffs, as we had done to get at the bridge, would find attackers on the arched walkways pouring molten lead or arrows or burning oil on them, which could be most effective in discouraging an attack.

A second, higher wall all but circled the peninsula's heart. The only gap in it opened at the harbor. Between the shore and this second wall lay Draconis township. It served as home to the masons, armorers, fletchers, bowyers, clerics, merchants, tavernkeepers, and prostitutes—all the support personnel that made life in such a place possible. The township itself looked fairly unremarkable save that its roadways made little or no sense, since they curled around and cut off at odd angles—a carter's nightmare if ever I'd seen one. It would only occur to me later that this tangle of streets meant that collapsing a house or raising a barricade would make progress of an attacking army quite difficult.

In the area between the second wall and the wall of the original fortress lay the garrison town. Here were the barracks for troops, warehouses for weapons and armor, a temple to Kedyn, and storehouses full of food, wine, oil, and other necessities for withstanding a siege. In this section of town the architecture changed, with each building having a heavy, blocky profile. Windows were arrowslits, doors were iron and deep set, allowing defenders to use murderholes cut above them to discourage attackers. Each one of the buildings, constructed of grey granite blocks, was a fortress unto itself. As I would find out later, a regular warren of tunnels linked the warehouses and storehouses with the tower, allowing the shifting of troops and materiels as needed.

The tower complex, strong and dark and ancient in its majesty, rivaled the architecture of Svarskya and Yslin. Whereas they had an artistry about them, the sheer power of the buttressed monstrosity thrusting up into the sky allowed it to dominate the landscape. Balconies ringed it. At the top, a conical leaded roof ended in a spike upon which flew a blue flag with a dragon rampant emblazoned on it.

A taller, thicker wall surrounded the base of the tower, with enough space between the tower's base and the wall to allow for several city streets and normal buildings, though I imagined they would all have the heavy construction I'd seen in the garrison town. Eight smaller towers split the walls at the cardinal points, providing a command of the surrounding area.

If Fortress Draconis had a *weirun*, I would have expected it to be a martial spirit Kedyn would be happy to claim as a son.

The Croquelf leading Cavarre's scouts pointed out a path across the dike holding the sea back. "We will move along there and enter through the harbor."

Lord Norrington frowned. "The outer wall has water lapping at the edge of it. An Aurolani charge could drive us off the dike and into the sea. In armor we're not going to swim well."

The Croquelf laughed. "Fear not, the Snow Fox thinks of everything."

"The Snow Fox?" Prince Kirill frowned. "This is Dothan Cavarre?"

"Yes. His father was Baron before him and called the Fox. His son is very much his heir; you will see."

A flag went up on the lower battlements and the elf summoned us forward along the dike. It was broad enough to be a road, and level, too, so we were able to make good progress along it. While the lowlands between us and the Aurolani host was smooth land, suitable for a charge, we took the Croquelf at his word and cautiously set worry aside. After all, the lowlands were supposed to be flooded as the enemy came at us.

And come they did. As we started along the dike, trumpets blared and flags waved. Company after company of gibberers and vylaens ran this way and that to form up in good order. We faced a front of ten companies and, if my count of flags was right, it ran nine companies deep, pitting us against nine battalions, or a force of almost 2,500 creatures. While that number did daunt me, what disturbed me more was that barely a tenth of the Aurolani camp roused itself to deal with us.

We kept moving and I waited for the secret tunnels leading from the river to burst open. I wanted to see white foaming water wash away the front ranks, sending gibberers rolling and bobbing. I wanted to see the other ranks turn in their panic, shattering the ranks behind them. I wanted to see a lake fill the lowlands, dotted with gibberer corpses like so many mottled islands.

The floods did not come. The gibberers did, marching ever closer. While we outnumbered them, we were stretched out on the dike. Their charge against us would be as deadly as our ambush had been. I eased my bow from across my body and fingered an arrow. I noticed the other archers among us make similar preparations, and even Lord Norrington loosened his sword in its scabbard.

Our guide did not seem concerned at all, which made me feel no better. Prince Augustus formed his cavalry up at the northern end of the dike, ready to mount a suicidal charge to break the enemy formation from the flank. The horsemen wouldn't get very far before they were overwhelmed, but Augustus' forethought was characteristic of the sort of leader he was.

The gibberers, now only a thousand yards from us, sped up their pace. They began trotting toward us, eating up ground. I nocked an arrow, cursing myself for being so nervous. The elven archers further back had not yet set arrow to bow, knowing that even our best shots wouldn't kill until the gibberers closed to within a hundred yards. I swallowed hard and licked my lips, flexed my right hand and continued walking, but I was always ready to stop and shoot.

At five hundred yards the gibberers began to run, and it was then that trumpets blasted from the fortress's walls. Flags shot to the top of poles mounted on towers. The distant shouts of orders could be heard, and I'd have despaired save that the flags and shouts coaxed a laugh from our guide.

Siege machines, big and small, hidden behind walls and ramparts, arched their loads into the air. I saw casks fly out, trailing stout line. When it went taut, the barrels burst, their staves opening like the petals of a flower. From within them flew countless calthrops, made of nails welded together so no matter which way they landed, a spike always faced up. This rain of pointed metal spread out in the gibberers' path, with front ranks pulling up lame, and those following battering them down or tripping over them—dodging only to skewer their own feet.

Clouds of arrows and spears arched over the battlefield. Lead weights had been mounted behind the points, some larger, some smaller, so that the projectile rain spread itself in a line that cut across the battlefield. Whole companies died at once, leaving huge gaps in the enemy formation.

Massive logs arched into the sky, but did not fly as an arrow might. They came broadside. They smashed down into the gibberers, pulping those upon whom they landed, then rolled on, out away from the walls, flattening whole companies. One log, which developed a wobble in flight, hit at one end first, then the other, pitching broken bodies and sod into the air as the ends alternately touched down.

Mismatched stones linked by chains were hurled through the sky. I'd seem similar missiles used in our sea battle, designed to take down a mast and sails, but in the lowlands it had another, more curious effect. The heavier stone would strike first, squashing gibberers beneath it, and would anchor the second stone. Its momentum would stretch the chain taut, then the second stone would roll in a great arc, scything down warriors in a bloody circle.

Even more devastating than those weapons were the *napthalm* spitters. The bronze nozzles had been fashioned to resemble the heads of serpents and had been mounted midway down the tower walls. Torches guttered in the serpent's nostrils. They sprayed out a great stream of *napthalm* which the torches ignited, transforming the dark liquid into a cascade of fire. One tower projected a fiery curtain in front of the Aurolani warriors, while two others played their flaming torrents over the gibberers. Fire-touched warriors screamed and ran, or curled up into little balls and burned.

Nothing got through the firewall to challenge us. More arrows and spears, stones and logs flew from within the fortress to break the gibberers, but their formations had dissolved. Their retreat was headlong and fast.

I looked past the burning field at the rest of the Aurolani host. It didn't matter that they had twenty thousand or thirty thousand warriors out there. There was no way they could successfully lay siege to Fortress Draconis. Chytrine had to know that, had to know her troops could not break the fortress.

I shivered because despite that certain knowledge, she had sent her troops out and that meant she knew something I did not. I took that realization as a harbinger of disaster.

CHAPTER 32

As we neared the outer wall, a trio of barges slid into place and were lashed together to form a floating bridge. It then funneled the whole of our host into the township. The elven guide brought Lord Norrington, Prince Kirill, Nay, Leigh, Seethe, and me over to meet Dothan Cavarre, the Draconis Baron.

It was not hard to see why he was also known as the Snow Fox, for he was a small man with hair so blond it seemed almost white. His sharp features were accentuated by the meticulously trimmed white moustache and goatee that brought his chin to a point. High cheekbones hollowed his cheeks. Hints of blue flecked his grey eyes—the eyes themselves being restless and constantly shifting from wide-eyed wonderment to a focused narrowing to study something or someone.

The fact that he was small—a good head shorter than me—was emphasized by the fact that he wore a loose-fitting silken tunic of blue, black silk pantaloons, and knee-high black leather boots. An oversized belt slanted across his waistline and a dagger hung in a sheath at his right hip. It had no sword to balance it at the left, though a folded pair of gloves did reside there. His hands had long, slender fingers, but they were uncalloused as if he'd never done a day of work in his life.

Judging by the seamless nature of his face, his life had not been that long, either. If he was five years my senior, I could have spit fire at gibberers myself and watched them run. How someone like him became the commander of Fortress Draconis, I could not imagine. Then, just at the point when I was judging him the most harshly, a shift of the wind carried the scent of roasting gibberer to me and I did have to credit his methods for their efficacy.

"Ah, yes, Lord Norrington, at last." He grasped Lord Norrington's hand in both of his and pumped it mightily. "I have enjoyed our correspondence via *arcanslata* very much. I am so glad to have you here. You've brought thirty-five hundred men, yes? Good. That brings us nearly to ten thousand in the garrison here, not counting the militia raised from the township. They're really not useful for much, but . . . Yes?"

Lord Norrington held up his free hand. "I am pleased to be here, but before we continue, I would introduce to you Prince Kirill of Okrannel . . ."

"My pleasure, Highness." The Snow Fox shook his hand and smiled, then killed the smile instantly. "I was sorry to hear of your wife's passing, and of the loss of your city." The smile returned in a flash. "I have had word that your daughter has arrived in the south unharmed."

Kirill's face brightened. "Thank you for telling me that."

Dothan moved on and brought Seethe's right hand to his mouth for a kiss. "A Vorquelf. You would be Seethe, sister to Oracle, who produced the Norrington prophecy?"

Seethe's eyes widened. "I am."

"Good, very good. I like the sound of the prophecy, but would prefer to hear it in the native Elvish. Mine is weak, of course. I'm out of practice, and speak with a dreadful Croquelf accent, but if you wish to converse . . ."

"Thank you, my lord." A hint of confusion ran through Seethe's voice. "Perhaps we will have a chance."

"I'm sure of it." Dothan released her hand, then opened his arms to take in Nay, Leigh, and me. "And here they are, all birds of a feather, as it were. You would be Naysmith Carver, giant-slayer, if reports are right."

"Arrows would have killed him eventually."

"Modest, too; splendid. And you, you are Bosleigh Norrington. You wield Temmer and have killed two—TWO—*sullanciri*. Perhaps your presence here can give the two out there something to fear."

Leigh nodded wearily. "That would be my hope."

"Of course it would, my boy, of course it would." The Snow Fox turned and faced me. "And you are Tarrant Hawkins. I've heard you reached into a temeryx's chest and squeezed its heart until it died. I see by the bow you've impressed Loquelven archers—not easy to do for a man."

"I've done no more than anyone else."

"Extraordinary times demand the extraordinary from everyone." He clapped his hands, then turned back to Lord Norrington. "Well, then, I should love to take you on a tour of the fortress, if you don't mind. I have people who will bring your troops to their billets—no dearth of room here. We'll get them fed and to bed, then give them assignments that will familiarize them with the fortress. No heavy work yet; some relaxation, yes?"

Lord Norrington nodded. "That sounds right. Ah, here are Princes Augustus and Scrainwood. My lords, this is our host, Dothan Cavarre."

"Prince Augustus, your cavalry looked very smart drawn up there on the plain. I almost let some of the gibberers through to watch you work, but I was too selfish. Forgive me."

Prince Augustus smiled. "I'm sure we will have another chance to show you our skill."

"Indeed." Dothan looked at Prince Scrainwood. "I hope you will enjoy your stay with us."

Prince Kirill adjusted the sling holding his left arm. "You said you almost let some of the gibberers through. We thought you were going to flood the lowlands."

"Oh, I was, I was . . ."

"Preparations went awry?"

"No, Prince Kirill, not at all. They went very well." Dothan smiled. "I'll show you, of course, but I decided to save the flood for another time. Couldn't have used the calthrops since the land would get too marshy, you see. Wouldn't have worked at all. I wanted to give them something to think about, so I gave them a little taste of what we have in store for them."

Leigh's father nodded. "It was an impressive display."

"If you liked that, then come, let me show you everything else." The Snow Fox started toward the outer wall, saw he'd have to march us through the troops streaming in, so he spun about and started off in another direction, then shifted to a third. "Come along, this is it."

The Fortress Draconis he toured us through is hard to imagine now for anyone who had not seen it previously. The changes made over the years did not so much overshadow the brilliance of the original design, but rather just layered excess over it. It was like dipping a candle in wax over and over again, sometimes all the way, sometimes not, ending up with a bloated thing that lacks the elegance of its core.

For instance, he showed us how he had small catapults mounted on a turntable that allowed him to swivel them around. Or how the *napthalm* spitters were nozzles in the center of a tower that could move up and down or side to side, but were connected via a stout hose to a tank in a chamber higher in the tower. The weight of the fluid forced it out through the hose without any pumps to break down. In yet other places he had long metal rails running in parallel, and along them were drawn carts carrying arrows or spears or stones or canisters of calthrops to the ballistae.

Quoting Dothan Cavarre exactly is difficult, given how he runs on with his words so. Any one of his monologues might touch on dozens of subjects, and sorting out fact from opinion and linking them to the right subjects was enough work to keep me silent throughout the tour. I was able to confirm that he was only four years older than me, which made him Princess Ryhope's age, yet his knowledge of the world surpassed that of the eldest man in Valsina.

He had become the Draconis Baron because his father, Raakin, had been the Draconis Baron before him; but the post was not one passed on via a bloodline. When his father prepared to retire, he notified the Harvest Council and they began

to look for a replacement. Dothan, who had spent his entire
life in Fortress Draconis, applied for the position, submitting
his application under an assumed name. His father, who
helped choose a successor, did not know his own son was one
of the candidates.

"You see, I did not have the military experience of the
other candidates, no, indeed. But then, no one had repulsed
an Aurolani attack in almost a century, so no one had the
experience needed, really. But I had spent my whole life here,
growing up in the fortress, exploring every nook and cranny.
I'd watched all the troops, become a mascot for some, learned
Elvish and urZrethi—which is a gods-awful tongue for a man
to try—and discovered I had no skill with weapons, save to
invent them and perfect them and imagine how to use them."

Dothan's smile broadened, his steps lengthened, and his
arms swung wide as he turned circles and led us through the
fortress. His right hand lovingly caressed the central spine of
the Crown Tower as he ascended the spiral steps through its
heart. At each level he'd have us leave the stairs and move to
the balconies so we could get a better look at the carvings on
the walls, or the tapestries hung there, or some little treasure
brought from this nation or that.

He was quite proud of everything, as well he should have
been.

I think I found the flying buttresses the most impressive.
They had not been carved, but poured of a mixture of lime-
stone and sand, which was blended into a slurry and fed into
wooden forms that had been carved with designs. He called it
acretestone. Metal posts ran through the mixture, which hardened and set, then the next piece was poured. The forms produced a stone in the shape of a dragon, which stood on the
head of the one below it, and so on down to the ground, with
the dragons getting slightly smaller as the buttress went up.
When we got to the top, the uppermost dragons leaned in to
hold the tower upright. We could have easily walked out on
their broad backs—Dothan offered us the chance to do so, in
fact—but I demurred.

"It is quite solid, Hawkins. It can support a lot of weight."

"That's fine, I believe you." I held my hands up. "After all we have been through, walking out there is one more chance than I want to take."

"Very good point, Hawkins." Dothan laughed aloud. "Why drink from the cask of luck now when you might need a mouthful later?"

The Crown Chamber capped the tower, as one might expect. Stout wooden rafters supported the leaded, conical roof. The chamber itself had no decoration or furnishings aside from a round firepit at the floor's heart in which burned a small votive fire and three small plinths arranged around it. On each plinth rested a dazzling stone bound in gold—almost identical matches for the piece of the DragonCrown I'd seen in Svarskya. One stone was a ruby, another a bright yellow sapphirelike stone, and the last a green stone resembling the one I'd seen before. It had hints of blue in it, the significance of which I did not know.

We looked at the room through a wall made of the same iron bars that covered the windows in a crosshatched pattern. Dothan smiled and rested his hand on the iron-bar door in the center of the wall. "I would invite you in to look at the pieces of the crown more closely, but the effort of disarming the thief traps would take far too long. If you would like a closer look, however, I can bring you along on my weekly inspection."

Lord Norrington gave him a quick nod. "That would be appreciated, but only if it is no trouble."

"None whatsoever, not at all, not at all." The master of Fortress Draconis waved us back toward the stairs. "You have come a long way and have accomplished much. Let me see you to your accommodations. Please, consider the fortress your home. Make yourselves at home—use the gardens, raid my wine cellar, whatever suits your fancy."

Prince Kirill smiled. "You are most generous."

"I would like to think so, but everything I have here has come from the nations of the world—your nations. Our supply often exceeds our demand, so we have excess for times like this. Giving it to you, to repay what you have done, it is the least I can do."

• • •

Dothan Cavarre's *least* was by far the most luxurious treatment I'd had in my entire life. The apartments he led us to were small, but filled with ornate furnishings. I had a big bed with a canopy over it and a heavy down quilt covering it. A wardrobe and a matching chest of drawers stood as sentries on either side of the door, then a sideboard, a small table, and four upholstered chairs took over the half of the room next to the bed. A small iron stove functioned in place of a hearth and hugged the wall right beside the bed, with the stovepipe burrowing into the wall and, I presumed, linking up with some flue hidden therein. A couple of rugs covered most of the floor. The window, which was functionally narrow, gave me a distant glimpse of the harbor.

The sideboard had three decanters full of wine and four goblets, as well as some cheese and a small basket of dried fruit. I'd just unstoppered a crystal decanter to sniff at the red wine therein, when a gentle knock preceded a servant slipping into my room. He was older than me, but not by much, and held himself erect—making me wonder if he weren't a soldier pressed into auxiliary duty.

"Begging your pardon, sir, but the Baron, he asked that I conduct you to the bathing center."

I returned the stopper to the decanter, then set it back on the sideboard. He opened the door and I followed. We took a stairway worked in the external wall and descended to ground level. He led me past the arched doorway to a vast room tiled in ivory, with mosaics on the walls and along the bottom of pools. Steam rising from most of the pools prevented me from getting a good look at the art, but the general theme seemed to have something to do with the slaying of Aurolani beasts.

I disrobed in the alcove the servant indicated. I left my mask hanging from a peg and donned a slender cloth bathing mask of brown. I cut down through a cool corridor and slipped into a pool of warm water—one of several, each hidden from the rest of the room and each other by a low wall. The brushes and soap tucked into niches around the rim led me to believe I was supposed to scrub myself in this pool before visiting any of the others, and the wall allowed me the privacy I wanted to remove my mask to bathe. I took the hint to heart, pulled my mask off, and plied the soap and brush over my skin with serious effort. In fairly short order my skin shed the brown hue I'd mistaken as sun-tint from my journey.

Feeling truly clean for the first time in ages, I tied my bathing mask back into place and slipped from that pool to one that was slightly hotter, and from there into another that was hotter still. I closed my eyes and floated there blissfully, drawing the warm wet air deep into my lungs. The heat melted away the knots in my muscles and returned to me a sense of peace I'd all but forgotten existed.

I bobbed up and down as someone else's entry sent ripples through the pool. I rolled over and smiled as both Leigh and Nay entered the pool. Nay was smiling broadly and groaned delightedly as he sank to his neck in the steaming water. Leigh still moved a bit slowly, but even his face lit up as the water wrapped him in a hot cocoon. Me, I was just happy to see him without Temmer.

Nay sighed aloud. "There were nights on the ships, in the rain, that this was just a dream."

Leigh nodded. "The cold, it just sinks into your bones, but this burns it out again." He lowered his face into the water, then came up with his face dripping and his blue eyes bright. "Well, lads, who would have thought we'd be here, doing this, a scant three months ago? Hawkins, you were hoping you'd be a Scout, and Nay, well, I don't know what you were hoping."

"Being a Scout would do."

"Those are still goals we can attain."

I frowned at Leigh. "What were you hoping for yourself?"

He shrugged. "Does it matter? Now I have new goals. Marry a princess, start a dynasty—the usual, you know."

"Oh, indeed." I affected the lilting tone of his voice. "Slay a dragon, conquer Aurolan: trivial matters."

"Quite so, quite so." Nay's attempt at aping Leigh's tone had enough enthusiasm to cover the stiffness therein. I expected him to continue, but he stopped and his face drained of color. I whirled around to see what he was staring at, then had to lunge for the edge of the pool to catch myself.

A man stood in the mists, wearing the ceremonial cloak of a Knight of the Phoenix. His left hand came up, touched just below his left eye, descended and rose again—the signal for us to follow him. He spun on his heel, his cloak swirling through the mist, then he disappeared out of the room.

The three of us got over our astonishment rather quickly and hauled ourselves out of the pool. I went immediately for the alcove where I'd left my true mask. I wasn't so much concerned about being naked as I was about having a bathing mask on. The other two followed. We found our masks, and Phoenix Knight cloaks where our clothes had been. Pulling them on, we ran through the hall to try and find the person who had summoned us, but he was gone.

Leigh pointed to wet bootprints on the stone. We quickly followed them and descended a stairway, then found the Fledgling sign worked in a stone along the side of a narrow corridor. Nay pushed on the stone, then pulled his hand away as if it had been stung. "Not liking that at all."

A magickal glow began in the stone. Further down the corridor a section of the wall pulled back and tipped down, providing us a drawbridge into another corridor. I led us across the section of wall, then had to turn immediately to the left to continue even though the corridor looked as if it extended for a good long distance. Had a breach been opened in the wall and I'd tried to leap across the chasm, I'd have slammed into a wall that had been ingeniously painted to look like a corridor. I'd have either dashed my brains out, or fallen to my death below, and I wasn't certain which fate I would have preferred.

We descended a spiral staircase and came out onto a narrow platform. Steep stairs ran up from it to a broader, deeper platform, perhaps five feet above us and fifteen feet back. Starting level with it, a semicircular series of benches rose in five steps. Upon these benches sat men and women in a rainbow of hooded cloaks.

The small man standing in the middle of the dais could have been no one other than the Draconis Baron. He wore a cloak of red trimmed in gold. He extended a gloved hand toward us and filled the room with a voice that took on a resonance I'd not have thought possible from having heard him earlier.

"Behold three who were, just weeks ago, made Minor Fledglings in Oriosa. In Alcida they were given instruction, and since then they have been in service to the world. The first has slain two *sullanciri*, a feat unequaled in the annals of heroism. The second has slain a giant, crushing it in three blows. And the third has confronted *sullanciri* and has proved to be an archer of such skill that Loquelves fashioned for him a bow of silverwood. Their selfless efforts have brought great glory upon us."

The assembled Knights applauded politely. Their cloaks had enough variation to mark them as coming from different nations. Some had hems trimmed in gibberer fur. Others sported dangling temeryx feathers of white, and at least one hood was made of a vylaen pelt. That they applauded us at all struck me as odd, for these were men and women who, by the very virtue of their being at Fortress Draconis, had likely seen and done more than we would ever do. As with Cavarre's earlier praise, I did not think what I had done was worthy of such acclaim.

Nay seemed to be similarly uncomfortable, but Leigh beamed proudly. I couldn't fault him for that—he'd eliminated half of Chytrine's leadership cadre, which was a momentous accomplishment. There was no doubting he was a hero and the acclaim seemed to infuse back into him some of the life the sword had drained.

"As the acting Flock Lord for the precinct of Fortress Draconis, I ask if there is anyone who would speak."

A man stepped forward in the first rank wearing a scarlet cloak trimmed in black; the quilted feathers on his cloak were likewise outlined in black. Until he spoke I couldn't recognize him, but his voice permitted no mistake.

Prince Augustus cleared his throat. "I have witnessed the actions of these three. They have acquitted themselves far better than their youth or rank would suggest possible. It is my thought that elevation to the rank of Wing is in order."

"Thank you, Grand Black Phoenix." Cavarre slowly turned and looked around the room. "Is there anyone who would speak against this elevation?"

The other Knights remained silent.

The acting Flock Lord came around to look at us again. "It is my pleasure to welcome you to the rank of Wing." At his signal three other Knights moved from their places and stood in a line behind him. Each one bore a folded cloak. The Flock Lord beckoned us forward, and as we stepped toward the stairs, the clasps on our cloaks failed, leaving them behind. Naked, we climbed the stairs in the order of our initial recognition.

The new cloaks, which were brown except for a red course of feathers above the yellow course we'd worn before, were draped over our shoulders. Cavarre stood before each of us and reached up to fasten our clasps. Once that was done, he retreated a step and bowed his head to us.

He spoke in a solemn voice that filled the amphitheatre easily. "In the course of your time here at Fortress Draconis, you will be tutored in that which you must know to fulfill the duties and shoulder the responsibilities of your new rank. It should make you proud to know that seldom has any one person reached this rank this swiftly. Never before, to my knowledge, has a trio of Knights risen this far, this fast. On the eve of the battles we will face here, we consider this a most fortuitous omen."

CHAPTER 33

After our elevation—an event that surprised and pleased me—I got some food, returned to my room alone, and promptly fell asleep. While I'd certainly slept onboard the ships and caught as much rest as I could on the road, there was no denying I was exhausted. The sun was just setting as I crawled into my bed, and it was long past dawn when I awakened.

I got dressed from the clothes in my wardrobe—which did not include the ragged garments I'd worn since we left Yslin. Someone had filled my wardrobe with tunics and trousers that fit pretty well and were dyed Oriosan green. I slipped the boot knife Nay had given me into the top of my right boot.

I wandered down into the dining hall and found it fairly full. As Cavarre had explained the day before, the garrison troops ate in shifts, so food was always available. I grabbed a bowl of thick stew and half a round of bread, then retreated to an empty side table to eat. I was fairly certain that I could have joined any of the groups of men and women seated elsewhere, but I kept my distance on purpose.

Despite the praises sung of us in the Phoenix Knight assembly, I knew the reality of the world. The men and women serving here had bonded through their experiences. They trained together and every day were willing to fight and even die to defend the fortress. Their sacrifices were greater than any I had made. I was just a youth off on an adventure, and to be touted as somehow their equal or superior was simply wrong.

Part of me wanted very much to join them, and I took great solace in the warm laughter that echoed throughout the room. Brags were shouted from one table to the next, with individual challenging individual and unit challenging unit. Wagers were offered and taken concerning the numbers of enemy each would slay, the number of prisoners to be taken, the number of citations to be won, the honors that would be awarded, and even the number of stitches to sew up wounds. The warriors gathered there exuded a buoyant confidence that would do more to defend Fortress Draconis than walls and weapons.

I finished my breakfast quickly, cleared away my bowl and crumbs—having pitched the last piece of bread to one of the various curs slinking about. I began to wander around and inquire if anyone had seen Nay. The first few folks I asked had not, but one of the Guards who had been with us on the ship said he'd seen him in the fortress's armory.

The armory itself wasn't in the tower, but a walled and covered walkway connected the two buildings. Even before I reached the building I could smell the smoke from the forges and feel the heat. As I climbed the steps to the entrance, the clangor of smiths at work vibrated through me, sounding as pure and deadly as the thunder of war drums.

My eyes watered as I paused in the entrance. Directly before me, glowing red with a sweaty sheen, Nay hammered a length of yellow-orange steel. Sparks shot down with each blow, and each blow came in a cadence that was regular and insistent. It didn't race, nor did it plod along, but matched the heartbeat of a man hard at work.

The steel dulled to a deep red, so Nay thrust it back into the forge. Two apprentices worked the bellows, sprouting bright yellow flames from the hot coals. Nay swiped at his sweaty brow with his gloved left hand, then he reached into a pocket of his leather apron and pulled out the stone that was Tsamoc. He stared intently at the stone, and the faint hint of a glow started from within it. This brought a smile to his face. He returned the stone to his pocket, picked up his tongs again, and rescued the swordblade from the coals. He eyed it carefully, then began to pound on it again.

So intent was he on his work that he did not notice me—not that he had much of a chance to do so since I must just have been a silhouette in the doorway. I chose not to disturb him and moved on. A smile grew on my face as I realized Nay had returned to what he did and what he was before his Moon Month, as a way to get back in touch with reality. I guessed he was as confused about our situation as I was, and I was happy he found a way to deal with the problem.

I decided to do the same thing, and since I spent most of my spare time with Leigh in the past, I searched him out.

One aspect of Fortress Draconis that I did not describe previously was the series of gardens that ringed the western half of the tower's base. Two of the five were conventional gardens, with herbs and vegetables and flowers. The one near the armory did have a couple of apple trees, but the apples were just shy of ripe.

Big, thick hedges split the gardens one from another. I moved around the circuit, passing through a wrought-iron gate into the second garden. White stones had been sown over the ground and raked to a smoothness that almost made the place seem covered in snow. Two trees, one by the outer wall and the other kitty-corner back by the tower offered some shade, but did not overshadow much of the garden. Flat stones provided a meandering walkway that linked this gate with the next and with a doorway into the tower. A dry river of stones split the white expanse, with a stone bridge arching over it. Elsewhere bigger stones stood like islands in a white ocean.

Here I found Leigh, sitting cross-legged on the bridge's railing. He wore only a loose robe and some silk pants—no boots, nothing else. Nowhere could I see Temmer. My friend just sat there, staring down at the dry streambed with dark-rimmed eyes, as if he could see water swirling through it.

I tried to close the gate silently behind me, and thought I

had done so, until I turned and saw Leigh looking at me. "Sorry. I didn't want to disturb you."

He shook his head. "You didn't. I was just thinking. Thinking a lot. About things. About how things have been going." His voice carried a sadness to it that made my heart ache.

"Any interesting conclusions?"

Leigh smiled carefully. "I feel very much at peace here. I don't know if you can feel it, too, but I feel secure. Before there was this oppressive air around me. Unless I had Temmer in hand, I didn't feel safe."

"I feel the peace here, yes." I stepped from stone to stone in my slow approach to the bridge. "I think it's good you don't have the sword with you."

"So do I, but there is a cost." He held his right hand out, palm open, parallel to the ground. Little tremors shook it, like an old man's palsy. "Even though I don't need it here, I still want it. I feel crippled without it."

"It's a fell thing, that sword. It does great things, but the price . . ." I reached the bridge and leaned against the railing on which he sat. "If only you'd known when you found it."

Leigh gave me a half smile and stared down at the stone-strewn gully. "I did know, Tarrant, I did. When I saw it there, the way the skeleton's hands clutched the hilt, I knew I shouldn't touch it. With one hand the skeleton pulled it to himself, but with the other he was pushing it away. I knew there was something wrong, something bad about it, but that didn't deter me. I was a child again, looking at something I knew wasn't mine, something I knew I shouldn't take, like it was a pie cooling on a window sill. Part of me knew I'd be caught, that I'd be punished, but I went ahead and took it anyway."

I shook my head. "But the story Resolute told, the bargain struck with the wielder, you didn't know that. The cost isn't worth the gain."

Leigh laughed weakly, rocking back. "But it is, Tarrant, it *is* worth it. When you've drawn Temmer—and I pray to all the gods that you never do—you feel such power that you know nothing can stand against you. You know, as I did in Atval, that your enemies will fall and your friends will live. You are the arbiter of life and death—and in that moment, for that time, Temmer is worth the future of pain."

"But what happened in the Ghost Marches . . ."

"Yes, the woman protecting the little girl." Leigh closed his eyes and ran a hand over his mouth. "I want you to know I would not have attacked the child. I knew she was no threat. I . . . the mother had a knife and I saw it . . . There was no time to think, I just struck and then she was dead and the child started crying."

He looked over at me for a second, sucking on his lower lip. "I owe you thanks for stopping me, for getting me down. Twice you've risked Temmer's wrath to save me. I couldn't have a better friend."

I gave him a quick grin. "We've been friends forever, Leigh. No reason to let a magick sword come between us. I just don't want you getting hurt."

"Me? Hurt?" He shrugged. "Part of the bargain with the sword."

"Yes, but there are ways to be hurt and ways to be hurt."

His blue eyes narrowed. "What are you talking about?"

I folded my arms over my chest. "The Ghost Marches thing I was talking about wasn't the woman and the child. What I was talking about was the *hoargoun*. You stood there, waiting for it to crush you."

Leigh's voice sank to a whisper. "You think I wanted to die."

"I don't know what you were thinking, Leigh, but I know what I want you to think." I reached out and rested a hand on his shoulder. "I want you to think that there are other ways to beat Temmer than dying."

"Sure, never draw it again. Never go into battle again. That will beat it." He pointed off to the east with his left hand. "Of course, that would let them win. It might cost you and Nay and my father your lives, but I'd win. I'd be alive to savor my victory for the rest of time."

"Right, fine, that solution doesn't work, but there are others. We'll think of them."

"Will we, Tarrant?" Leigh looked through me. "While I've

been sitting here, I've come up with a piece of a rhyme. Want to hear it?"

"Please." I smiled and lowered my hand. If Leigh was feeling good enough to be coming up with poetry, I knew things weren't totally lost. "What is it?"

"It's only a piece, but here it is:

> *Weak heart faints*
> *When trouble rises.*
> *Brave heart soars,*
> *Steals all the prizes.*
> *False heart, it*
> *Shrinks small in peace*
> *And finds in*
> *Fear no surcease.*"

He smiled at me. "What do you think?"

"More serious than most of your other poems, Leigh." I sighed and tried to see past his hollow-eyed visage to the friend I'd grown up with. "We will find another solution to the Temmer problem."

"Of course we will, Hawkins." Leigh nodded slowly. "Count on it."

He returned to staring at the dry river and I left him alone. To my mind came Resolute's comment about Leigh, that he was one of the walking dead. It wasn't so much that he'd given up on life as he was trapped by it. Given a choice he would have thrown away the sword, but that would let Chytrine live. Trapped between saving himself and the world, Leigh's spirit was being pounded into gravel.

I moved through the next garden, which featured steaming pools of water and a variety of plants that thrived in hot, moist areas. From there I came into a sunken area that had been flooded. Rocks created islands and little wooden bridges and walkways connected them. The clear water in the pools below permitted crystal views of the fish swimming lazily along. I recognized none of them, but the fish I knew had come from local lakes and rivers, so tended to be sleek and powerful. These fish had fancy fins and swam slowly, though their gold scales did glint brightly.

Watching them promoted a sense of peace, and I took it as a bad sign that Leigh was spending his time in the barren garden instead of this one full of life. The old Leigh would have been here, sitting on the walkways, dangling his toes like fat little worms in the water. He'd have named each of the fish, would have made up vast stories about them and their relationships with each other. He would have tempted them with his toes and rewarded any quick enough to nip him with a nickname and a verse in its honor.

"You look so pensive, Hawkins."

I turned and forced a smile on my face. "Seethe. I didn't hear you come up."

She winked at me with a gold eye. "Have to watch us Vorquelves all the time. We've learned to be sneaky."

"They say that's why Chytrine doesn't sleep whole nights through."

"Oh, very good." She gave me a little laugh, which nibbled away at the chill I'd felt in Leigh's presence. Her golden eyes burned with life, and her smile shared it with me. As much as Leigh might have been glad to have me as a friend, more so was I glad to have her.

She'd gathered her long black hair into a single thick braid that snaked over her right shoulder. She played with the end of it in both hands. Seethe, too, wore a silken robe, but this one was blue and trimmed in black, matching the long skirt she had on. Like Leigh, she was barefoot.

I frowned. "Did I miss a sign that said boots weren't allowed in the gardens?"

"No, I don't think so, Hawkins." She smiled and playfully flicked her braid in my direction. "I think it's just that you like to be prepared for emergencies. You think ahead like that. You have a knife, I have none. You have boots, I have none. In the back of your mind you have worries; right now I have none."

"None?" I blinked my eyes. "No worries at all?"

Seethe wrinkled her nose and shrugged slightly. "Well, perhaps a few, but they are packed away in my room for the moment." She leaned against the walkway railing, resting her elbows on it. "Well, there is one worry that I didn't pack away, and it's this: I worry that I never expressed my gratitude to you for staying with me as we sailed past Vorquellyn."

"It was no problem."

"Not that you would say if it had been, would you, Hawkins?" She smiled at me, then turned away and looked down at the fish. "I had seen Vorquellyn before, you know. Ages ago, well before you were born and perhaps even before your parents were born. I was with a number of other Vorquelves—Resolute was there; he's the only one you know—in a small boat. We were heading for the Ghost Marches, to go north and try to kill Chytrine. We were close but couldn't land. We knew it would be suicide and that insulated us from the pain and disappointment. What we were heading out to do would be the first step in liberating our homeland.

"This time, with a fleet and warriors, I knew we could have attacked. We could have driven the Aurolani forces from Vorquellyn. We could have saved it, we could have made it ours again, yet that was not the object of our expedition."

She turned and looked up into my eyes, peering at me as if her gaze could see past my mask and even into my soul. "Right then I wanted to hate everyone in the expedition. I knew why Resolute had withdrawn. I understood him as I never have before, his militancy, his insistence. I hated the fact that we were passing so close, yet would leave Vorquellyn behind, and I wanted to hate all men for not having taken action before now.

"You didn't let that happen. You were there with me. You took care of me. This trip was my second sailing from Vorquellyn and again a man saw me through it." Seethe straightened up and closed the distance between us. She leaned forward and I felt the feather-light brush of her breath on my face a second before she kissed me.

I had kissed and been kissed before, but this kiss was different—and not just because Seethe was a Vorquelf. Her kiss came light and slow. For a moment I was free to wonder if our lips had actually touched, but the tingle running through my body confirmed they had. She kissed me again, then, a bit more insistently, and I slipped my arms around her. I drew her to me and we kissed a third time.

I have never forgotten the warm press of her body against mine, the way her hands held my face, the taste of her lips and the warmth of her breath. Her taut body fit perfectly within my arms. I clung to her fiercely and she to me, our shared experience on the expedition being more important in that moment than all the differences that might have separated us.

Arm in arm, stealing kisses as we went, we retreated from the garden and secreted ourselves away in the room she'd been given. Morning bled into afternoon and then evening as we lay together, touching, whispering, giggling at the things lovers find funny. We drank little and ate less, but neither of us noticed time passing or the lack of food. We satisfied each other in warm and gentle, steaming and passionate ways that made physical hunger irrelevant.

As night fell, with her head on my chest, I drew the sheets up around her shoulders and stroked her now unbound hair. I leaned down and kissed her on the crown. "Seethe, I need to ask you something."

"Yes?"

"How do we . . . The others will notice that you and I . . . What do we tell . . . ?"

She kissed me on the chest, then rolled over onto her belly and smiled at me. Her gold eyes glowed with a muted reflection of the sinking sun's light. "Are you worried that someone might gossip about our liaison? That my reputation will be tarnished?"

I blushed. "I don't want anyone to hurt you."

Her throaty laugh warmed me, as did the quick kiss with which she punctuated it. "Fear not, my gallant one, for Vorquelves are known for being different. The other elves here will see our dalliance as a sign of my immaturity, a tragic remnant of my being unhomed. Your people—those who are hopelessly jealous of you and driven to cruelty because of it—will know that we have found in each other strength and peace. Thus they will envy us, but they will also understand."

I raised an eyebrow. "Ummm, I think you're thinking far better of men than I do."

"Ah, but you inspire confidence in me for your people, Tarrant." She half-lidded her eyes, then rested her chin on my chest. "It doesn't matter what they say. We can't be hurt unless we let ourselves be hurt. Here, with you, I am beyond hurting and that is all that matters. Other elves avoid unions with men because fleeting pleasure scares them. It doesn't me and shouldn't you. Right now we need each other, and that is enough reason to be together. Remember that always, no matter what happens, and no one will be able to hurt you again."

CHAPTER 34

As far north as Fortress Draconis is, the autumn mornings start crisp, making me even more reluctant to slip from a warm bed. As it was no one said anything to me about my liaison with Seethe—aside from congratulating me. I gathered, from a comment Seethe made, that Lord Norrington had spoken to her about our involvement. I ended up being flattered by the fact that he never spoke to me about it—which I took as an indication of his trust in my judgment.

Leigh did kid me about it a bit, but that was fine, too, since it heralded a return of the Leigh I'd known. "She's a fine catch, Hawkins. I'd have cast my eye in her direction too, if I weren't set to marry a princess. But you shouldn't feel disappointed in your choice because of that."

"Who me? No. I know that courting someone who has a century on you is a rare art."

"An acquired taste, really, and one I'm not sure I want to acquire."

I smiled. "But women are like wine, getting better with age . . ."

"Ah, but young vintages have their charms, too." Leigh gave me a smile that emerged free of the air of doom that had settled over him. "Once we lift the siege here and destroy Chytrine, I think I will formally court Ryhope. Scrainwood says he favors me in that regard."

"With friends like that at court, then . . ."

Leigh's eyes sharpened and his voice shrank to a whisper. "I know there is no love lost between you. He's spoken badly of you, so I've got his full measure, my friend. Have no doubt of that. Still, using a bridge—no matter how weak—to cross a river beats getting wet."

I had to allow as how that was true, though I still hitched a bit when I saw Scrainwood and Leigh walking together along battlements or sharing a laugh over a meal. The only good thing I could see from their conspiracy to marry Leigh off to Ryhope was that it gave Leigh something to think about. He was very good at assuming roles and postures that would get him what he wanted, and paying court to Scrainwood distracted him from Temmer and the problems that came with it.

It struck me that perhaps Leigh's ability to shift his personality to suit a given situation was the reason the sword was able to exert as much control as it could over him. While that idea had some appeal for me, the appeal was but a thin layer of ice over a very deep, dark lake. The only solution to the problem was for Leigh to become more rigid, more mature, stronger in mind and soul. That would destroy the Leigh I'd known, but so would the sword.

I diverted myself from such dire thoughts by focusing on the situation at the fortress. I kept watches with the men and women of the Seventh Oriosan Guards. Units from the various nations served at Fortress Draconis for a one year term, at which time they rotated home. It wasn't then as it became, with permanent garrison units being reinforced piecemeal with raw recruits or *meckanshii*. Things were not yet that desperate, so the warriors I served with had not yet developed the grim, fatalistic sense that came to dominate Fortress Draconis.

Occasionally Dothan Cavarre would pull me aside and have me join him, Lord Norrington, and Princes Augustus and Kirill in inspections of various parts of the fortress. By and large the inspections were purely routine, and I was very impressed with the stockpile of food and weapons in the warehouses. Each nation contributed to the fortress's support and the result was enough supplies to last a dozen years.

Our most interesting excursion came three days after our arrival. The Draconis Baron sent a message telling me to armor up and arm myself with a dagger or two, then to meet him in the outer town. I did as requested, adding one of the captured gibberer longknives to my belt so I could have something a bit more substantial than a dagger. I came to the appointed house and entered, discovering piles of dirt packing it from floor to rafters save for a set of stairs leading down into the ground. At the base of the stairs I found Cavarre, Lord Norrington, Prince Augustus, Prince Kirill, and Faryaah-Tse Kimp. All of them were armored and armed, with the ur-Zrethi's weapons a pair of nasty spikes growing out of her right wrist and extending nearly two feet beyond her hand. Even Cavarre wore quilted silk armor with a mail surcoat over it and had a pair of daggers with him, so I knew some danger was expected.

Cavarre led us out and down through a reinforced tunnel that ran to the northeast. Lanterns hung from rafters to provide light, though seeing where I was going was difficult because I was last in line and the tunnel was low enough that I had to constantly stoop or bump my head. Those in front of me eclipsed the light. Because of the tunnel's tight confines I realized the only swordwork I'd have managed would have been thrusting, so bringing the longknife was the better way to go.

The tunnel broadened into a small opening off which three more tunnels extended. As we moved into the opening, a dozen urZrethi marched past us, hauling sacks of dirt strapped to their backs. Unlike Faryaah-Tse, they were duller colors, the red of earth, the grey of ash, and black of coal. Their hands ended in shovel-like blades, while their eyes and ears had become oversized. They paid us no mind as they went on their way, presumably to dump their dirt and return to dig more.

Cavarre dropped into a crouch and pointed at the tunnels. "We are now just beyond our walls, perhaps twenty feet down. We have crews digging all the time, working to find the tunnels the Aurolani sappers are creating to take down our walls. We shore up our tunnels, of course, so we won't do their work for them, then we hunt the Aurolani. The reason for the larger ears on the urZrethi diggers is so they can hear sappers and dig toward them. I was sent word that they were close to a tunnel to the east here, and that they expected to break through this morning. I thought you might like to observe."

He raised a finger to his lips, then pointed down the central tunnel, the one leading almost directly east. Faryaah-Tse went first, followed by Augustus, Lord Norrington, and Kirill. I came next and Cavarre dropped into line behind me. That struck me as odd until I recalled that he knew little or nothing about combat. If any of the Aurolani did get into our tunnel, they'd be hard-pressed to reach him, which was actually a good thing as far as the leadership of the fortress was concerned.

We passed through a couple of zigs and zags in the tunnel, then descended through a steep dip and back up. The dip served as a flood-stop, since the next section of tunnel was lower than the first, while the cutbacks were designed to slow attackers and give defenders time to hold them off. It also struck me that defenders further back could probably collapse the tunnel fairly easily, preventing entry into the fortress.

The air in the tunnel tasted foul and even the lanterns seemed dimmer. I've never been one to fear small, enclosed spaces, but scraping my back along the roof of a tunnel did begin to wear on me. Poor Cavarre reaped the reward for my discomfort, as bits and pieces of dirt rained on his head, but he didn't complain.

At the far end of the tunnel—and I have no idea how far out we were—we stopped at the rear of an urZrethi formation. The urZrethi arrayed before us had the same shape as the diggers, but that began to change. Bumps and hard edges rose through their flesh, as if it were wet cloth being pulled taut over armor. Turtle-shell plates came to cover them; hooks and spurs grew on shoulders, elbows, and wrists. Their ears shrank away to nothing while their eye-sockets deepened. Their faces projected muzzles forward, with a hard bony ridge running the length of them. The snout tapered, making it not as blocky as that of a gibberer, and giving them more reach. Some grew fangs or tusks, others drew back lips to reveal ranks of serrated teeth. Their hands curled down into at least one spike, usually short and very stout. Many transformed their off hand into a two-fingered, one-thumbed grasping tool with big claws that could hit hard as a fist, or reach into a chest and pluck out organs. Their legs thickened and shrank as their upper bodies expanded and their arms bulked with muscle.

In less than a minute they'd gone from diggers to warriors perfectly suited to fighting in the enclosed tunnels. They couldn't run fast, but they wouldn't need to. The combat would all be close and nasty, full of biting, tearing, and stabbing.

As quietly as possible I drew my longknife, then, almost as an afterthought, I shucked off my left glove and tucked it down inside my jerkin.

Cavarre watched me do that for a moment, then nodded. "Yes, in the dark, touch will count for more than any other sense. Very good, Hawkins."

"If it has fur, I can stab it."

Ahead of us, near the wall of the tunnel, Faryaah-Tse shone like a beacon compared to the other urZrethi. She maintained the shape she had taken when she joined us, which left her looking very childlike and innocent. She raised her arms and crossed them, then pulled them apart sharply.

Two diggers at the front of the tunnel stabbed their hands deep into the dirt and clawed it back. A little hole opened up, but before they could expand on it, the urZrethi warriors surged forward, blasting through with their shoulders. "For Boragul," shouted one, and a half-dozen voices answered, "Varagul for Victory." Other war cries I could not understand, though the guttural pulsing of "kang vatt ki-det" really needed no translation. Through the wall and into the enemy tunnel they poured, with snarls and snaps and howls greeting them.

Of that combat there was not much to see, as swaying lanterns only gave me occasional glimpses of the action. I remember most the scent, the thick, musky odor of gibberers and the sweet, sharp tang of blood. I remember the sounds as well: the snarls evaporating into whimpers, the wet splash of blood spurting rhythmically, the crunch of bones breaking, the grunt of someone having the breath driven from him, and the dying sighs of creatures as they went down with crushed skulls.

I shifted to the right side of the tunnel and moved to the fore, but found nothing to do. We had been brought along as observers, and the urZrethi meant for us to do just that. I suspected the reason we had been invited along was so we could see how well the urZrethi fought—as if that could dispel any concerns we might have over them because of the Man-urZrethi War fought centuries before. But I had no reservations to begin with, and all this display managed to do was make me wonder how men managed to fight the urZrethi to a standstill.

The battle ended quickly. We'd entered the tunnel behind the digging party and, though they were armed, the tight confines gave them little room to fight. The urZrethi slaughtered them with the loss of only two of their own. No one bothered to count Aurolani bodies, but both vylaens and gibberers had been slain. Judging by the number of longknives hauled back, at least two dozen of the enemy had died.

The urZrethi sent a half-dozen people back up the tunnel with rope. This they fastened to support beams in the Aurolani tunnel. When they got back to our tunnel, the urZrethi formed a line and pulled on the ropes, tugging away the posts and beams to collapse the tunnel. A great rush of air and dust blew back into our tunnel and I coughed for a bit while blinking my eyes to clear them.

Up above us—well east of the fortress—a snakelike track of sunken turf would mark the Aurolani graves.

The Draconis Baron led us all back to the surface and we looked a frightful mess. Dust caked us all over, save for the twin tear tracks down our faces. Augustus spat out a fair amount of dirt, then joined me at a cistern in the street, where I dunked my head and washed it off.

I relished the feel of water dripping down my neck and over my spine. It felt good to be back out of the tunnel, back in the cool, fresh air. I wanted nothing so much as to run off and relax in one of the steaming pools in the Crown Tower, but I remained there, watching Cavarre and the urZrethi.

The diminutive Baron greeted each of the urZrethi as they exited the house. He thanked them and appeared to be addressing each by name. That struck me as remarkable because of how they had shifted shape. Still, if he had a way to recognize them, if he was able to speak to each of them as he had each of us when we arrived, that would explain why the garrison felt confidence in his leadership despite his youth and martial inexperience.

I walked over to Faryaah-Tse and dropped to a knee beside her. "What will you do for a memorial for the two who died?"

She shook her head. "They were buried where they fell. That is the fate of warriors, to be returned to the earth where they died, or as close to it as possible. Because we shift shape, and remain changed when we die, we do not have the cultural attachment to seeing the dead that men seem to. We will simply go off, eat a meal, share stories and remember, so we can tell their kin how they passed."

"A memorial meal, that's a good idea." I nodded. "Men do that."

"It is also vital for us." She looked at me with black eyes. "Shifting is not easy for us. It tires us out and strains our bodies. We need to eat to regain our strength so we can change back. If we could not, we would be stuck like this."

"Oh." I stood as the bandy-legged urZrethi troop began walking past. Some actually leaned forward on their hands to walk on all fours, while most just struggled along on two. "I shan't keep you, then. It is good to see you up and about."

"And it is good to be up and about." She gave me a quick smile. "Find me later; I have something for you—a relic of our adventures that you might find useful. Until then, be well."

"And you."

I watched her go and wondered what she was talking about. Before I could figure it out, I turned and found Lord Norrington approaching me. "What did you think, Hawkins, of the fighting down there?"

"Seemed to me to be like fighting in a grave. I didn't much care for it."

"Neither did I, but as a result of seeing it I'm fairly certain the walls will stand until Chytrine batters them down." He laughed. "It will be quite a while before that happens, though. We've a long siege ahead of us."

I nodded in agreement, not realizing how quickly the both of us would be proved wrong.

Later that afternoon a great cry rose from the enemy camp. I was walking with Seethe in the outermost section of the city and quickly mounted the walls near the main gate. Because of the press of people, the closest we got to them was a hundred yards. Even so, we did have a decent view of what was going on and quickly understood why the Aurolani host was elated.

Chytrine had arrived.

Six magnificent drearbeasts pulled her gilded carriage, with vylaens serving as coachmen and footmen. The bulbous carriage had been shaped like a dragon in white, with its head and long neck extending out over the fearsome team drawing it. The wings flowed back to form the roof and the tail sailed behind to counterbalance the head. All four paws clutched axles and windows had been cut in the side, but curtains hid her from curious gazes. Gold traced every scale and edge on the carriage, allowing the afternoon sun to sparkle off it the way it ripples off gentle sea swells.

Above it all flew a white banner with the black image of a man wreathed in red, yellow, and orange dragonfire. I'd seen that banner before, in some of the fortress' murals, and knew it to be the banner beneath which Kirûn had invaded the south. That she still used it even though he'd been dead for centuries made me wonder if she was not so much interested in conquest as vengeance. Which, if true, made her more dangerous in my mind.

Seethe shielded her eyes against the glare. "So there she is. Things will begin soon, I expect."

"I agree, but I think we can hold." I pointed out at the entourage that had traveled with her. "She didn't bring that much in the way of troops. She's not got enough to take this fortress."

"I hope you're right, and I hope Kedyn sees no reason to test your faith in him."

Part of the company that came with Chytrine split off and moved forward, drawing itself up near a pyramidal stack of round stone balls. We'd seen the stones there for days, but they were too far back and too light to be of much use with the siege machinery the troops had built. Two drearbeasts hauled a long, narrow, canvas-shrouded cart into position beside the stones, then vylaens shouted at gibberers as they turned it around and started off-loading barrels from one of the wagons.

A vylaen stripped the canvas off the cart with an air of grave solemnity that prompted a tittering from the defenders. What we saw was a stout cart bearing a long bronze tube with a rounded end at the back, which seemed scarcely worth the care the vylaen seemed to lavish upon it. The entire cylinder had been worked with a dragon-scale pattern and the mouth of the thing had a big dragon's head on it, with the mouth open. It didn't look beautiful or terrifying, and none of us had any idea what it was.

"What's this now?" Cavarre shouldered his way in between Seethe and me. "What has she brought us?"

I shrugged. "I don't know. Could she keep the fragment of the DragonCrown in there?"

"Perhaps it's a cup for a dragon." Seethe frowned. "I've not seen its like before."

Cavarre said nothing and just stared intently at it.

A group of vylaens filled buckets with a black powder, which they poured into the dragon's mouth. Another one pushed a long stick with a thick end into the dragon's throat, packing the powder down in there. Finally four gibberers lifted one of the stone balls and rolled it into the tube, but I gathered they didn't do such a good job because two vylaens used the packing stick to force it down further.

Back up the hill a door opened in the side of the carriage and Chytrine emerged. Being as how she was a mile or so distant, making her out was tough, but she had bright gold hair that seemed to flow down to mid-back. She wore boots and a skirt and a blouse, and even though I knew she was over a hundred years old, she didn't show any signs of her age in how she stood or walked. In many ways she seemed as ageless as Seethe, and that scared me a little.

Chytrine walked forward to the metal dragon and a vylaen handed her a torch that had been kindled in a nearby fire. She waved it back and forth, as if in a salute to the fortress. People standing along the wall, me included, waved back. Some added shouted epithets to our acknowledgment of her presence. The Aurolani troops started to shout back at us, but orders snapped by vylaens quieted them.

Chytrine gently kissed the dragon-tube's tail with the torch, and the world changed forever.

I saw a flash of fire from the dragon's mouth and saw a billow of grey-white smoke shoot out, as if the dragon had vomited. Then, barely a heartbeat later, a loud boom shuddered through my chest. I felt it hit me, harder than a gust of wind, and vibrate its way through me. It was as if I'd been slammed into a wall suddenly and fast, without having moved at all.

Then the stone ball hit. It struck the wall above the gate, striking one of the merlons. The ball crushed the stone and itself shattered into thousands of deadly fragments. People standing there were reduced to a red mist. Arms and legs flew. Bodies, torn in half, linked only by entrails, toppled from the walls. Beyond them, in the streets below, stone chips blasted through people, pulverizing bone, laying flesh open. Rocks struck houses, breaking bricks, bursting through windows and cracking doors.

Bile bubbled up in my throat and I reached a trembling hand out for Seethe. "What is it?"

"I don't know."

Pressed against the battlements, leaning forward through a crennel to study it as best he could, Cavarre shook his head. "That is the weapon that will lay waste to this fortress and, damn me, I don't think there is anything we can do to stop it."

CHAPTER 35

It was of considerable interest, but little comfort, to learn that the dragonel was not magickal in nature. Had it been, our sorcerers could have analyzed the spells that made it work and created counterspells. As it was, the range to the target made hitting it or the loaders, packers, and firebeasts with combat spells impossible. There was some thought that magickers might be able to affect the stone balls in flight, but not without shards of them to provide links to them.

The only bit of luck we had came because of Cavarre's foresight. The streets and houses nearest the outer wall had long since been evacuated and many were already filled with dirt and debris. The dragonel shots that arced up over the walls plowed into these buildings, crushing facades and sending broken roof tiles whirling off in all directions, but the buildings themselves did not collapse. In essence they formed a wall inside the wall, limiting damage done deeper into the city, which prompted Chytrine to shoot further, with higher arcs, until she bounced a shot off the fortress's second wall.

The dragonel's rate of fire was low, but its accuracy made it devastating. A catapult or trebuchet would hurl stones and firepots and debris *toward* a target. Depending on the weight of the load being flung, it would fly over, or land short and often drift side to side a fair amount. But the dragonel directed shots and kept them on target. Two shots shattered the fortress gates. Subsequent shots pulverized the barricades we raised in their place. If the dragonel's crew could see a target they could hit it, which made defending the fortress difficult and hazardous.

The Aurolani forces rolled forward the siege towers they'd created. These were remarkable things, for they rose a good ten feet above the level of the outer wall. Gibberkin archers were placed atop the crenelated wooden towers. Wet canvas hung in great sheets over the towers themselves, so any *napthalm* would have a hard time sticking and catching the towers on fire. Walls in the front of the tower were hinged to open down into platforms that would allow the warriors inside to cross onto our battlements.

Chytrine used the dragonel throughout that first night. The slow, steady, rhythmic booming deprived us all of sleep. Shot after shot slammed into buildings and walls. A careful series of shots opened breaches north and south of the main gate, giving the Aurolani host three avenues of attack, with the siege towers supplementing them. Her troops organized themselves through the night, dividing into three forces.

By dawn we expected them to come.

Dothan Cavarre impressed me with his determined calm despite the situation. He divided his forces into three commands, granting Lord Norrington the northern command while entrusting the southern command to Prince Augustus. He maintained control of the central command, which pitted him against the Aurolani force commanded by Chytrine.

Throughout the night, workers tore down houses in the outer city's interior, creating channels into which the Aurolani hosts would flow. Where the siege towers seemed headed, he set up barricades so those troops would find themselves in blind alleys and trapped in killing zones. Siege machines on the second set of walls were prepared to target those areas. Troops were dispatched to wait in stronghouses until trumpeters could call them forth to their stations.

The day dawned dim and cold, with low fog clinging to

the landscape. I waited with Prince Kirill, Lord Norrington, Seethe, Leigh, and Nay on the battlements near the north wall breach. In front of us, five hundred yards off, the Aurolani legions arrayed themselves in hideous splendor. Banners rose at the head of their ranks, huge drums on wheels boomed and massive trumpets blared obscenely. Guttural war cries were snapped and snarled, making the enemy host sound like a pack of dogs fighting over scraps—and they didn't look or smell much better at that.

To the head of their formation moved a creature I knew instantly to be a *sullanciri*. It had a huge mannish torso joined at the waist to the body of a gigantic horse. The upper body sprouted four arms, each of which had a serrated bony blade running the length of the forearms and two longer blades curving out three feet past its massive, clawed hands. The creature's beetling brows and saberlike fangs stole from it any sense of civilization. Armor plates, as if inlays of turtle shell, covered it from head to tail.

As impressive a sight as that was, what made it all the more eyecatching was the fact that he glowed white. All the urZrethi I had seen before had been the color of minerals or dirt, and this one was as well, but it was the color of iron that lay in a forge. The incandescent color dominated its core, but yellowed slightly in some cooler areas. I could feel no heat radiating off it, but I didn't want to get any closer to determine if that lack was only a function of range.

My hand sought Seethe's, or hers mine—I don't remember after all this time. I gave her a brave smile. "We'll get through this, you know."

"One way or the other, I suspect." She reached over and plucked at the bowstring lying across my chest. "If it comes down to it, save an arrow for me. Don't let them take me."

I shook my head. "They won't take you, I promise." I gave her a quick kiss, which she turned into a longer one. When we broke apart I blushed, and Prince Kirill turned away with a smile on his face.

Leigh stared tight-eyed at the *sullanciri* and clasped Temmer's hilt the way Seethe held my hand. "Yes, my pet, I understand . . . That one is Vank-dae Ynl. He was exiled from

Boragul for reasons of sedition. Chytrine made him the first of her Dark Lancers. He, I suppose, will be mine."

Lord Norrington laid his hand on Leigh's shoulder. "You're not the only one who will be fighting here today, my son."

"But I'm the only one who can kill him."

Leigh's father smiled. "If he joins the battle, then you are free to engage him, but killing gibberers will win us this battle."

"Won't be wanting for gibberers to kill." Nay shouldered his maul. "Hawkins can feather vylaens and we'll kill the rest, Leigh and me."

Leigh turned his head to look at Nay. "Was that a rhyme?"

"Might could be." Nay grinned slowly. "Forge work doesn't demand a lot of thinking. Played with words for a bit."

A smile broke on Leigh's face. "Very good, Nay, very good. A wager, then. A point per creature we kill—the loser composes a poem to the glory of the winner."

"Done and done."

"Done and done." Leigh looked over at me. "We'd invite you in on this, Hawkins, but you'll claim every arrow-stuck body as your own."

I shrugged. "Just as well. I couldn't stand the two of you offering praises to me. Good luck."

Leigh nodded. "May Kedyn's will be done."

I glanced at Nay. "For this contest are you sure you don't want to be using the sword you've been working on?"

He smiled, then glanced down at his feet. "This would be a great battle for Tsamoc, but I yet need to put an edge on it. Next battle, after we beat them back here."

"Next battle, indeed." I nodded, then turned back to the Aurolani host. From the east blatted a harsh trumpet blast, and horns to the north and south repeated it. A thunderclap echoed from the east, then a stone ball hit on the gate towers, toppling men to the street below. The image of their falling, and of arrows spilling from their quivers, froze itself in my mind forever.

"They're coming." Lord Norrington drew his sword and

pointed down at the catapults and trebuchets behind the wall. "Ready your missiles; launch on my command."

The northern Aurolani army started forward. All but the banners of their lead ranks disappeared as they dipped into the fog-bound lowlands. We watched the banners draw closer, as if they were held by the vanguard of a ghostly army. At the other side of the river of fog the *sullanciri* waved its arms, urging troops on in a shrill, undulating voice that cracked and popped despite being almost too high to hear.

Lord Norrington raised his sword, then slashed it down. "Launch!"

The husky whisper of logs and stones being hurled through the air sounded impossibly low compared to the exhortations from the *sullanciri*. A hail of calthrops arced through the sky, jingling and jangling like a pouch full of coins. Even the harsh clack of catapult arms against stop-beams didn't have a martial quality, though the sounds of men cranking the arms back into place for another shot certainly did.

As did the results of those first shots.

I saw a log vanish in the fog, then bounce up once and flick off a bloody vapor before disappearing again. Banners snapped and fell in its path and screams erupted in its wake. A huge stone likewise rolled through the Aurolani formation, flinging broken bodies into the air behind it. Then the calthrops sowed more pain.

The enemy cut loose with their siege machines, launching rocks and flights of arrows. I ducked down behind a merlon as arrows rattled off the wall around me. A tremor rippled through the wall as a stone struck solidly below me, but it rebounded and rolled into the fog to crush one of the enemy. It was a good thing, too, because we had underestimated the *sullanciri*'s craftiness.

The banners had all been in the front of each company, but as they entered the fog, the warriors ran forward while the banners marched on slowly. As we shot into the thick of things, we did hit a few running warriors, but they were all from ranks further back. The lead gibberers had sprinted forward, boiling up out of the fog to come at us.

I drew and shot, spitting a vylaen. Other archers shot as well, sinking arrows into running gibberers and vylaens, but they were coming too fast for us. They headed for the breach in the wall created by the dragonel's shots. The rubble on the outside formed a perfect causeway. Clutching longknives in their teeth, they scrambled up on all fours, leaping over the bodies of arrow-stuck comrades or sliding them off into the fog.

The Aurolani horde poured into the breach without hesitation. Unthinking beasts that they were, they did not wonder why we had no warriors rising to oppose them. They crested the ragged gap in the wall and started down the other side, which is when Lord Norrington gave the order for the ballistae to shoot.

Lanyards were pulled, catches slipped, and torsion-bars twisted, propelling a broad, flat hammer against the ends of spears which had been mounted in racks of tubes. The spears hurled out and would normally have arced through the air to impale soldiers, but here found their targets before much of their force was spent. Many spears ripped through one gibberer to become lodged in one behind him. Because the ballistae had been positioned at a variety of angles, they raked the breach with missiles, clearing the inside and top of the gap.

Still they came, a motley rabble yipping and howling. Vylaens clapped off spells that washed the walls in brilliant green flame or splashed gouts of reeking acid on defenders. I nocked arrow after arrow and shot, knowing I could not miss a target in the roiling mass of creatures below. An arrow would hit, a gibberer would sink in the crush of his fellows, and the ranks would close again.

When I found myself down to my last arrow—a gift from Faryaah-Tse—I started harvesting others from the battlements and shooting the Aurolani's arrows back at them. Quickly enough I ran out of those missiles, so I slung my bow across my chest and drew my sword, which was just as well as the swarming gibberers had climbed up the walls and were nearing us.

Seethe stepped forward to engage them and was magnificent. Her surcoat of silver-washed mail glowed with what little sunlight made it through the clouds. She wore a winged helm that had a spike mounted in the crown and her black hair flew from beneath the edges. Her sword slashed and stabbed with unerring accuracy. Gibberers reeled away from her clutching shattered faces, blood spurting from split arteries and gaping chest wounds. She spun and cut, whirled and lunged as if she could see all around her at once. Bodies toppled off the battlements near her and a bloody circle described the range of her lethal reach.

Nay and Leigh had taken up positions below, defending one of the ballistae while its crew reloaded it. Nay fought with a savagery that challenged the gibberers in their own domain. His maul landed heavily, crushing limbs, denting heads, driving armor back through fur and flesh. Rents opened in his mail and in the padded leather jerkin beneath it, but no gibberer got a chance to press a deadly attack. Beasts that got close enough were hideously wounded, whether by a jab with the spike, a poke with the butt-cap, or a bone-shattering strike from the maul's heavy end.

While everyone in that place fought valiantly, there was no equal to Leigh. As if inspired by the *sullanciri*, Leigh and Temmer glowed gold and I *did* feel a heat coming from the blade. Gibberer flesh sizzled as Leigh lopped off limbs and popped heads from bodies. One cut would be enough to send any of the Aurolani soldiers to the ground, but Leigh was so quick that he could get in two or sometimes three cuts on a body before it fell. Blood stained Temmer for only a second before combusting into a ghastly choking cloud. Leigh laughed aloud, beckoning gibberers forward, nattering at them about his contest with Nay, beseeching them to come to him and die, which many of them did.

Down below us, the Aurolani warriors flowed into a corridor constricted by buildings and piles of rubble. Archers, both elven and human, shot at them from upper-story windows. Okrans spearmen defended piles of rubble, jabbing and poking and stabbing the gibberers that tried to break past. Elsewhere, further down the corridor, Oriosan Guards armed with sword and ax fought fiercely. Grudgingly men gave ground and the Aurolani host pressed forward in a thick stream of bodies.

Fighting raged everywhere and I was forced to do some serious cutting. Gibberers came up over the wall and I slashed at them. I traded blows with one, then dodged aside, letting his lunge at me carry him off the rampart. Another gibberer's cut sliced me just above the right knee, but I gutted him and pitched his body back onto the ground below.

Trumpets blared outside the walls and the last of the Aurolani forces started to move forward. One of our trumpeters blew a blast announcing that fact. I spared a glance in toward the advancing troops, but couldn't see the *sullanciri*. An immediate chill sank into my guts and the happy yips of the gibberers below told me where it was.

The *sullanciri* leaped from the depths of the fog to the top of the breach, its hooves scattering rocks that felled gibberer and man alike. Leigh, whose magickal blade had scythed down countless gibberers, had hacked a swath in the enemy formation and through it the Dark Lancer launched itself. The gibberers retreated at the *sullanciri*'s shrill command, opening an arena around the paired combatants. Raising all four of its arms, the Aurolani leader shrieked a challenge.

A low laugh rolled from Leigh's throat. His blade trailed smoke and hung loosely from his right hand. Leigh moved easily, almost clumsily, as if he were drunk, and casually waved the *sullanciri* forward with his left hand. Though his mask hid his expression, the light in his eyes blazed wildly.

The *sullanciri* charged, slashing at Leigh with the blades on its right arms. Leigh ducked beneath the upper blades, then swung his blade low and to the left as he moved in that direction. His parry caught the lower blades with the sound of steel ringing on steel, then Leigh leaped into the air, tucking his legs beneath him and hopping over the Dark Lancer's lower arm. Temmer came up and around in a blazing golden arc that swept through the *sullanciri*'s low right wrist, and Leigh bounced off to his left.

The blade-bearing fist rolled into the gibberer ranks, causing the first one it touched to burst into flame. Molten metal dripped from the stump, bubbling up the pools of blood into which it fell. The Dark Lancer screamed in pain and spun to face Leigh. My friend, in turn, flicked his blade toward the Aurolani horde, spattering them with their leaders' incendiary blood.

Hugging the wounded limb to its chest, the *sullanciri* again came at Leigh. It slashed at the man with the upper right arm, making the cut a diagonal one that should have sundered Leigh from left shoulder to right hip, but Leigh danced back out of range easily, then darted forward. He lunged up with Temmer, driving the point into the Dark Lancer's side. Molten blood gushed. The *sullanciri* squealed, then struck.

It backhanded Leigh with its lower right arm, catching him in the ribs below his sword-arm and spinning him back toward the breach. Leigh stumbled and fell, but did not lose his grip on Temmer. He clutched at his right side with his left hand and I could see a cough wrack him with pain. He was far enough away that I couldn't tell if there was blood on his lips, but I knew he was hurt more seriously than ever before.

The *sullanciri* keened triumphantly, raising its three good arms. It slowly stalked forward and looked around, daring any of us to interfere. Men shrank from its hot gaze, then its eyes met mine.

In mine, it could see my soul.

In its, I could see it had none.

Casting aside my blade, I brought my bow to hand and nocked that last arrow. I held the *sullanciri*'s gaze as I drew my silverwood bow. I stared at it past the broadhead and aimed for its chest. It smiled at me mockingly, working its jaw to show me how it would eat my heart when it was through with Leigh. I shook my head ever so slightly in reply, then let fly my last arrow, the one I had been saving.

That arrow, the one that had been cut free of Faryaah-Tse's flesh in Okrannel, flew straight and true. The magick that had been worked on it by the other *sullanciri* had not abated—whether because it had not killed the urZrethi for which it was intended, or just because that was the nature of the enchantment, I do not know. The black arrow took the *sullanciri* high in the chest, between both pairs of shoulders, and when it screamed, burning blood cascaded from its mouth like molten lead being poured from a crucible.

It leaped forward blindly, yet still almost crushed Leigh beneath its hooves. It landed in the gap, then dashed beyond the walls. Its hands clutched at the arrow, trying to break it off, but it remained whole. It pranced angrily, hopping back and forth in evident agony, its torso and back high enough to rise above the thinning fog.

It moved from trying to break the arrow to pulling it out, but it defied the *sullanciri* in that as well. Chytrine's creature smiled, a most horrible thing to behold, and looked up at me. Its smile broadened as it pounded a fist against the end of the arrow, driving it deeper into its body. The pain that action caused made it shift and dance, twisting it around enough to let me see the arrow's tip protruding from its back. Another blow extended it six inches more, then the Aurolani leader reached a hand back and started to draw the arrow from itself.

More blood flowed, coursing down its back and belly, and ran from its mouth as it laughed. I had no idea how long it would take it to recover from its wounds, but I did know that as long as it had the spark of life in it, it would heal. It might be vulnerable to Leigh's sword or that one arrow, but once it was whole again it would destroy us.

Fortunately, it ran out of time to heal.

The trumpet blast alerting us to the commitment of the Aurolani reinforcements had long since signaled others among us to act. The tunnels that would allow the Dûrgrue River to flood the lowlands were opened. Water burst through the grasses in great muddy brown gouts, pitching turf and stones, corpses and debris into the air. Water pounced on the fog, churning it into tan froth, then rolled forward in a wave that crashed into the *sullanciri*.

Steam hissed from it in great sibilant clouds. What had been white hot dulled to red, then grey and black, then cracked. A torrent swirled around it, splashing over its face, cooling blood into black icicles hanging from its chin. The Dark Lancer sat back, as if preparing to rear up, but its hind legs collapsed. Its forelegs disintegrated as they came up out of the water, then it toppled over onto its side and exploded.

The flood swallowed it in an unmarked grave and rolled on, sweeping through the swollen ranks of gibberers and vylaens. A few temeryces squawked and clawed at gibberers to try to rise above the flood, but their dying perches sank. The frostclaws nipped at the water as if they could drive it away, but it pulled them down and rolled them over, mixing them with the struggling, sputtering Aurolani host.

The trumpet blast also summoned our reinforcements from the stronghouses. Crossbowmen and archers filled the ranks of spearmen. Their shots ripped through gibberers and broke the tide of the Aurolani advance. More archers flanked the column and newly reloaded ballistae cut down dozens. Nay and an Oriosan company surged forward, driving a wedge into the Aurolani flank. They reached Leigh, who had already gained his feet and, despite shifting Temmer to his left hand, had killed a few more gibberers.

Both of the towers located on either side of the gap started the flow of *napthalm*, covering the water with a burning coat. Gibberers striking for the surface and those swimming in retreat suddenly found the lowlands impassable. Further along the wall one of the siege towers began to topple as the rising water softened the land beneath it. It splashed down grandly, casting archers from the top, and began to burn as flaming water hit it.

In less than an hour we had broken the army of the north and sealed our breach with a fiery lake. The other battles still raged in the city, their outcome yet to be decided. It was our job to compound our victory with theirs, and to accomplish that task we grimly set forth.

CHAPTER 36

All of our troops, save the garrison we left to hold the breach, swept south and slammed into Chytrine's right flank. Her force, which had been channeled into the city much as the northern army had, began to crumble. To counter our attack she loosed a flock of grand temeryces. Sporting brilliantly colored plumage, these frostclaws were a bit bigger than those we'd seen before. Their attack on our central formation was nothing short of suicidal, but they broke our momentum and blunted our drive to nip off a portion of her force.

She also fired the outer city. With my own eyes I saw vylaens use magick to ignite the blazes. Despite what has been rumored, Cavarre did not start the fire, nor did any of our forces. He had, of course, long since figured out how to deal with such an eventuality, and before the smoke could settle over everything in a choking fog, trumpets blew retreats, pulling us back to the inner city. Chytrine also pulled her troops back, including the southern force, which had come to a stalemate with Augustus' force.

The fire provided Chytrine's forces with a respite, and we likewise won one, though resting up and trying to breathe in the smoky inner fortress was very difficult. The food all tasted burned and keeping bits of ash off it was impossible. Many veterans just smiled and said it would put hair on our chests or give us good singing voices, but I failed to see how either thing would be relevant in our current situation.

I searched for a long time to find Leigh, mistakenly having assumed he would be at the aid station set up for Oriosan troops. Most of our men had faired pretty well, with the majority of the wounds being like mine: minor cuts. A few had been lung-struck with arrows or swords, and more had deep gashes from the temeryx attack, but all seemed in good spirits and busied themselves sewing up wounds, creating poultices at healers' instructions or just calming hurt friends who had to wait for elven magickers to appear.

I found Leigh in a small blockhouse near the inner fortress gate. I'd been directed to it because it was the aid station that had been set up for nobles. Few enough of them had been hurt that, had I been of a cynical mindset, I would have assumed that instead of being lucky, most of the nobles had never put themselves in jeopardy. Being young as I was, and with the examples of Prince Kirill and Lord Norrington fresh in my mind, I assumed good training and intelligence had preserved most of the nobles from injury.

I found Leigh on a cot in the corner of a room with Prince Scrainwood perched at the foot of his bed. The Prince scowled at me instantly, but Leigh gave me a smile. He levered himself higher in the bed using Temmer. He'd been stripped to the waist and had a bandage wrapped around his ribs. I could see the dark angry purple of a bruise all over his right flank, and despite his brave smile, I knew he was in a lot of pain.

"*Metholanth* could ease that, you know."

Leigh waved away the suggestion. "Others have more need."

Scrainwood, who had been holding a poultice against a nasty bruise on his forehead, glared at me. "This place is for nobles. You'll have to get your leg looked after elsewhere."

I looked at him and poured as much contempt as I could into my stare, then shook my head and nodded at Leigh. "How bad is it?"

"Ribs broke, definitely. I've not coughed up blood." He

winced, his breath coming short and hard. "An elf's on the way. Once the Prince is taken care of . . ."

"I see." I again regarded Scrainwood. "What happened to you?"

"I was unhorsed and hit my head."

I did my best to hide my surprise since I knew he'd been with Augustus and I didn't see Scrainwood tucking himself into combat. Regardless, warriors generally mention *what* or *who* hit them, which suggested to me it hadn't been an enemy warrior. As I had the story afterward—not from the Prince, of course—Scrainwood managed to lead a small knot of men into the wrong place at the wrong time. A roving gibberer squad attacked them, his horse went down and he hit his head on a watering trough. His men managed to get him clear, but at the cost of two lives.

Leigh coughed weakly, then hissed with pain. "The Prince tells me the *sullanciri* leading the southern army was a hoargoun. He says it has a most hideous power. Fear spreads from it in this miasma. Worse, it cannot be killed."

Scrainwood nodded enthusiastically. "Yes, it is already dead, so it cannot die again. Our arrows had no effect. The narrow streets restricted the swing of its club, otherwise it would have smashed us."

"How fared Augustus?"

"Well."

"Prince Scrainwood told me that Augustus managed to have a catapult hit the *sullanciri* with *napthalm* and set it afire. That drove it back but didn't consume it."

I nodded, then pointed at Temmer. "Magick weapons seem to be all that works against them. You best be up and about when he comes again."

"That is my plan." He smiled and looked past me toward the door. "And here is the first step in that plan."

I turned as a rustling of skirts came to me, and immediately felt out of place. The elf entering the room wore a brown gown that, while not festive, seemed far removed from combat. Here I stood reeking of smoke, with soot and blood staining me and my clothes, and she clean and fresh, with bright eyes and a beautiful smile. She seemed the utter opposite of what we all represented.

She came immediately to Leigh, but he shook his head. "You should see to Prince Scrainwood."

She smiled indulgently. "You will forgive me, but I choose who I heal and of what. My strength is limited, and I wish to put it to its best use."

"But my head, it hurts." Scrainwood pulled away the compress to show her the bump.

"And I see one possible cause." She reached out and brushed the middle finger of her left hand on Scrainwood's bump. I saw a flash of blue, akin to a woolspark. Scrainwood yelped and jumped back, banging his head on the wall.

The Prince snarled at her. "What did you do?"

"Magicks require an expenditure of energy to fuel them. I can draw on my own reserves or, in the case where someone is receptive, I can use their body's own strength to help. In your case, I reduced the swelling and repaired the damage, but it had a cost. In that one instant you felt all the pain the wound would have caused you if it had healed naturally."

Scrainwood frowned and slumped against the wall, rubbing the back of his head.

The elf smiled at Leigh. "I am Jilandessa. With you I need to determine what is wrong before I can weave a spell to heal you."

Leigh smiled. "I am at your disposal."

Jilandessa brushed her raven hair back past her shoulders, then spread her long-fingered hands out and held them over his ribcage. A soft red glow began to spread out from them, but failed to touch Leigh's flesh. She pulled back, narrowing her steel-blue eyes. "There is interference. I cannot work spells on you."

Leigh frowned, then glanced at the sheathed sword he clutched in his right hand. "Could this be the cause?"

The elf nodded. "Very possible. You and it have a bond. As long as you are touching it, I cannot heal you. No simple magicks can work on you."

Leigh smiled and glanced at me. "See, Hawkins, you needn't have gotten yourself roasted at the bridge."

"Nice to know now."

Leigh looked again at the sword. "Well, if I must give you up . . ."

Scrainwood got up on his knees at Leigh's right, his hands poised to grab the sword. "I will hold it for you."

"You are very kind, Prince Scrainwood, but . . ." Leigh shook his head, "I would not make a servant of you." He shifted the blade to his left hand, then held it out to me. "Hawkins, would you hold this for me?"

I almost protested the implication that I was his servant, but I knew he didn't mean that. I accepted the sword from his hand, keeping my grip firm on the scabbard and refraining from touching any part of Temmer itself. The blade did feel light—far lighter than it should have—and well balanced. In and of itself, even without the magick, it was a formidable weapon.

The second it left Leigh's grasp, his expression slackened and his eyes lost focus. Pain tightened his eyes and he sagged. He tried to smile, but his teeth were gritted. "I'm ready."

Jilandessa bent to her task quickly and this time the red magick did penetrate his flesh. I saw a silver line glowing on his right flank, glowing right up through the bandage, and it seemed as if that might be outlining the broken ribs. It looked a bit like lightning and probably hurt as much.

The red changed to green, which dulled the silver lightning, then subsumed it. The bruises on Leigh's chest faded, pulling back like an army in retreat. Leigh's breathing eased and his jaw unclenched. He remained slumped in the bed, but that seemed more because of fatigue than an inability to move.

He nodded sleepily at her. "I feel much better. Thank you."

Jilandessa smiled. "You'll need to sleep now, for a while, but you will be recovered when you waken."

Leigh smiled, then held his left hand out toward me. "Temmer, please."

He struck me very much as a child asking for a favored toy at bedtime. I hesitated, not because I coveted the blade for myself, but because I wished him the peace he'd known earlier without it. Something inside of me said that such peace would never be his again, so I gave him back Temmer and tried to smile as he clutched the blade to his breast, much in the same way he had described it lying in the sepulchre where he found it.

The elf turned to me. "Shall I deal with your leg?"

I looked up at her, surprised. "No, my lady, I am not a noble."

"Spells do not discriminate." She shrugged slightly. "And you bear a silverwood bow. Your actions have proved you worthy of my ministrations."

"But I would not have you tire yourself on my account. It's a flesh wound—one suited to needle and thread, not magick."

Jilandessa smiled carefully. "Then I will use your own strength, as I did with Prince Scrainwood."

Well, there was an opportunity I could not pass up. I nodded to her and steeled myself for the pain. I had always thought I had a high threshold of pain—things did not seem to hurt me as much as they had others, and I'd played that to my advantage, cultivating a reputation for being quite stoic. I set my face and stared past her at Scrainwood.

Jilandessa flicked a finger over the gash on my thigh. It felt to me as if she had jammed a glass auger into the wound and kept turning and turning it, driving the pain deeper and deeper. It built for one heartbeat, then two, and I expected it to subside then, but it kept going. I wanted to curse the pain, I wanted to blaspheme Fesyin's name, but I held it in. I forced myself to remain expressionless and to continue breathing as the pain spiked high, then did not let my relief show as it began to drain away.

"There, gone." The elf smiled at me, then drew back a step and curtsied to the Prince and Leigh. "Good day, fine men."

I nodded to her. "Thank you very much for your help."

She swept from the room. I watched her go, then turned back to look at Leigh, who was sleeping. I caught Scrainwood staring angrily at me. His face looked as if the pain I had endured were a bitter draught he'd been forced to drink down.

I ignored him, bent and kissed Leigh on the forehead. 'Sleep well, Leigh. Tomorrow your actions will decide the fate of Fortress Draconis."

• • • •

Somehow, in the chaos that was the inner fortress, I found Seethe and we retreated to the Crown Tower. We sought sanctuary in her room. Though both of us were grimy and hungry and exhausted, we stripped off our clothes and fell into her bed together. We went at each other with a fierce passion and intensity that matched the ferocity of combat and I knew greater pleasures than I had known before.

I've heard men speculate about why people are so eager to couple in such circumstances. Some say battle, with all its horror and blood and death, reminds us of our own mortality. Procreation, or at least the act of it, is the only answer to staring your own death in the face. Others contend that the joy of surviving is so great that words and thoughts and songs alone cannot express it. It requires the whole of a person to sing it, body and soul. And yet others suggest it is a way to anchor yourself in normalcy after having ventured into the twisted and mind-breaking crucible of warfare.

To me, it seems, it was all of those things and more. Though young and absolutely entranced with all that Seethe was, the clarity of mind Kedyn granted me left me no doubt about the ultimate fate of our relationship. Even if we did both survive this war, I would age and she would not. Eventually she would tire of me or, if I was fortunate, she would clutch my hand while I lay on my deathbed. I think I wanted to share passion with her at that time, in that place, under those circumstances, so she would have something to remember. I did not want her to be able to forget me because I knew I would never forget her.

Her motivation I can only guess at. When she did notice, during a pause in our frenzy, that my thigh had been sealed with magick, she playfully accused me of seeing another elf. "Have we spoiled you now, Hawkins, that no woman will satisfy you?"

We laughed over that and plunged back into our lovemaking, but I'd noted a hint of sadness in her as she chided me. Being a Vorquelf meant she always felt she was an outsider, so the idea that another elf, one bound to a homeland, would somehow be more attractive to me than she was an idea that easily took root in her heart. I did all I could, in word and deed, to eradicate it—and in the end, I think it had withered and died. Still, because of it, I think she clung to me so she could belong with someone, to be more than an outsider.

While we were together the world did continue on around us and even affected us. As dusk fell—prematurely because of the smoke blotting out the sun—a loud blast ripped through the outer city and shook the tower sufficiently to bounce me out of bed. My ears rang, both with the sound of the explosion and Seethe's laughter. I spared a mock-angry glance at her, then stripped off a blanket and wrapped myself in it. I heard people scurrying about in the hallway and I inquired of them what had happened.

No one knew then, but the way Dothan Cavarre reconstructed events provided a plausible explanation for what had happened. It appeared that in the haste to bring the dragonel into the city to blast the inner fortress gate down, a vylaen in charge of the powder wagon had raced it into the burning city. He made a wrong turn, found himself in a cul-de-sac of burning buildings and one collapsed on his wagon. It ignited the powder, resulting in an explosion that leveled six blocks of the city.

Some good came out of that explosion, for it snuffed some of the fires—most of which were burning out anyway. As the sun sank and the moon rose, the smoke began to clear and blow back over Chytrine's camp. That *did* make it difficult to assess how much we had weakened her forces, but the bodies scattered through the streets and the reports by various commanders suggested she had lost at least half her force.

The blast also deprived her of the powder that made the dragonel work. We didn't realize she had no extra at the time, of course, but the cessation of dragonel shots was a welcome relief in and of itself. We braced for their resumption at any time, but as none came our confidence in the fortress' strength increased.

The loss of the dragonel as a weapon did force Chytrine to do something I think she would have preferred not to do. Our first inkling that she had acted came when a winged form momentarily blotted out the moon. I'd not seen it, but others started howling about having seen a dragon. Cavarre immediately isolated and interrogated those who had seen it, but the rumor spread and even the elves and urZrethi seemed unsettled by it. I knew of dragons from legend, but it is hard to invest a lot of fear in a creature you think of as all but mythical.

Reflecting back on what I had seen at Atval, I really should have been out of my mind with fear. I'd seen what dragons were capable of doing to a city and really should have seen how easily one would devastate the fortress. Still, it was not until dawn, when this massive creature unfurled bat-wings and hurled itself into the air, that I began to quake.

The legends and bard's tales that describe dragons as huge, scaled beasts with horns and spiked tails, claws and wings and breath of fire are not wrong. What they miss falls into two areas, one of which is the graceful ease with which a dragon moves. I would never describe a dragon as being playful, but the way the tail curled around in flight, the way it ducked its head left and right when flying over the fortress, mirrored the curiosity of cats or dogs, or the suppleness of a marten.

The other thing the legends do not address is the intelligence in a dragon's eyes. As it landed before the inner fortress' gate, its claws digging up cobblestones and its body crushing the smoldering ruins of houses, the dragon swept its gaze over us. Gold flecked its luminously green eyes, a pattern that was reversed on its scales. It watched us, and as those massive eyes met mine, I knew it could read me and through me my parents and their parents and so on, back to the dawn of time. I saw no sympathy there, or compassion. Merely curiosity and, perhaps, a hint of intellectual satisfaction at seeing how some lines had bred down through the ages.

Then its eyes dulled and its chest expanded. Standing on the battlements well north of the gate, I could feel air rushing past as the dragon breathed in. Then the breeze stopped, much as the air stills before a storm. Only the panicked screams of men running from the battlements near the gate split the silence.

Then the dragon breathed out.

A blast of heat hit me, just like stepping into a warm house on a cold winter night, only much hotter and much harder. My eyes watered and narrowed as a brilliant jet of flame shot from the beast's mouth. The iron binding the oak beams in the gate went from black to red, then boiled away in an eye-blink. The beams resisted for a moment, still held in place against the massive beam holding the gates shut. Then they combusted, and a second later the beam did too. I heard it snap and burning chunks of oak scattered themselves through the courtyard as if someone had carelessly kicked embers from a campfire across it.

Men who had been slow to run were blown off the battlements, but burned to ash before their bodies ever hit the ground. More peculiarly—and faintly reminiscent of Atval—the stones near the gate began to melt and then froze in place. The gate looked as if a stone wave had been splashed against it, but before the stone could flow away, it had been solidified. These new crenelations gave a look of surprise to the gate, as if it could not believe what would be passing through it.

The dragon launched itself into the air, screamed once defiantly, then circled the fortress and flew back to Chytrine's camp. It settled there, behind her pavilion, and roared exultantly.

Seethe slipped into my arms and shivered. Lord Norrington appeared next to me on the wall. "The piece of the DragonCrown that she got from Okrannel allows her to control that dragon. If she gets the pieces stored here, her power will be multiplied. Instead of controlling one dragon, she will control a legion of them."

I nodded. "We can't let that happen."

"No, we can't."

As if to mock our resolve, war drums began pounding in the Aurolani camp, and her legions began their advance.

CHAPTER 37

Seethe, Lord Norrington, and I rushed down the steps to where Cavarre and Prince Kirill were ordering men to swing ballistae into place to defend the open gateway. Elsewhere Nay, Leigh, Augustus, and even Scrainwood helped people situate barricades. Wagons were rolled into place and overturned, log spindles with spikes on all sides were laid out—men even kicked and poked burning remnants of the gate into place to hold back the armies that were coming in.

Down on the ground we couldn't see the line of Aurolani forces snaking its way through the city, but the action of catapults and fire-towers told us when they began to draw near. Stones arced through the sky, clouds of calthrops flew, and streams of fire poured out. We heard screams in the distance and saw greasy black smoke curl up, but the *boom, boom, boom* of the drums never ceased.

A figure loomed in the smoke, all tall and unsteady, moping along with a heavy club dragged behind it. As it drew closer, smoke clung to it and reluctantly drifted off. The creature's flesh matched the smoke, while rents in its skin revealed blackened muscles. When it clumsily sagged against a building, its shoulder catching and breaking the frame of a second-story window, I realized how big it was. It was a hoargoun, and as the stench of it finally reached me I realized it really was undead, a revived corpse, and a *sullanciri*.

Two things happened as it hove into view. The first felt akin to the sensation I had after that first dragonel shot. This time, though, the wall that slammed into me hit on an intangible level. I couldn't feel it physically. It didn't shake me, but I know it went through me. I shivered in its wake, then I felt pain.

Down in my right leg, where it had been wounded. Where it had been healed.

I could see through the cut in my breeches that the wound had reopened. All around me—on the walls, in the courtyard—men crumpled. Blood began pouring from wounds magick had closed. Leigh collapsed, clutching his arms around his middle.

Lord Norrington's eyes narrowed. "Chytrine managed to dispel all the healing magick. Evacuate the wounded. Get them off the walls and into the tower. Move them, now!"

I glanced over at Leigh. Nay helped him to his feet and another man already had Leigh's left arm over his shoulders and was hustling him away. It took me a half-second to figure out who was helping Leigh, then I bristled. *Scrainwood!* The coward was using Leigh as an excuse to get himself off the battlefield.

I started after them, vaulting a wagon, then leaping above burning logs when the second thing hit me. Fear poured off the *sullanciri* in waves, like echoes in a hall. People all around me got a wild expression in their eyes. Some dropped their weapons and covered their faces in their hands, too afraid to look at what was coming. Others spun and vomited while yet others began to scream.

I could feel the *sullanciri's* magick pick at me, trying to find some sort of fear that would resonate within me. Any fear would do, big or small—it needed something to open a wound in my soul. From there it could expand, carrying me over into panic. I'd lose my mind and become a helpless victim of the Aurolani host.

I flashed past a ballistae as Prince Kirill pulled the lanyard and sent a score of yard-and-a-half-long spears hurtling out at the shambling giant. Many hit, skewering its thighs and arms, piercing its belly and chest. One passed through its throat. The *sullanciri* did stumble back under the force of the assault and crashed into a chimney. It fell apart beneath the *sullanciri*, but the creature slowly gathered itself to stand again.

My run carried me out of sight of the creature, though fear still assaulted me. I think I did not go mad right then and there because I was more concerned for Leigh than I was myself. So, I guess, in some way I was affected by the magick, but its bidding and mine were the same, so little harm was done.

I almost missed them because Scrainwood had dragged Leigh down an alley and deposited him against a wall. The Prince squatted beside him with both hands on Temmer's scabbarded length. Leigh clung to the sword's hilt with one hand and weakly tried to push Scrainwood away with the other.

My backhand slap caught Scrainwood across the face and spun him deeper into the alley. He came to rest on his ass, with his knees drawn up to his chest. I'd split his lip. The pink tip of his tongue came out and tasted blood, then retreated as if the wound were a nettle and it had been stung.

I dropped to a knee beside Leigh and rested my hands on his shoulders. "Leigh, *Leigh*! You have to get up. You have to kill the *sullanciri*."

He shook his head wildly, looking at me and past me. "No, no, no!"

"Leigh!" I raised my hand to strike him.

He snarled at me and made as if to draw his sword, but then he coughed and pain wracked him. It also brought him to his senses. "I can't, Hawkins."

"You must. You have Temmer. You can kill it."

"I can't, Hawkins." Leigh clutched at my mail surcoat. "Don't you see, the sword didn't protect me from magick. It never has. If I . . . the *sullanciri* . . . Hawkins, I can't do it. I'll die. The curse will be true."

"If you don't draw it, your friends and your father will

die!" I shook him, not too hard, but firmly nonetheless. "You have to do it, Leigh."

"I *can't!*"

Scrainwood crawled forward on his hands and knees. "He can't do it, Hawkins, you can see that. Leigh, give the sword to me. I'll do it."

Leigh's eyes widened and terror shot through his voice. "No, no, no, no!" He held the sword tightly. "No, no, no!"

"Leigh!" I clapped my hands on his head and forced him to look at me. "You must come fight."

His eyes never focused. "No, no, no, no . . ."

"He's not going to do it, Hawkins. Give the sword to me."

I snorted and slapped Scrainwood again. "You're a fool."

He'd fallen back on his right haunch and held his left hand to his face. "A fool, me? Without that sword . . ."

"Yes, I know." I looked down at my friend cringing there. He clung to the sword like ivy, like a babe to his mother. I remembered Leigh laughing, rhyming, making an entrance at the gala, gallantly accepting Ryhope's scarf as a prize.

That Leigh was as close to me as any of my brothers.

The man curled around the sword at my feet was not that Leigh.

"I'm sorry, so sorry." I rapped my right hand hard against Leigh's ribs, wringing a howl from him. The pain drained all the strength from his body, making it easy for me to rip Temmer from his grasp.

I snarled and brandished Temmer at the Oriosan Prince. "You're a fool because you *asked* for the sword, Scrainwood. A sword like this can only be *taken*."

I drew Temmer and caught my reflection in its golden length. My heart ached for Leigh because suddenly I comprehended all of what he'd been living with. Temmer was at once wonderful and terrible, a best friend and a vile enemy. I lusted after it, I hated it, and I was awed by it.

With that hilt in my hand, the golden blade bared, the world shifted in my sight. I could suddenly see a rainbow of colors that had not existed before. Fear and pain tinted Leigh, while hatred burned brightly from Scrainwood's exposed flesh. In an instant I saw him as an enemy and knew killing him would be justified, but I also felt there was bigger prey in the area and Temmer demanded I seek it out.

I stripped off my old sword, casting it aside. I had Temmer, I had no need of another sword. It could only slow me, trip me, and steal from me the glory I would win with Temmer.

I ran from the alley and stemmed the tide of fleeing warriors. As I turned the corner and entered the courtyard, the *sullanciri* ducked its head and passed through the gate. A few arrows, mostly elven, shot at it. Shafts bristled from the giant, but its slack-jawed, empty-eyed face gave no sign if it felt pain or not.

As it came closer, with each ponderous step loosening the cobbles beneath its feet, the miasma of fear became more powerful. The assaults increased in speed and intensity, searching minds for any possible fear it could exploit. I relived countless fearful situations in a heartbeat and might have succumbed to any of them, save for having Temmer in my right hand.

I have Temmer. What have I to fear?

A man leaped over a barricade and dashed forward with a sword in hand. It was Kirill and I knew that, but Temmer overlaid him with new colors. Courage boiled off him like steam on a lake, and fury seemed to be the fire in his heart. His sword cut left and right, slicing muscle, hewing bone as he dashed beneath the swung club and slashed the hoargoun's legs. He got behind the giant and gashed the creature in the back of a leg, hoping to hobble it. His effort might have worked, too, had the hoargoun simply been a creature of flesh and blood.

It wasn't. It was a *sullanciri* and its most insidious weapon finally found its mark.

Fear. Fear for his daughter. Fear for what would happen to her if he failed. It curled up in his belly and struck like a snake. Kirill hesitated, didn't move. I could see the fear of never seeing his daughter again well up in him, paralyzing him just for a moment.

For a moment too long.

The Dark Lancer's cudgel came around and smashed Kirill against the inside of the fortress wall. His legs thrashed on the ground. The rest of him dripped out of the crater the club's impact had left in the wall.

As I sprinted within striking range, Temmer displayed its full powers to me. The *sullanciri* seemed to move more slowly and I could see flows of motion around it, indicating where it was going to go, where the club would be. Dodging to one side was simple. I ducked beneath the club strike and was in between the creature's legs.

I swept the blade up and around in a two-handed strike at the Dark Lancer's left knee. As the edge bit into the creature's flesh the skin and muscle became almost transparent to my eyes. I could see the blade cutting through sinew and with a wiggle here or a twist there, I guided it through the kneejoint without burying the blade in bone. Temmer came out the other side, spraying the fetid fluid that served as the Dark Lancer's blood over the wall.

I dashed forward as the hoargoun began to fall, and spun into another attack. I slashed through the back of its left thigh, letting Temmer's tip barely score the bone. I leaped into the air and landed on the *sullanciri*'s buttocks as its hips hit the ground, then I scurried up its back. It tried to keep itself off the ground with its arms, but a quick slash up through the left armpit, and then some sawing with Temmer, and that arm came away.

The *sullanciri* crashed down to the left and flung me off, but I landed easily, tucked into a ball and rolled. At the end of it I came up on my feet and danced back toward the creature's head. It reared up, pushing off with its right arm. It managed to raise its head up about six feet. Though the *sullanciri* was huge and ugly and reeked of death, I dashed in and stabbed upward, driving Temmer through the empty left eye-socket and deep into whatever it had remaining for a brain.

A dark, stinking fluid gushed out, drenching me. I tried to tug Temmer free but could not, and the greasy ooze made my hand slip from the sword's hilt. The *sullanciri*'s thrashing tore the blade from my grip and I sailed back, bouncing down hard on the cobbles. I spun, pummeled by fear, and watched the hoargoun heave itself to its feet.

It was a testament to the fearful strength of the creature

that with only one arm it could push itself upright. The right leg straightened and the giant would have remained upright, save that without a left arm it could not balance itself, nor could it brace itself against the gateway. Its head smashed into the battlement above the gate, then the *sullanciri* listed to the right, drove the stump of its left leg into the ground, and fell full forward for a second time.

The *sullanciri*'s head slammed hard into the courtyard's paving stones. I heard a pop and a crack, then saw the tip of Temmer's blade poke up through the back of the giant's skull. A second later the sword's hilt, with only a couple of inches of blade attached, skittered and danced across the stones and spun to a rest near my right hand.

The gibberer horde at the gateway howled and, brandishing their longknives, sprinted forward.

"Hawkins, stay down!"

I flattened as ballistae behind me shot, speeding spears and arrows above the *sullanciri*'s corpse. The volleys tore holes in the Aurolani line, but gibberers still came hard. I tried to scramble to my feet, but the Dark Lancer's blood made the ground slippery and kept me down. I sprawled there, with two inches of broken sword all I had to defend myself.

Then Lord Norrington appeared above me, sword in hand, and slashed the face from the gibberer closest to me. He parried another blade aside, kicked the gibberer carrying it in the gut, then crushed the creature's head with his pommel. Lord Norrington's blade swung in a broad arc, cleaving skulls, severing limbs, opening bellies, and spilling blood—one man against a wall, holding them back from me.

I rolled to my right, getting past the arc of his blade, then appropriated a longknife. I twisted to the left, lunging across my body to throat-stick a gibberer going at Lord Norrington's back. It gurgled and died, but not before I had to kick it away from clutching at his legs. I settled in at Lord Norrington's back. He acknowledged me with a nod. Together we stood there and slew anything within reach.

We should have died because the whole of the Aurolani horde poured through that gateway—at least it seemed so to me. I heard men and women shouting all around us. Bows thrummed, catapults cracked, swords cut, axes chopped, spears stabbed, and magick sizzled, yet all I could see around Lord Norrington and me were gibberers—rank upon rank of them flowing around us like a stream around a rock. Bodies were deposited around us like silt, building up a barrier that couldn't be crossed, and our blades still licked out to inflict as much damage as we could.

With our forces scattered, I thought we had lost the day. As it turned out, though, men and women now free of fear returned to the battle. They'd been so enwrapped in terror that anything seemed a relief and even a change for the better. The absence of fear substituted for courage in many, so they returned to fight and the river flowing around us slowed, then began to thin and reverse course.

The thunder of hoofbeats on paving stones filled the courtyard as Augustus and his cavalry charged into the gibberer throng through an opening they'd torn in barricades. Archers on the walls, or raised on any high point like stairs or nearby rooftops, shot down into the gibberers. Combative roars dwindled to painful squeals then, somewhere distant, trumpets began to blow a recall and the gibberers fled.

A cheer arose from our people, but it lasted only a moment. As if summoned by the same trumpet that had sounded an Aurolani retreat, the dragon took wing and soared above us. It screamed defiantly, then tightened its circle and descended toward the Crown Tower.

I saw in an instant what had happened. Chytrine had wished to raze Fortress Draconis, for it was an affront to her. It had been built after Kirûn's defeat to forever challenge any invasion from the north. Its very presence was a pebble in her shoe and she had been determined to have it gone. It had proved more formidable than she had anticipated, however, and with her generals all dead, her army began to fall apart.

She had not, however, lost sight of the great prize in Fortress Draconis. Three pieces of the DragonCrown had been housed there. Along with the one portion she already possessed, these three would give her half of it. The power to control one dragon had already proved devastating, and using that dragon to get the other three pieces would be simple.

We had won the battle on the ground, but she would have her prize.

The dragon flared his wings out, then settled on the tower. All four of his claws found ample purchase on the buttresses, while the tip of the tower just barely scraped against his belly. He craned his head back, roaring triumphantly, then snaked his long neck forward and down. Like a dog devouring a hen's egg, the dragon snapped his jaws shut on the tower's roof, crushing it and tearing it away. He flung his head back and forth, scattering debris all over the fortress, then let the lead-sheathed remnants fly deep out into the ocean.

I remember two things with crystal clarity from that moment. One was the light from the crown fragments playing over the dragon's golden belly scales. The dragon looked down and in beneath himself at them, almost with the gentleness of a bitch nuzzling suckling puppies. The light seemed to dazzle it for a moment.

The other thing I recall was the serene expression on Dothan Cavarre's face as, with the rest of us, he stared up at the tower top. Though the others around him had their mouths open in horror and defeat, he watched peacefully and expectantly. He knew what would happen and waited to see if centuries of preparation would pay off.

While placing items of great value in a tower made sense for men, it was because we were creatures who did not soar. Hiding the DragonCrown fragments at the top of a tower, on the other hand, made no sense especially if it were a dragon that might come to steal them away. From the very first the architects who had planned the fortress realized this, and they took precautions which the centuries had hidden from everyone save the Draconis Barons and a few trusted aides.

The removal of the tower's roof loosed four massive counterweights that fell down through shafts built in the tower's external walls. These counterweights pulled cables magickally spun of steel. Those cables were linked through a pulley system to a needle-sharp steel spike over thirty feet in length that had been housed in the central shaft of the circular stairway that ran up the tower. As the weights fell toward the earth, the spike flew up from the depths. It stabbed up through the firepit in the Crown Chamber and pierced the dragon's heart.

The dragon leaped up and away, and had it been free of Chytrine's control, it might have gotten off with only a pinking. It beat its wings hard twice, lifting it from the tower and backing it to the north, then its tail twisted and lashed in pain. The dragon roared again, though muted and abruptly cut off. Then one wing flailed, the other half-furled, and the dragon fell from the sky.

It hit the ground in the new, man-made lake north of the fortress. None of us could see it crash down, though droplets of water from the splash reached us even as far away as we were. We all stood there in stunned silence, none of us certain about what we had seen. Then, from here and there, someone cursed or shouted, and cheers began to drown out the moans and mews and whimpers of the wounded and dying. I began to laugh and hugged Lord Norrington, and he, me.

All of us, the survivors of the siege, yelped for joy. And then, just as quickly as pandemonium had erupted, it subsided, and we set about the brutal task of driving the Aurolani host from our land.

CHAPTER 38

The dragon died just after noon. Prince Augustus led the fortress's cavalry in a series of harassing charges at the Aurolani rear guard, but Chytrine refused to let a retreat turn into a rout. She kept vylaens and temeryces active on the flanks, so that when the cavalry charged at the gibberer formations, the threat of attacks from their sides made them break off their runs at the enemy. Even so, the horsemen drove the guards off the dragonel, allowing a small squad of Nalesk cavalry to capture the weapon. Augustus' people then chased the Aurolani forces into the woods and onto the road north for two hours, then returned.

By the time he came back, the Aurolani fleet had broken up and we were able to land our own ships. Better yet, Oriosan Scouts, Muroson Heavy Guards, and Sebcian Light Foot arrived from the south. Their intent had been to lift the siege, but their presence as reinforcements was more than welcome.

I sought Leigh to apologize for what I had done. I headed first for the aid station where I'd found him after the previous fight. The place was filled to overflowing with the wounded, some who just sat glassy-eyed, staring off at nothing, others keening in voices no long human, but filled with pain. Bodies were sprawled everywhere. Men clutched at me as I moved past, mistaking me for friends. I slipped their grasping hands and continued my search.

Finally, in the small room that had housed him before, I found Leigh. I caught a glimpse of him through the doorway. He sat up on the bed, shivering—at least, I told myself he was shivering, not suffering from the palsy for which Temmer was the cure. Grey blankets enshrouded him, emphasizing the pallor of his skin. He sat there, rocking back and forth, clutching to himself a stick, caressing it as if it were his sword. Speaking to it.

I made as if to enter the room, but a hand caught my wrist, spinning me about. Jilandessa, haggard and bloodstained, shook her head at me. "You can't go in there."

"But, Leigh . . ."

"Physically he is well, Hawkins." The elf lowered her eyes for a moment. "There are other wounds I cannot heal. They will take time."

"Perhaps I can—"

"No, Hawkins. Seeing you would not help him right now." She clasped me by the shoulders. "You have to give him time. . . ."

Her words, though offered softly and sympathetically, left me hollow inside. As per the price paid by those who wielded Temmer, Leigh had been broken in his last battle. The problem was, I'd done the breaking. I'd broken his trust, I'd betrayed him and, for the life of me, I couldn't imagine a way to repair that damage.

I glanced back over my shoulder at Leigh, at his swaying, and a shiver shook me. "Thank you, Jilandessa. Take good care of him." She nodded in reply, then let me slip past and out into the sunlight.

Finding Nay was easier, and I was pleased to see him in good spirits despite his waiting at an aid station for help. He sat on a broken piece of wall with his left leg extended before him. His left ankle had been savaged. Blood well stained the bandages wrapped around it and had even soaked into his trousers. He held his maul the way an old man might hold a cane and smiled at me.

"Kill a *sullanciri* and you're not hurt? You *are* a hero, Hawkins."

"Just a survivor, Nay. What happened to you?"

He laughed through pain. "Broke gibberers left and right. Had one crawl forward and lock his jaws on my ankle. Crushed it. Don't hurt much sitting."

"They'll fix you up." I glanced back at the blockhouse where Leigh was recuperating. "Have you seen Leigh yet?"

He nodded solemnly. "Hobbled over. He's going to live."

"So I heard." I glanced down at the ground. "They said my seeing him wouldn't help."

Nay glanced down at the ground. "He's hurt in the head, Hawkins, mixed up and afraid. Don't help much Scrainwood sitting with him up there."

"I missed that. Great." I shook my head and turned Temmer's hilt over in my hands. "I know I shouldn't have—"

Nay struck the ground hard with the butt of his maul. "Stop that talk now. You did what we needed. Leigh knows it. Told him so; think he heard it." Nay dropped his voice to a whisper. "Back that first day of our Moon Month I prayed for courage. Kedyn gave it to me, but when that *sullanciri* came near, it failed. Trembled and shook, I did; I peed myself."

He laughed and raised his left foot. "Only good thing about the bite was it holed my boot. No more sloshing around."

"Silver lining to a cloud."

Nay's eyes hardened as he reached out and took the hilt from me. "I'da shit myself, too, when it come through the gate, but I seen you coming round the corner with Temmer. Saw you kill it. Saw the sword break. Been thinking on that and have an idea."

"Why it broke?"

He nodded slowly. "Sword was said to break everyone in their last battle. Don't know about others, but Leigh, he's broke. He took the blade, hoping to be a hero. For himself he took it, so it could break him. You, you took it not for yourself, but to save others. It had no hold to break you, so *it* broke."

A chill ran down my spine. "I don't know that you're right, but I'd be happy if you are. I can't say I'm sorry it's gone."

"It was a sword. In the right hands it was dangerous." He tilted his head and smiled. "In the wrong hands it was more dangerous."

I nodded slowly, then held up a hand to stop him from giving the hilt back to me. "No, keep it. I don't want it. I don't imagine the blade can be repaired, but even if it could, after what I did to Leigh, I don't think I'm the man to carry it."

"We'll differ over that, but . . ." Nay nodded and tucked the hilt through his belt. "They're coming for me now. You did the right thing, Hawkins. Don't doubt it. See you later."

I stood there as two other men came and helped him hobble to the aid station, then I slipped from the inner city and wandered north through the ruins of the outer city. All around me were signs of life—curs tearing at corpses, ragged men and women looting bodies, ravens plucking out eyes. Squads of men moved through the city, gathering up bodies and dumping them into piles which were then doused with *napthalm* and set alight. I kept upwind of those pyres as well as I could, for the sweet scent of burning flesh made me want to vomit.

I mounted the stairs and climbed to the top of the battlement from which I'd shot the urZrethi *sullanciri*. The dragon had landed in the flooded plain there and lay on its left side, half submerged. Its head had finally flopped down at an angle, so that water lapped at the lower teeth. Its tongue rolled out like a carpet over the right side of its face and disappeared in the water.

Three boys poled a makeshift raft toward it. Dirty water washed over the raft and their bare feet. They quarreled among themselves as to what the best way to approach it might be, with the smallest insisting loudly that they had to go to the half-open mouth because he wanted to crawl inside. The other two, who were larger and larger still, exchanged glances, then sent the raft in that direction, with their smaller companion eagerly waiting at the front of the raft.

It struck me, of course, that those three boys could have been Leigh, Nay, and me, all off on our grand adventure. We had approached it with the same awe these boys did, heedless of the dangers. We'd all accepted the challenge that had been offered to us, not realizing there would be a price to pay for it.

I cupped my hands to my mouth. "Hey, you, boys, don't go there. Stay away. You could get hurt."

They turned and looked at me with the sort of contemptuous disregard the young give elders. *You might be afraid*, their eyes said, *but we are not. We are immortal.*

Luckily for me, and for them, a gibberer corpse chose that moment to bob up in front of the raft. The smaller boy yelped and leaped back. That knocked the other two into the water. All three of them screamed in terror. The two wet ones crawled onto the raft again and lay there shivering while the currents coming around the dragon slowly pushed them away from it.

"It was a good thing you did that. They might have truly been hurt."

I spun, then bowed my head. "My lord, I didn't hear you approach."

Lord Norrington smiled and rested his left hand on my right shoulder. "You and I have stood back-to-back in battle. We have endured much together, and will endure more. You shall call me by my given name, Kenwick."

My mouth open with surprise, I looked up. "Thank you, my lord; I mean, Ken— I can't."

Lord Norrington's smile shrank to a bemused grin. "Whyever not?"

"My father would have my hide off me if he ever heard me address you so familiarly. He'd be hurt and . . ."

Lord Norrington's hand squeezed my shoulder. "I understand, Tarrant. Neither of us would ever want to hurt your father. Perhaps, when we are alone, like this, you need not be so formal."

"As you wish, Kenwick." I tried his name tentatively and it fit in my mouth without too much trouble. "I think you grant me this reward too freely, however."

He crossed his arms over his chest. "What do you mean?"

"What I did to your son . . ."

His head came up and his eyes narrowed, then he nodded.

"You freed him of a curse, Tarrant, and for that I cannot thank you enough. Ever since Atval I have been afraid he would die on this campaign. I know my son is not perfect, but I love him nonetheless. That he is hurt does pain me, but the fact that he will still hurt rather than burn in a pyre, this makes me very happy. He will heal, Tarrant, the Norrington bloodline will continue. Doing what you did preserved our future, so I bear you no ill will at all."

"You love him and were afraid for him because of the sword, but you let him fight?"

Lord Norrington nodded, then turned and leaned on a merlon to look to the north. "My duty to my nation and to the Council of Kings—indeed, my duty to all civilized peoples—demanded I field the best forces I could for each battle we faced. With the sword, Leigh became the one tool I had to destroy *sullanciri*. As much as I wanted to keep him out of danger, I had to place him in it. I had to hope that the next battle would not be his last.

"I hated putting you and Nay in danger the way I did as well, but without the two of you, Leigh would not have acted as he did. Do you know that when he ran through the woods to summon help for you two and Rounce, I think that was the first selfless thing I ever saw Leigh do? Something in him refused to surrender as long as you were in danger. As much as his feet hurt that night, as much as he was exhausted, I could see his concern and pleasure at having acted to save you. In saving you, he took responsibility for you, and throughout this campaign that sense of responsibility drove him on."

He glanced sidelong at me as I leaned next to him on the merlon. "Someday, Tarrant, when you have children of your own, you'll see their potential and you'll see their limitations. You'll want to steer them toward the things you know they can do and you'll want to shield them from the things they can't. The difficulty is that they won't see things the way you do. They won't acknowledge the same potential and problems you see. And then, at some point, they will surprise you, going places you never expected. That's been Leigh, here, on this expedition. Though it did not end as well as it might have, he still lives and can still realize the new potentials he has."

Another voice broke in, all snarling and harsh. "How dare you, Kenwick Norrington, deny me my right!" Prince Scrainwood stamped his way up onto the battlement, waving clenched fists. "You have denied me a place in your expedition north. And why? So you can take this mongrel who assaulted your son, who assaulted *me*?"

I frowned. "What?"

Lord Norrington placed his right hand on my chest, holding me back. "You learned this how, my Prince?"

Scrainwood waved a hand back toward the tower. "It's all over, the gossips have it now. You'll be leaving me behind, but you'll take Augustus and the others. I asked Augustus to demand that you take me with you, but he said you had been adamant about my being abandoned here. *And* equally adamant about taking Hawkins with you."

"I see." Lord Norrington's words came with a coldness to them that made me shiver. "There are a couple of things you should remember, Prince Scrainwood. First and foremost is that I am truly in command of the expedition to destroy Chytrine, not you."

"Because of that damned elven prophecy."

"For whatever reason, yes, and do not imagine my experience in leading men had a *small* part in that decision. The fact is, Prince Scrainwood, throughout this expedition you have done little more than dispatch the wounded or fall off a horse. Now you may hire bards to create songs that praise your efforts, but you and I and every soldier who has watched you flee knows what I say is true."

The portion of Scrainwood's face that remained unmasked went white. "Why that is, that is, that is base slander!" He pointed a finger at me. "He's filled your head with lies about me. I watched him assault your son and steal his sword. I tried to stop him but—"

"But you failed to do that just as you failed in every other martial endeavor you've attempted." Lord Norrington waved away Scrainwood's sputtering. "And it's not Hawkins who has spoken against you, but everyone else. My own son told me what happened in the alley, and even his account does you no credit. Your presence costs lives, my Prince, and I will not put my people in jeopardy to save you. If you press your suit and do come along, you will die. I can all but guarantee that."

"You threaten me, sir."

"No, I merely state realities." Lord Norrington pressed his hands together. "You have a choice. You can have it said that I left you behind here with the Oriosan Scouts to set about the rehabilitation of Fortress Draconis, or I will call together all the armies we have here and denounce you as a coward. Moreover, as a reward for what has been accomplished here, I will demand that your sister is wedded to my son, and that your mother should pass you over and let the crown go to Ryhope. And don't think for a heartbeat she'd not do it."

Scrainwood staggered back and pressed his hands to his heart. "You wouldn't!"

"Without hesitation." He turned to me. "Fetch me an *arcanslata* and a magicker to work it."

"No! Stop, Hawkins; go no further." Scrainwood's eyes grew as tight as his voice. "So, this is the way it will be, then? I remain here and you do not denounce me?"

Lord Norrington nodded. "It is more than you deserve, but it does not mean you are fully free. If ever I do not like how you rule Oriosa, my 'memoirs' will be distributed and you will be discredited."

"Will you press for your son to marry my sister?"

Lord Norrington hesitated for a moment. "That is an issue to explore when my son is well again. We will discuss it upon my return."

Scrainwood's lips puckered for a moment, then he nodded. "Are you certain you wish to play at being a politician like this?"

"No, but since you wish to play at being a soldier, I have little choice." Lord Norrington waved him away. "Be gone, my Prince. Annoy someone else."

Scrainwood clearly did not like being dismissed, but he withdrew. He spared me a last glare, but I met it with expressionless silence. The last I saw of him the smoke from a pyre had settled over him as he stomped off.

Lord Norrington smiled as he turned back toward me. "Well, as you have heard, we will be sending a force north to chase down Chytrine. We will leave in the morning. I want you with me. Seethe, Faryaah-Tse Kimp, and some of the others will be going along."

"Nay, too?"

"No, I'm afraid he cannot go." He sighed. "Nay will have magick used to heal his leg. If Chytrine were to employ the spell that canceled the healings while we were in Aurolan, we could do nothing for her victims. We're making our force out of people whose wounds were so minor they did not require magick to heal. The rest will remain here and serve as part of the garrison, or will be sent back home. Nay will end up back in Valsina."

"You'll be sending him with Leigh?"

"Yes."

I nodded. "How did Chytrine cast that spell?"

He shrugged. "There are many things about magick I don't understand. All spells, apparently, are akin to knots in ropes. If you know how it was tied, it is easy to untie. Some knots are very complex and therefore hard to undo, but healing spells are relatively simple so many people can master them. It may take years to do so, of course, but Chytrine has had those years and then some. The magickers are convinced the scholars at Vilwan can devise new healing spells she can't undo, but that will take time."

"Time we don't have if we want to catch her."

"Unfortunately."

I nodded, then hooked my thumbs in my belt. "If we're leaving tomorrow, I'd best run and make preparations."

"Good idea, but it can wait a bit." Lord Norrington pointed off toward the tower. "Your brother Sallitt came up with the Scouts. I thought you might like to see him before we left, so I have arranged for you to share dinner."

"You will join us?"

"No. I would love to, but while you spend time with your family, I will spend time with mine." He pointed a hand idly toward the north. "Get your fill of warm memories, Tarrant, because, out there, they will be few and very far between."

CHAPTER 39

I was a bit nervous about meeting my brother, and I'm not sure why. I went back to my room in the tower and washed up, then changed into the sort of light clothes Cavarre favored. I knew that I'd not have a chance to wear such things on the road and, somehow, putting on things that had nothing to do with warfare helped convince me that Chytrine's force really *had* been broken.

My apprehension at seeing my brother spiked when I found him waiting outside the dining hall in the tower with some of the other Oriosan Scouts. Sallitt looked at me a bit uncertainly, then he cracked a big smile when one of his mates shoved him forward. We hugged each other, slapped each other's back, then he introduced me to his friends. I promptly forgot all of their names, but it didn't matter since they excused themselves and left the two of us to get food and find a quiet table—of which there were too many because of the casualties caused by the siege.

Sal looked tired, which made sense since the Scouts had been marching hard for the better part of a month. Still, his hazel eyes remained bright and the sort of animation I was used to returned as we talked. "And when word came through who was leading the expedition, well, Father's chest swelled fair to bursting. He knew Leigh and you would be along, too, and it was all we could do to get him to remain as Peaceward instead of forming up his own militia company and coming north with us."

I smiled. "It would have been grand to see him here."

"It would have." My brother reached over and patted my left hand. "You'll be seeing him soon enough when you go back with Leigh."

I shook my head. "I'm going north with Lord Norrington. Nay will go back with Leigh."

Sal could tell, given my flat tone of voice, that there was some hardship there, but he didn't press. "We're being assigned to garrison duty here for a bit, under Prince Scrainwood."

"Do yourself a favor, Sal, and don't let him know you're my brother. Or, if he finds out, tell him you've never liked me."

"What?" Sal laughed aloud. "Not like you? You're a hero. You don't know it, but when we arrived, Captain Cross called me by name and all sorts of folks started cheering for me. They thought I was you, and just the mention of the Hawkins name was enough to put a smile on their faces. What could the Prince have against you?"

I almost told him the truth. "Fact is, Sal, we never got along. I'm just a country bumpkin to him—not even noble. Just avoid him, please."

My brother studied me for a bit, then nodded. "You've grown up a lot, Tarrant and I'm proud of you for that."

"Thanks."

We passed the rest of the dinner in conversations that covered subjects a bit more trivial than Princes and wars. I did take some ribbing over having an elf for a lover, but Sal told me he'd been paying court to two women in Valsina, so we moved quickly away from love lives to other subjects. He told me a lot of stories about the Scouts and their time on the road, which had me laughing. I was grateful for his tales because that meant I didn't have to share too much of my experiences—none of which really would encourage laughter.

After dinner we parted and I returned to my room. I packed up all my equipment and had it ready to go. It took me the longest time to tie the blanket Leigh had given me into a bundle. Part of me figured I didn't deserve it, but another part refused to leave it behind. Once I'd gotten the things all together, a porter came around to take them away. He also carried my longknives off to have new edges put on them.

From there I went to Seethe's room and we spent the evening in luxurious abandon, as if the next morning would never come. We bathed together, then returned to her room and engaged in long, slow lovemaking by the light of a constellation of candles. Though I think we both felt some urgency, we shunted it aside and made every moment last as long as we could. I remember the golden glow of candlelight on her body, her strength as she moved against me and with me and the sweet warmth of her whispered words. Our fingers intertwined as did our bodies, and I knew that any time I held her hand I would be carried back to that night.

We woke with the dawn, dressed, ate, and joined the other members of the command company in the courtyard before the tower. Well-wishers had gathered there to see us go. Dothan Cavarre left off his study of Chytrine's captured dragonel to bid us farewell. He gave Lord Norrington a silver flask filled with a fine brandy. To me he presented a quiver of thirty arrows with wide broadheads that had been washed in silver. "The size of the head should make killing shots on temeryces easier, I think, Hawkins. Good hunting to you."

"Thank you." I tied the quiver to my saddle and slipped my bow into the scabbard. I was about to haul myself into the saddle when I noticed that while my longknives hung from the belt looped over the saddle pommel, there was no sword attached to it. I frowned and was about to complain when a voice stopped me.

"Missing something, Hawkins?"

I turned and smiled as Nay walked over to me. He held out a scabbarded blade that I knew wasn't the one I'd tossed away. I also knew it wasn't Temmer. "What's this?"

Nay gave me a weak grin. "Made a promise at the bridge, but never made good on it. I'll be going back, you know, with

Leigh. I have a favor to ask you. Take Tsamoc here. This blade won't fail you."

I accepted the sword and slid it from the scabbard slowly and a bit apprehensively. There, incorporated in the blade itself, lay the keystone that had been Tsamoc's heart. Little lights moved through it and I knew magick resided there, but I didn't feel the way I did when I wielded Temmer. The blade had been reinforced around the stone and I had no fears of it breaking. The crossguard and pommel repeated the keystone design in brass. Leather wrapped the hilt, and I knew the blade would stay with me even if both hands were drenched in pig fat and numb from the cold.

I resheathed the sword, and swallowed past the lump in my throat. "You take good care of Leigh, and I'll take care of Tsamoc."

Nay nodded. "That's a fair bargain." He gave me a half grin, then clapped me on the shoulders. "That night, when we first met, you were the one I figured to be the best of us. Didn't think Leigh would end up this way. Didn't think I'd get this far. You I figured for great things. Glad to know that judgment was right."

I shook my head. "*We* have done great things, Giant-slayer, all of us. That's what will be remembered, not me."

Nay steadied my horse as I mounted up, then slapped me on the leg. "When you come back to Valsina, find me. Tell me how Tsamoc fared and how Chytrine died."

"Another fair bargain." I shook his hand, then reined my horse about and trotted him after the others exiting the court-yard. As we moved into the inner city, people cheered us from the roadside, doorways, rooftops, and windows. They cheered as if we were a conquering army returning from victory, not heading out to chase down an enemy. What struck me as even odder was that their enthusiasm mocked the black ruins of the outer city and the body-strewn fields beyond. Intoxicated with their survival, they cheered us off on a task that would result in more death.

But it is not their deaths.

I shrugged my shoulders, gave my horse a touch of spur, and rode out of Fortress Draconis at Seethe's side. I wanted to look back, to see if Leigh stood in a window and watched us depart, but I refrained for fear of what I might see on his face. Instead I just imagined him sitting on the bridge in the tower garden, studying a riverbed that carried no water, beginning to heal.

Bards who have sung of this second expedition have immortalized the command company in countless songs. Of Lord Norrington, Seethe, Faryaah-Tse Kimp, and Prince Augustus I have written much. Winfellis, the Croquelf magicker who'd been with us from the start, also came along. The others were heroes in their own right and had not participated in our earlier adventure because they had been occupied elsewhere.

Duke Brencis Galacos had been at Fortress Draconis serving with the Jeranese Crown Guards who were just finishing their deployment when Chytrine invaded. The Crown Guards had taken heavy casualties in the first day's fighting by the southern breach, but the white-haired warrior had pulled them back in good order and prevented the slaughter of more of his people. Bringing him along not only gave us a good tactician, but honored the sacrifice his warriors had made at the fortress.

Lady Jeturna Costasi of Viarca was something of a soldier of fortune. She had led her family's house guard unit out against the gibberers that had made it into Viarca, much as Lord Norrington had done. She chased them north into Nybal, where she joined forces with a Nybali Warden and rode for Fortress Draconis. They hooked up with our reinforcements on the road and were ready to go after Chytrine.

Aren Asvaldget was the Nybali Warden who had ridden with Lady Jeturna. Smaller than me and lean, with long blond hair and blue eyes, Aren reminded me a lot of a wolf, and it wasn't just because wolf pelts had been used to make his cloak. He was a shaman, which I gathered was to a Vilwanese magicker what a street-brawler was to a trained warrior. His chief asset, aside from his quick laugh, was a very good knowledge of the northlands and a lot of smarts concerning plants and healing. I saw him as taking over one of Nay's roles in our company.

The last two members of the company often get short shrift in the songs, and I can't say that I imagine it's something they find discomfiting, all things considered. Drugi Oldach was a warrior from far Valsogon who had taken up residence in Fortress Draconis after a stint of hiring on there as a mercenary. From his base in the outer city he would head out north and spend much of the year trapping animals, prospecting for gold, or hunting up rare plants for drying and shipping south. He claimed to be only forty-five years old, but his white hair and leathery skin suggested to me he just couldn't count past forty-five and had long since given up trying to learn how. He favored a double-bitted ax and had enough gibberer fur worked into his cloak and patching his clothes that I figured he knew how to use it to his advantage.

Edamis Vilkaso was a golden-haired warrior up all the way from Naliserro. She'd actually led the squad of Nalesk cavalry that charged out of the fortress and took Chytrine's dragonel. They held it despite opposition. What prompted Lord Norrington to invite her along was the fact that she'd been smart enough to figure out that the dragonel was likely the most valuable artifact of the invasion. That was something the other commanders had overlooked—they'd reverted to old ways of thinking when the dragonel stopped shooting and the gibberers broke. She made good use of forethought, and there was no doubt in my mind we'd have ample need of it on our expedition.

For troops we took three units: Muroson Heavy Guards, Sebcian Light Foot, and a cavalry unit cobbled together from those who had traveled with us all the way and others at Fortress Draconis. They were designated the Draconis Lancers and bore shields hastily emblazoned with a lance that looked remarkably like the Crown Tower. Prince Augustus led them, giving us a total force of roughly a thousand foot soldiers and five hundred cavalry. Another three hundred people came with our supplies, which consisted of forty wagons and over a thousand horses.

The sun broke through clouds to warm us as we marched north. Most took that as a good omen. I guess I did too, at the time.

Now I just remember it was the last time I felt anything but cold.

CHAPTER 40

As difficult as our expedition had been so far, the trek north made it seem like a child's garden romp. The distance to the pass in the Boreal Mountains was not far, and Fortress Draconis yielded an abundance of food, supplies, and cold-weather gear. We should have been able to make the journey in half a week or so. And yet, at that point, only five days out, we were only halfway to our goal.

I do recall turning in my saddle and looking back at Fortress Draconis as we rode from it. The outer town formed a charcoal ring around the inner city. The needle that had killed the dragon gleamed in the sunlight. Teams of men swarmed over the dragon, taking it to pieces. While I knew Cavarre had ordered its dissection so he could understand it, from this distance the butchers had the look of insects feeding on a corpse.

North we headed, constantly on alert. This is where our previous experience served us well, as we took precautions against ambushes. When we neared any likely place, squads of men spread out and moved through the forests to sweep them of Aurolani forces. We uncovered and dispersed a number of ambushes set to kill Lord Norrington and our other leaders. Ruining Chytrine's plans heartened all of us greatly.

Chytrine did learn, however. As we sent squads out, other hidden gibberer groups ambushed them, slowing us further. The fighting grew fierce in some spots, but the gibberers always ended up being overwhelmed. The problem with engagements deep in the woods was that our cavalry couldn't be employed well, nor could our archers. It was simple cut-and-crush warfare, to which our men took just fine, but deploying men, recovering the wounded, and getting everyone moving again cut our expected rate of advance.

By midday a half a week out of Fortress Draconis, the weather had turned bitter, with a cold wind bringing snow from the north. Ahead of us lay the pass. We could reach it by week's-end, but now we could barely see it. Clouds shrouded the dulled rock fangs, and white snow covered all the slopes we could see. If the snow let up, it was possible we could still sneak through the pass. If it snowed after that, however, we'd have five long months of winter to survive before we could return south.

Chytrine forced us to make a decision at that point, one that turned out to be as fateful as any we had faced so far. Our scouts found ample evidence that the bulk of her army had set off west into the Ghost Marches. Prince Augustus and Lord Norrington immediately realized she had sent her army in that direction to draw us off. Her troops might be able to make it to Okrannel and link up with the army that had been left behind there. That put Jerana in jeopardy, not to mention all the people living in the Ghost Marches.

At the same time we found evidence that Chytrine and her entourage continued north. If we went after her, we might or might not make it in time to catch and kill her. No one doubted she was the greater evil, and that her death would render the known world safe for a long time. Regardless of our success in getting her, the Aurolani army would still be operating at our rear. They could sweep back and trap us against the Boreal Mountains; they could again assault Fortress Draconis or campaign in Okrannel. As long as they were out there, people would die.

It was that realization that prompted Lord Norrington to split our main force off under Prince Augustus' command. Riders were sent back to Fortress Draconis with orders to bring the Oriosan Scouts—albeit without Prince Scrainwood—and our fleet and land them in the Ghost Marches. As many popular songs have chronicled the Ghost Campaign, I need not detail it here. None of the songs I have heard could ever exaggerate the heroic effort Prince Augustus and his command exerted to track down and destroy the Aurolani host. They fought their way from the Dûrgrue River to the Jerana border. The fact that along the way he managed to win himself a wife and save the Okrans refugees who now have communities in civilized cities everywhere merely speaks to his courage and intelligence.

The rest of us, what had become known as the command company, were to head north with all possible speed to catch Chytrine and kill her. The ten of us drew two extra horses apiece and ample supplies to see us through a month of travels. We all joked that we would be able to eat well since we expected to return not a week hence and ride to join up with Augustus. Those who were heading west abetted us in this joke, since all of us knew that chances were we'd never return.

It can seem self-serving for me to say that, especially since I did survive, but Augustus—King Augustus, now—can attest to this fact. In fact, it was he who approached me the eve before we left the main group. The command company had all assembled around a vast bonfire and was eating boiled beans and salt pork when Augustus leaned forward and pointed a fork at Lord Norrington.

"My lord, there is only one more thing I wish you would grant me for my campaign."

Lord Norrington barely looked up from his plate. "And that is, Prince Augustus?"

"We know the Aurolani warriors are a sullen and stupid lot, given to panic and breaking in terror." Augustus' eyes narrowed and he glanced at me. "I would like to have with me a *sullanciri*-slayer. Give me your aide, young Hawkins here. His presence alone would be worth another battalion of men."

Lord Norrington nodded. "Your reasoning is sound, Prince Augustus."

My hands were trembling as I set my plate down. "Don't do this, my lord, don't send me away."

Lord Norrington looked up and fixed me with a compassionate stare. "You think I am willing to send you away because what we are going to do will likely result in our deaths, don't you? You think I wish to spare you that pain, to preserve your life."

"Yes, Lord Norrington."

"You're wrong, Hawkins." He looked around the circle, past the leaping flames that hissed and snapped. The others had stopped eating and regarded us carefully. I remember Drugi wiping food from his white beard with the back of his hand, watching me to see how I was reacting. All of them knew Lord Norrington was, in fact, attempting to save my life, and they seemed ready and willing to aid him in that effort.

"You're wrong, Hawkins, because the battles Prince Augustus will fight could just as easily destroy you as any we will engage in. You will not be spared hazardous duty. You will be there, fighting along with the others. You will be spared nothing."

I stood slowly, fighting to hold back tears. "Respectfully, my lord, I submit you are wrong. I will be spared a chance to put an end to the evil that has taken over my life. You cannot have forgotten how, on the first night I wore a moonmask, I slew a temeryx to save a friend—only to find his life had been ruined by the beast. My family, back in Valsina, thrills to tales of this expedition, but I know fear gnaws at them, the same way it gnaws at each of us. Friends have died because of Chytrine, and friends have been broken, and the whole of my adult life has been centered around stopping her. While what Prince Augustus sets out to do is right and necessary to blunt her evil, what you will do will be the thing that puts an end to it. If I go with him and, somehow, you fail, I will know it was because I was not there."

Lord Norrington's eyes narrowed. "And what if we all fail, Hawkins? What if the cold kills us? What if we never find her and are trapped in the mountains, waiting to starve? There are a thousand ways we can fail. Those of us who are going have lived our lives and can assess the risks. We know what we are doing. You do not."

I raised my chin. "I tell you, my lord, that in the last months I have lived a lifetime as well. I know the risks. There may be a thousand ways the effort can fail, but the thousand and first would be to leave me behind. Narrow the odds at least that much."

Lord Norrington stared into the fire for a while, then looked over at Prince Augustus. "I thank you, my friend, for your asking after Hawkins. I apologize for putting you up to that."

Augustus nodded once. "It was my pleasure to help you. And, Hawkins, know that what I said concerning you was the truth. I would gladly have you beside me."

Lord Norrington smiled, then looked around the circle again. "I should have known better than to ask what I did, and I apologize to all of you for this public display. Tarrant Hawkins here is someone I have known since before he could walk. Among us, as you may know, when a youth receives his first adult mask—like the one he wears now—it is customary for friends to offer gifts. I offered him the choice of anything it was my ability to grant. Hawkins here asked for only one thing: my trust. I gave it to him and now reaffirm it. It is my hope you will join me in that trust, for he is very much a worthy companion on this quest of ours."

Those gathered at the fire, those who would brave Aurolan, grumbled and nodded their assent, then went back to eating. Occasionally one or the other of them would look at me and nod, not the nod of an elder indulging a child, but the nod of a peer to a peer. In that fire burned any doubts they may have had about me.

Over the years I have had time to reflect on that incident. I do not yet know if Lord Norrington meant truly to offer me a chance to escape, or if he wanted a way for me to show the others that I was as committed to the quest as they were. Perhaps it was a bit of both, but the core of it came down to his letting me take responsibility for my own life.

Had I, at that point, come to believe my own legend? It

was easy to be humble in such heroic company, but their easy acceptance of me did let me believe I deserved to be there. I *did* believe my role would be critical in hunting down Chytrine, though never would I have expected my role to be warped the way it was. And while I will not say there are not days when I wish I had gone with Augustus, I do believe the choice made at that fire was the right one, despite everything that flowed from it.

Leavetaking that next morning was full of cheers and hearty brags. A thousand locks of Chytrine's hair were promised that morning, I figure, and twice that number of sword cuts to her heart. I'm sure most of them saw us as riding off to reap glory, but by the same token, I don't think but a handful of them would have come along with us if offered the chance.

It took us three days to reach the pass. Life settled into an easy routine during that time, and the falling snow softened the landscape so effectively that it was almost possible to forget the business we were about. The snow brought with it a silence that made every forested stretch we rode through into a peaceful temple. I let myself think about the good times in my past and project them forward, seeing myself with Seethe at my side. In those moments I did not doubt my ability to survive and, rather foolishly, I assumed that if *I* could survive, all of us would.

Because of the snow we did not push on as hard as we might. While I was used to winters in Oriosa and dealing with snow, Drugi and Aren taught me a great deal about surviving in the colder north. Some things were simple, like learning not to build a fire beneath snow-laden branches, since the snow, when warmed by the fire, would fall into it and smother it. They also showed me how to read tracks in the snow, and we all rejoiced that there were no temeryx tracks for me to learn from.

Other things were more important. We melted snow for water and had to stir so it wouldn't scorch. More importantly, we never ate snow and, as much as possible, drank only teas or water that had been heated. Toward that end we kept waterskins between our coats and us, letting our bodies warm the water. Cold water would chill us and, given our circumstances, that would kill us, too.

At night we slept two to a tent, sharing body heat beneath thick blankets and skins. Drugi showed us how to make shelters of snow, so we often built a wall to the windward side of our tents. Seethe and I shared a tent. We were more than companions but less than lovers. Though we huddled together, our naked bodies pressed tightly to each other, we did not make love. It really wasn't necessary—we had each other and that was more than enough. We slept in each other's arms, woke to warm and heartfelt greetings, and then rejoined our other companions to continue our journey.

At noon on the third day, as we crested a hill, Lord Norrington called a halt. The skies had cleared and ahead of us, barely a half-day's ride away, lay the pass. Snow blurred details of the pass' steep sides, but could not erase the impression that the mountains had been cloven with a giant ax. Snow filled the pass, and even though we could see everything very clearly, we caught no sign of Chytrine.

"Either she's already made it through, or she got buried in it." Drugi nipped off a piece of dried beef and tucked it inside his left cheek. He pointed the rest of the beef stick toward the pass. "Could be a snowtide caught her."

Lord Norrington's breath came white through the green wool of his scarf. "Doesn't matter what she did, as long as she didn't turn back. The question is, can we make it through?"

Aren Asvaldget tossed back his wolf's-head hood and looked north. "Snowtide might have let her pass, but it would get us. See the wind curling snow out into ledges to the east there? Those come down and they'll never find us."

Drugi nodded his agreement.

Lord Norrington reined his horse around. "Faryaah-Tse, the mountains forming the eastern side of the pass are part of Boragul, aren't they?"

The diminutive urZrethi nodded. "The advent of cooler weather was what drove urZrethi south long ago. Boragul was abandoned."

"Abandoned completely? There's no one in there?"

Drugi shook his head. "I've seen sign in them mountains. Something lives there."

Faryaah-Tse held up a hand. "By abandoned I mean that those who could or were brave enough left and went south. Those who were left behind were of no consequence. I do not know if they have died out."

"Are there ways through Boragul?" Lord Norrington patted his horse on the neck. "Could Chytrine have used Boragul to return north, or to bring reinforcements south?"

The urZrethi sat back in the saddle, bringing her left leg up and laying her shin across the horse's shoulders. "There *are* ways through Boragul, unless they have collapsed because of age. I would imagine we can even find an entrance. As for Chytrine and her use of Boragul, I do not know."

She hesitated for a moment, then plunged into an explanation. "You men, you think of the urZrethi or elves as all being the same. I shall confess to you that men often seem the same to me. However, you all come from different nations and have different customs. Would it surprise you to know a man of Valsogon who knew nothing of Oriosa? So it is with us. I come from Tsagul. We reached furthest south in the invasion and are proud of that. For those left behind we have little concern."

"I understand, and do not consider your lack of knowledge a flaw." Lord Norrington opened his arms. "Our choices, then, are this: we turn back now, or we go forward and seek to enter Boragul. We will see if we can travel north from there and, if there are any urZrethi still living there, we shall determine if they know of Chytrine's fate. I am for pushing on, but I shall abide by the wishes of the majority."

No one dissented and so, with Faryaah-Tse Kimp leading us, we rode forward toward the destiny that would consume us all.

CHAPTER 41

Faryaah-Tse's trail took us east for an hour and then north toward Boragul, along the banks of a stream that gurgled beneath snow and ice. Ahead of us lay a deep, narrow canyon that had its southern face exposed to the sun. Whatever snow had been deposited there had long since melted to fill the stream beside which we rode. As nightfall approached, we came to the mouth of the canyon.

"We have to stop here." The urZrethi turned in her saddle and held up a hand. "You can go no further for the moment."

Drugi pulled down his grey scarf and spat. "There's no entrance to nothing in there. I've been in there afore and seen nothing."

"This surprises me not at all." Faryaah-Tse tossed the reins of her horse to me, then tugged off her boots. Before any of us could question what she was doing, her feet broadened out into a spoon shape and her legs lengthened so she didn't have to hop down off the horse. She stood up and the snow supported her. She crunched her way to a standing stone on the west side of the canyon mouth, touched it, then walked over to one on the east side and touched that one, too. Then she returned to the center of the canyon and waved us forward.

I saw nothing different until I reached the line linking the two stones. As I passed through it a light dazzled me, almost as if the setting sun had risen again and left me snowblind. I felt my stomach roil and tasted my luncheon broth again, but choked it back down. When I looked around I saw much of the same little canyon I had before, but toward the back, down somewhat low, it curved to the west.

Faryaah-Tse took the reins from me and led her horse on foot. "Not far now."

Drugi kind of hunkered down in his saddle as he looked around. "I've not seen this before, and I was here."

The urZrethi looked at him. "You were not meant to see this, Drugi Oldach. No man was, nor elf. This was meant for urZrethi eyes alone."

As we came around the corner and could see into the western branch, my breath caught in my throat. There, not a hundred yards off, stood a massive stone portal carved out of the rock. It was round, and water that had dripped down from above coated the rim in ice. The circular portal's edge had been carved from the living rock and worked with odd runes and sigils. The door itself, which appeared to be a big round slab of black rock, was recessed several feet. Broad steps led up to the platform before the door.

But more impressive than the portal itself were the paired statues beside it. They showed two female figures, naked, kneeling. Instead of arms they had wings and had raised them high above their heads, as if trying to touch the sun. The figures looked serene and powerful.

"Who are they?"

Faryaah-Tse turned at my question. "There is a myth among the urZrethi that the truly powerful and complete ur-Zrethi will be able to assume a shape that will permit flight. It has less to do with the size of the wings than the nature of the spirit that will allow the person to soar. It is perhaps not unexpected that those who dwell largely within the earth wish to fly."

I slowly nodded and wondered to myself if this myth did not also explain why the urZrethi courted the wrath of the elves when they created Gyrvirgul as a home for the Gyrkyme.

As much as the elves saw the Gyrkyme as bestial abominations, perhaps the urZrethi saw them as an embodiment of their dream. Regardless, even Winfellis seemed to be rendered breathless by the statues' beauty.

We rode in solemn silence to the portal. Lord Norrington dismounted and, along with Faryaah-Tse, mounted the steps. The urZrethi studied the runes around the portal, which had a diameter of at least a dozen feet, then shucked a glove and extended an arm up to touch the arch's keystone. Both of them stepped back as a grinding started from within, then slowly the black doorstone rolled to the left and warm air gushed out to wash over us.

The warmth was welcome, but the scent was not. Part musty and a bit sharp, it reminded me of a barn that had not been mucked out recently enough. I suppose I should have taken the sharp scent as a good sign, since that meant there were living creatures about. I would have, too, I think, but the Boragul urZrethi quickly showed themselves.

Four of them came hobbling out. Their flesh varied between the yellow of old bones and the white-grey of cold ash. Some had mismatched feet, others had a spare joint in a leg, and one even had a second, smaller pair of arms sprouting from its waist. They all seemed to be female, or at least, some of them had breasts, though too many had an odd number. Their eyes usually rested on either side of their noses and often lined up with each other, which couldn't be said of their ears—in the case of those who had any.

That they were misshapen was patently obvious to anyone who cared to look, for their ratty clothes barely covered them. Still, it took me a second or two to figure out what the problem really was. I recalled Faryaah-Tse mentioning that changing shape was tiring and consumed energy. To me they all looked underfed, so I suspected they had become stuck between changes.

One, bearing a rusty spear and what once might have been a round shield, stepped forward to challenge us. "Who dares open the way to Boragul?"

Faryaah-Tse swept her stick-thin yellow arm out and pressed her hand to her breast. "I do. I am Faryaah-Tse Kimp, come far from Tsagul. I ask for me and my companions the hospitality of Boragul."

Though the lead urZrethi gave no sign of being impressed by Faryaah-Tse, his trio of seconds began to quake. They studied her legs and right arm, then their eyes grew wide as she shrank her arm down to fill her sleeve and match the other arm. They watched her, then pointed to the sky and jabbered among themselves.

The leader whirled around and smacked one of them on the back of the head with the haft of her spear. "Be quiet. Still your tongues or they'll be shrunk in your heads. This is a matter for the queen."

The leader came back around and stumbled for a step, then righted herself. "The queen will decide. Follow."

We dismounted and led our horses into the heart of the mountain. Seethe gasped and pressed her hand to her throat as she looked about. I could see little, as shadows shrouded what must have been tall galleries with high arches and intricate carvings worked throughout, but even what I saw down low impressed me: friezes of battles so intricately carved that the figures in them seemed to shift position as we moved along. From every corner and recess a playful face grinned or a warrior scowled. I saw statues representing urZrethi as normally shaped as Faryaah-Tse and yet others mutated into forms suited to combat or mining or any of countless other occupations.

Other things in the halls of Boragul did not impress and, in fact, prompted pity, surprise, and anger. The halls could not be described as anything but filthy. Half-gnawed bones and shards of broken crockery lined the walkways. Feathers and dust and hair all rolled together into little balls that trailed in our wake. Flies hovered over mounds of offal, and likewise circled piles of dung. Mangy curs snarled from the darkness and feral cats—easily spotted by the glow in their eyes—spat hisses. Bird guano stained statues and streaked the floor, while somewhere in the darkness above I heard the leather flap of bats' wings.

I wondered for a moment at the feathers and bird droppings, then got the shock of my life as miniature temeryces came trotting out in a pack to pace beside us. I dropped a hand to Tsamoc's hilt and would have drawn the blade, but our guide reached out with a hand and chuckled one under the chin. The little creature, which had a uniform color matching the brown of a bruised mushroom, tootled contentedly at this treatment.

Our guide led us along through series of halls, twisting and turning through smaller ones where I could almost make out the ceiling, then back into larger, more grand ones. It did become apparent that as we headed toward wherever the queen made her lair, things seemed cleaner and were even better lit. Even so, I still maintained the impression that garbage was merely hauled to the nearest convenient passage that saw little use.

The increased lighting allowed me to see what Seethe had looked at before. In the hallways the urZrethi had worked massive mosaics that displayed grand battles, scenes from romances and history, and even myths such as the progression of urZrethi from their earliest form up to taking flight. Each tiny piece of the mosaics seemed to be made of gemstones, with any small portion of it being enough to allow a man to live well for decades. Even as that thought came to me, though, I couldn't imagine despoiling such beauty.

Finally we reached another round portal that glowed with golden light. A number of urZrethi accepted the reins of our horses and led them off while we advanced to the queen's throne room. I refer to it as a room because that's what the round chamber was, though once inside it was easy to forget that fact.

The first thing I noticed was the sheer amount of gold present. There was no area that was not gilded, no flat surface that did not have piled on it a golden urn or statuette or have golden mail draped over it. Even the throne, which had the aspect of being a giant egg with one side carved out, had been layered in gold and encrusted with gemstones. Gold velvet pillows filled it.

The second inescapable aspect of the room was how a bird theme tied everything together. The walls, from floor to the top of the wainscoting, had been covered with a screen of golden twigs and branches. They'd been fashioned well above life-size, but woven together the way a bird might interlace them to form a nest. It even widened at the base to suggest the bowl of a nest, and the gold inlay on the floor continued this theme. Above, hanging down from the ceiling on nearly invisible wires were golden leaves, and above them were stars and the moon and sun. Feather patterns covered rugs and pillows, while the statuary and other appointments were birds, had birds on them, or touched on some other bird attribute.

Even the gown the queen wore was made of cloth of gold and embroidered with birds. It took me a moment or two to recognize that fact, however, because where her sleeves ended I could see arms covered with feathers. They matched the grey of her face and other exposed flesh, so I assumed they were part of her. She had none of the dignity or bearing of the Gyrkyme I had seen in Okrannel and Fortress Draconis, but she did have feathers.

Our guide ran forward and slid to an uneven stop on her knees at the foot of the throne. She spoke quickly to the queen, who answered with a sharp, crowlike *caw!* Our guide recoiled, then spun herself about and knelt with head pressed to the floor as the Queen stood.

"I am Tzindr-Coraxoc Vlay, Queen of Boragul." The queen, who stooped at the shoulders and had a figure like a brandy cask, glanced at our guide. "I have been told that you, one of the outcasts who resides in Tsagul, has asked for our hospitality."

Faryaah-Tse stiffened with the word outcast, but merely bowed her head. "The generosity of Boragul and its queen is well known, even in far Tsagul, though we tremble so at your greatness that we dare not speak your name."

Tzindr-Coraxoc seemed mollified by that comment. "I shall consider your petition. For now I will grant you an abode. You are bound on your word to remain there until summoned."

Faryaah-Tse nodded. "It shall be as you wish."

The queen snapped an order at our guide, who immediately herded us back out of the throne room and led us down a dark corridor. We mounted a wide stairway and went up several flights, then were pointed to a round doorway. "You will wait within."

Faryaah-Tse led us into the doorway which, on the other side, broadened and grew into a round tunnel perhaps ten yards in length. A stripe down the center of the ceiling began to glow a yellow-orange, providing me with enough light to see the images painted on the walls. They reminded me of the ancestral statues in Alcida and I assumed they were all of a family. Despite my being unable to read urZrethi runes, I did notice the repetition of a pattern that I took to represent the surname of those depicted.

The portraits, despite the grime and spiderwebs covering them, were quite heroic, showing people with enemies crushed underfoot or flowers growing around them with the blossoms facing them as they might face the sun. Flesh color varied on all of them, and the light was not the best for picking it out, but most of them did seem to be very similar to Faryaah-Tse in skin tone.

The tunnel ended in a curious chamber made of two spheres linked like soap bubbles in the middle. The entry sphere was big and featured a large hearth to the immediate left of the entryway. A ring of glowing panels surrounded the room beyond my head height, passing just above the circular portal that marked the intersection of the two spheres. A flat floor made of set stones cut the bottom off both spheres, but the floor level of the second one was a good three feet higher than that of the entry sphere. Both spheres had round portals that led off into side rooms and the painted designs in both had representations of flowers and animals—including but not limited to birds—woven together in intricate braids of legs, tails, and bodies. Following any one line was a hypnotic pursuit that could have occupied me for hours.

Faryaah-Tse moved to the center of the entry sphere and stones in the hearth began a soft red glowing that pulsed out heat. She smiled, that warm, familiar sort of smile that comes from fond memories or unexpected discoveries. She held her hands out toward the hearth, then nodded to the rest of us. "Welcome home."

We'd spread throughout the room and started to strip off

our heavy winter clothing. Lord Norrington unfastened his woolen cloak and shook off droplets of melted snow. "You say 'home' as if you recognize this place."

"More that it recognizes me." She turned and silhouetted herself against the hearth's growing glow. "There were magicks worked into this chamber a long time ago, magicks that would be triggered in the presence of one of the Kimp bloodline. When we left ten generations ago to head south, we never expected to return—or so I am told. That the queen has placed us in this chamber either is a sign of respect, or she mocks me for being a pureblood returning."

Brencis Galacos stroked his white goatee. "Pureblood?"

Faryaah-Tse hesitated for a moment, then turned and stared into the hearth. "The urZrethi do not approach life as do men or elves. This place we have been given is called a *coric*. Here the matriarch of a family would be in residence, back, up there, in one of the rooms off the inner chamber. Her daughters would live with her, as would her sisters, all working to help raise her children. On occasion, if alliances were wished with this family, other sisters or daughters would be allowed to bear children, creating ties between families."

Seethe arched an eyebrow in her direction. "Males are sent to live apart, with each wife's family?"

"Usually, yes, after they reach maturity." She opened her arms and pointed to the rooms off the lower sphere. "These rooms house the males, both family and visitors who are here to get a female with child. Most males accept the way of things, but when they rebel, they are exiled. Tales you have heard of solitary urZrethi working mines or lurking beneath bridges, these are the outcasts."

I frowned. "But those stories depict them as monsters."

"So they are, and so they become." Faryaah-Tse shrugged. "Cut off from civilization they become malignant, much as the urZrethi here have become, I fear."

She turned her back to the hearth and moved to the side so we could see her face again. "Imagine if you abandoned a city—Yslin, for example—and all that were left in it were the halt, the lame, the beggars, and the scoundrels. In a thousand years, this is what you would have."

Jeturna laughed aloud. "You underestimate the human capacity to distort society. We'd have this in a month or two."

We all laughed, men, urZrethi, and elves, breaking the tension. Faryaah-Tse's explanations clearly had not been easy for her, and had revealed more to me about urZrethi than I had heard in a lifetime of living in the shadow of the Bokagul. The urZrethi were known for being very private. She had shared much with us, and I took that as a sign of how much she had come to trust us.

UrZrethi bearers soon brought us our baggage and we hauled it into our rooms. I shared one of the upper chambers with Seethe. Those rooms were more elegant than the long, blocky rooms given over to male urZrethi. While all the elements of it had been hewn from stone, in our chamber the edges had been rounded, and expanses had been painted. We had a small hearth that projected a little warmth into the room, and more than enough space under our sleeping platforms to store all of our gear.

The male rooms looked more like warehouses with shelves that served as sleeping space. There looked to be enough slabs to fit ten men—and twice that many urZrethi, I suppose—and the edges and corners had the hardness of weapons to them. These rooms were also unheated, but this deep in the mountains they never got that cold, so blankets and furs would be enough to keep people snug and warm.

After we had settled ourselves in, Tzindr-Coraxoc sent for us. A misshapen guide limped her way through corridors and brought us to another chamber that must have been linked to the Kimp family because it warmed immediately in Faryaah-Tse's presence. The long room had a curved ceiling painted with images of urZrethi broken into panels by the same sort of twisted knotwork I'd seen in the *coric*. Running down the center of it was a stone table that clearly had been carved from the rock as the room was made. Wooden chairs and benches sat at it and thick candles had been run down its spine. Battered plates, bowls, and goblets of gold had been set at each place, and food—some of which I suspected had been pilfered from our stores—had been heaped steaming on platters large enough to serve as shields in battle.

Tzindr-Coraxoc, rising from the tall chair set at the table's far end, spread her arms wide. "You asked for the hospitality of Boragul and we give it to you. This is the best we have to offer."

Each of us had our own bodyservant allotted to us. Mine took me by the hand and guided me to my place at the table. I seated myself in the chair there, and found my knees higher than my hips because the chair had been built to accommodate an urZrethi. This still left me ridiculously high in comparison to the table, so I just shifted the chair out from under me and sat on the floor.

The Boragul queen regarded me coldly and snarled something in a tongue I could not understand.

Faryaah-Tse, who had been seated at her right hand, leaned forward. "It is not a dishonor, my queen, but these men have taken an oath that they will only sit in a saddle until their mission has been accomplished."

The queen nodded and the rest of our company also abandoned their chairs, though Seethe and Winfellis remained on the bench they shared. By shifting forward a bit, they tucked their legs beneath them and all but kneeled at the table. Drugi mumbled something about having the cold seep from the floor into his old bones.

Brencis glanced at him and snorted. "Given where we've been, it's likely to seep bone to stone and not the other way around, my friend."

Even the queen liked that joke, so she laughed then clapped her hands and the feasting began. The food was not the strangest part of it, but rather having a servant whose body shifted to become the proper utensil. My servant's right hand became a ladle to provide me soup, then made the shift to pincers to get me meat. As I ate, I saw her eyeing my food with a certain desire. Since I had guessed the urZrethi here were not eating well and getting stuck between transitions, I always left something on my plate that she might gobble down later.

As bizarre as the setting and servants were, the food was very good and very spicy. The soup, which was a rather thin broth with mushrooms, some vegetables, and a bit of other stuff I didn't want to recognize floating in it, still tasted very rich and hot enough to make my lips throb. Leaving some of it behind for my servant was harder than I would have imagined.

Most of the other dishes came covered in brown sauces, which I considered a virtue when I couldn't clearly identify some of the bones which came in the meat. It all tasted rather exotic and not bad at all, but I was certain I wasn't eating chicken, pork, beef, or even mutton. Whatever it was, it tasted better than dried beef, so I wolfed it down.

The wine proved to be surprisingly good. I didn't have Leigh's facility for guessing vintages and ages from a single sniff, but I very much liked it. The dark wine had good body and just a tickle of berry flavor to it. It didn't strike me as anything that had laid in casks for ten centuries, so either the urZrethi of Boragul had vineyards hidden in high mountain meadows, or they maintained some limited trade with peoples outside the mountains.

The centerpiece of the feast came later, after soup and a few preliminary dishes. From a gourmet's point of view it might well have been a spectacular dish, but it was served in a manner that left no mystery to its origin. The main beast lay on a platter as it might lie before a hearth. Into it had been stuffed a smaller creature and into that a yet smaller creature, much in the way we might expect one to end up in the other's stomach if swallowed whole. Most damnably of all, the dog stuffed with cat that was stuffed with a rat had been so deliciously spiced that my mouth watered even as I wanted to recoil from the table.

The queen looked at me. "It is my understanding, Tarrant Hawkins, that you are the youngest person here. To you, then, goes the honor of the choice cut."

I coughed into my hand to cover my surprise. I glanced at Faryaah-Tse, but she only stared at me and nodded curtly once. My mind reeled. I'd never considered eating a dog before, so thinking of a dog as food was completely beyond me. And the choicest cut, what would that be? I wasn't a butcher given to knowing what part of an animal tasted best. I didn't know what choice to make, but I knew I had to make one, and

having the image of every dog I'd ever petted flying through
my mind didn't help. I could feel their heads under my hand,
see their eager eyes looking up at me. I was lost.

Faryaah-Tse's second nod forced me to make a decision.
"Queen Tzindr-Coraxoc, in Oriosa, from whence I come,
there is only one tidbit that can be considered the choice cut."
I pointed to the dog's skull. "There, the little strip of muscle
on the top. I'll only take the right side, leaving the left for
someone else."

The queen smiled slowly. "Excellent choice."

I bowed my head to her. "Thank you."

She tapped a finger against the table. "You will tell me *why*
it is the choice cut."

Muscles bunched at my jaws as I sought to cover my surprise and consternation. I'd been lucky once, but again?

I looked over at her and calmed myself as inspiration
struck. "It is the choice cut because that is the muscle with
which the dog chews, and we must chew it. It is the only cut
that works on us as it works on the dog."

The queen clapped her hands. "Splendid, splendid! Now
you will all enjoy our main course."

We all ate of it, but sparingly. It struck me as odd that they
would eat dog and cat and rat but keep temeryces as pets. It
would have probably struck the Boragul urZrethi as odd to
know I'd eaten temeryx, and you can rest assured that
temeryx, though gamier, tastes better than dog.

Once the main dish was cleared we were served a sweet
wine and tarts filled with berries and nuts. These combined to
wash away the last of the dog taste from my mouth and I did
not leave any for my servant to finish. The wine did relax us
and loosen tongues. We spun tales of our adventures, leaving
the queen agog at all we had done and how far we had come.

In the perpetual twilight that was Boragul, we had no idea
how much time had passed. Soon enough, though, yawns
came to match laughs and we knew it was time to retire. After
thanking our hostess, we followed Faryaah-Tse back to our
rooms and, save for Drugi who wanted to wander around
until his stomach settled down, we headed off to bed.

Seethe and I did make love that night, half blaming our

ardor on the wine and the other half on the urZrethi enchantments worked into these rooms for the convenience of ur-
Zrethi females who wanted to breed. Everything came slowly
that night, soft and warm and slow. There was no urgency, no
sense of holding off death or doom, just the chance for the
two of us to share pleasure with and in each other.

I awoke, assuming it was morning, but having no way of
knowing. I pulled on my clothes and wandered out into the
main chamber, finding others of our company rising and
brushing sleepsand from their eyes. None of us were hung-
over, which was good, and all of us agreed we'd eaten enough
dog to stand us for a lifetime.

Brencis looked around and frowned. "Hawkins, did you
see Drugi?"

I shook my head. "He's not back in that room?"

"His blankets are laid out, but he did that before we left for
the feast."

Lord Norrington descended the steps from the upper
sphere. "Did anyone see Drugi return last night?"

No one had.

I shivered. "I don't like this."

"Nor do I." Lord Norrington regarded those of us who
were awake. "We'll need to search for him. We'll do it under
the pretext of enjoying the splendor that is Boragul. We'll go
out in pairs."

Aren Asvaldget raised a hand. "With Drugi gone we are
one shy of a final pair. I will go alone."

"No, I'll be alone." Lord Norrington smiled. "You work
well together with Edamis. I'd rather have you together. All of
you, go armed. We don't know what's wrong, and with any
luck nothing is, but I don't want to take any chances."

I returned to the chamber I shared with Seethe, woke her
and told her what had happened. She quickly dressed and
strapped on Tsamoc. I scabbarded a gibberer longknife on my
right hip and tucked the boot dagger Nay had given me in my
right boot. She belted on her sword and dagger, and we went
out for our search.

The pretext Lord Norrington had given us wasn't as thin a

it might have sounded. The halls were certainly stupendous, and though I could not see much, Seethe described many things to me in exquisite detail. I heard awe in her voice at what she saw, and disgust, too, for how it had been allowed to be soiled by bats and other feral creatures.

"What they have allowed to happen here is akin to what the Aurolani have done to Vorquellyn. It is evil."

As we moved through the hallways I took the precaution of looking around and committing to memory the nature of the turns we'd taken. In places where the dust lay thick I used my bootheel to scrape a cross. The dust also proved useful because it held tracks, and I looked for Drugi's footprints wherever traffic had moved off the main thoroughfare.

Up some stairs and around some corners I saw some tracks that I wasn't sure I recognized. They were not made by booted feet, and though most of the urZrethi seemed to go around unshod, their feet tended to be smaller than these. Moreover, these steps had an even gait which was highly unusual since most of the urZrethi were lame. Seethe crouched and studied them for a moment, then silently waved me on down the dark corridor into which they led.

The tracks continued for twenty yards, past several portals, then curved in toward one to the right. A big stone door blocked it and though we listened, we could hear nothing. I pantomimed knocking on the stone, but Seethe shook that idea off. Instead she had me stoop down and take hold of her legs around the knees. As I stood up again she was able to reach up and touch the keystone in the round portal.

As the stone rolled back, a musky scent I recognized very well rolled out of the room. I stumbled back and fell, Seethe landing on my chest. I coughed in spite of myself, then let her bounce off to the left. I twisted around, coming up on my knees and drew Tsamoc.

"It can't be," she breathed as she armed herself.

"It is, Seethe." Bile burned my throat. "It's all been a trap."

The portal opened onto a massive room with muted lights playing along into its depth. Raised platforms dotted the floor, but could barely be seen for what, at first glance, appeared to be thick carpet covering everything. The problem was that the carpet moved—wriggled really—in little bits and pieces working their way up to the summit of each platform.

Mounted atop the platform were huge creatures, as fat as sows but with the size of oxen to them. The white fur on their bellies revealed a dozen red teats. The brood mothers did not move much at all, but their offspring, hundreds of puling mottled kitts, clawed and snapped at each other in their quest to feed.

"Boragul, nursery to gibberkin." Seethe shook her head. "Run, Hawkins, and hope we can run far and fast enough."

CHAPTER 42

Run we did, but not far enough or fast enough. Tsamoc sang as it parried short spears, then cut up through the bellies of gibberers. One lunged at my gut, but with both hands on Tsamoc's hilt I took the longknife around and carried it high, then shifted my grip and chopped down, hard. The blow carved a third of the gibberer's face off, sending him reeling, trying to piece it back together.

Seethe grinned a terrible grin, her white teeth shining in a face splashed with gibberer blood. We ran from that knot of gibberers, the dead and whimpering, and sped through the corridors. Mostly we found gibberers, but occasionally ur-Crethi with packs of little temeryces came after us. They'd shifted themselves into what they thought warriors should be, which left them half-armored and under-armed. Faryaah-Tse would have ridiculed them if she'd seen them.

They came at us recklessly. I assume it was because they thought us beneath them. We took their sense of superiority and carved it into little bits, leaving them on the cold stone floors with their pets delicately picking at them.

We knew we were dead and we both howled at the insanity of it. Our howls matched those of the gibberers hunting us.

We called all the louder to them, challenging them, and they howled back.

Had they been men, I would have said the ferocity and daring of our attacks were what surprised them, but these beasts had little intelligence. Their surprise came when we did not shy from their snarling, when we dared attack, and from the fact that the blood of their kind drenched us.

I followed Seethe, running hard to keep her in sight. Her eyesight allowed her to see more than I could, and in some ways, I was happy I could see so little. Just the bits and pieces of her tunic flapping loose meant she'd been nicked up as badly as I had. No mortal wounds, but enough to eventually slow me down and let them catch me.

Urging me along, Seethe ran ahead, into an intersection. She twisted to the right and a gibberer lunged with a spear and stuck her through the chest, high on the flank. I heard her scream and saw the spear-point poke through her tunic at her back. He hoisted her up, her legs kicking, her arms flailing, and shook the spear to harvest more screams from her.

In a heartbeat I was on her attacker. Tsamoc slashed down, cutting through the spear. I hit the gibberer with my right shoulder, knocking him back and down.

I spun around to the left and brought Tsamoc up, sliding the blade beneath another spear—this one meant to catch me. I slashed a gibberer across the belly, then parried another spear wide to my left. Dodging right I let that gibberer dash past me, then I whipped my blade around in a flat arc. The sword sang as it excised a bowl-like hunk from the back of his skull.

A slash caught me across the back of my left leg, but scored nothing more than flesh. I continued my spin and hacked Tsamoc down. I caught the gibberer between shoulder and neck, cutting enough to free a geyser of blood. He collapsed and I turned, slashing high right to low left. The blow caught the first gibberer, the one who speared Seethe, cutting off his hands and slicing through his neck. It would have opened him from shoulder to hip, had he not been on his knees mewing for mercy.

I ran to where Seethe had dragged herself against the wall.

She'd left a smear of blood behind her and the broken spear-shaft still quivered with each breath. A glistening blackness welled up around it. I reached out to press my hands against the wound, to do something, but her hands closed on mine.

"Go, Tarrant, go. Leave me."

"I can't leave you."

Her chest heaved heavily with each labored breath. "You can't carry me. I can't run. Go. Go!"

Tears blurred her image, softening it. "I can't go. I love you."

She laughed and, if not for the pain tingeing it, I'd have thought it beautiful. "Dear Tarrant. You must go. If you love me, grant me this." She coughed lightly and blood flecked her lips. "Let me die knowing you are free."

"Seethe, I can't leave you."

"You must." She reached up and stroked my cheek. Her thumb brushed away a tear. "Go, Tarrant. Find help for me, yes?"

I nodded. "Don't die on me. I'll be back for you."

"I know you will." She kicked weakly at me. "Hurry, Tarrant. Find the others. And come back."

I picked Tsamoc up and stood, then turned away because I did not want to see her die. I looked around and recognized nothing, so I picked a direction and started off. I made myself run hard and strong, so she could see that I was going to get help. It didn't matter that we both knew help would never arrive in time. I just wanted her to die with hope, and to comfort myself knowing I'd supplied it.

As Seethe had bidden, I did find some of the others, here and there, with bits and pieces of them scattered yet further. Winfellis had given a good account of herself, leaving a trail of burned and blasted gibberers and vylaens in her wake. Eventually, I guess, she ran out of strength, which let gibberers catch up with her and haul her down.

Brencis Galacos and Jeturna Costasi died fighting side by side. A half-dozen spears had taken him down. She'd lost her sword arm, then her head had been taken. I had no idea where it was, but her body lay sprawled over his legs. I closed his eyes and continued on.

In my search I did run into gibberers, but I felt less prey than predator. The rules by which I was playing were simple: I had to kill everything I met or I would die. I had no reason to hold back, no reason to be cautious. I snarled and snapped at them with the same ferocity they did me. I hacked them with my sword, stabbed them with my longknife, kicked and punched, bit and cursed. I did everything I could, took every advantage I could, and it saw me through.

Eventually I found my trial-blazes and descended stairs. I hauled myself back to our quarters. A gibberer lay dead outside the portal, and from his orientation I knew he had dragged himself clear. Cautiously I stepped over him and entered the tunnel. More bodies filled it, all gibberers.

I found five more dead in the lower sphere and one lying on its back on the stairs. Droplets of blood formed a trail to the chamber Lord Norrington had stayed in. I rushed to the portal, couldn't suppress a gasp, then nipped in and dropped to my knees.

Lord Norrington lay slumped against the shelf where he had slept the night before. I could tell from the blood smeared on the edge that he'd tried to climb onto it, but his strength had failed him. I thought for a second that he was dead, but an eyelid flickered open.

"Hawkins?" He barely got the word out. "Alive?"

"Alive, yes."

"Others?"

"Some dead; some, I don't know." I looped his right arm around my neck. "Hold on, I'll get you onto the bed."

He hissed with pain as I lifted him. He managed to lay his left arm across his belly and, as he did so, I could see it was badly broken across the forearm. I eased him down and he sighed as he straightened out. As he did that I noticed his right ankle didn't seem to work either.

"My lord, I'll get the herbs from Aren's pack. I know enough to identify *metholanth*."

"No, Tarrant." He clutched at my arm with his right hand. "Don't go."

"But you'll need the medicine to make you better."

He shook his head slowly. "I'm not getting better." He

lifted his left arm at the elbow. "I'm stuck through the stomach. Without magick I won't heal. I can already feel the infection."

"But *metholanth* will help."

"Too little, too late." Lord Norrington gave me a brave smile. "I need you to do something. A Phoenix Knight must be burned, not buried. Burned. You have to burn my body."

I nodded. "Burn it, I understand. I will, but first I'm going to get the herbs and buy some time to find you help." I forced out of my mind the fact that Winfellis was dead because there had to be some way to save him. "Then, years from now, in Valsina, I'll burn your body. I promise with my heart and soul."

His brown eyes sparkled. "Remove my mask. I want to share with you what I look like."

"No, my lord, I couldn't."

"Do it, Tarrant. And say my name."

I nodded and slid his mask off. Nothing I saw surprised me, really. I'd not imagined his nose was quite that straight, or that his hairline had pulled back quite that far. It should have seemed to me that I was looking at a complete stranger, but it wasn't. It seemed as if I'd known this face all my life.

"There, Kenwick, is that better?"

"Yes. Thank you." He pressed the mask in my hands against my chest. "Take that mask to Leigh."

"As you wish."

His eyes closed. "And I would have you do one more thing, Tarrant."

"What is it, Kenwick?"

His hand slid to my left wrist and gripped it tightly. "I want you to kill me."

"What? No!"

"Yes, Tarrant. Just open an artery. Let me bleed and fall asleep."

"I can't."

"You must." Lord Norrington's mouth gaped open and his eyes widened as his body shook. The look of agony on his face was unmistakable and when his body slackened I felt the strength in his grip fade away. "The pain. I can't . . ."

"But you are Lord Norrington. How can you surrender to something like pain?"

A short laugh wheezed between his lips. "You speak of a legend. I am just flesh and blood. Aching flesh. Draining blood. Don't let me die this way."

"No. You gave me your trust, and I'm going to hold you to that gift. I will find a way to save you. You have to trust me in that."

"Hawkins, Hawkins." He smiled at me and closed his eyes. "You have to kill me. This is why."

As he lay there dying, Lord Kenwick Norrington revealed to me the secret he said was known only to one other living person. His secret, he said, was the reason the final bit of our quest was bound to fail. He said he'd known that from the beginning, but had persuaded himself it could be otherwise because of the victories we'd won. In his arrogance he'd doomed us all. He'd led Seethe to her death. He'd even put me in jeopardy, all because he needed to prove something to himself and the world.

What he told me left me cold inside, but also answered many tiny little questions I'd never thought to ask before. I do not share that secret here, in these pages, because there are still people who could be hurt by its revelation. The only reason I mention it at all is because that secret, which he hoped would motivate me to kill him, convinced me I could do nothing less than take every step possible to see to it that he lived.

His confession wore him out, so I slipped my arm from his grip and retrieved herbs from Aren's gear. I mixed the *metholanth* with water and packed his wounds, including the two nasty stab wounds in his stomach. I bound his wounds as best I could, then set about shifting all our packs and supplies into his room. We had enough food to last us for a long time, but very little water. Of course, all Tzindr-Coraxoc needed to do was to send more gibberers after us and they'd eventually wear me down.

At some point as I sat there with Lord Norrington, I fell asleep. I know this because I awoke when an urZrethi poked me with a long finger. I started and almost slashed the ur

Zrethi, but I recognized her as the servant I'd had the night before at the feast.

"You are to come." She turned and shuffled from the room.

I stood and sheathed Tsamoc. I looked down at Lord Norrington, taking some satisfaction in his even breathing. I kissed him on the forehead, made sure a bowl of water was near enough to his right hand that he could drink if he wanted to, then strode from the room. I kept my tread even as I walked through the bodies and followed my guide.

Why would I trust one of the urZrethi? I really had nothing else to do. Had they wanted me dead they could have slain me while I slept. That they wanted to talk to me meant there was a chance Lord Norrington might live, and I had to take that chance. It was my only hope

We wandered through the halls for a long time, taking a roundabout path that led me through long corridors, up and down stairs, and through galleries. I relished the click of my boots on the floors and the echoes from the walls. I looked for signs of fighting, but I saw none. In fact, the filth that had clogged the corners and edges of the walkways was gone. Statuary I was certain had been caked with bat droppings and bird guano were clean. The lights seemed a bit stronger, the shadows sharper, and in many ways, the whole place more stark and forbidding than before.

Cold.

Sterile.

Dead.

My guide led me into a long chamber that struck me as being a proper throne room. The columns holding up the ceiling were carved in the shape of urZrethi with massive shoulders and arms. The other statues formed whole tableaux in wall niches, showing great urZrethi in battles out of legend. In one, an urZrethi had closed with and managed to drive handspikes up through the lower jaw of a dragon. The idea that any creature could get close enough to kill a dragon with bare hands left me in awe.

My guide abandoned me in the entryway, but the clear path down to the golden throne in the center of the room left

no doubt as to where I was bound. I did my best to ignore the
ranks of gibberers and vylaens lining the spaces between the
columns. Temeryces, from the small brown ones the urZrethi
raised through those I'd killed and on up to the grand temeryces with their colorful plumage, paced back and forth behind
the gibberer lines, with the small ones occasionally poking
their heads between knees to look at me. A pair of hoargoun
stood in the shadows of the final pillars. Their muscles
bunched as they held a pair of chained drearbeasts back.

As fearsome as was the gauntlet through which I walked,
what waited for me scared me even more. Tzindr-Coraxoc
slumped in a big throne, one far too large for her. Behind her,
hanging there in the air, five to a side, were my companions,
including Lord Norrington and the wizard, Heslin. Seethe,
Lord Norrington, and Heslin seemed alive, as did others,
though Brencis and Jeturna were clearly dead. Of Drugi I saw
no sign at all, but I did not find this heartening.

As I came within a dozen steps of the throne, Tzindr-
Coraxoc's head came up and her body began to change. Her
legs and arms lost their feathers and grew thicker, more
shapely. Her barrel torso stretched and filled out the cloth of
gold robe she wore. Her hair, which had been short and grey,
lengthened into a golden cascade. Her features sharpened, taking up the excess flesh that had hung on Tzindr-Coraxoc's
face. Her eyes became an exotic blue-green, with little swirls
working through the color.

She leaned heavily on one of the throne's arms and looked
down at me. "You have amused me, Tarrant Hawkins." Her
voice had the softness of velvet, but none of its warmth.

"I would not think anything amuses you, Chytrine."

"But you do, by being clever, just like that, just like with
the dog." She laughed easily, like the rustle of wind in a tree,
though to me it sounded like the rasp of a snake crawling
through dead leaves. "I see all that my *sullanciri* saw, and what
I saw of you amused me. You, barely a man, attacked my
sullanciri. The grapnel and anchor, that was inventive. The
bowshot was likewise inspired. Even using one of my arrows
against one of my creations, that was very good. And the last
one, using the sword, I could not have done better myself."

"You mean that as high praise."

Her eyes narrowed and the movement in them increased. "I do, boy, I do. You should take it as such."

"You give me too much credit." I did my best to match her stare and only managed it because I was able to hide behind my mask.

"Leigh slew your *sullanciri*. I only did what I did to save him and others."

"Oh, I know, Tarrant. Your selflessness has touched me, deeply." As she spoke she played a hand down between her breasts. "Because of it I will give you a chance to save your friends."

She gestured behind her and each one of them twitched as if invisible lightning had played from her fingers. Seethe half opened her eyes and looked down at me, but I don't think she really saw me. Lord Norrington did and frowned, but couldn't hold the expression for very long. The others' heads just lolled on their necks, including Jeturna's, which had been crudely sewn back into place.

"Some of them are dead."

"And they will remain dead, but there are worse things than death, and I will put them through each and every one if you fail." She gestured casually then beckoned, drawing hooked fingers toward the palm of her outstretched right hand. I heard a snort from my right, and one of the grand temeryces came trotting past the drearbeasts. Its talons clicked against the floor, then it stopped beside me, all but resting its muzzle on my right shoulder. Its breath blew thunder into my ears.

Chytrine's stare bored into me. "The game is this: if you do not fail, those who live will live, those who are dead will be dead. Do you understand?"

"I do."

"Do you accept?"

I looked at them, hanging there, and nodded. "I do."

"Good, then all you must do is show me your strength. Make no sound through your ordeal, do not move, and you will save your friends."

She hissed something and the temeryx moved to where it

stood in front of me, but toward my right. The beast lifted its right leg and extended the great hooked claw toward me. I felt it punch into my scalp and start down, slowly, letting droplets of blood outpace it. The claw hitched for a moment, then scratched its way down over my mask. I saw a curled ribbon of leather rising from the claw as it swept past my right eye, then dug in again on my cheek.

It scored flesh below my cheekbone and on to my jaw. The temeryx's foot moved toward me to catch my throat and bump the line down over my collarbone. There the other two claws joined in response to a new sibilant command from Chytrine. The claws raked their way down over my flesh, shredding my clothes, tearing bloody furrows in my skin.

The pain was hardly indescribable, for it matched the cuts I'd won earlier that day. It wasn't the worst I'd ever felt, either, but there was just more of it. Every inch the creature clawed open compounded the pain. I wanted to yell, to twitch, to do something, *anything*, so my attention did not have to be focused just on the lines burning down my body.

Looking past Chytrine I found my focus. Aren Asvaldget appeared as if they'd broken every bone in his body. The spear still twitched in Seethe's chest. Lord Norrington's left arm still dangled uselessly, his ankle still twisted at an unnatural angle. Even Heslin, with a *sullanciri* arrow in him, all of them were worse off than I was and they said nothing. By holding firm, I could save them, and save them I would. To twitch, to cry out would be to allow Chytrine a victory, and I'd denied her the same so far.

I felt detached from my body. I couldn't step out of it and look back at it, but I withdrew from it as if it were a mask being worn by my spirit. The pain still registered, but made no more of an impression than the *pit-pit-pit* of blood droplets dripping from my jaw to splash against my chest. The pain was just part of what I was, who I had become. I could not escape it, nor did I see a reason to. If I fled, my friends would suffer, and that I would not allow.

The grand temeryx's claws curled away as they scrabbled at my boot. The beast bounced back a step and peered at me curiously, then jutted its nose forward and sniffed at the blood seeping into the long scratches it had carved in my flesh. The heat of its breath seemed a distant echo of the fire burning a line from my scalp to my shin.

The staccato dripping of blood down my cheek and off my jaw marked time for me. I think the droplets slowed as blood clotted, but I had no trust of my senses. Chytrine watched me, her eyes roiling as blood collected in my boot. A chill settled into my flesh through the rents in my clothes, but the fire in my skin did not diminish and I knew the wounds would putrefy.

Finally she shifted in her throne, with her eyes widening somewhat. "Before you amused, now you impress. Your stoicism amazes me."

I allowed myself one nod and somehow restrained myself from leaping back and around in a furious dance designed to bleed the pain out. I had no doubt such action would amuse her, but I thought impressing her was preferential given the circumstances.

"The bargain."

She nodded. "I shall keep to it. Those of your friends who are dead will remain dead. Those who live will remain alive." Chytrine let a light chuckle roll from her throat. "Of course, your actions have determined their fate. It is clear my invasion of the south was premature, for my leaders were dull and my troops insufficient to accomplish all I set out for them. Since you destroyed my *sullanciri*, I must replace them, and I would have good leaders, heroic leaders, in their places. Your friends will serve me well in that capacity."

"No, no, you can't do that." My hands curled into fists. "They deserve better. They deserve their freedom."

"Do they?" She snorted sharply, her flared nostrils eroding her beauty. "Perhaps another bargain. I will grant them their freedom in exchange for something only you can give me."

I felt as if thorny vines had wrapped themselves around my heart. "And that would be?"

"Your allegiance and service." She leaned forward and smiled most seductively. "You will become my new *sullanciri*. You've certainly won the right, having destroyed the others. I will make you over into that which you wish to be, and I will grant your friends their freedom in the bargain. You will serve as my warlord and consort, and the world will be ours."

Such an offer, it would seem, would require long deliberation before a decision was made. If I agreed, my friends would be given their freedom. They—they who knew so much more than I did and who knew me—could certainly muster the strength and devise the strategies needed to defeat me. And to appear in the south with an army that would make Scrainwood melt into a trembling puddle had appeal. I could even direct the invasion so it accomplished her ends while minimizing the damage to my people.

Those thoughts did occur to me at the time, but they evaporated in a heartbeat because I knew I could never trust Chytrine. I had agreed to her first contest and she remained true to her word, but not the spirit of her words. She had tricked me once and I knew a second trick lurked there, waiting to take me. I had given her a minor victory, and even if denying her another would cost me my life, I deemed denying it to her a goal worthy of being so dearly purchased.

I shook my head. "No. I won't join you. I will never join you."

Chytrine straightened up in her throne. "Every man has his price. I would have thought saving your friends was yours."

"Oh, it would be, but I have no doubt your offer will trap me while cheating me out of that price."

She laughed once, and it probably came out more harsh than expected. "Very good, Hawkins, very good. I tell you this now, each one of these, your friends, came to me willingly. I met their price. The Vorquelf, in her last moment, allowed herself to believe you had abandoned her, so she accepted my fellowship. And your Lord Norrington, in his pain he dearly sought the surcease you denied him. I promised him an end to pain and he swore to serve me. So it was with the others, even the dead, who merely wished to remain in this world.

"So, you were right. If I granted them their freedom, they would still serve me as *sullanciri*. They *would* have served *you* as *your sullanciri*, but you have chosen to oppose me." He thick-lidded eyes half closed. "You have proved clever and stalwart so far, but will you have the stomach for what will come?"

I transformed my personal pain into the pain she had caused so many others, then used that anger to fuel my words. "If it means defeating you, I will gladly do my part. I will always oppose you."

"I am certain you think you will, but you should beware such irrational beliefs. They leave you prey to folly." She opened her arms to take in the hall. "The urZrethi of Boragul believed themselves the only ones worthy of becoming fledged. I appeared to them as Tzindr-Coraxoc, fletched on arms and legs, and they accepted me as their leader. You men of the south are just as foolish and, to my advantage, you are more than capable of playing yourselves off, one against another."

"Even the most stupid leader in the south can recognize the threat you pose, Chytrine."

"Is that so? We shall see." She smiled at me again, leaning forward like an adult about to indulge a child in some kindness. "I will give you two days' headstart, then I will send my hunters after you. If you make it south, you can warn your kings and queens that I am coming. You can give them the most dire warning you can think of, and tell them that I've said my next appearance will be worse than that. *Their* champions are now *my* champions, and unless they find a way to breed heroes as quickly as I can breed *grichothka*—what you style as gibberkin—the children of today will never see their own offspring mature."

Sitting back, Chytrine arched an eyebrow at me. "Do you understand this message?"

"I do, and I will deliver it."

"Will you, or will my hunters find you first?" She watched me with boiling eyes. "I almost hope you do survive."

"I will, and you will regret it."

"Never, Hawkins." She stood and descended from her throne. "I always win, and victory over you is something I will savor."

She leaned toward me and licked blood from my cheek. I

recoiled from the touch of her tongue, but not quickly enough. She caught my jaw in one hand, then kissed me on the lips.

The burning on them surpassed the pain from my wounds, and my world went black.

CHAPTER 43

That I actually awoke again is a miracle for which I cannot account. Perhaps one of the godlings—Arel of luck or Nilin of perversity, or even Fesyin of pain—decided I was entertaining enough to continue my mortal trials. The oath I swore Resolute to help him liberate Vorquellyn, that, too, could have been powerful enough to rouse me. How I came to wake really matters not at all, but just the fact that I did waken is important.

Chytrine clearly did not intend it to be so. I had been carried from her throne room and tossed bodily from Boragul, wearing only that which I'd had on in my audience with her. Frostbite had already numbed my fingers, toes, nose, and cheeks, and likely would have gnawed clean through me had I not regained consciousness. The pain from my cuts did get dulled by the cold, but that was a small comfort.

I found myself in the shadows of Boragul, and this worried me greatly since their shadows only point north. In that direction a vast ice field spread out, featureless save for snowdrifts discernible only by hints of blue shadows. For me to make my way home I would have to struggle west, to the pass which we had previously decided was impassable, and win my way south with legions of gibberkin hounding my every step.

I forced myself to my feet and balanced unsteadily on the snow's thick crust. I drew Tsamoc and set about chopping out thick blocks of snow, which I shifted into position to build a snow den of the type Drugi had showed us how to make. Though I knew little about building a dome, Tsamoc cut blocks that fit perfectly together. As I worked, my body warmed, and in two hours I had a snow den somewhat larger than a coffin.

It might not seem as if a shelter built of snow could prevent someone from freezing, but the body produces heat of its own and the shelter trapped the warm air. It was clear to me that being protected from the northern winds that had begun to howl meant I would not freeze to death quickly, but freezing slowly has little more appeal. I tried to keep moving, at least as much as my shelter would allow, but as night fell, fatigue and pain ate away at my resolve to remain active. I told myself I would just close my eyes for a moment or two, to husband my strength, and somehow I made myself believe that whatever force had awakened me the first time would do so again.

Awaken again I did, and I felt much warmer. This was undoubtedly because of the tallow candle burning near my head and the thick wool blanket spread over me. At my feet I found the heavier winter clothes I'd worn when coming north and a pack stuffed with a jumble of supplies, including a skin of wine, a packet of dried meat, another with cheese and some biscuits. Most important was a pouch containing *metholanth*. My silverwood bow and the quiver of arrows Cavarre had given me lay beside Tsamoc on the snowy shelf I'd carved in the sword's honor.

Of equal import were a gold plate piled high with meat and next to it another with a berry tart. I can only assume my benefactor was the feast servant with whom I shared part of my food. The meat could not have been dog, for it tasted far too good. And the tart, which had been delicious previously, now convinced me that it really was the food of the gods.

I mixed *metholanth* with some of the wine and packed it

into the most gaping portions of the wounds. I shredded the tunic and trousers into rags and bound my wounds with them, then slipped on my warm clothing. I held my hands over the small yellow flame, drinking in its warmth. I mumbled a prayer to Aren, asking for my benefactress to go unpunished and, to this day, I hope that prayer was answered.

The next morning I gathered up my things and started out. The snow supported me and, by keeping Boragul to my left, I knew I was moving west. The featurelessness of the landscape was disheartening in that it made it difficult for me to determine how far I'd come. I accepted that burden, however, since the landscape also offered my enemies nowhere to hide. Any that wanted to get me—the first thirty, anyway—had to be better archers than I was, and I doubted any of them had my motivation to make shots count.

True to her word, Chytrine didn't send her hunters after me for two days, which meant I might have outrun them until I was trying to make my way through the pass, save for a savage storm that blew up out of the north. I was able to dig myself another shelter and just hunkered down to wait it out. I have no idea how long it took to pass, but it was enough time for some of the wounds to begin to suppurate and for me to become feverish.

I knew the infection and fever was not good, but my supply of *metholanth* had dwindled away to nothing. With the rising fever came delirium, which I fully expected to kill me. As it turned out, it actually saved my life.

Of the days after the storm I remember very little, and what I do remember comes in flashes. The storm, it seems, covered my trail so well that Chytrine's hunters actually moved past my shelter, never detecting me. Then, in my feverwalks, I headed directly west and actually overshot the mouth of the pass. Somehow I realized my mistake and cut back to the southeast, where I made contact with the fringes of a hunting party.

A fevermad bowman is not one I would expect to shoot well, and I have no recollection of what I shot where, though my supply of arrows shrank to five. I do know I did not kill all the hunters after me because we did engage in running battles.

I was more an animal than a man, learning all manner of ways to hide myself from hunters when they moved in packs, then darting out to pick off the stragglers.

I'd reached the northern foothills of the Boreal Mountains, just west of the pass, and was moving through a sparse bit of forest when the core of the pack that had been hunting me finally tracked me down. I remember seeing shadows flitting between small pines and hearing the crunch of feet on snowy crusts. The stone set in Tsamoc glowed softly, supplementing the moon's weak light. It did draw the enemy to me, but I didn't care since the only way I could deal with them was if they came within sword's-reach.

The last of them—there were four, I think—came hard and fast. I parried a spear-thrust down to my right, then brought Tsamoc up and around in a slash that split the gibberer's spine at his waist. He crashed down through the snow's crust as I turned to my left and swatted a longknife aside with my mittened left hand. I slashed weakly at him, cutting his flank. Then, as I tried to turn further to the left to continue to engage him, the crust parted beneath my feet, sinking me in snow to my knees. Though my weight was shifting directions, my feet couldn't, and I toppled onto my right side, Tsamoc slicing deep into the snow.

The gibberer loomed up over me, raising its longknife in both hands, set to plunge it down through my belly. I snarled and tugged at Tsamoc. I tried to kick out with my feet, but they were trapped deep. I looked up into the gibberer's feral eyes and I knew my fight was over.

Then a whirring buzz drilled into me and something flashed through the night. The gibberer screamed and clutched at its eyes. It reeled away, stumbling and breaking through the crust. A different whirring sound built and faded, ending in a wet *thunk*. The blind gibberer's wailing ceased, its spine arched against a metal cross half buried in its back. It flopped forward and lay still.

The whirring buzz returned and I knew myself to be in the full and probably fatal throes of fever, for only delirium could account for the thing that landed on my stomach. A foot and a half tall and appearing to be largely armored with glossy black casing segments—like those on an insect—the creature folded all four of his arms over his chest. His four wings, which resembled those of a dragonfly, folded back down toward his feet. Two antennae rose from his forehead, just before the bristly shock of hair covering his head. He regarded me with two jewel-faceted eyes.

"Quick, quick," he piped in a high voice. "Alive, he alive. Quick, quick."

I heard the crunch of heavy feet punching through the snow crust with each step. "Damn those gibberers for breaking the crust."

I recognized the voice and turned my head toward it. The moonlight lent an iridescence to Resolute's white hair and silver eyes. I reached my left hand toward him. I wanted to call his name, but words refused to come. I let my arm flop down across my chest and began to cry.

Resolute crouched beside me and smiled. "Don't worry, Hawkins. You've promised to liberate Vorquellyn and I'm going to make sure you live long enough to do it."

Resolute bundled me aboard a long sled of the sort used for travel in the winter. Usually dogs are used to pull it, and given my condition I could be wrong, but for part of our journey I'm fairly certain the beasts drawing us along were gibberers that he'd magicked back to life.

None of his magick could heal me, but his companion managed to help me recover. Sprynt was a Spritha and gathered *metholanth* and other herbs despite their being buried under feet of snow. Somehow he knew where they were, and Resolute told me that was a thing about Spritha, that there were times when they just knew they had to be someplace, and so they went.

"After you left Yslin, Sprynt found me and told me he knew he was to be with me in Aurolan to save you." The Vorquelf shook his head. "There was no doubting him, and you might imagine that he could be something of a pest if you try to ignore him."

"Adamant, adamant." The Spritha posted his lower arms on his hips as his upper arms worked at sewing my scalp shut.

In the flickering light of the small fire Resolute had built I could see that Sprynt was not black but a bright red, and his eyes ruby. His hair was black, and the leathery bits of flesh between segments of his exoskeleton were the color of dried blood. The creature smiled frequently and worked on me with a delicate touch, which seemed to compensate for his disappointment over the fact that I would certainly bear scars from my wounds.

Resolute had come north through the pass. He'd started with enspelled wolves to pull the sled, but had switched to gibberers once he'd killed enough of them. "I felt sorry for using the wolves so."

He assumed, and as my fever broke I agreed, that Chytrine would set troops in the pass to prevent my escape. To thwart her we worked our way south through the Boreal Mountains. Our journey took us through high passes that, while treacherous, did not betray the three of us. We eventually came down into the Ghost Marches almost due north of Vorquellyn. There Sprynt led us to some horses which we used to bring us to Fortress Draconis.

It is perhaps a sign of how weak I was that the fortress seemed to me to be the most beautiful building I'd ever seen. Though I'd only been a month absent from it, nearly all the rubble from the wall breaches had been cleared, and the walls were in the process of being rebuilt. Moreover, the fortress was being expanded, with new walls spreading out in a zig-zag pattern.

Within the walls reconstruction had also taken place. While empty lots marked the destruction Chytrine's forces had caused, the streets had been cleared and life appeared normal for a town of this size. Washing hung from lines, flowers in pots decorated windows, and many buildings had been brightened up with splashes of paint.

Though I alone of the command company returned, those who recognized me seemed oblivious to the import of my solo return. Soldiers saluted me, and children ran in front of my horse, shrieking out the news of my return. Sprynt darted on ahead, presumably to tell the Draconis Baron of my arrival, as Dothan Cavarre met me at the tower gate. He helped me off my horse and inside, once again ensconcing me in the rooms I'd had before.

After a rest, I told the tale of our expedition to Cavarre and Prince Scrainwood. My story had little of the organization of this account and probably did sound like the ravings of a madman. At that time I was truly exhausted and as I told them what had happened, the grief I felt for my lost friends hammered me and ground down my spirit.

I relapsed into fever and Dothan Cavarre saw to my care. He insisted I remain as his guest until my health was again restored. It was not until later that I discovered he did this at Prince Scrainwood's order—though, truth be told, Cavarre was the sort of man to have kept me there if he felt it was the best thing.

It certainly was not bad for me. Nay and Leigh had long since headed south to Valsina, wishing to make it home before winter set in. Still, there were enough people around who I knew to provide me ample visitors, and Cavarre took great delight in showing me all the steps being taken to restore Fortress Draconis. Resolute and Sprynt even stayed for a while, though they left on a ship for Yslin when word came through of Prince Augustus' triumphant campaign in Okrannel and his return to Yslin.

Prince Scrainwood had left for Yslin the day after I told my story. I had not been sorry to learn of his departure. I had heard, of course, the old saw that one should keep friends close and enemies closer, but somehow the only enemies I thought I had in the world were to the north.

I learned my error when, in the spring, a ship came to Fortress Draconis with orders to take me to Yslin.

CHAPTER 44

I suppose I should have known things were odd well before I
stepped onto the *Tectus* for the journey to Yslin. During my
time at Fortress Draconis I was never summoned to the
Phoenix Knights' hall. To be perfectly honest I never sought to
make contact with the Knights because my memory of all the
rituals was bound up with images of Leigh and Nay and Lord
Norrington. I spent a lot of time that winter doing all I could
to avoid revisiting those memories.

Even so, I would have thought the Knights would have
called me before them to praise me for surviving or to ask
after Lord Norrington's demise, or even to chasten me for
failing to die with my comrades. At the very least they could
have summoned me so I could learn more of my rank duties.
From them I heard nothing, and even though I spent a lot of
time with Cavarre, he never gave me any sign that he even
knew what the Knights were, much less ran the lodge at Fortress Draconis.

The ship that had been sent for me, the *Tectus*, was a small
ship with a single mast and only eight oars. It could not make
a lot of speed unless the wind or sea ran in our favor.
Tagothcha allowed us to sail on unmolested and an unseason-

able wind from the north propelled us south. We skirted Vorquellyn, then slid past Wruona, Vael, and Vilwan as if we were
invisible.

The fare of dried meat, fish stew, and hard-baked biscuits
proved slightly more tolerable than the company I was given.
The crew ignored me almost entirely and the captain only
spoke to me when it would have been painfully awkward not
to acknowledge my existence. The only person who regularly
did speak with me was an Oriosan who had been the envoy to
bring my summons to me.

Cabot Marsham was and yet is an odious little man who
has grown more sour and scheming over the years. I mistook
the contempt in which he held me for some sort of jealousy,
or pique over the fact that I, someone a good five years his
junior, had been the reason he had to endure two long weeks
on the sea while it was still so cold. The only things about him
that were softer and thinner than his hair—which he still had
then—were his arms and legs. In many ways he seemed to me
to be a child playing at being an adult, and the faint little
moustache that dusted his upper lip did nothing to dispel this
impression.

Marsham asked incessantly about my adventures and, for
lack of any other companionship, I made the mistake of indulging him. I confided in him many details—of conversations and encounters—that I consider so trivial to have
omitted from this record, yet he wove them into a web that,
before I knew it, had me all entangled.

We reached Yslin without incident and I was conducted to
Fortress Gryps straight away. I was given a suite of rooms to
myself and two servants so I would never be left unaccompa-
nied. They saw to my every need and I discovered many of
them had been anticipated. The wardrobe in my suite had
already been filled with clothes cut to fit me perfectly.

Within two days of my arrival I was deemed "recovered"
enough from my long voyage to be summoned. In the company of guards I descended to the Great Hall and received my
first substantial shock when I entered the room. I last remembered it as the home to the Council of Kings, with a dozen
nations represented at the time of the Harvest Festival. Here

now, though, tables had been arranged in long rows, akin to the oar-benches on a galley, with the leaders or ambassadors from every nation in the world represented. Each sat beneath a national banner hung from the ceiling, with all three elven homelands and even a couple of urZrethi homelands represented.

Duke Reed Larner, Chamberlain to Queen Lanivette of Oriosa, introduced me to the royal assemblage. He asked me to swear an oath to tell the truth, which I did, then he asked me to tell the leaders of the world about the expedition. I did so, as best I was able, and certainly made a better job of it that time than I did when speaking to Dothan Cavarre and Prince Scrainwood at Fortress Draconis.

I think I realized I was on trial as my narrative ended and the questions began. An ambassador from Nybal stood toward the back of the room. "Is it true that at Fortress Draconis you struck Prince Scrainwood of Oriosa not once, but twice?"

I hesitated, since that had not been part of my tale. "It is true. He'd run in terror in the face of the enemy. I wanted to bring him to his senses, so I slapped him. Twice."

My response raced a murmur through the royals. I decided, albeit too late, that telling royalty that I'd decided one of their number needed to be slapped was not a good idea. At least, I hoped they were protesting my slapping him. If they were protesting the possibility of one of their company needing to be brought to his senses, well, the world was lost.

Another person asked if it were true that I discarded a powerful weapon, one that could have killed *sullanciri*, by cavalierly tossing it into the sea. Yet another wanted to know how it was that all my fellows, who were far more experienced than I in the ways of warfare, died in Boragul and I survived.

"That is a question I have asked myself every day since then."

"And the answer you have come up with is?"

"If I had an answer, would I keep asking the question?"

The questions tailed off into inquiries about obscure details asked, I think, just so members of delegations could prove they had listened to me and, apparently, listened to others who spoke about me. When no more questions were offered, I was escorted back to my suite and locked in. While I did not want for material needs, a lack of freedom weighs one down more than any chains ever could. I was permitted no visitors and could neither send nor receive messages.

And I am assuming that at least one person, someone, *anyone*, did wish to speak with me.

The fact that I was not allowed visitors did not mean people were prevented from entering my apartments. My last morning there I awoke to find a fine black ash on my bedroom floor. It was laid out in the shape of a ceremonial robe and I knew no Phoenix Knight would be rising from those ashes. The message delivered in that way got through to me as nothing else had, and in that moment I think I grew up more than I had even through the events of the previous year.

I presented a problem for the rulers of the world. The previous year, at their command, a task force had gone forth and, at great cost, broken the Aurolani army. Prince Augustus had undertaken an operation that rescued the refugee population of Okrannel, though Aurolani forces, now reduced to roving bandit bands and local warlord militias, still controlled Okrannel. Jerana had held them back at their border and expatriate Okrans gathered there preparing to win their homeland back. Even the siege of Fortress Draconis had been lifted and Chytrine had fled.

In fact, everything had gone perfectly, save for the last strike at her, and I was the only person who tarnished the image of the heroes who had been sent forth. I was the one who said they had succumbed to Chytrine's temptations. I was the one who reported they had become her creatures, but I could offer no proof. I can see that my story sounded suspect.

Or could easily have been made to sound suspect.

I was summoned back to the Council that day and ordered to stand before the assembly as Duke Larner read a list of refutations to what I had told others.

"The royal personages assembled here have decided and concluded the following to be facts:

"First, it is inconceivable that the persons entrusted with seeing to the well-being of the nations assembled here would, at any time, under any circumstances, join forces with the evil they were sent to destroy.

"Second, according to testimony offered by other witnesses, the Boreal Pass has such snowfall in it that it will take thirty years for it to be passable again, eliminating any threat from Aurolan beyond the rovers who slip through the mountains from time to time."

I laughed aloud. "You can say that to ease the fears of the common folks, but you know it's not true. And, even if it was, she could come through Boragul."

The Duke stared down at the foolscap upon which the refutations had been written and refused to look at me. "Third, according to urZrethi scouts who, in the company of the Vorquelf, Resolute, traveled to Boragul, that urZrethi stronghold is completely abandoned. It is open to the weather and completely uninhabitable. No gibberkin nurseries were located, no temeryces or any other creature were seen, and no urZrethi were in residence.

"Fourth, it is deduced that Tarrant Hawkins of Oriosa, a man who has admitted to striking the Prince of his nation, a man who is notorious for having stolen the sword Temmer to reap glory for himself at Fortress Draconis, a man who clearly was not prepared for the difficulties of the trek north, did get separated from the company of heroes and survived the horrible fate that overtook them. It is deduced that they sent him away, to preserve his life or even to summon help, and that in a confused state he himself was attacked and would have been slain save for the intervention of others. To believe otherwise of him would be to believe he had actively betrayed his companions, having allied himself with Chytrine, thereby committing treason against every civilized nation and earning the just rewards of same."

I stiffened as he read that final article. I marveled at the work of politicians because I found it as deadly and beautiful as a master swordsman's bladework. They would allow me to admit I had been sent back by my fellows and, through no fault of my own, had failed to bring them help. The only alternative was to be branded a traitor, and actually being *branded* a traitor was the least of the punishments I could face for that crime. In essence they were telling me that if I disputed their findings, I'd be put to death.

Even I could see how futile a gesture that would be.

Duke Larner looked up at me. "Do you understand what has been read to you?"

"I do."

"Do you accept these conclusions as the truth?"

"Are they the truth?" I looked out at the rulers assembled there. "The pass will reopen, we know that. Boragul may be abandoned now, but always? You know that the story I told you is true, but it is a story you cannot allow to be told. If it is told, if I go out and tell it, then your people will know that the security they believe they have now is a lie. Perhaps this generation is safe, but what of the next?"

I opened my hands. "I will accept what you say of me provided *you* know that Chytrine will return, whether in five years or ten or thirty. If you do nothing to prepare for her return, the blood of thousands, of hundreds of thousands, will be on your hands. Whether you are alive or dead, your names will become a curse and your memories will be mocked."

Scrainwood shot to his feet at his mother's side. Rage purpled the lower parts of his face and sent a quiver through the finger he pointed at me. "You are in no position to dictate to us, traitor!"

The pure venom in his voice was meant to hurt me, but instead it made me laugh. "And you, Prince Scrainwood, know better than the others the horror that will descend upon us when Chytrine comes back. Don't let your cowardice shield you from what you know to be true."

His voice dropped to a cruel whisper. "What I know to be true is this, Tarrant Hawkins. I know the rulers here gathered have decided, in their wisdom, to set you free, to let you live out your life as you might. But we of Oriosa are not so kindly disposed to those who flout authority, strike their betters, and bully the reputations of heroes. You are henceforth and forevermore banished from Oriosa."

Scrainwood waved someone into the room. I heard bootheels click across the floor, then found myself facing my father. A smile lit my face, then drained away as it found no mate on his face.

I saw no warmth in his eyes. "Father?"

"You left Kenwick Norrington to die and lied about it."

"Father, I . . ."

He raised a hand as if to strike me. "I have no son named Tarrant." Reaching his hand out, he grasped the top edge of my mask and tore it away.

The day they took my mask was the day Tarrant Hawkins died.